Praise for *Sea of Ghosts*

-ri-L

'A stonking good time, rip-roaring and boundlessly
ambitious – a breathless, whistle-stop tour of a
wonderfully moldering world'
Speculative Scotsman

'A truly fantastic tale'
The Times

'Rampant imagination is allied with unusually rich writing'
Morning Star

'Vivid, bloody, enthralling and utterly atmospheric . . . the first
of what should be a fantastic new series. Bravo'
Book Geeks

Alan Campbell was born in Falkirk and went to
Edinburgh University. He worked as a designer/coder on
the hugely successful Grand Theft Auto video games before
deciding to pursue a career in writing and photography.
His previous novels are the Deepgate Codex series,
Scar Night, *Iron Angel* and *God of Clocks*. He now
lives in south Lanarkshire.

Also by Alan Campbell

The Deepgate Codex

SCAR NIGHT

IRON ANGEL

GOD OF CLOCKS

ALAN CAMPBELL

SEA OF GHOSTS

BOOK ONE OF THE GRAVEDIGGER CHRONICLES

TOR

First published 2011 by Tor

This paperback edition published 2012 by Tor
an imprint of Pan Macmillan, a division of Macmillan Publishers Limited
Pan Macmillan, 20 New Wharf Road, London N1 9RR
Basingstoke and Oxford
Associated companies throughout the world
www.panmacmillan.com

ISBN 978-0-330-50878-0

1 3 5 7 9 8 6 4 2

A CIP catalogue record for this book is available from
the British Library.

Typeset by CPI Typesetting
Printed and bound by CPI Group (UK) Ltd, Croydon, CR0 4YY

Visit **www.panmacmillan.com** to read more about all our books
and to buy them. You will also find features, author interviews and
news of any author events, and you can sign up for e-newsletters
so that you're always first to hear about our new releases.

'Let my skill with a bow be judged when the stars flare and die, for I have shot arrows at all of them'

Argusto Conquillas, *The Art of Hunting*, 8/4/900

'Ballistic weapons can be used effectively against a sorcerer, provided they are not aimed directly at the sorcerer'

Colonel Thomas Granger, *Treatise on the Use of Imperial Ordnance against Entropic Trickery*, 12/HA/1420

Thanks to Simon Kavanagh and Julie Crisp, and to my good friends at the Edinburgh writers' group who read those early chapters and set me on the right course.

This book is dedicated to
William Campbell

PROLOGUE

A TAPESTRY OF SEX

The shopkeeper stood seven feet tall and wore a fantastic turban, a twist of ice-cream silk laced with pearls. He ran his hand along the bookcase until he found the volume he was looking for and extracted it with the deft flourish of a carnival magician. 'This is the book you want,' he said. '*A Tapestry of Sex* explores the art of seduction; it was penned by the greatest lover who ever lived.' He paused in affected wonder. 'Herein lie the secrets of Lord Herian Goodman – the methods by which he won the hearts of every man, woman and cauldron abomination he desired. Take it, read it, allow yourself to be seduced by it.'

Ida pressed the pages to her lips and breathed in odours of perspiration and exotic perfume. She could still hear the hubbub of commerce in the cavernous gloom around her, but the noise seemed suddenly distant. As her eye followed the neat printed words, her heart began to race. She had to buy this book.

The Trove Market had grown into a network of enormous brick vaults and sinuous passages that reached underneath the Imperial city of Losoto, its cluttered aisles defining tributaries through which endless streams of tourists flowed. They wandered through vast arched spaces, gaping at shelves ablaze with gold and silver trinkets, at glass orchids and jewelled clocks and alabaster birdcages, at endless stacks of boiled-black dragon bones. Painted

1

saints and figureheads smiled back at them with eyes of candle-flame and lips like glazed cherries. Tiny brass machines chuckled and chirruped meaningless words, pulsing colourful lights to no apparent purpose. Old swords waited in cabinets for new owners. There were boxes of feathers and jars of colourful dust, bottles of jellyfish wine and cloaks woven from the hair of dead princesses. Manatee skulls lay next to miniature tombstones. Sharkskin men and women writhed and danced in tanks of brine, their grey limbs sliding fluidly behind the curved glass walls, their hair like green pennants. A million customers might pass through Losoto's underground market, plucking at the banks of treasure, and yet the stock never diminished. It could not be eroded. Every artefact in the empire found its way here eventually, to lie in wait for a spark of desire.

Ida clutched her book as fiercely as a mother holds a long-lost child. 'Goodman was an Unmer Lord?' she asked the shopkeeper.

'Lord, libertine and a formidable sorcerer to boot. He lived in a house up there, less than a hundred yards from here.' He jabbed a finger up at the vaulted brick ceiling, beyond which the streets of Losoto would be basking in the sunshine.

'Then this book is magical?'

The shopkeeper smiled broadly, displaying the diamonds set in his teeth. 'Who can say? The Unmer invested so many of their creations with magic. You must read it all to discover its value. Passion, sexual ecstasy, horror and peril. Anything is possible between the covers of such a book.'

She nodded urgently.

'But there's more,' he added. 'Now that you possess a map of seduction, you must acquire a compass and a sextant, so to speak, to facilitate your success.' He steered her towards a dark cabinet stuffed with bulbous phials that gleamed like squid. 'These Unmer potions have been dredged from the beds of sixteen seas.

Look here.' He picked up a green bottle. 'Drink this to cleanse and revitalize your mind; it tastes like spring rain. And this –' He chose a tiny, empty jar '– is a singularly precious ointment.'

'What is it?'

'Clarity.'

'How much do they cost? I don't know—'

'And here is stamina.' This bottle was sunflower-yellow, the next one pink. He scooped them into his arms like glazed fruit sweets. 'And lucid dreams and lightness of step – ah, here is an enigma. This tincture allows one to see colours hidden in other people's shadows and thus perceive hidden intentions. These three are the bottled auras of young boys sacrificed at Unmer altars; their ghosts will be lingering nearby. How long do you plan to stay?'

'Excuse me?'

'Will you be in Losoto a week from now?'

She shook her head. 'My ship leaves tomorrow.'

The shopkeeper threw up his hands with mock regret. Suddenly he seemed taller and wilder, an enormous blue-lipped djinn at the centre of the universe. Lanterns suspended from the ceiling whirled around his head like flaming bolas. His eyes blazed. 'But you'll miss the rarest treasure of them all. My agent in Valcinder is sending me a jealous knife. They dragged it up from sixty fathoms down. A man died to procure it, and I am told it is superb.'

Her head spun. 'Is it an Unmer artefact? What does it do?'

'What does it *do*? The jealous knife allows two lovers to exchange tactile sensation. Prick each partner's finger and thereafter each will experience the other's pleasure or pain. Thus a lonely wife might please her husband across great gulfs of separation, or a brave man endure the pain of childbirth in his woman's stead.'

'But why is it called—'

3

He made a dismissive gesture. 'The effect is everlasting. Relationships are not.'

Perhaps Ida could remain a few days and return home on a later boat? She had spent so much money already on this trip, but she absolutely had to have that knife. And possibly an aura or two, an Unmer sonnet, a dragon's eye, or a few vials of passion drained from a corpse. Leave the gold to the magpies; she would indulge her taste for Unmer sorcery. Yes. She simply must stay. She was about to say as much when she heard a great commotion from another part of the market. A woman screamed.

The shopkeeper stared past her, over the tops of the nearest shelves. And then he turned and walked briskly away down the aisle.

'Mr Sa'mael?' Ida called after him. 'Mr Sa'mael?'

Other people were shoving past her now, quickly. Ida sensed a swell of panic building under the vaulted ceiling. She heard another scream, and what sounded like an explosion. Glass smashed. Suddenly the crowd surged, and someone knocked her to the floor. Ida cried out and cowered under her book as boots thudded past her head.

Silence followed.

Ida wobbled to her feet and swept back the tangled mess of her hair. Dirty footprints bruised her dress. Her arms and legs smarted. The aisles all around were clogged with wreckage from fallen shelves. It looked as if a tsunami had swept through here. The crowds had fled, but the marketplace was not deserted.

Ten yards away a little girl stood at the junction of four aisles, cradling a metal doll in her arms. She wore a red frock composed of many layers and frills that flared out around her boots like the petals of a rose. Her hair and skin were as white as bone dust, and her huge dark eyes brimmed with tears.

'Oh, you poor tyke.' Ida moved towards the child.

From behind came the calm sound of a man's voice: 'Ma'am.' Ida turned.

Five Imperial soldiers perched upon the tops of the shelves above her. They had climbed up among the boxes of treasure, three on one side of the aisle, two on the opposite bank. As motley a group as Ida had ever seen, they wore tattered black uniforms adorned with old clasps, buckles and pins. They wore whaleskin boots and gloves and carried swords, gutting knives and hand-cannons fashioned from dragon-bone and silver – these latter clearly salvaged from the seabed, for the stocks still bore the scars of barnacles. The man who had spoken crouched over a leather satchel, gripping the stub of a cigar between his teeth and holding his firearm upright in one fist like a staff. His own uniform bore the bee-stripe epaulettes of an Imperial Guard colonel. He was wiry, tough-looking but ungainly, with oversized joints and a neat cap of brown hair. Grey spots of sharkskin marred one side of his neck, and yet his pale blue eyes were as clear and hard as glass. His raggedy appearance seemed so much at odds with his apparent rank that for a moment Ida wondered if he'd mugged one of Emperor Hu's finest and stolen the fellow's getup.

'She's Unmer,' he said. 'She'll kill you without meaning to.'

'She can't be Unmer,' Ida retorted. 'The Haurstaf would have sensed her.'

The colonel looked at her without the faintest glimmer of emotion. 'If you say so,' he said. 'Debating the situation further serves no purpose, ma'am. Please move aside, or we will remove you by force.'

Ida did as she was told, stepping through the piles of glittering junk. Now that she thought about it, the girl's frock did look old enough to be an antique. An original Unmer garment, intact and undamaged by the sea? The sheer value of it astonished her. And wasn't there an odd graveyard smell in the air?

'But how did she get out?' she said.

'Crawled straight through a wall, I imagine.'

'But the Haurstaf would have sensed that!'

The colonel puffed on his cigar. 'The Haurstaf always seem a trifle lax when the emperor neglects to pay his dues on time. If you would be so kind as to make your way towards the nearest exit, we will handle the crisis from here.'

The soldier beside him grunted. 'Fucking extortion is what it is.' A great dark brute of a man, he crouched on his high perch like some enormous ape, with the butt of his firearm pressed firmly into his massive shoulder and the barrel aimed at the child. On the back of his hand he bore a small black tattoo. It looked like a shovel.

'Language, Sergeant Creedy.'

'Well, it is,' the other man persisted. 'They let this one escape to teach Hu a lesson.'

'Then they're not coming?' Ida said.

'It seems unlikely, ma'am,' the colonel replied.

She was about to protest the woeful inadequacy of this when the child cried out suddenly, 'I want my mother.' Her voice reverberated strangely in the vast space; it was accompanied by a queer crackling sound, like distant cannon fire.

The colonel reached into his satchel and pulled out a fist-sized ball of baked clay. A short fuse extended from its wax-sealed top. He examined the munition carefully, then glanced up at the vaulted ceiling. 'Banks,' he said to the second man sharing his side of the aisle. 'I'd like your opinion on the roof.'

This soldier was much younger than his companions, but he surveyed the gloomy space above them with the grim demeanour and confidence of a much older man. He sniffed and rubbed at his nose. 'The Unmer built this whole place,' he replied. 'Those corbels date back to the Lucian Wars. The problem is, I can't tell exactly what's above them from down here. We blow that roof, and we might bring down more than just rubble.' He paused and sneezed into his hand. 'Dragonfire would be better.'

'Did you bring a dragon, Banks?' the colonel said.

The younger soldier looked as if he was about to say something, then he shook his head wearily and returned his gaze to the ceiling. 'We must be close to the Unmer ghetto, sir,' he said. 'Bring *that* down on our heads and the emperor will not be happy.'

'What do the maps say?'

He blinked watery eyes, then gave a grunt. 'What maps? Hu doesn't consider the Trove Market close enough to his palace to warrant the expense of a survey. The Haurstaf would know, but '

'Blow the roof?' Ida exclaimed. 'What do you mean, *blow the roof?*'

'Standard procedure, ma'am,' the colonel said. 'Nothing for you to be concerned about.' He stood up, stared intently at the little girl for a moment, then turned to the big soldier by his side. 'Fire a round at the child, Sergeant Creedy. Aim for her head.'

'Aye, sir.' The huge soldier pulled back the weapon's firing lever, with a click.

Ida rushed in front of the child to block his shot. 'What in heavens do you think you're doing?' she said, brandishing her book. 'She's just a little girl.'

'I need you to stand aside, ma'am,' the colonel said.

Ida didn't budge.

'We are here on Emperor's Hu's orders,' he added. 'If you fail to comply we will arrest you for resisting Imperial troops in a time of war. The punishment for such a crime is typically six to nine months' incarceration.'

She folded her arms.

He observed her for a moment with cold eyes. 'I don't think you fully comprehend the danger,' he said. 'That crackling noise you heard when she spoke was the sound of air turning to vacuum in her lungs. She can't help herself. Unmer children lack the restraint of adults.'

Ida glared at him. 'She's not doing anybody any harm.' From the corner of her eye she noticed the child move close behind her.

The colonel glanced across at the two men perched on the shelves on the opposite side of the aisle and raised his eyebrows. These two were like ancient crows: scrawny, bow-legged creatures with wild black hair and noses shaped for pecking. They might both have been the sons of the same unfortunate woman. They held their heavy guns easily enough, but their narrowed, squinting eyes did not inspire confidence. One of them shook his head and spoke in a thick Greenbay accent, 'Not without hitting the woman, sir.'

Creedy grunted. 'You couldn't hit the ocean from a boat, Swan. I can end all this time-wasting with one shot. If we dynamite the woman's body afterwards, it'll look like the Unmer child killed her.'

The colonel raised his hand. 'No, Sergeant,' he said. 'We will adhere to the law.' He thought for a moment, before turning his attention back to Ida. 'Do you have a receipt for that book, ma'am?'

She blinked. 'I hadn't bought it yet.'

'We *are* authorized to shoot looters on sight.'

Creedy laughed.

Ida felt strength draining from her legs. She cried out, 'It doesn't give you the right to shoot an unarmed—'

She didn't get a chance to finish. The girl bolted away from her, down the aisle.

Ida half-turned.

And Creedy fired.

A flash erupted from the weapon, accompanied by a tremendous *boom*. The child shrieked as a second burst of light bloomed against her back. She dropped like a rag doll. Ida's heart clenched in desperate panic. She felt as if the air had been sucked from her lungs.

Smoke leaked from the barrel of Creedy's gun. He lowered the weapon and said, 'Damn.'

Ida's ears still rang with the sound of the detonation. It took her a moment to realize that the Unmer girl had not been harmed. Still clutching her doll, the poor child was trying to push herself upright amidst the piles of fallen treasure.

'I shot her in the back,' Creedy said.

'Reload your weapon, Sergeant,' the colonel said.

Creedy was shaking his head. 'The round just *vanished*.'

The child was sobbing. She got to her feet and edged backwards away from the men. Behind her loomed one of the Trove Market's many brine tanks, twelve tons of poisonous seawater glowing faintly behind its glass walls. A sharkskin woman stood in that brown gloom, watching the child approach. She thumped a fist against the inside of her container, but her warning made no sound.

Banks shouted, 'The tank, Colonel.'

Creedy was hurriedly pouring powder into his gun.

The colonel nodded to the crows on the opposite bank. 'Swan, Tummel, please do try to avoid any sort of mess.'

They raised their weapons.

The child wailed.

Explosions rattled the air. A hail of pellets crackled against the child's red frock and flared out of existence. She screamed and dropped her doll. Through a veil of white smoke Ida saw her turn and flee.

'Slippery little bitch,' Creedy said.

Whether the girl was unable to perceive the brine tank, or whether she simply did not notice it in her panic, Ida didn't know. But she doubted that what happened next was deliberate. The child ran straight into the container's curved glass wall.

There was a blaze of white light, a sharp *bang* . . .

And the tank shattered.

A wave of brine erupted out onto the market floor, washing artefacts aside as it surged between the aisles. Ida leapt for the safety of the nearest set of shelves and tried to clamber up among the trove. Her foot slipped, and she felt cold seawater close around the heel of her shoe. The metal stink of brine filled her nostrils. She yelped, snatching her foot away, but it was too late. Her ankle had already begun to itch.

Strong hands gripped her, pulled her up. 'Relax, ma'am. It's only your ankle.'

The itching became a strange prickling sensation. Ida's heart-beat quickened.

She heard Creedy's voice. 'That wasn't our fault. Hu can't blame us for breaking that.'

'There she is,' said another man. '*She's splashing through the stuff.*'

The prickling sensation in Ida's foot intensified. She began to shiver with fear. Was this shock? How long did she have before her skin began to change? 'I need fresh water,' she said. 'I need to—'

'The guns aren't working, sir. Our shots don't have enough mass. We're going to have to overwhelm her.'

Ida pulled off her slipper and stared at her ankle. She couldn't see any damage yet, but the skin on her heel felt like it was tight-ening over the bones inside.

'. . . for something her size?'

'Five or six tons. But, like I said, it's a hell of a risk. Hu is still looking for an excuse to bury us. A hole in his city pretty much fits that bill.'

Ida tried to swallow her revulsion, but visions of sharkskin assailed her. Was she turning into one of the Drowned? She felt nauseous, dizzy, as though racked by the effects of some hideous drug. The Trove Market whirled around her in glittering wheels of gold and silver. She leaned over and vomited.

From nearby came a long low wail. The sharkskin woman lying at the bottom of the smashed tank was beginning to dry out. She was writhing about, scooping up brine and rubbing it into her leathery grey flesh. Ida tore her gaze away from the unfortunate creature. Her own ankle was nipping quite fiercely now. So soon? She needed fresh water to clean the wound. She searched around frantically for something, somewhere. . . .

'Take Swan and Tummel and find the breach. It'll be a small hole, child-sized. If we scare her enough we might just manage to steer her back there.'

'We're supposed to kill any escapees. Hu was very specific about that.'

'Emperor Hu is not here.'

'Right, sir.'

'Creedy, you're with me.'

'They can't blame us for that mess, can they, sir?'

'Ma'am?'

Ida looked up.

The colonel was holding out a bottle. 'It's wine,' he said.

She gazed at him dumbly.

'Use it on your ankle. It'll help.'

Ida took the bottle and poured pink wine over her ankle. Had her skin already begun to toughen and change? Wasn't that a patch of grey, there, on the side of her heel? Hurriedly, she massaged the wine into her foot, then felt a jab of panic as her fingers began to itch. 'Colonel,' she began.

But the colonel did not reply. He was looking past her.

A hundred paces beyond the smashed tank stood a man. He was aiming a bow at the colonel. He was dressed up like a noble from a bygone era: a jewel-studded black jerkin spun about with a platinum sash, black breeches over white hose and sandals of soft dark leather. Rouge coloured his cheeks, but the powdered make-up did little to dampen the sharpness of his features. His out-thrust chin and dagger-like nose were too severe to be considered handsome. He wore his long grey hair in a tight plait pulled back from his face and he glared at them with sharp violet eyes. Ida found him strangely mesmerizing. He seemed somehow more *solid* than the world around him, a fixed point in a spinning world. She felt her nausea diminish.

The Unmer child had her arms wrapped around the bowman's leg.

And behind them both stood a berserker dragon.

The beast was small for its species, perhaps sixty feet from its snout to the tip of its tail. It wore a suit of glazed white armour chased with silver, each plate exquisitely shaped to hug its serpentine body and its short, powerful limbs. Shards of crystal glinted on its gauntlets and again on its long, tapered helmet, wherein burned blood-red eyes. It nuzzled the Unmer child until she giggled.

Like all dragons, it had been human once – a warrior remade by Unmer sorcery into this new and bestial form. It unfolded great nacreous wings that glittered like rainbows, and then it lowered its equine head and began to lap at the poisonous brine. In creating this species for war, the Unmer had given it unholy addictions. The seawater would be acting like a drug, fuelling its rage in preparation for battle. When it raised its head again, brine dripped from ranks of bared white teeth.

The bowman smiled. 'Do you enjoy tormenting children?'

Creedy said, 'Fuck.'

Now the colonel hefted his own hand-cannon. 'The child was in no danger from us,' he said. 'Take her back to the ghetto, and we'll allow you to leave here unharmed.'

'*Allow* me to leave?' the archer said incredulously. 'In what way do you suppose you can harm me? Your weapons are like those of ghosts.' Behind him, the dragon growled words in a strange, guttural language. The archer listened and then replied in the same twisted speech. Finally he turned back to the colonel. 'Yva is hungry,' he said. 'She has begged me to allow her to remain here, so that she may devour you at her leisure.' He smiled again, inclining his head towards the sharkskin woman writhing on the ground. 'Of course Yva is lying. She wants that Drowned woman and is too ashamed of her addiction to admit it.'

'Who are you?' Ida asked.

The bowman looked at her with utter disdain, as though the question was one that ought to have required no answer. 'I am Argusto Conquillas,' he said, 'Lord of Herica and the Sumran Islands.'

'I know who you are,' the colonel said. 'You're a long way from Herica.'

Creedy grunted. 'He's Lord of shit now, a dragon fetishist and a Haurstaf toy.'

Conquillas shot him.

Creedy tried to turn away. He was fast, but not fast enough. The arrow tore through the air like a thunderbolt, crackling with black fire. It passed clean through the bridge of Creedy's nose and then out of the right side of his skull behind his eye, before disappearing *into* the vaulted wall sixty yards behind with a sudden *bang*. Ida gaped at the spot where it had vanished. She could still hear a furious snapping sound receding into the distance as it continued on its path beyond that wall and through the foundations of the city itself.

In the heartbeat before Creedy howled and clutched at his face, Ida glimpsed a bloody mess where his right eye had been.

The colonel's men reacted with uproar. Banks grabbed Creedy, who was screaming and worrying his head with bloody fingers. The crows yelled and lifted their hand-cannons. Wheellock dogs clicked back.

'Hold your fire!' the colonel shouted.

Conquillas was holding up a green glass bottle the size of his thumb. It had a small copper stopper wedged in its neck. An arrogant smirk formed on his lips. Behind him, the dragon leaned closer and purred deeply.

'You know what this is?' Conquillas said.

Ida's moistened her lips. Was that a *sea-bottle*? One could buy an apartment in Valcinder with one of those.

The colonel lowered his gun. 'There are innocent people in here.'

'No human is innocent.' Conquillas unplugged the stopper and threw the bottle high into the air, towards the soldiers. Great arcs of dark green brine sprayed out of its open neck – too much liquid, far more than such a tiny container could possibly hold. The bottle bounced three times, then clattered across the ground and, still spewing brine, disappeared under one of the shelves.

The colonel hissed. The liquid had splashed his shoulder, soaking his uniform. He jumped down, his whaleskin boots slapping into the wet floor, then turned to his men and said calmly, 'Find that ichusae and seal it, please.'

Banks clambered down after the officer and was quickly joined by the two crows. The colonel was already on his knees, crawling across the ground as he tried to reach under the opposite bank of shelves. But then he muttered in frustration and stood up again. 'Give me a hand to push it over.' He pressed his body against the shelf, heaving at it with his shoulder. The other three men joined him, and together they pushed.

The shelf tilted back and then slammed to the ground, spilling trove everywhere. Scores of relics fell and smashed. Brine coursed and bubbled across the floor between them. The four soldiers were raking through the treasure, kicking and flinging it aside. 'Here we are,' the colonel said, reaching down.

Ida felt a gust of wind batter her face. She looked up to see the dragon take to the air. Conquillas and the child had disappeared. With its wings shimmering, the beast seemed vague, illusory. Its crystal claws flashed. It roared.

'Wings!' Banks cried.

'Thank you, Private.' The colonel already had his hand-cannon trained on the dragon. In his other hand he held up the bottle. Gallons of brine continued to bubble and froth out of the tiny container, soaking his gloved fist. He forced his thumb down on to the open neck to try and stem the flow, but the pressure was too great. Jets of green liquid sprayed across the fallen treasure. 'I'll need that stopper, Private Swan,' he said. 'As soon as you can.'

'Here, Colonel!' One of the crows had located the stopper.

The great serpent spread out its wings and then fell upon the sharkskin woman lying on the ground sixty paces from the soldiers. Ida turned away just as its open jaws darted down. The woman's scream was cut short by the sound of crunching bones.

By now the colonel had sealed the Unmer bottle. He wiped it dry on the edge of his whaleskin boot and then slipped it into a pocket on the front of his uniform.

The dragon raised its head, blood and brine dripping from its maw. Nothing remained of the sharkskin woman's corpse but a few scraps of meat. It snapped its teeth; its neck reared back like a viper about to strike.

15

The colonel walked towards it, his hand-cannon levelled at its head, and spoke in that same guttural language the serpent had used. 'Yva feroo raka. Onolam nagir.'

'Onolam?' the dragon replied. A prolonged booming noise, perhaps a laugh, came from its throat. 'Nash, nagir seen awar. Bones and blood, little mortal. The laws of men mean nothing to me.'

'Conquillas was right,' the colonel said. 'You are ashamed of your addiction.'

The dragon lowered its long neck, hunched its body behind its forelegs and hissed. Ida could smell the sea upon its breath – the heady stench of salt and metals. Red eyes burned malevolently in the gloom.

And then it pounced.

The sheer power and speed of the creature was astonishing. It shot forward, a blaze of white armour and crystal, its bloody maw open wide.

The colonel fired his hand-cannon into the creature's mouth. To the sound of an enormous detonation, the dragon's head blew apart and spattered across the vaulted ceiling. Chunks of meat rained down far across the marketplace. The massive jaws slid to a stop against the colonel's boot.

He turned to face his men. 'How is Creedy?'

Banks was cradling the sergeant's shoulders. 'He's lost his looks, but he'll live. The pair of them were covered from head to foot in dragon blood. Banks looked around at the mess and grinned. 'Supper's on you then,' he said.

The colonel shook his head. 'I never much liked the taste of dragon.'

CHAPTER 1

HU

An aide held up the bottle for Emperor Hu's inspection. Sweat trails ran down his powdered blue cheeks and through the rouge around his eyes, and he clutched the Unmer container in both trembling hands, clearly terrified of dropping it. The emperor, for his part, looked just as uncomfortable. From a distance of five feet away, Hu leaned his long white face towards the cause of this morning's woes.

'A sea-bottle,' he remarked, rubbing his pointed chin. 'It never ceases to amaze me how such tiny things can cause so much trouble. What do the Unmer call them?'

'Ichusae, your Majesty,' the aide said.

The emperor's hall contained a great expanse of air so pungent with clashing perfumes that one wondered if it was safe to breathe. Sunlight slanted down through high windows in the opposite walls and baked wedges of pink marble floor. Several hundred courtiers had gathered to see the Unmer bottle: a score of the emperor's aides bedecked in jewels and silk kamarbands, legislators huddled together like great red bears in their fur-lined robes, administrators in white wool wigs and grey sacking, shipping magnates from Valcinder, and assorted noblemen and women, favoured artisans, poets and fools, military officers and concubines wearing little but beads. Sworn-blood representatives of at least three enemy warlords were also present, each heavily adorned with gold clasps and chains that had doubtlessly been stolen from Hu's own ships. Their crooked grins suggested mouths full of other men's teeth. Two lines of blind Samarol bodyguard stood between the emperor and his guests, clad in silver mail and eyeless silver helms forged into the likeness of snarling wolves and clutching Unmer seeing knives

'Which means what exactly?' Hu retorted.

The aide looked uncertain.

'It means a doorway.' This answer came from the Haurstaf witch standing nearby. Sister Briana Marks was fair-skinned and flushed with youth. A great tumble of golden hair gathered in the sinuous hollow at the back of her white frock, flashing with sunlight whenever she moved.

Granger's right shoulder was still burning from its exposure to the brine. The weird ichor was gnawing on his nerve-endings like an army of ants as it worked its spell on him, and it took a supreme effort of will to maintain his composure. He did not wish to show weakness in front of Banks, Tummel and Swan. The three privates waited six paces behind him. Sergeant Creedy had remained with the barrack surgeon.

'Doorway,' the emperor muttered. 'What strange creatures the Unmer are.'

A general mutter of agreement passed through the assembled crowd. Fans waved and heads nodded. Strange creatures indeed.

'One sea-bottle hardly matters when thousands more remain scattered across the ocean floors,' Sister Marks said. She gave the emperor a perfect smile, her blue eyes gleaming with impudence, and strolled across the dais to the throne. For a moment Granger thought she was actually going to *sit* in it. But she simply hovered there, one slender hand resting on the gilded arm rest.

'My navy is occupied,' the emperor retorted.

'If your navy was less intent on expanding your empire and more focused on finding these ichusae,' the witch replied, 'there would be no further *need* for expansion. But you'd have them respond to the symptoms rather than cure the disease.'

Emperor Hu dismissed his aide and fixed a look of disdain on the witch. 'Where would the Haurstaf have me search?'

'Why, everywhere, of course.'

A fresh jolt of pain stabbed Granger's damaged shoulder. His collar bone felt like hot iron, and his nerves screamed. *Three more days.* Three more days before it healed or turned to sharkskin. He'd washed the wound thoroughly in clean water, but not soon enough after exposure to be certain it wouldn't alter his flesh for good. Either way, he'd probably lose a great deal of flexibility in the right arm. And that would mean retraining to bring his fencing skills up to par.

The emperor snorted. He raised his voice for the benefit everyone present. 'The Haurstaf would have me leave my empire unguarded while I hunt the seabed for little green bottles.'

A nervous laugh swept through the crowd.

Sister Marks only smiled. 'Without the Haurstaf,' she said carefully, 'you would not have an empire to guard.'

Hu was turning red. 'I could afford a hundred dredgers for what you charge for your services,' he said through his teeth. 'If you would only kill the last of the Unmer and take your witches back to Awl, I would have the resources with which to search the seas.'

'*Kill* the Unmer?' Marks said in affected tones. 'But that would be wrong.'

He glared at her.

'If you're not happy with our little arrangement,' she said. 'We'll gladly leave you to deal with the Unmer yourselves. After all, we do have other clients.'

Granger noted a sharp intake of breath from a few of the assembled guests. One of the warlords' men chuckled. The witch simply regarded Hu with a vague air of contempt. *No ordinary telepath, this one.* Few Haurstaf would have been so arrogant as to humiliate the emperor in his own hall.

Hu's expression darkened. 'Warlords and privateers,' he growled. He flashed a look at the representatives of these same men, before his attention settled on Granger. 'What is *wrong* with you?'

'A minor injury, Emperor,' Granger replied.

'Did I give you permission to speak?'

Granger looked at him coldly. Evidently the witch wasn't the only one who needed a lesson in diplomacy. 'You addressed the hall, Emperor,' he said. 'And I was the logical person to answer your question.' From the corner of his eye, he saw Banks cringe.

Hu glared at him. 'I know you, don't I?'

'Colonel Granger, Emperor.'

A knowing smirk came to the emperor's lips. 'Weaverbrook,' he said. '1432. You're one of the Gravediggers.'

Granger nodded.

'Weaverbrook 1432,' Hu said. 'The largest loss of Imperial troops in my whole campaign.'

'I believe it was the second-largest loss, Emperor.'

Hu snorted a laugh. 'Is that so? For a man who spent more time digging holes for his dead comrades than actually fighting, you don't sound particularly remorseful, Colonel.'

'My men fought bravely,' Granger replied. He could see Banks shaking his head urgently, Swan and Tummel shifting uncomfortably. They didn't want Granger to say what he was about to say. But he said it anyway. 'We took the villages and the outlying farms, as ordered. We secured the peninsula to Coomb, as ordered. We arranged an armistice, and I delivered your terms to the Evensraum Council myself. My men were jubilant but exhausted, and I regret we were ill equipped to withstand the naval bombardment you ordered on our position, Emperor.'

Silence filled the hall, only to be broken a moment later by a laugh from the Haurstaf witch.

'Forgive me, Colonel,' Banks said, 'but why did you have to open your goddamned mouth?'

They were walking along a corridor in the City Fortress. Gem lanterns hung from the rafters, but they were ancient and provided scant illumination in this gloom. Moonlight filtered through a line of small grimy windows that overlooked the Naval Dockyards and the dragon cannery. Even from here, Granger could hear the pounding of the factory machines and smell the blood and salt.

'Did you not see the warlords' men?'

Granger marched ahead.

Banks went on, 'You might as well as commented on the size of the emperor's cock.'

Granger's boots splashed through a puddle. The floor above held tanks of Mare Lux brine to accommodate sharkskin prisoners of war for experimentation, but the old vats leaked constantly, sending trickles of toxic seawater down through the fabric of the building. Damp stained the corridor walls. Chocolate-coloured ichusan crystals had already begun to form in places.

'Actually,' Banks said, 'it might have been less of a problem if you *had*—'

'That's enough,' Granger said.

Banks blew between his teeth. 'Hell,' he said. 'At least I'll take the image of his face to my grave. However soon that'll be.'

'I said, that's enough.'

They found the surgeon in Recovery Room 4. He was leaning over Creedy's head, feeding gauze into the wounded man's eye socket. The sergeant reclined on an enormous adjustable chair, clutching a tray full of bloody surgical implements in his lap.

'That looks like a good clean wound, Sergeant,' Granger observed.

'Hurts like a bastard, sir,' Creedy replied. 'But I've had worse.'

The surgeon looked up. 'I thought it best to avoid the risk of anaesthetic,' he said. 'In this case the arrow has cauterized the wound quite nicely.' He sighed. 'We don't see many injuries like this any more.'

'You sound disappointed,' Granger said.

The other man made a non-committal gesture. 'Void arrows make such lovely wounds. Much cleaner than a sword cut. Much less prone to infection.' He withdrew his bloody fingers from Creedy's eye socket. 'Hand me one of those bandages, will you?'

Granger took a bandage and a couple of snap-pins from a box on a nearby trolley. 'I'll finish this off,' he said. 'Get yourself cleaned up.' He wrapped the bandage around Creedy's head and secured it with a pin.

The recovery room plumbing had been rudely extended to reposition an array of washbasins a foot out from the wall, away from the brine-riddled stonework. The ceiling plaster along the western edge of the room had collapsed, and glassy brown contusions had appeared around the metal window frames. The surgeon washed his hands in fresh water and shook them dry. 'I don't suppose you recovered the arrow?' he asked Granger.

'It disappeared into the vault wall.'

'Shame, shame. Skywards or seawards?'

'A very slight inclination. It must have passed through the city in an instant.'

The surgeon nodded. 'Heading for the stars.' He turned back to Creedy. 'Your eye socket will take an implant, Sergeant. I can have one made up in a couple of weeks. Nothing fancy, just clay and resin.'

'I like the hole just fine.' Creedy thought for a moment. 'Maybe I can keep something useful in there . . . tobacco, ammunition.' He laughed. 'Would it hold a grenade?'

'I have one you could try,' Banks said. 'You can have it for free, Creedy.'

The surgeon made a sound of disapproval. 'I would not recommend that, Sergeant. Colonel, would you like me to take a look at your shoulder?'

Before Granger could reply, the door of the recovery room opened, and a young girl walked in. She couldn't have been more than sixteen, but she wore the robes of a Haurstaf cadet and carried herself with all the authority that implied. She approached the colonel and handed him a sealed envelope. 'Sister Marks asked me to deliver this,' she said. 'It's already in circulation.'

Creedy sat up.

Granger opened the envelope and read the note inside.

24/Hu-Suarin/1441

NOTICE OF WARRANT(110334)

Imperial Infiltration Unit 7 (the 'Gravediggers' – Cmdr Colonel Thomas Granger) is summarily disbanded with immediate effect, pending investigation of article 118 malfeasance. Warrants have been issued for the arrest of the following men:

Colonel Thomas Granger – RN348384793888

Sergeant William Patrick Creedy – RN934308459839

Private Merrad Banks – RN239852389578

Able Seaman Gerhard Tummel – RN934783898

Able Seaman Swan Tummel – RN09859080908

Issued without prejudice on behalf of his Majesty Emperor
Jilak Hu.

He stared at the note for a long time. His shoulder began to
throb with renewed vigour as his heart rate quickened, but he
barely noticed it. He felt strangely numb. He looked at the young
witch. 'How did Sister Marks get this?'

The girl just shrugged. 'She's Haurstaf.'

'What is it?' Creedy asked.

Granger ignored him. 'And why is she helping us?' he said to
the witch.

'She—' The girl suddenly stopped. 'I'm not allowed to say.'
She paused for a minute, then nodded. 'Politics.'

Creedy leaned forward. 'You getting love letters from psychics now?'

'She was the only one who liked his joke,' Banks muttered.

'What joke was that?' Creedy asked.

'The one about the emperor's cock.'

'Be quiet,' Granger said. He took a deep breath. 'Private
Banks, Sergeant Creedy, we are now civilians. Emperor Hu has
disbanded the Gravediggers.'

Nobody spoke.

'We've been charged under article 118,' Granger went on.
'Attempting to escape active duty through self-inflicted injuries.
Warrants already issued. They'll be coming for us at any moment.'

Creedy roared. 'Warrants?'

'We're fugitives.'

'Son of a bitch.'

Granger felt suddenly light-headed. 'Language, Sergeant,' he said. 'A direct insult to the emperor—'

'Fuck him,' Creedy snarled. 'Fuck him and fuck the law. We ought to wring that powdered bastard's neck.' His eye had begun to bleed again, and a red patch was spreading into the bandage. He looked up again in disbelief. 'Self-inflicted injuries?'

'It's close enough to the truth,' Granger said. 'I'm afraid I've let us down.'

'You're not taking sole responsibility for this one, Colonel,' Swan said. 'It was about time somebody said it to his face.'

'I've been itching to have it out with him myself,' Tummel said. 'That pond lily has been living in a fantasy too long.'

Swan gave a derisory grunt. 'Admiral of the Fleet.'

'Captain of War,' Tummel added.

The pair of them chuckled. They were taking great care to move silently through the yard behind the Fenwick Ale House, which only seemed to help their drunken voices carry all the further in the darkness. Private Banks shuffled along beside Granger, wrapped in his own thoughts, but Sergeant Creedy's anger could be heard in the thump of his boots a short distance behind them.

When they reached the yard gate, Tummel glanced over his shoulder to where a yellow outline in the gloom marked the back door of the ale house. 'When did you last clear the tab?' he asked his brother.

'Three days ago,' Swan replied.

'Shame. Noril's usually good for a week.'

'Quiet now,' Granger said. He listened for a few moments at the gate, then eased it open. The five men filed out into the alleyway behind. All was silent, but for a tolling bell down by the harbour. Overhead, the city rooftops and chimneys sawed a jagged silhouette across the grand sweep of the cosmos, where the stars sparkled like fine particles of glass. The smell of brine filled Granger's nostrils. He hefted his kitbag higher onto his shoulder and started walking.

They hurried along the alleyway without another word, until they reach the junction with the main thoroughfare. Granger held up his hand to halt his men. He peered from the shadows. Lamps burned in the windows of the traders' houses on Wicklow Street, throwing cross-hatch patterns across the paving stones all the way down the hill to the harbour. The masts of trawlers and whalers cluttered the water's edge like cattails. Stevedores were working on the quayside down there, unloading crates by the light from whale-oil braziers. On the peninsula side of the bay, the dock warehouses and sailors' hostels clung to the cliffs under the shadow of the City Fortress.

Granger scanned the buildings around that black-water basin until he found what he was looking for. A group of nine Imperial soldiers were waiting outside the Harbour Freight Office, carbine rifles slung across their backs. He traced the road around to the shadowy mass of the dragon cannery situated at the breakwater side of the bay and spotted another unit guarding the entrance to the deepwater docks. This group was smaller – only two men.

'Samarol,' he muttered.

Banks moved to his side. 'I always wondered if they could see in the dark.'

'Better than most men,' Granger replied. He thought for a moment. 'We'll reach it by sea.' He pointed to an area several hundred yards west of the harbour, where a great expanse of partially submerged and roofless houses stretched out into the sea. 'Out through the Sunken Quarter, around the breakwater and back in to the cannery landing ramp itself.'

'You want to steal a trover's boat?'

'Borrow,' Granger said. 'There should be dozens of them hidden down there.'

'That'll be because trovers are shot on sight, Colonel.'

'The emperor's men will be looking landward tonight.'

Banks shrugged his agreement.

They cut straight across Wicklow Street and delved into the network of cobbled lanes that ran like veins down towards the Sunken Quarter. The town houses, like all those in Upper Losoto, were Unmer built, and their pillared marble façades reeked of arrogance. Many had been slavers' homes, and the brick foundations of the old stock pens could still be seen in a few of the adjoining courtyards, now converted into gazebos, pergolas or fountains by the new owners. Granger wondered how many of those slaves had gone on to occupy their former masters' homes after the Uprising. Not many, he supposed. The Unmer slavers had butchered their human chattel after the Battle of Awl, when the victorious Haurstaf navy had turned their ships east towards Losoto.

These streets had run with blood.

They passed through a small quadrangle where four grand, shuttered houses faced each other across the spider-web remains of an ancient spell garden. A faintly bitter aroma still surrounded the dead winter-wools, peregollins, spleenworts and liverworts. Sergeant Creedy covered his mouth and nose and muttered something about the inducement of dark dreams. Tummel and Swan ribbed him for the next two streets until Granger ordered them to be quiet.

The houses became more dilapidated as the men drew near to the sea. Smashed windows looked out into the lanes, the rooms inside dark. The stench of brine overpowered everything else. Granger found Banks at his side again. 'The trovers in Ratpen Pennow hide their boats on the rooftops,' the private said. 'Small canoes. They lower them down at night.'

Granger shook his head. 'This isn't the Ratpen,' he said. 'We should be able to find an illegal mooring in one of the sunken ruins. By the last Imperial reckoning, there were two or three dozen of them.'

'Planks on the wall?'

'That's what I was thinking.'

The private nodded. 'With any luck we'll find a cache as well. What did Creedy tell you about his cannery man?'

'A cousin of a cousin,' Granger said. 'Ex-navy. Works as a descaler now.' He shrugged. 'Creedy trusts him, and the price is fair.'

'I've been meaning to talk to you about that,' Banks said. He hesitated for a long moment. 'I never did get a chance to put very much away, sir. My old man back in the Ratpen lost his pension to some bad investments, so most of my salary went home to him and his sisters.' He glanced back over his shoulder. 'I don't suppose Swan and Tummel are in much of a better state. You've seen them play cards.'

'Don't worry about it, Private,' Granger said. 'It's been taken care of.'

Banks seemed about to say something, then changed his mind. Finally he said, 'I'll pay you back somehow, sir.'

'I know,' Granger said.

They arrived at a street running parallel to the coast. The houses here were utterly derelict, a crumbling bank of boarded-up windows and partially collapsed roofs. Graffiti covered the walls. Across the façade immediately before them, someone had scrawled in huge black letters:

WHY ARE WE PAYING TO KEEP THE UNMER ALIVE?

Most of the doors had been staved in, revealing cavernous rooms beyond. Granger poked his head through the nearest doorway. The reck of brine filled the darkness. Through an open doorway in the opposite wall, he heard the gentle slosh of seawater coming from the rooms beyond. He glanced around. Nothing but wet rubble and the remains of an old fire.

They set off down the street, peering into each of the houses. After a short while Banks gave a low whistle and beckoned the others over to one particular house.

Inside, the room was as damp and miserable as any other, a gloomy, rubble-filled shell with two doorways in the opposite wall. The only thing different was a wooden plank leaning against the wall to the left of the door. Granger set down his kitbag, then picked up the plank and carried it over to the first of the doorways opposite.

It had been a kitchen once. The sinks had been ripped out and taken, but a rusted iron stove remained under the chimney stack. Most of the ceiling had collapsed, along with a good part of the roof above, and heavy beams lay strewn across the floor. A doorway led out into what must have once been a back garden or courtyard. The floor here was an inch deep in brine. In this gloom the brown water looked like tar.

'There,' Banks said. He was pointing to a place low on the back door frame. 'You see those marks? Something has been knocked against the wood.'

Granger returned for his kitbag. He opened it and handed out hemp face masks and sailors' goggles to his men. They wouldn't need them unless the wind picked up, but it was best to be safe. With the lenses resting on his forehead, and the mask slung loosely around his neck, he traversed the kitchen again, stepping between mounds of rubble to keep his boots out of the brine. The back doorway led to a courtyard full of dark seawater. Steps vanished down into that toxic murk. Granger couldn't tell how deep the water was, but it was unlikely to be more than a few feet here. Small waves came through an open gate in the back wall of the yard, pushing in from the lane beyond, and lapping around the edges of the enclosed space. Someone had built a number of stone piles leading out through that gate, like widely spaced stepping stones.

Granger lowered the plank between the doorway and the first pile, then turned back into the kitchen. 'Bring me some of those ceiling beams,' he said.

Soon they had constructed a rudimentary walkway out into the lane, which turned out to be a narrow channel running between the courtyards of opposing ranks of houses. The buildings further out were little more than roofless shells, all of them Unmer dwellings, except for the twelve Haurstaf watchtowers that loomed like a great henge over a walled section the Sunken Quarter. From here, the stone piles led away in both directions. They would have to lift planks and beams from the start of the walkway and lay them down in the lane ahead to progress any further.

Granger stared up at the watchtowers.

Banks followed his gaze. 'It's the size of that place gets me,' he said.

'You mean how large it is, or how small?'

'Both,' Banks replied. 'That used to be the largest Unmer ghetto in the world. Sixty blocks in all.' He blew through his teeth, then shrugged. 'Doesn't seem so big when you think how many Unmer they managed to squeeze in there.'

Granger nodded. After the Uprising, the Haurstaf had refused to allow the liberated Losotan slaves to execute their former masters. Such genocide would have offered them no profit. Instead, they'd confined half a million Unmer souls to that one small part of the city and left twelve telepaths behind to form a psychic cordon around them. *The Veil of Screams.* How many Unmer had died trying to pass through that invisible barrier? It

30

had been more effective than any tangible wall could ever have been. Losoto's taxpayers had been paying for it dearly ever since.

Creedy frowned. 'So we're going the other way? That whole place is likely to stink of sorcery.'

Banks laughed. 'An Unmer ghetto? There can't be many places *less* likely to stink of sorcery. You try weaving a spell with a witch sticking psychic needles into your brain. The Unmer couldn't even take a shit without Haurstaf approval.' He shook his head. 'I'll tell you what, though, if I was a trover, that's exactly the sort of place I'd hide my stash.'

Creedy's frown dissolved. 'You reckon there's treasure in there?'

Banks shrugged. 'Creepy old places like that have an aura of mystery about them. And that keeps the idiots out.'

Creedy turned to Granger. 'We could check it out, Colonel.'

Granger shook his head. 'We're here to look for a boat, Sergeant. And that means locating an illegal mooring. Banks?'

'It's this way,' the private said, jabbing his thumb in the opposite direction to the watchtowers.

'That's a crapping guess,' Creedy said.

Banks sighed. 'Look at those piles,' he said, pointing further down the lane. 'You see where the ichusan crystals are broken? Someone put down planks.'

They set off again, lifting beams from behind them and laying them down on the stone piles ahead. Soon they reached an opening in the seaward wall which led into another yard. The stepping stones vanished through the kitchen door of the house beyond. Banks crouched to study the surroundings closely, then nodded to Granger. They made a bridge over to the house.

The kitchen opened into a hallway blocked by a collapsed staircase. Someone had left a ladder in its place. Granger's unit manhandled their planks and beams up to the first floor and

31

carried them over rotten floorboards to the front of the house. Here an empty room overlooked a black canal clogged with mats of seaweed and rubbish from the still-living city. Brine sucked at the brickwork. It smelled like a sewer. The gap between this house and the one opposite was narrow enough to be spanned by the longest of their beams.

'Goddamn rat's maze,' Creedy muttered as he slid the beam across to the first-floor window of the opposite house.

'Nothing wrong with rats,' Tummel said. 'There's good meat on rats.'

'Very good,' Swan agreed. 'We had a little farm going in our attic. Rats as big as dogs we had, hundreds of them. We were going to sell them down the market.'

'Rat stew with dumplings,' Tummel said.

'Rat on a stick,' Swan added.

Creedy glared at them. 'You pair make me sick,' he said. He climbed up on to one end of the beam, tested it with his foot and then strolled across to the opposite house.

'The man has no taste,' Swan said. 'It's not as if he hasn't eaten rat before.'

'Best keep that quiet,' Tummel said.

As Granger stomped over the makeshift bridge after Sergeant Creedy, he experienced a moment of dizziness. For an instant he wavered between the black, sucking brine and the stars cartwheeling across the heavens above. He halted and crouched on the beam until the moment passed.

'Colonel?' Banks was clinging to the window frame of the house behind, his hand outstretched.

Granger shook his head. 'Lack of sleep,' he muttered. But it had seemed to him something far more profound, as if the universe had just *shifted* around him. He looked down at the beam and noticed an old Unmer sigil carved into the grain: an eye encircled. This particular lump of wood had once been part of an Unmer ship. Hadn't eye sigils been used to observe a ship's crew from afar? Granger wasn't entirely sure. So much of their understanding of Unmer sorcery was little more than conjecture. He stood up, careful to keep his heavy kitbag from unbalancing him. Creedy waited in the opposite room with his fists on his hips.

Granger crossed over the remainder of the bridge and ducked through the window into another dark bedroom.

'Signs of life here, Colonel,' Creedy said, shifting a pile of empty cans with the toe of his boot. 'Trovers used this place recently.' It was an observation that need not have been said, but Granger gave his sergeant a nod. Creedy had a habit of taking even the smallest opportunity to prove his worth when Banks was around.

The other three men arrived. Now that they were far enough from the occupied city to avoid detection, Granger opened his kitbag and took out a gem lantern. He handed it to Banks, who opened its shutters. Light flooded the dismal chamber. Tummel helped Swan pull the bridge across to their side, and then the whole group set off through the derelict house. The rooms had all been stripped bare. They filed along passageways still clad in peeling wallpaper with floral or mathematical designs. They peered out of glassless windows into drowned lanes and gardens steeped in darkness. They stepped over the skeleton of a dog. Openings smashed through the outer walls gave them access to adjacent buildings. And always Banks's keen eyes kept them on the correct path through this brine-sodden labyrinth.

Finally they came to the doorway of a large attic. A square trapdoor occupied the centre of the floor beyond. The hatch was padlocked shut, but marks in the dust around it indicated it had been opened recently. Creedy was about to step through, when Granger seized his arm.

Creedy froze.

Granger slid his kitbag down from his shoulder. He held it out at arm's length over the floorboards inside the doorway. Then, keeping a hold of the strap, he let the heavy bag drop.

The floorboards shattered where it hit the floor, falling into the darkness below. Granger heard the splash of water.

Banks looked down at the hole and blew through his teeth. 'They must have chiselled into the floorboards from below.'

Granger nodded. 'That's what I would do.'

The men stepped over the hole and into the attic. Creedy broke the lock hinge with the butt of his hand-cannon and opened the trapdoor.

Two wooden canoes floated on brine four feet below the opening. Their mooring lines had been tied to a bent nail under the floor. Creedy moved to ease himself down through the opening, but Granger stopped him. He opening his kitbag again and pulled out a length of wire cord, which he attached to the handle of the gem lantern. Then he lay down on the floor, lowered the light down through the trapdoor and poked his head through after it.

The smell of that black brine made him cough. The canoes rocked gently in the centre of a broad chamber. Treasure-hunting equipment packed each narrow hull – the nets, lines and hooks the trovers used to haul up Unmer artefacts from the deep. A hole on the northern wall led out to the sunken lanes beyond.

Granger lowered the lantern even further, allowing it sink down beneath the surface of the poisonous seawater. As the light descended, it illuminated the flooded room below the canoes: bare brick walls, a rubble-strewn floor.

Banks's voice came suddenly from behind. 'Bloody hell.'

Three women and a boy stood under the surface of the brine, their corpse-eyes gazing up at the lantern above them. They waited, immobile and expressionless, their grey sharkskin flesh draped in the last tatters of their former clothing. Slowly, one of the women reached up her hands towards the light.

'That one's fresh,' Tummel said. 'Can't be more than three or four days since they drowned her. The others are just about gone. The little one's probably her son. Looks enough like her.'

Granger stared down at the people under the water. He'd heard of trovers drowning people to scour the seabed for treasure, but he'd never seen any until now. The victims' personalities couldn't survive for more than a few days. After that, they'd forget who they were. They'd drift away, become part of the sea itself.

'Fucking trovers,' Banks said.

Creedy peered down over his shoulder and laughed. 'That is one phenomenally ugly bitch,' he said. 'You ask me, they did her a favour.'

Banks wheeled round and took a swing at Creedy. But the big man was way too fast for him. He knocked Banks's blow aside with his elbow and then drove his fist into the smaller man's stomach. Banks doubled over, gasping, and dropped to his knees. Creedy raised his hand to strike him across the back of the neck.

'Sergeant!' Granger said.

Creedy lowered his hand. He looked abashed. 'Fucker started it,' he said. He spat on the floor and then walked over to the doorway to be by himself.

Granger pulled up the lantern. He couldn't do anything for the Drowned but leave them in peace. 'Banks, Swan and Tummel, take the first canoe,' he said. 'Sergeant Creedy, you're with me in the second.'

One by one they dropped down into the small craft. Granger passed down his kitbag to Creedy. Once it was safely stowed, he eased himself down into the tiny boat, untied the lines and then pushed off against the low ceiling with the paddle. Both canoes slid across the dark water and passed through the hole in the wall.

Stars glimmered above. They paddled through a large glass-less greenhouse, where the branches of sunken trees reached out to pluck at them. Granger glanced back to see Swan edging the other canoe along behind with all the skill of an old smuggler. Banks sat between the two brothers, wrapped in sullen silence. They glided out of the greenhouse into another yard, slipped through a set of tall iron gates and reached a channel where the walls and railings on the far side side barely broke the surface of the water. The tide was going out, Granger noted. He could see ichusan crystals clinging to the metalwork, glinting as Creedy moved the gem lantern across the brine.

'Eyes ahead, Sergeant,' Granger said. 'This is no time to search for trove.'

Creedy glanced back over his shoulder. 'I saw bubbles, sir. Could have been a sea-bottle down there.'

Granger shook his head. 'It's just the Drowned,' he said. 'The Unmer sank all their ichusae in deep water.' After they'd realized that defeat was inevitable, the Unmer had seeded the oceans with god-only-knew how many millions of these toxic little bottles. It had been an act of astonishing spite, so typical of the Unmer. They would watch the world drown in poison rather than leave it to their enemies.

Creedy peered down into the black water. 'You reckon those women are following us?' he said.

Granger nodded. 'It's what they were trained to do.'

Creedy wrapped his cloak more tightly around his shoulders and said nothing more about it for a while. He gazed up at the blazing heavens. He sniffed and spat into the water. Finally he said, 'How did you know they were down there at all? Why lower the lantern into *that* pool of brine?'

36

'Intuition.'

'Like that time in Weaverbrook? The food panic?'

Granger shrugged.

'Or when you got us out of the Fall Caves?' Creedy looked at him intently. 'Or Ancillor? What was that bloody warlord called? Captain something?' He shook his head and grinned. 'I reckon you've got some Haurstaf blood in you somewhere, Colonel. If you'd been born a woman, they'd have snatched you away to Awl a long time ago.'

Granger said nothing. His great-grandmother had indeed come from Port Awl, but he never talked about it. That sort of heritage wasn't likely to win him many favours in the Imperial Army. Not that the old woman had ever belonged to the Guild, or shown even a glimmer of psychic ability. She'd made her money dressing corpses.

They reached the end of the lane and paddled out into a glooming quadrangle where the town houses had been scorched by dragonfire an age ago. Brine lapped the front-door lintels. Four human skeletons hung from an upper window. Granger spied residues of red paint on their bones. *A trovers' territory marker.* A battle had been fought here over treasure rights. Man's liberation from slavery had merely given them the freedom to slaughter each other. *Our world is drowning, and we squabble over trinkets.* He wondered if mankind had always been so flawed.

A mound of rubble blocked any passage to the south. Banks looked around and then gave a short whistle. He pointed to a window fronting one particular house, where the panes and lead cames had been smashed out, leaving a wide gap. The men steered the canoes between jutting shards of glass and into a room that must have once been a grand entrance hall. A sweeping marble staircase sank into the brine. The rising seas had drowned everything but the uppermost four feet. Creedy held up his lantern to inspect a chandelier depending from the ceiling rose. Its lowest candles were submerged in brine. Ichusan crystals covered the curlicues of brass and ran up the chain itself.

'The tide must be going out,' he said.

A ragged hole in the back wall gave them access to an inner corridor behind the staircase, where the hulls of their small craft knocked and scraped the stonework on either side. Someone had fixed a rope to the ceiling, which they used to pull themselves along. They negotiated the boats around a tight corner and into a further passageway flanked by doorways on both sides. Through the last of these openings, Granger spotted the unmistakable glow of a lantern.

Trovers?

Creedy must have seen it too, for he immediately shuttered their own light. He looked back at Granger, his huge body now silhouetted against the dim yellow illumination at the end of the passageway. Then he reached inside his jacket and withdrew his hand-cannon. Granger heard the *click* of the weapon's wheel-lock.

Granger pulled the canoe along silently towards the source of the light. He couldn't identify any man-made sounds coming from that room, just the slosh of seawater against their own hull. As the bow of the canoe reached the doorway, he reached out and braced the craft against the wall to accommodate any recoil from the sergeant's cannon.

Creedy's face became illuminated – a battlefield corpse face with its mess of bloody bandages and teeth bared as if in a rictus of death. He held his weapon in one powerful fist, training it on the room behind the doorway. He scanned the room for an instant and then turned back to Granger and placed a finger against his lips. Then he grabbed the sides of the door frame and pulled the canoe through.

They were in a ballroom. Huge windows occupied the southern wall, the panes all broken to provide exits from the building. Long chains fixed to the ceiling supported gem lanterns, but the seawater had risen above them and they now shone underwater. Ripples of light chased each other across faded scenes painted onto the corbelled plaster overhead. There were images of long-dead Unmer kings and queens at court, pale exquisite palaces set among woodlands or ornamental gardens, depictions of ships at sea and then moored at harbour, where human slaves unloaded chests of jewels and strange golden machines. The painted heavens above these scenes contained a great mass of stars joined by interconnected lines and mathematical symbols. Taken as a whole, the artwork seemed to tell the story of the Unmer's arrival from the East and the subsequent enslavement of the human race.

The ballroom itself was empty, but for a floating platform being used as a mooring for three blood-red dragon-hide skiffs. Upon this makeshift dock lay a man wrapped in a dirty blanket. He appeared to be asleep.

Creedy inclined his head toward the skiffs. Granger nodded. Those vessels were more suited to the open sea. He glanced back to see Tummel manoeuvring the other canoe quietly through the doorway. Banks and Swan had their own weapons out.

Without a sound, they paddled across the room to the dock.

Granger peered down at the ballroom floor two fathoms below. It was littered with rubble, opened cans, snarls of wire and broken nets. He couldn't see any of the Drowned, but he spotted a pile of bones from at least three more human skeletons. A chain rose from a concrete anchor to the underside of the platform. Shoals of small silver fish glided through the murky water.

The sleeping trover did not stir as Granger slid his canoe alongside. His mouth was open. He was snoring softly. He wore soiled whaleskins, too large for his narrow shoulders, and sported an uneven beard that grew only from the few remaining patches of his jaw not burned by seawater. Sergeant Creedy disembarked silently, then walked over and jammed the barrel of his hand-cannon down over the trover's mouth.

'Wakey wakey, son,' he said.

The man's eyes flicked open. He would surely have screamed if Creedy's gun hadn't entirely obscured his lips. He managed a gasp and tried to get up, but the sergeant just shook his head. 'Where do you hide your trove?'

Granger stepped onto the platform and dragged his kitbag after him. He inspected the skiffs. One was leaking from holes in the hide, but the remaining two looked sound enough. He helped Banks and Swan out of the other canoe, then reached an arm down to assist Tummel. The old soldier groaned and complained about stiffness in his legs.

'More brine than blood in my veins,' he muttered.

'More whisky, you mean,' Swan said. 'Give me hand with that skiff.'

'Your stash,' Creedy said, holding the barrel of his weapon firmly over the trover's mouth. 'Where d'you keep it?'

The man began to choke.

'Leave it,' Granger said. 'We're only here for the boats.'

Creedy spat. 'We'll need money where we're going, sir.'

'We're not thieves, Sergeant.'

Swan and Tummel had untied the soundest of the skiffs. It was also packed with nets, hooks and lines – larger versions of the equipment in the canoes – along with goggles and whaleskin cloaks to protect the treasure hunters from caustic sea spray. Granger unfastened the other boats and kicked them away from the dock. Then he shoved the two canoes out after them.

The four men clambered into the open-decked craft, leaving Creedy pinning the trover to the dock.

'Sergeant,' Granger said.

Creedy leaned his big ugly face closer to his captive. 'Tell me where it is, you son of a bitch.'

'Sergeant.'

Creedy gave a growl of frustration, then released the trover and stood up. He kicked the man hard in the ribs and swung back his boot to do it again.

'We're leaving, Sergeant,' Granger said. 'Right now.'

Creedy stomped over and got into the stern seat beside Tummel, while Swan and Banks slotted oars into the rowlocks midway along the hull. Granger stuffed his kitbag down by his feet and pushed off from the bow.

They crossed the ballroom, leaving the stranded trover gazing after them.

'Who the hell are you?' he shouted. 'You're not Imperial soldiers.'

Creedy raised his hand-cannon.

'Lower you weapon, Sergeant,' Granger said.

They rowed the skiff out through one of the windows.

The street outside was broader, and the sea noticeably rougher, here. Waves washed through the roof spaces of ruined houses. The land below must have fallen away more steeply beyond this point, because the five men reached the edge of the Sunken Quarter after only three blocks. Ahead lay open ocean, silver in the star-light. To the west they could see foam thrashing against the dark ridge of the harbour breakwater. On the landward side stood the cannery, with the Fortress peninsula behind. Lanterns burned on the decks of an old iron dragon-hunter moored at the cannery loading ramp.

The skiff pitched and rolled, but Banks and Swan kept her bow pointed towards the waves. The wind was fresh, but manage-able, and they made good progress. Every man aboard had sailed in worse. They wore the trovers' goggles and whaleskin cloaks to guard against sea spray, and they stuffed scraps of sackcloth into the rowlocks to muffle the sound of the oars. They didn't speak, lest the wind carry their voices back to the shore. Soon they had cleared the breakwater and were heading back into the harbour.

Unseen in the dark, they slipped past the port side of the dragon-hunter. The silhouettes of her harpoons could be seen overhead, pointing at the stars. Her engines throbbed inside her iron belly. The rich odour of meat filled the air here, mingling with the ever-present shipyard aromas of brine and oil.

Creedy directed them to a ladder beside the cannery loading ramp at the rear of the ship, where the sea was red with blood. Granger held the skiff while his men disembarked, then tied her bow line to the ladder and hefted his kitbag over his shoulder before climbing up the greasy rungs after them.

The sea door at the rear of the dragon-hunter had been lowered onto the loading ramp below, revealing the ship's cavernous interior. At the top of the ramp, a massive steel winch waited beside an overhead conveyor system of hooks and chains designed to uplift carcasses and carry them through an enormous doorway obscured by flaps of whaleskin.

Three big stevedores worked to unload the vessel. Two of them dragged a pair of hooked chains down the blood-soaked loading ramp below the winch and disappeared with them into the darkness of the ship's hold. After a moment, one of them called out, 'Pull.'

The third man had remained at the winch. He clanked a lever forward, whereupon the chains tightened and then slowly began to reel back onto a huge spool. As Granger watched, the carcass of a dragon emerged from the ship's hold. It was a common red from the Sea of Kings, about eighty feet from snout to tail-tip. The chain hooks had been rammed into the flesh between the scales at the nape of its neck. Its crumpled wings scraped over the bloody concrete as the chain dragged it up the ramp towards the huge factory doorway. The stevedores emerged from the ship again, following a few yards behind. The dragon was still bleeding out from a harpoon wound in its chest. At the top of the ramp, the third man stopped the winch. His two comrades unhooked the carcass from one set of chains and hooked it up to another pair fixed to the conveyor system above.

'That's Davy,' Creedy said, pointing to a fourth man who had just appeared through the factory doorway. He was a lean, hard-faced fellow, draped in bloody oilskins. A cheroot hung from the corner of his mouth. He carried a head-spade like a staff. He glanced at the carcass, then pulled a lever on the wall behind.

Another *clunk*, and the dragon carcass rose from the concrete floor, pulled up onto the overhead conveyor system by hooks in its neck and in the base of its tail. When it was fully off the ground, Davy halted the mechanism and then threw another switch.

The conveyor gave a jerk, a rattle, and then rumbled forward, carrying the suspended carcass through the whale-hide doorway.

'Davy!' Creedy called.

The hard-faced man looked up. He frowned and then jerked his head over his shoulder. And then he disappeared back through the doorway into the factory.

'Come on,' Creedy said.

Granger and the others followed the sergeant along the edge of the loading ramp, while the two stevedores below returned the chains to the ship to hook up another carcass. Creedy pushed through the whaleskin flaps covering the conveyor doorway.

Davy was waiting for them on the other side. He glared at Creedy and growled, 'I said two.'

They were in an enormous butchering hall, where dozens of dragon carcasses trundled along the overhead conveyor system. Workers slewed off scales with head-spades and opened bellies to spill out guts and hacked off wings and flesh with heavy machetes. White bones glistened among red meat. Blood ran in runnels across the floor and collected in frothing channels. The smell and heat was overpowering.

'Two, five, what's the difference?' Creedy said.

'The difference is, I only got two suits,' Davy replied. 'The price was for two. We already agreed that.'

Granger stepped between them. 'What does he mean?' he said to Creedy. 'The arrangement was for all five of us.'

Creedy looked at the ground. 'You couldn't afford five,' he said. 'Those suits aren't cheap.'

Granger took a deep breath. 'What did you think was going to happen when we got here?'

Creedy shrugged. 'I dunno,' he said. 'Maybe whaleskins. Hell, what was I supposed to say? I thought you'd figure something out. You always figure something out.'

Davy laughed. 'Whaleskins? You'll be dead in a day.'

Granger turned to him. 'Show me.'

He led them through the butchering hall and through a set of hangar doors into a cold room. Here, lying among blocks of ice, was an enormous green dragon. It was twice the size of the reds. Its mouth had been propped open with a head-spade, revealing the pink tunnel of its throat. One of its eyes stared glassily at the ceiling, the other had been mangled into red pulp. On the floor beside it lay two bulky brass diving suits. They looked perilously old and rotten.

'You were lucky,' Davy said. 'We've not seen a monster like this in months.' He rested a hand on the dragon's snout. 'She sank two ships, dragged them straight to the bottom, before the third put a harpoon through her eye.'

Banks blew through his teeth. 'That is one phenomenally ugly bitch,' he said. 'She reminds me of someone.' He looked over at Creedy. 'Can't think who, though.'

44

Creedy gave him a grim smile.

'You aren't gonna survive in there without a suit,' Davy said. 'Not all the way to Ethugra, anyways. These greens have guts like acid. Burn a man alive.'

'Can you get more suits?' Granger said.

Davy snorted. 'Tonight?' He stared at the dragon for a long moment. 'Maybe for sixteen thousand, I can get one.'

'I don't have that sort of money.'

'Then you're screwed, aren't you? Ship sails at dawn.'

Banks stepped up to Granger. 'You and Creedy go,' he said. 'We'll follow when we can.'

Granger shook his head.

'Creedy knows Ethugra,' Banks said. 'You'll need him once you get there.'

'Makes sense to me,' Creedy said.

'No,' Granger insisted. 'I'm not leaving anyone behind. Banks and Swan can use the diving suits. The rest of us will have to wrap up in whaleskins. Once the carcass is aboard, we'll climb out and look for another place to hide.'

Creedy grunted. 'It's a goddamn prison ship. Where you going to hide?'

'We'll deal with that problem when we have to,' Granger said.

'The sergeant's right for once,' Swan said. 'We wouldn't stand a chance on a ship like that, not outside that big green bastard. You and Creedy take the suits.' He sniffed and wiped his nose on his sleeve. 'To be honest, I never much liked the idea of Ethugra anyway.'

'Absolute shit-hole,' Tummel agreed. 'Too many jailers and not enough publicans.'

'Gambling's illegal in Ethugra,' Swan muttered.

'Everything's illegal in Ethugra,' Tummel said.

Banks nodded. 'We'll take our chances here.'

Creedy had already chosen the better of the two diving suits and began to pull it on.

Granger wouldn't have ordered them to obey him if he still had the power to do so. They were his men – the last and best of his men – but more than that, they were their own men. He couldn't order them, but he didn't have to abandon them either. 'I'm staying here,' he said. 'One of you can have that suit.'

'I don't think you understand, sir,' Banks said. 'If you don't go, the suit stays empty.' He glanced over at Swan and Tummel, and then the three of them turned around and walked away.

Banks looked back once over his shoulder. 'Tell Creedy we're going to find the trover's stash.'

The sergeant had lifted the heavy brass helmet onto his shoulders, but hadn't yet clamped it down. 'Son of a bitch,' he muttered, his voice muffled by the cumbersome headpiece. 'Just our luck if the bastard finds it.'

'The suit filters will take worst of the brine out of the air,' Davy said, 'and there's a jerry can of water already in there. Don't take off your helmets except when you need to drink. And for god's sake, don't damage the dragon. It's going to a collector.' He glanced between the two men. 'That's it, except for the money.'

Granger pulled out a wad of gilders from his kitbag and gave it to Davy. It was everything he had. Then he gathered up the other diving suit and began to clamber inside it. Creedy snapped down the last of his helmet clamps and peered out through the circular window at his own gloved hands. 'How do I take a piss?' he said.

'The usual way,' Davy said. 'Good luck.'

Creedy got on his hands and knees and crawled inside the dragon's mouth. After a moment, he called back, 'Holy shit, Colonel, you'll never guess what this thing has eaten.'

SIX YEARS LATER

CHAPTER 2

A OO A APEE

Dear Margaret,

Thanks to Mr Swinekicker, I'm now officially dead. This means you can make the payments directly to him without losing half of it to tax, which will save you money and allow me to remain here in prison for twice as long. Yesterday I saw a bird soaring above my cell window. I don't know what sort it was, but it was white and it had something clutched in its claws. Didn't birds like that once dive for fish?

I wonder what this one had?

All my love,
Alfred

The brine had risen another inch in the week since he'd last been down here. All the books he'd piled upon the floorboards to act as stepping stones had now vanished under its toxic brown surface. Granger stood at the bottom of the steps with his lantern raised and peered along the flooded corridor, wondering how he was going to get the prison register out of the storage room at the far end. He only had one more book left, and sacrificing that one wouldn't help. The air down here had a burned-salt, chemical aroma, like the air in a whaling station. He pulled his goggles over his eyes, then squatted down as close to the water as he dared, swinging the light around him. Dead beetles floated everywhere. Blisters of green paint and brown ichusan crystals marred the walls along the waterline, but the cell doors on either side of the passage looked intact.

'Anyone still alive down here?' he called.

He heard a thump and a splash, as if something had been thrown against one of the doors, then a man's voice called back from the shadows: 'Give me some food, you son of a bitch.'

Granger raised his goggles and went back up the stairs.

Creedy had tilted his chair back on its rear legs and sat with his boots resting on the munitions crate Granger used as a table. A huge man with a boxer's face and hair shaved close to his skull, he still possessed an aura of brute savagery. Even now he was gnawing on a dragon knuckle, sucking at the cartilage and ripping shreds of meat free with soft, bestial grunts. Most men with a past like his would have chosen to hide it, but William Patrick Creedy still wore the Gravediggers' tattoo on the back of his hand openly, proudly, challenging anyone who saw it to betray him to the emperor's men. It was an attitude that had almost killed him more than once. Grey patches of sharkskin marred one side of his jaw – an injury sustained when six privateers had pinned him, momentarily, to a wet dockside in Tallship. His left ear was missing, hacked off in that same brawl. Creedy simply didn't give a shit. His clockwork eye ticked with the steady precision of a detonator, the small blue lens shuttling back and forth in its socket, but his good eye – the cunning one – was watching Granger. 'What's the situation, Colonel?' he asked.

'The brine's risen another inch,' he replied.

'I meant, are any of your guests still breathing?'

Granger shrugged. 'I didn't hear anything.'

'Good,' Creedy said. 'You're officially a priority now. Since they can't expect a man to make a living from an empty jail, they are obliged do something about it.' He leaned forward and spat out a piece of gristle. 'That's the law.'

Granger hung his lantern on a wall hook. 'I can't get to the register,' he said.

'The hell you keep it down there for anyway?'

The truth was Granger hadn't thought about going back for it, not since the old man's death. But Creedy would never have understood that. All but one of the names in the register had lines scored through them, and after that final one he didn't think he wanted to add any more. If he accepted more prisoners he'd have to feed them, and it might be years before their families ran out of money to send. And then it would be Granger himself who'd have to carry down the last meal; Thomas Granger who'd have to watch them die. The hardest part of job was the part he did for free.

He wasn't running a prison so much as a tomb.

'You should have built that other storey like old Swinekicker said,' Creedy remarked. 'Another couple of winters like the last one, and the Mare Lux will be lapping your balls. What are you going to do when you run out of space? Where are you going to live? I mean, look at this place, man.'

The detritus of Granger's life filled a series of cramped spaces under the building's coombed attic ceilings. A jumble of wood, whale- and dragon-bones supported the roof. Morning light fell through the windows facing Halcine Canal, illuminating piles of spent shell casings, drip-pans positioned under leaks, carpentry tools, oarlocks and old engine parts from the Trove Market in Losoto. In the centre of the room sat a massive anchor, too heavy for Granger to lift on his own. God knows how Swinekicker had got it in here. A flap of whaleskin covered the hole leading out to the eaves, while the wooden hatch it had replaced rested against the wall nearby. He'd been forced to rip the little door off its

51

hinges to drag the old man's coffin out. You could still see the scrapes the heavy box had left in the floorboards; they looked like gouges left by fingernails.

'It's a prison,' he said. 'What do you expect it to look like?'

Creedy grunted. 'Other people manage to keep themselves in comfort. You're letting this place slip under.' He looked around. 'That hatch'll go back on easy enough.'

Granger didn't reply.

'And you could raise the floors in the cells downstairs.'

Granger shrugged. 'Some people build things . . .'

'. . . and other people break them,' Creedy finished, with an oafish laugh. 'Do you remember Dunbar?'

Granger was looking for a crowbar among his tools. 'Dunbar's underwater now,' he said. He couldn't find the crowbar so he picked up a head-spade instead and carried it over to a spot at the far end of the living room, about forty paces from the front gable. He got down on his knees and crawled around, squinting down through the gaps in the floorboards. When he spotted the top of the wardrobe in the storage room below, he jammed the head of the spade between two boards and began ripping up wood.

'Banks found that silverfin's egg in the cave under the cliff,' the other man went on, 'and there you were, boiling it up in an old concussion shell when Hu's Lancers came up the path. I'll never forget the look on that young officer's face. You stared right at him. You remember what you said?'

Granger tossed a plank aside and pulled up another.

'Would you be kind enough to keep an eye out for the mother?' Creedy said in an affected tone. Then he guffawed. 'Would you be kind enough?' He tore another shred of meat from the bone and chewed it thoughtfully. 'Tenacious bastards, though, I'll give them that.'

'Hu's Lancers?'

'Dragons, man. You ever hear the stories about that green?'

Granger eased himself down through the hole he'd made in the floor, planting his feet on the top of the wardrobe underneath. It creaked under him. 'Maskelyne just makes those up,' he said. 'He'll sell the beast on to another collector once he's given it a reputation as a monster.'

'It *was* a monster,' Creedy said. 'Sank seven ships before they harpooned it in the eye.'

'Two ships,' Granger said.

'Well,' Creedy said. 'But you saw what it ate.'

Grunting, Granger manoeuvred his shoulders down through the gap in the floor. 'Saw it?' he said. 'I disarmed the bloody thing.'

Creedy laughed. 'I don't think Davy even knew what it was.'

Granger dropped to a squatting position. It was a tight squeeze, but he managed to duck his head under the joists. Apart from the wardrobe, some shelves stuffed with moth-eaten blankets and a stack of old tin pails, the storage room was empty.

'What are you doing?' Creedy said. 'I've got galoshes you could have borrowed. You don't have to rip the goddamn house apart to get down there.'

Granger opened the wardrobe door, then, turning to face the wall, he lowered himself down on splayed elbows. His boots scuffed the sides of the wardrobe and kicked against the open door, knocking it back against the wall. Finally the air under his heels gave way to a solid surface. With another grunt, he hopped down inside the narrow wooden space.

It was musty and dark, but his fumbling hands located the tin box at once. He picked it up and slid it on top of the wardrobe, then stopped as pain seized his chest. It hit him like a punch. 'Could you give me a hand back up, Mr Creedy?'

'You got your own self down there.'

'I can't . . . breathe.'

Granger heard a chair scrape across the floor above. A moment later, a shadow fell across the gap above, and he saw his former sergeant's big, ugly face staring down. 'You're never going to fix this hole, are you?'

'Grab that box and give me a hand.'

Once he was back up in the garret, he took a drink of water straight from the spigot and then sat down on the floor, breathing slow until the cramps in his chest relaxed. He'd been inhaling this sea air for too long, living too close to the brine. The Mare Lux had got into his lungs, and there was nothing to be done about it now.

'You don't look well,' Creedy said.

'The register's in that box.'

Creedy opened it. 'What's all this?'

He pulled out an assortment of objects. There were two books: the prison register and an old Unmer tome in raggedy script. And there was a child's doll. This last was a representation of a human infant, fashioned out of silver and brass. Tiny joints allowed its head and arms to swivel. One of its eye sockets was empty, but the other held a glass copy of the real thing – a finer replica than Creedy's old clockwork lens. A faint yellow light glowed behind its remaining iris.

'You don't remember it?' Granger said.

Creedy thought for a moment, then frowned. 'The Unmer child,' he said, unconsciously lifting his hand to his eye. 'What did you keep this for?'

'I don't know,' Granger said. 'Evidence. Lift its arm. No, the other one.'

A tinny voice came from the thing: 'A oo a apee.'

'I'll be damned,' Creedy said. 'That sounded like speech.' He lifted the arm again.

'Oo oo uv ee.'

'It is speech,' Granger said. 'There's a mechanism inside.'

'You *opened* it?'

Granger shrugged. 'Why not?'

Creedy looked incredulous. 'It's Unmer made. God knows what sort of sorcery is woven into this thing.'

'Do you suppose it's worth anything?'

The other man examined the doll. 'Maybe,' he said. 'If you could figure out what it's saying. A lot of people will pay good money for something like that. Don't let Maskelyne's buyers rip you off, though. No offence, Colonel, but you need the money.' He looked pointedly around the room, before returning his attention to the doll.

'A is oo oo.'

'I doubt it's even speaking Anean,' he said. 'Sounds like one of those old Unmer languages.'

'Don't wear it out, Mr Creedy.' Granger got to his feet and picked up the prison register – a heavy book bound in blue cloth. He thumbed through hundreds of pages, the columns of convicts' names and dates all written in Swinekicker's fastidious handwriting and then scored through with neat lines. Coffin nails, the old soldier had called those marks. Only the last half-page had been written in Granger's own hand. In the six years since he'd been here in Ethugra, he'd drawn nine coffin nails of his own. The final entry remained unmarked.

Duka, Eric. 3/HA/07. Evensraum. E-Com. #44-WR15102. III 30/HA/46 – 13/HR/47

Eric Duka, born in Evensraum in 1407. Fought as an enemy combatant, one of twenty thousand soldiers captured by the emperor's forces at Whiterock Bay during the Forty-fourth War of Liberation. Granger made a clicking sound with his tongue. According to this, he'd received three initial payments from Evensraum Council, followed by ten more from Duka's own family. Funds ceased on the 13th Hu-Rain 1447 – three weeks ago. No explanation given. Granger took a pencil from the box and drew a shaky line through the text. The chances of the prisoner's relations sending any more money now were as good as nil. If they petitioned the Council, they might get another one or two compassion payments. But Granger could always claim those had arrived too late.

The pages after this entry were empty, space enough for a thousand more lives, if he wanted them on his conscience. He looked around at his dismal apartment, at the drip-pans, and then at the hole he'd just ripped in the floor. 'What time does the *Alabaster Sound* get here?' he asked Creedy.

'We got hours yet.'

'Have they posted the lists?'

Creedy shrugged. 'No point checking them. We're still getting combatants from Evensraum and Calloway. Hu ships them over as soon as Interrogation's done with them. They're all piss-poor farmers.'

They'd been in Evensraum in the thirties. Granger recalled a farm near Weaverbrook, a place tucked right in behind the sea-wall with twelve acres turned over to wheat and corn and another two for grazing. There had been an old stone house with a kitchen garden, an orchard and a wooden hay barn. Living trees on the hills. Rabbits. His orders had been to burn and shell nothing, to take the island by boot and sword, one smallholding at a time. But then Emperor Hu had grown impatient with their progress.

He remembered the smell of mud all around, the clean, cold taste of well water, his brother John gathering apples in his helmet. A good place, Evensraum. They said all good things were worth fighting for. But then he remembered the bombardment, the fires and the screaming, and the cholera that followed.

'Let's get over there anyway,' he said. 'It's best to be early.'

Creedy was frowning at the doll. 'You've had this thing all these years?' he said. 'And you didn't think to tell me about it till now? I might have been able to find you a buyer.'

'I meant to repair it first,' Granger said.

The other man grunted. 'Right,' he said, twisting the doll's arm again.

'Oo oo uv ee,' said the hopeless little voice.

Outside upon the roof of Granger's prison it was a fine blue day, but the two men wore their whaleskin cloaks out of habit. You never could tell when the wind might pick up. They hadn't worn their uniforms in years, and in their seaman's breeches and Ethugran jerkins they looked like the jailers they'd become. Swinekicker's old brine purifier squatted upon a clutter of lead pipes beside the cistern, its faceted lenses gleaming in the sun like the eyes of a spider. It badly needed cleaning, he noted, as he always did. Ten yards below, Halcine Canal and its many branches formed a web of tea-coloured channels between Ethugra's jails, the banks all crooked by pontoons and wickers of flotsam. Boats waited in shadowy moorings, the brine under their hulls as darkly lustrous as bronze.

In places where sunlight fell between the buildings, Granger could see hazy details under the surface of the water: rows of iron-barred windows, and here and there a doorway through which old Swinekicker might once have stepped. Deeper still lay ordinary windows like the ones in Old Losoto. As a boy he'd clambered over Unmer façades that looked just like that, or swung from the mooring hooks, shrieking, while the other boys thrilled at the thought of Old Man Ghoul reaching up from the depths to grab him. It seemed like another world now. The Mare Lux smothered the past. Fish now glided though spaces that were once kitchens and bedrooms. Crabs and eels traversed the old cell floors in search of food.

The majority of Swinekicker's neighbours had kept pace with the rising seas, and their buildings cast shadows over the old man's jail. Dun-coloured façades loomed two or three storeys above him. There was Hoeken's, and Dan Cuttle's jail, and there the round-tower Mrs Pursewearer was having built with her husband's inheritance. A bare-chested labourer stood on the tower scaffold, slapping down mortar with a trowel while his companion carried blocks of stone up a ladder and laid them at his feet. This endless construction was part of Ethugran life. Masonry reclaimed from the seabed lay drying on palettes against a hundred half-built eaves, or stood in silhouette upon the rooftops like gravestones. A few of the buildings had cracked and subsided, broken by the Mare Lux tides. Others had given up the fight entirely. Thirty yards further along the canal, nothing of Ma Bitter's place remained above the waterline but a lone chimneypot. Someone had stuffed it full of rubbish.

'Look.' Creedy was pointing down at the canal.

Granger looked and immediately spotted a yellow light moving through the murky waters between the prison foundations. Five fathoms down, a sharkskin man was carrying a small child in his arms. He clutched a gem lantern in one upraised fist, using it to light his way across the drowned street. Both he and the child wore rags. His trouser legs flapped against his scarred grey shins. The child's hair wafted like a yellow flame behind its head. They moved lethargically through the brine, crossing the boulder-strewn seabed with great care, before disappearing through an open doorway into the opposite building.

'Someone ought to tell Dan Cuttle,' Creedy said. 'That was his place they went into.'

'I'll mention it to him.'

'It's not right, the Drowned moving the hell into wherever they please.'

Granger continued to peer down at the doorway through which they'd disappeared. They'd come from *this* side of the street, which meant they might be living in his own foundations. The law required him to inform Maskelyne's Hookmen, but that would mean inspections, and Granger didn't want inspections.

Creedy insisted they take his own launch to Averley Plaza because he said Swinekicker's old boat was bowed and splitting along the keel and was likely to sink with the two of them in it. Granger looked down at the places in the hull he'd filled with resin. He still owed the boatyard a thousand gilders for repairing the engine.

The launch puttered along. A former Imperial Navy tender, it still bore the scars of cannon-fire across its metal hull. Creedy claimed to have bought it cheap from a cousin who'd been a cox-swain under Admiral Lamont, but Granger suspected he'd stolen it. He didn't want to know. They'd all done desperate things these last six years.

Granger sat dead centre, away from the sides of the vessel. Creedy slouched over the helm, with one hand on the wheel. With his other hand he absently twisted the lens of his clockwork eye, as though the reappearance of that Unmer doll had stirred unwelcome memories. 'You ever wonder what happened to the other guys?' he said. 'I heard Banks stayed on in Losoto, right under Hu's nose.'

'Banks was smart enough to look after himself,' Granger replied. 'He's probably worked his way into Administration by now.'

'Smarter than us, eh?' Creedy steered the launch around Ma Bitter's chimneypot. Massive prison buildings glided past on either side, trapping great dark slabs of shadow between them. Behind them, the propeller churned the canal waters into an ochre froth. 'We should get the last of the Gravediggers together again,' Creedy said. 'Get them out here, I mean. Banks would know how to fix up that place of yours. Swan and Tummel could help dredge up stone for the walls. We could go after trove while we're at it. Get an operation going.'

An illegal operation, Granger thought. 'I don't have anything to pay them with,' he said.

'They wouldn't ask for nothing, not from you, Colonel. You could offer them a lay of the trove.'

'There's nothing valuable left in these canals,' Granger said. 'And we'd need a ton of equipment for deepwater salvage: cranes, steel-nets, dredging hooks. A bigger boat.' He shook his head. 'We'd be putting ourselves in competition with Maskelyne. Somehow, I don't think he'd be pleased.'

Creedy spat over the side, but said nothing more.

This talk made Granger wonder how the other man's business was faring. Creedy had grown up here, and his family still ran four or five prisons out on the edge of Tallship. They'd hooked Creedy up with a distant relation, some poor second cousin who owed the grandfather money. Didn't want him brandishing that tattoo in the family's own neighbourhood, they said. Not with the emperor's spies around. The cousin's place was big enough to be profitable, Granger supposed, but then Creedy had a talent for making money disappear.

Swinekicker had been kind to Granger. The old soldier hadn't wanted anything from him but a hard day's work and an ear to listen to his army stories. He been riddled with brine rot when Granger had first been introduced to him. Maybe he'd just wanted someone to carry his coffin out.

The launch turned west out of Halcine Canal and into

Francialle, where the buildings brawled for space, abandoning the waterways between them in a warren of perpetual gloom. Creedy switched off the engine and took up his boat hook, pushing it against the stonework on either side as he eased the vessel through channels barely wider than its hull. In some places the clover-leaf windows of ancient palazzos could be seen dimly underwater, but mostly the brine was as impenetrable as dreamless sleep. These old drowned avenues of Francialle had once resounded with the hammers of Unmer weapon-smiths and metalworkers, and the chants of Brutalist and Entropic sorcerers as they imbued their creations with treacherous powers. Granger couldn't help but wonder what strange devices still lay down there, chattering mindlessly to the fish. Even now it seemed perilous to disturb the silence.

A rat scampered along ledges above the water's edge, its scarred grey snout sniffing after water-beetles. Granger watched it for a while. Once he thought he spied another lantern moving slowly through the deep. Another Drowned soul on an unknowable errand? If Creedy noticed it, he chose not to comment.

At length they left the shadows of Francialle and steered the boat out into a wide quadrangle open to the full glare of the midday sun.

Averley Plaza formed a great sunlit harbour in the centre of the city, flanked on three sides by the grand façades of Ethugra's Imperial jails and administration buildings. Ships from Losoto, Valcinder, Chandel and the liberated territories of Cog-Ellis and Evensraum reached this place by way of the Glot Madera – a deepwater channel that meandered south through the heart of the city to the open sea. The whole basin teemed with boats: merchantmen, trawlers and dragon-claves from all corners of the empire; dredgers, squid lanterns, crane-ships and barges loaded with reclaimed stone, earth and firewood dragged up from undersea forests. A fleet of smaller vessels wove between the larger craft, from hardwood yachts to whaleskin coracles and old Unmer crystal-hulls; they bobbed and danced like bright mirages upon the bronze waters.

On the north embankment Ethugra's weekly market was already underway. Several hundred tents and stalls crammed the broad swathe of flagstones along the wharf side, selling everything from soil-grown produce to flame coral, thrice-boiled fish and trove. At the water's edge stood the stony figures of men and women – not statues, but the corpses of sharkskin men and women, each netted in Ethugra's own canals and left out to harden in the glare of the sun.

Creedy was looking south. 'Lucky we got here when we did,' he said. 'The *Baster*'s early.'

A former Imperial battleship, the *Alabaster Sound* was now one of the largest of Emperor Hu's prisoner transport vessels. Two steam tugs were nudging her battle-scarred steel bow through the gates of the Glot Madera and into Averley Plaza. She had been decommissioned after the Forty-third War of Liberation, but her iron guns still loomed over her deck rails, the shadows of their barrels sweeping across the brine like black banners. Her massive sloping funnel towered above the roofs of even the tallest buildings, disgorging fumes into the blue sky. A blast from her horn announced her arrival to the whole city, and her engines began to rumble like an earthquake as she turned. The captain stood on her wheelhouse deck, clad in emerald storm armour, his bulbous glass faceplate gleaming in the sun like the eye of a frog.

Ethugra's prison administrators were busy preparing for the *Alabaster Sound*'s arrival, laying out their ledgers and inkwells on long tables under canopies facing the waterfront. The harbour master shouted orders to his stevedores, who ran to positions beside stanchions, ready to haul in mooring ropes. Sailors scrambled to move smaller boats and coracles out of the former battleship's way. An expectant crowd began to gather behind them.

Creedy steered the launch across the plaza and into a public berth at the westernmost end of the docks, where he and Granger alighted. A dozen hawkers assailed Creedy at once, shoving all manner of cheap food and worthless trove into his face.

'Chariot ballast, Mr Creedy?'

'Catspin claws, sir. Original claws – see the brass work on this . . .'

'. . . dredged from the Mare Verdant . . .'

'Mr Creedy?'

'Six gilders an ounce, my friend.'

A fat man wearing spectacles stepped in front of Granger. He had dozens of similar pairs of eyeglasses arranged on a tray hung from his neck. 'See the past through the eyes of a dead sorcerer,' he said. 'Genuine Unmer lenses. They'll show you where to find lost trove, sir.' His voice dropped to a whisper. 'Unholy rituals, human sacrifices, Unmer sex, dragon sex.'

Granger ignored them all. Creedy hesitated, ogling the dizzying array of goods with his rapidly stuttering eye. He glanced back, spotted the spectacle seller, and then shoved him aside to let Granger past. 'Fakes,' he muttered. 'You don't see shit through them.' He was about to go, but then became distracted by a man selling silver puzzle boxes.

Granger urged him on.

Scores of other jailers had gathered around the administrators' desks by now. They sat on the harbour's edge with their legs dangling over the poisonous water, or leaned on the corpse-statues, watching the stevedores secure the ship and lower her loading ramps. Granger recognized a few faces and nodded greetings. They were all small-timers. Nobody from the larger prisons would bother with such low-value captives. There wasn't enough profit in peasants. Creedy fell into conversation with a man Granger didn't know, so Granger turned back to watch the *Alabaster Sound.*

The captain stomped down the gangplank, his helmet gripped in the crook of his arm, his lacquered steel boots clanking. He was typical Losotan, dark-haired with fine features. He grinned broadly, wiped sweat from his brow and called out, 'Grech.'

The head administrator peered up from his desk with darkly suspicious little eyes. 'You're early,' he said. He was all joints, this man – a great shambling preying mantis. He wore a dusty wig, woven into plaits, and an ash-coloured Imperial robe enriched with silver and lead chain-links around the shoulders. His chin hovered over his ledger like a stalactite.

The captain handed him a scroll. 'One hundred and sixty-three redundants. Eighteen twenty-eight still breathing, and another eighteen lawbreakers pickling in our seawater tanks. That's two thousand and nine bodies delivered.'

'Eighteen lawbreakers?' the administrator said. 'That seems excessive.'

'Discipline,' the captain replied. 'You give these people an inch and their lawlessness starts to infect the crew. Besides, I know how much you like to watch them dry out.' His gaze wandered to the nearest stone figure – the stone body of a woman curled up on the ground, her face a rictus of agony – and he gave a little smile.

The administrator examined the document, then scrawled something across the bottom and handed it back to the other man. The captain turned and gestured to one of the *Alabaster Sound*'s deck crew, who began unloading their human cargo.

The prisoners were much as Granger had expected: a rabble of Evensraum farm labourers, militia, women and old men. Hardly a trained combatant among them. Shackled hand to foot and linked by chains, they shuffled down the loading ramps under the watchful eyes of the ship's overseer. The crew lined them up on the dockside, while Ethugra's jailers crowded around the administrators' desks to collect the numbered tickets necessary to claim new arrivals. Granger was about to join them, when Creedy came forward, holding out two slips of paper.

'You're sorted,' he said.

Granger hesitated. 'How did you get these?'

The sergeant grunted. 'My first cousin's husband knows a man who knows a man,' he said. 'Just take them, Colonel, or we'll be here all day. It's too damn hot to hang around here any longer than we need to.'

Granger accepted the tickets and examined them. He was to be allocated prisoners forty-three and forty-four from the first batch. 'Is there anyone in this city your family doesn't know?'

Creedy thought for a moment. 'Aye, but they're all below water.'

The two men waited their turn as the first prisoners were brought, one by one, before the administrators. Documents were signed and passed along the line to be stamped and countersigned. Numbers were called out, whereupon the jailer holding the appropriate ticket claimed his captive and herded them further down the line to finalize the paperwork. The *Alabaster Sound*'s overseer unlocked chains, lashing his whip at his charges when they delayed.

The sun hammered them without mercy. The smell of whale oil from the ship's funnels lingered in the air and clung to the roof of Granger's mouth. He watched the boats bobbing in the bay. He eyed a beer seller and rummaged in his pocket for coins, but his hand came out empty. He tugged at his collar and wiped sweat from his brow and peered down the line of prisoners.

Fewer than thirty had been processed. Underfed and dejected, half of them wouldn't last a year in Ethugra.

'Thomas?'

A female captive at the front of the line was staring at Granger. Evidently she had been troublesome on the voyage, for the face under her bonfire of black hair had been beaten black and yellow. Dried blood caked her lower lip. She was clinging fiercely to a girl of fifteen or sixteen, trying to stop the overseer from separating them. 'Thomas?' she said quickly. 'It's you, isn't it?'

Granger shook his head. 'I don't know you, ma'am.'

The overseer wrenched the young girl away from the older woman and thrust her towards a waiting jailer. The woman shrieked, 'Ianthe,' and tried to follow, but the overseer kicked her to the ground. She reached out her arms and wailed. 'She's my daughter!'

Both mother and daughter wore simple Evensraum peasant clothes, as torn and filthy as any of the other captives, and yet the girl's boots were exceptionally fine, certainly not the sort of footwear one might expect a farm girl to own. Even in rags she was a striking young woman, olive-skinned with full lips, and a slender nose under a riot of black hair. She was terrified, confused, her eyes wild and brimming with tears. She didn't even appear to see the jailer as he grabbed her wrist and dragged her quickly down the line of tables. Something about her appearance struck a chord in Granger's heart. She looked strangely *familiar*.

'Please,' the woman on the ground begged him. 'Don't let them take her away from me. It would kill her.'

'Ma'am . . .' Granger began.

'My name is Hana,' she cried. 'You know me, Thomas. You know me from Weaverbrook.'

A slow, horrible realization came over Granger as he looked down at the beaten woman, at the face behind the bruises. She hadn't aged well. Suddenly he found himself staring after the girl in the hands of the other jailer. She had her mother's hair and skin, but what about the rest? The almond shape of that face, the tiny bump in the bridge of her nose, the strong line of her chin. Anyone could see the girl had some Losotan blood. And her eyes? Not dark like her mother's, but the same pale shade of blue Granger looked at in his shaving mirror every day. Fifteen years old? God help him. *Fifteen years. Not here, not now. Not in this godforsaken place.*

Creedy must have seen Granger's expression change, because he grabbed his arm and whispered, 'Fucking hell, Colonel. Don't even think about it. You're not Granger no longer. What happens in wartime happens. This has nothing to do with you now.'

The woman was sobbing. 'Please help her.'

The grip on Granger's arm tightened. 'Not a good idea, *Mr Swinekicker.*'

Granger wrenched away from the other man. He walked up to the administrator's desk and laid down his tickets. 'Give me these two,' he said.

The administrator didn't even glance at the tickets. 'I'm sorry, sir. These prisoners have already been claimed.'

'What difference does it make?' Granger insisted. 'They're randomly allocated.'

One of the men standing nearby glanced at the sobbing peasant woman, then turned to him and said, 'She's supposed to come with me, but I don't need the trouble, mate.' He held out his ticket. 'I'll trade you.'

Granger swapped tickets with the man. Then he approached the jailer holding the young girl. 'What do you say?'

The other man made a dismissive gesture. 'Forget it. I ain't queuing up again.' He handed his prison ledger to one of the administrators and stood there, studiously avoiding Granger's eye. The administrator looked at the ledger, then looked at Granger.

Granger leaned close to the jailer and said, 'One prisoner is as good as another.'

The other man shook his head. 'I told you,' he replied weakly. 'I'm not interested.' He rubbed sweat from his brow and stared intently down at the desk. Still, the official did nothing. The sun beat down on the plaza, on the administrators' desks, on the assembled crowds. Finally the jailer turned to Granger and whispered, 'I got another business to run, you know?' He moistened his lips. 'I can't trade her for some old man.'

'You paid extra for her?'

'You know how it is, man.'

Granger placed his remaining ticket and his ledger on the desk. 'Sign her over to me,' he said to the administrator.

The administrator gazed blankly at the scrap of paper.

'Do it,' Granger hissed, 'before I start using words like *corruption* and *prostitution*. Those terms are quite clearly defined in the Evensraum Convention.'

The jailer threw his ticket down. 'Fine,' he said. 'Have her. What do I care?' He snatched up his ledger and stormed away into the crowd.

Back in the launch, Granger felt like shivering despite the sun. What had he just done? His heart seemed to stutter as it wavered between feelings of responsibility and regret. He clutched his prison ledger in bloodless knuckles. Creedy steered the boat across the plaza, wrapped in a disapproving silence, while the two prisoners huddled together in the bow. Hana held her daughter tightly under a spare whaleskin cloak. She kept glancing over at Granger, a question burning in her eyes. The girl, Ianthe, stared absently across the brine, as though she wasn't really seeing anything at all, as though the world around her didn't really exist. She hadn't looked at Granger once.

68

Nobody spoke until they'd left the open water and plunged into the canals of Francialle, when Creedy suddenly said, 'Big mistake, Colonel. They're prisoners, for god's sake.' He picked up his boat hook and pushed the hull away from a wall with an angry grunt. 'They'd have been better off with *anyone* else in Ethugra.' He let out a sarcastic laugh. 'And it's against the fucking law.'

Creedy was right, of course, and it shamed Granger to think he had finally fallen so low. His own father would have raged and beaten him over it, would have forced him to hand Hana and Ianthe back to the prison administrators.

But his father was dead. And his mother was dead. His brother John killed in Weaverbrook, leaving a wife and child somewhere in Losoto. Even old Swinekicker had finally gone under the brine. The only family Granger had left was sitting in this boat.

CHAPTER 3

PERCEPTION

Dear Margaret,

There's been an unexpected turn of events. One of Maskelyne's Hookmen spotted me looking out of my cell window. He wants four hundred gilders to keep his mouth shut. Mr Swinekicker needs the money by the end of the month, or Maskelyne's man will let the authorities know I'm still alive. If that happens I'll be convicted of complicity in fraud and placed in one of the city plunge tanks. They drown you, and then they drag you out again and leave you to die in the sun. Sometimes the process can last for days. There's no time to write more. I need your help.

> *Love,*
> *Alfred*

The Evensraum woman and her daughter knelt on the floor in Granger's garret, their leg-irons chained to a water pipe running along the wall. He didn't know what he was going to do with them yet, and he was angry with himself for not having thought this through. The downstairs cells lay under six inches of poisonous brine. He'd have to fashion some kind of temporary platform, if he was going to keep them out of harm's way.

But Granger hesitated.

Creedy's parting words still rang in his ears. *Drown them both and say they tried to escape. Do it now and save yourself all the grief later on. They're nobodies, Tom. You'll be lucky if you get three payments for them.*

Ianthe stared into space like a girl in a trance, while her mother hugged her daughter's shoulders and rocked backwards and forwards, murmuring softly. They were surrounded by piles of rusting junk, broken tools and engine parts, all the things Granger had meant to fix up when he had a few spare gilders. The flap across the entrance hatch lifted in the breeze and then sank back down again.

'Listen—' Granger began.

'Thank you for doing this,' Hana said.

He tried to read the woman's face, searching for some hint of her expectations, but her bruises confounded him. He couldn't see past them. 'The cells are downstairs,' he said at last. 'That's what I do now. It's my job.'

She nodded.

'The name's Swinekicker, now,' he said. 'Don't call me Granger in public again.'

She nodded.

'I've got to sort things out,' he said. 'There's flooding down there. You stay here.' He was about to turn away, when he remembered his manners. 'Do you need something to eat? I have—'

'Some water, if you can spare it.'

He filled a jug from the spigot, then hunted for cups. They were all furred with mould, so he covered the sink with an old towel and handed her the jug. She accepted it hungrily and passed it to her daughter, who gulped down half before handing it back.

'Tastes like rust,' Ianthe said.

'The purifier is old,' Granger replied. 'I've been planning to replace it.'

71

She stared at him as if he didn't exist, her pale blue eyes so striking against her earthen complexion, and yet distant at the same time. She was as beautiful as her mother had been all those years ago: that same flawless skin, those dark eyebrows that tapered to perfect points, the black flame of her hair. Ianthe's gown had been ripped at one shoulder and hung loosely over her breasts.

Could he be wrong about her?

When Hana had fallen ill in those final days before his unit had been recalled from Weaverbrook, they hadn't talked about it. Disease already had a grip on the land. Hu's bombardment had caused uncountable deaths – the corpses left to rot in fields and drainage ditches. They had never been able to dig enough graves.

Had Hana known she was pregnant then? Would it have made a difference if she'd told him?

Ianthe's pale Losotan eyes belonged to him and no other. He could see that clearly, and it irked him that there was something wrong with her vision. She wasn't reacting to movement or light the way a normal person would. If he hadn't seen her reach for the water jug, he'd have thought she was blind.

That the fault in her should have come from him.

Hana watched them carefully. Underneath those bruises and the scars of age Granger thought he caught a glimpse of a nervous smile. Was she thinking about those nights fifteen years ago? His unit had commandeered her grandmother's farm for the duration of the campaign. In sixty-three days of fighting, he'd lost only seven men out of fifteen hundred, while the enemy mourned for four hundred of their own. It would have been an extraordinary victory for the empire, had the empire known about it.

But telepaths were expensive. And Emperor Hu had always been unwilling to pay.

He remembered Hana's terror when the shelling began. By

the time Hu's navy had finished there had been eight thousand more graves to dig, and scant few of his men left alive to dig them. Fewer still when the cholera took its toll.

That image just stirred his anger. Why was he doing this? He wasn't responsible for what had happened to her or her village. He'd kept her safe. He couldn't have taken her with him. He couldn't have stayed. He didn't *owe* her anything. He glanced at Ianthe again, but the sight of her just filled him with despair. A weight of expectation hung in the air between the three of them, and Granger could not define it. He didn't want to think about it. He had to get his boat repaired. He had to get away from this godforsaken city.

Drown them both and say they tried to escape.

He felt trapped and foolish. He snatched up his waterproof gloves and the galoshes Creedy had left for him. And then he grabbed his toolbox and trudged downstairs to see about fixing his prisoners somewhere to sleep.

Halfway down the steps he paused to put on the thick whale-skin gloves and to pull his galoshes over his boots. He fitted a hemp face mask over his mouth and nose and snapped his goggles into place. His breathing sounded heavy and erratic. He stared at the flooded passageway for a long time before he dropped down into the shallow brine and waded along the corridor. He planned to use the sleeping pallets from three or four vacant cells to build a higher platform for his two new captives.

The first two rooms contained nothing of use but the dragon-bones he'd stockpiled to repair his roof. Both the pallets here were partially submerged, and even the dry sections of wood looked rotten. Worms had eaten into the ends of the planks. Granger selected a couple of yard-long thigh bones and then stood for a moment wondering if could use them. Finally he threw them

73

away and left the room. The sound of his breaths came quicker. He could feel the icy chill of the water through his galoshes.

The pallet in the third cell was in better condition; he could use it. But the room itself was no good. The floorboards under the surface of the brine had collapsed, leaving a treacherous well that dropped into the flooded chamber below. Through this hole Granger spied dim beams of light slanting through a downstairs window and falling upon a heap of broken planks and plaster. Yellow particles hung suspended in the brown water. Something had disturbed the silt on that lower floor, for he could see foot-sized impressions around the rubble. Had the Drowned caused this damage? He doubted they were capable of such wilful destruction.

As Granger passed the fourth cell, he heard a splash coming from the other side of the door. He didn't stop to check on his prisoner. *No money, no food.* He wasn't running a goddamn soup kitchen here. There was nothing to be done for Duka now.

The floors in the remaining four cells looked sound, so he chose a cell facing Halcine Canal, where the barred window admitted more light. He gathered together all the solid pallets from the rest of the wing and nailed them down one upon the other to form a raised platform four yards long by two wide. It sloped badly towards the wall, but that was better than sloping the other way. When the construction was complete, Granger's breaths outpaced his heart. He leaned against the door jamb, wheezing, until the tightness left his chest. His shoulder throbbed. The platform he had built cleared the brine by six inches or so, enough to keep his prisoners dry for most of the coming year. It would have to do. He didn't have any more pallets.

He took some blankets from the storeroom cabinet and searched for a slop bucket in the deep lower drawers. He couldn't find a bucket so he pulled out the drawer and dumped that on the platform instead. It would have to do.

The two women hadn't moved. Hana held her daughter and rocked back and forward.

Ianthe said, 'I'm not going down there.'

Granger peeled off his gloves and let them drop to the floor. They were slick with brine and would have burned his captives' skin.

'Shush, Inny,' Hana said. 'We'll be fine.'

'It's thoroughly rotten. We won't survive.'

Her mother hugged her more tightly. 'We always survive.'

But Ianthe struggled out of Hana's embrace. 'There's a starving man in one of his cells,' she cried, pushing her mother away. 'And a drawer for a loo. How can you say we'll be fine when he treats his captives like that?' She took a breath as if to scream. 'The man in the boat told him to drown us!'

Granger stopped and stared at her, as helpless to respond to this sudden squall of teenage anger as he was to the words themselves. How did she know these things? She couldn't have heard Creedy. She couldn't be aware of the man in the cell.

Hana tried to restrain her daughter. 'Inny, please . . .'

But Ianthe would not be pacified. She stood up, her leg-irons clattering, then picked up the chain and pulled it. The locking cuff rattled against the water pipe, but it would not yield. Suddenly she spun round to face her mother again, her face flushed and savage. 'Who is he to you?' she demanded. 'Why do you look at him like that? He's hideous. You can't know him. You can't!'

'Inny—'

Granger felt his heart sink. 'She's psychic,' he said.

'No,' Hana replied.

'You *hid* her from the Haurstaf?'

The woman's expression tightened with frustration. 'No. You don't understand.'

'Do you know what they'll do to you when they find out?'

'She's not like them, I swear. They can't sense her. She—'

Ianthe cut her off with a yell. 'Don't you dare tell him!'

Hana reached for her daughter again. 'Sweetheart, maybe it's—'

Ianthe slapped her.

The sound of it snapped the argument to silence. For a long time Granger just stood there, listening to his own heart drumming in his ears. He didn't know what to say. Ianthe was trembling, breathing heavily as she gazed vacantly down at her mother. Hana sniffed and rubbed tears from her eyes.

'I'm *not* psychic,' Ianthe said bitterly.

'You're untrained,' Granger said, 'unfocused.'

She snorted. 'What difference does it make? You've already got it all planned out. Sell me to the Haurstaf, build yourself a proper jail. I don't care.'

A proper jail? She'd slipped that remark in with admirable ease. He'd been thinking of selling her to buy a new boat, as she well knew. Despite himself, he felt a twinge of admiration for the girl. 'Was that particular insight intended to convince me you're not psychic?'

Her hands tightened to fists. 'You just don't get it, do you?' She faced him and spoke with emphatic sarcasm, pronouncing each word as if he were retarded. '*I don't know what you are thinking.*'

'Then explain it to me.'

Ianthe sat back down on the floor beside her mother.

After a moment Hana clasped her daughter's fingers in her own. Then she wiped away more tears and said, 'Ianthe can see and hear things that other people can't.'

'That's obvious enough,' Granger said.

'That's not what I mean,' Hana said. 'Psychics read thoughts, but Ianthe only *sees* and *hears* whatever is around her. Her senses are just like yours or mine, only better. A lot better.'

Granger frowned. 'She *heard* Creedy whispering to me?'

Hana nodded.

'And the man downstairs?'

'Ianthe?'

The girl shrugged. 'I heard him sobbing.'

Had Duka been sobbing? Granger hadn't heard anything like that at all. He tried to think of a moment in which the starving man had made a sound that *might* have revealed his condition to the girl upstairs, but there simply wasn't one. *No money, no food,* Granger had thought. His every instinct told him he was being lied to.

'And the drawer?' he said.

Ianthe hesitated. 'What drawer?'

'The drawer in your cell,' he said. 'Did you hear that too?' He turned to find her glaring furiously at him and knew he'd trapped her. 'I'm sending a letter to Losoto tomorrow,' he said. 'I don't suppose I need to tell you who it's for and what I'm going to write.' The Haurstaf would pay a fortune for one of their own.

Her cold hard eyes narrowed. 'You don't have to tell me anything,' she growled. 'I know all about you. Your father was a beggar and your mother was Drowned when he took her. That's why you're so ugly. She squeezed you out of her womb like a fish. And your father took one look at you and wanted to vomit, so now you run this rotting prison because you can't do anything else. A sad little tinpot dictator who gets his thrills out of locking people up. You make me sick.'

Hana closed her eyes.

Granger took a deep breath. Then he unlocked the girl's leg-irons, seized her by the waist and pitched her over his shoulder. She wasn't heavy, but she fought like a cat in a kitbag, screaming and kicking and trying to scratch him. One of her boots flew off and smashed into the crockery in the sink. He carried the struggling girl down the stairs and along the flooded corridor and dumped her unceremoniously onto the platform he'd constructed in the fourth cell. And then he stood there wheezing while she scrambled back against the wall, her cheeks burning with embarrassment, her eyes mere pinpricks of hate.

'You . . . stay, while I get . . . your mother.'

'Bastard.'

He didn't bother to close the cell door behind her. The brine would damage her feet if she tried to escape. When he reached the bottom of the steps he sat down and rested his head against the wall. *Ten slow breaths.* The metal stench of seawater pinched his nostrils. He could hear her sobbing further down the corridor. He gnashed his teeth and dragged himself upright and went back upstairs.

Hana was sitting on the floor. 'We've been in one cell or another for the last six months,' she said. 'The detention centre, the ship, but the worst was Interrogation. When we didn't know the answer to their questions; they kept on asking until we did. The hard part was figuring out what they wanted to hear.'

'And that's what you've been doing with me?'

She looked at him directly. 'The Haurstaf will kill her.'

'They'll give her a good life.'

She shook her head defiantly.

Granger frowned. 'Is it so hard to let her go? Even if it means keeping her here?'

Hana closed her eyes. 'How do I convince you to trust me?'

'Tell me the truth.'

'We tried to!'

Granger unlocked her leg-irons and led her downstairs to the cell block. She didn't resist as he scooped her up in his arms. He carried her along the flooded corridor and across the threshold into the cell. Ianthe was curled up in the corner, crying into her elbows. Hana went over to her at once and embraced her.

Granger watched them for a moment, and then he eased the cell door closed behind him and turned the key in the lock out of habit.

Moonlight flooded the garret. Granger couldn't sleep. His prisoners would probably be awake in their cell below. No one slept well on the first night. They'd be looking at the walls and wondering what the dawn would bring. They'd be looking at the slop drawer. Granger lay in his cot, wrapped in blankets that didn't reach his feet, and stared at the head of a nail embedded in the ceiling. In this quiet darkness the smell of the sea always reminded him of his childhood in Losoto. The scent of brine was much stronger down in the cells, where there were bars instead of glass in the windows. Some nights it made you dream of drowning.

On the floor all around lay the scraps of wood and tools that he and Swinekicker had gathered over the years to fix the old man's boat. He'd dismantled most of the furniture last winter and burned what he decided couldn't use. His whaleskin cloak lay in a crumpled pile beside the heavy grey galoshes he'd borrowed from Creedy. In the gloom the dragon-bone joists in the ceiling looked like a sketch of a land at war with itself, a framework of pale borders dividing innumerable fiefdoms. It was a map of fear, lust and betrayal, just like any other map in Hu's empire.

Can you hear me?

The shadows gave no reply. Granger felt foolish. Perhaps Ianthe *was* asleep. Either way, the girl seemed determined to hide her powers from him. All Haurstaf could stare into the minds of their own kind, and an exceptional few could read the thoughts of humans. Their powers over an Unmer mind were akin to rape. And yet none of them possessed preternatural vision and hearing.

He shook his head. Ianthe *had* to be psychic, and a powerful one to boot. And that made her valuable to him. She was his ticket out of here.

A sturdy deepwater boat could take him across the Mare Lux, beyond Losoto and the reach of the empire. Valcinder still maintained some free ports, it was said. He could sell the boat there and buy passage on a vortex-class ship across the Strakebreaker Sea. In a year or so he might reach the Herican Peninsula, the last great wilderness – the place where gods once walked with men.

He could escape the brine.

The thought should have given him solace, and yet he found it impossible to sleep. Doubts continued to nag at him. Was there *any* way she could simply have heard him pull the drawer from the cabinet? He couldn't see how such a feat was possible. But if he was going to sell Ianthe to the Haurstaf, then he had to be *absolutely certain*. She was still too much of a mystery to him. The extent of her abilities remained untested, obscured by her lies. It was like peering into the depths of the sea. One never knew exactly what one might find down there.

He had to determine her limits.

But how do you test a psychic who knows your every thought and plans to confound you?

Granger got up and took the water jug from the sink. Then he walked downstairs to the flooded cell corridor. No windows opened onto the narrow space, and it was utterly dark down there, but Granger could have found his way in his sleep. He counted fifteen steps, then crouched. Slowly and carefully, he eased the lip of the jug into the brine, filling it with poison.

He slept later than usual. When he woke the sun was high and the room was already uncomfortably warm. He opened a window and pissed into the canal below. He still felt tired. He threw on a robe and pulled his borrowed galoshes over his bare feet. Then he picked up the jug of poisonous water and sniffed it. It smelled sulphurous and metallic, but so did everything else in his jail. He doubted any normal person would be able to detect the deception until it was too late. A psychic, however, would already know what he had done.

He carried it down to the flooded cell block.

Neither of his prisoners looked like they'd slept at all. Ianthe didn't seem to have the energy even to raise her head and scowl at him. She was still curled up in the corner, her head turned away, but breathing with such fierceness that Granger knew she was awake. Hana pushed herself up from the palette and tried to smile.

He handed her the jug and thought to himself, *I've poisoned the water, Ianthe.*

She set it down and rubbed her eyes. 'Do you feed us?' she said.

'In a minute.' He waited.

She picked up the jug.

'Hana.'

She lowered the jug and looked at him.

Don't count on me stopping her from drinking it, Ianthe. I'm not going to do it again. And don't pretend to be asleep. I can hear you breathing. 'How did you survive? In Evensraum, I mean. Cholera wiped out the colonies.'

She shrugged. 'Why did you change your name? Why Swinekicker?'

'Name of the guy who owned this place,' he said. 'I don't want to talk about that.'

'I walked east.' She raised the jug to her lips.

'East? To where?'

'Deslorn,' she said. 'Hundreds of us took that road.' She

was looking at him strangely now, trying to discover his motives. 'When the cholera took hold in Deslorn, I moved again. Temple Oak, Cannislaw, other places. A refugee camp in the woods, that's where Inny was born.' She lifted the jug again.

Damn you, Ianthe. You'd let her die to prove a point? Granger put his hand on the lip of the jug and lowered it. 'How did you end up here?'

She let out a deep sigh. 'Trove,' she said matter-of-factly. 'Inny can spot things lying on the seabed.' She set down the jug and looked at it. 'We got involved with this smuggler, Marcus Law. He was dredging the waters out past Port Vassar, the Ochre Sea and places like that. And he'd send the trove he found to the Losoto markets. Illegal, of course. But you always find buyers for exceptional finds, and a lot of Inny's finds were like that.'

Granger thought about this, now curious despite his misgivings. If Ianthe could do what her mother claimed, then what she was telling him made sense. Black-market salvage operations like these funnelled money into the Evensraum Resistance. The Imperial Navy had closed down dozens of them.

'You're telling me she can actually *see* trove down there?'

Hana nodded. 'Like you can see me now.' She picked up the water jug and held it out to her daughter. 'Inny . . .'

'I don't want anything from *him*,' the girl said. 'You drink it.'

Hana looked up at him helplessly, then she raised the jug to her own lips.

'Stop.' Granger took the jug away from her. His thoughts were reeling now. Had Ianthe been about to let her mother drink brine, simply *to conceal her talents*? Or was it more likely that Hana was telling the truth, that Ianthe simply didn't know about the poisoned water? He stared down at the jug in confusion. 'I have some wine, if you'd prefer.'

'Thank you,' Hana said. 'That would be nice.'

He emptied the jug in the corridor outside. Ianthe's behaviour continued to confound him. Had mother and daughter known about the poison all along and *planned* that whole display for his benefit? Had Hana *counted on him* preventing her from taking a sip? It was the only thing he could think of that made sense.

How do you test a psychic who knows your every thought and plans to confound you?

Had they simply outwitted him? Granger let out a growl of frustration and went to find them some wine.

At noon he cooked them thrice-boiled fish, adding oats to turn it into a thick porridge. If he was going to outwit his prisoners, he decided, it was best to earn their trust first. He found a little honey he'd been saving for himself and spooned that in too. It made the gruel more pleasant. He tasted it with his finger, then added salt and tasted it again. Not too bad. He felt quite pleased with himself. As he was ladling the mixture into bowls he heard the sound of a bell ringing outside. He went over to the open hatch and ducked outside.

The postboat was moving slowly along Halcine Canal, puffing steam from its short brass funnel. She was an old Valcinder coastal cruiser, slender and graceful. East Empire shipwrights had carved her hull from the jawbone of a hexen barracuda and fashioned her stem from hundreds of white and yellow angui bones that still gleamed like twists of marzipan. The waterway here was narrow enough to allow the postman's son, Ned, to toss bundles of letters onto the prison wharfs or into the open decks of the jailers' own tethered boats. Most of Granger's neighbours had postboxes fixed to their wharfs, but it wasn't raining so Ned wasn't bothering to use them. The Hoekens and Mrs Pursewearer would complain about that, and Ned would just laugh uproariously and carry on as usual.

On the opposite side of the canal Dan Cuttle was climbing down a series of ladders that zigzagged all the way down one side of his brick jail like huge iron stitches. He waved and called down, 'Fine hot day.'

'It's cooler down here in the shade,' Granger replied. 'Any time you want to swap your business for mine, I'd be happy to oblige you.'

Dan laughed and shouted back, 'I've got plenty of leftover bricks if you need them, Tom. Odd sizes, I'm afraid, but I'm sure you could use 'em. Rather give 'em to you than let the bloody Drowned have 'em back.'

'I might take you up on that, Dan. Thanks.' He thought about the Drowned family he'd seen going into the other man's basement, but then decided not to mention them. Dan would have Maskelyne's Hookmen down here in droves.

As the postboat slipped past, Ned threw a single envelope towards Granger's wharf. It looped momentarily in the air, before missing the wharf altogether and drifting down onto the open hull of Granger's rotten little boat.

Ned laughed. 'Sorry Tom.'

'Every time,' Granger muttered.

His vessel, *Hana*, was sitting lower in the water than ever before. He allowed his gaze to linger a moment on the name he'd painted across her bow. He could barely make out the faded letters among the cracks and blisters. The hull was in bad shape. Brine had leaked through cracks in the resin along the keel and pooled in the bottom. Thankfully the letter had landed on the centre board and remained dry. He balanced his foot on her port gunwale, but her hull tilted and the letter slid an inch closer to the brine. The toe rail cracked under his weight. A sloshing sound came from somewhere under the thwarts. Even at full stretch, he couldn't quite reach the letter, so he ripped loose a couple of long sections of toe rail and used them like pincers to grab the envelope.

It was addressed to *Mr Alfred Leach c/o Captain R. Swine-kicker, Halcine Canal* and it contained four hundred gilders in fifties, and a letter. Granger pocketed the money and wandered back upstairs, reading the letter.

Dearest Alfred,

Your last letter didn't give me much time to raise the money. I was forced to visit that money lender in the Trove Market. Please forgive me, I know how much you despise them. Sally spoke with him alone, and – god love her – she managed to convince him to lower his rates. Bright girl, that one. So you needn't worry too much. It's all done now. Ronald and Gunny send their love. They keep asking if you ever mention them in your letters.

I tell them yes, of course. I tell them that you miss them, as I'm sure, deep down, you do.

Love,
Margaret

Granger crumpled up the piece of paper and shoved it in his pocket. He went back to the stove and ladled the cooling porridge into two bowls. Then he washed and refilled the water jug and carried the lot down to his captives.

The moment he entered the cell he could see that Ianthe had mustered her rage for another outburst. Her jaw was tight, her eyes brimming with cruel intent.

He tried to pre-empt her. 'Should I just throw this into the brine and save you the effort of rejecting it?' By the time he'd closed his mouth he regretted ever opening it.

She actually snarled. 'Fish porridge? Isn't that like cannibalism for you? Boiling up your own relatives to feed to your prisoners?'

She was speaking through her teeth. 'I know beggars eat that muck, but they normally have the decency not to inflict it on others. Take it away and bring us something edible, or just leave us to starve to death.' She snorted. 'That's what you're going to do anyway, isn't it? When the council payments run out?'

'Inny, please!' Hana reached for her daughter, but the girl snatched her hand away.

Ianthe had adopted an air of smug self-righteousness. 'I can't believe you slept with him,' she said to her mother. 'Did he wear a bag over his head? Or did he rape you? That, at least, would be understandable. You're never *really* fulfilled unless you're somebody's victim.'

Hana's cheeks flushed.

'That's enough.' Granger stood there in the open doorway with an armload of crockery: a great lumbering, red-faced fool. Ianthe must have known about her parentage from the beginning. How do you keep secrets from a psychic? But he was surprised to find the girl's hostility directed at her mother, rather than him. He set their food down on the platform, weary and anxious to leave. 'I don't care if it's not what you're used to, it's all I can afford right now.'

'Poor you,' Ianthe scoffed. 'If only you had four hundred gilders in your pocket.'

He stopped. A slow grin spread across his face. 'Four hundred gilders, Ianthe?'

She snorted.

There was no doubt left in Granger's mind now. Only a psychic could have known about the money. 'I need it for something else.'

'Whores, I suppose.'

He took a deep breath. He was about to speak, but then he changed his mind and voiced his thoughts internally instead. *I didn't want be your father. I don't know you, and I don't want to.*

Tomorrow morning, I'm going to write to the Haurstaf. You'll be out of here in a couple of weeks and you can spend the rest of your life living in a marble tower, causing wars and blackmailing emperors and screwing the Unmer and whatever else it is you people do. He smiled grimly. 'Did you get all that? Or would you like me to repeat it out loud?'

Ianthe glared at him defiantly.

Hana glanced at her daughter, then back at Granger. 'I told you she doesn't read minds.'

Granger lost his temper. 'You've told me nothing but lies,' he exclaimed. 'It seems to me that *I'm* the only one who's acting in our daughter's interests. What is it with you? Pride? Selfishness? Are you so afraid of being alone that you'd keep her rotting in jail when she could be out of here in a heartbeat?' He set down the bowls roughly, spilling porridge everywhere. 'I don't get it, Hana. Do you think I'm suddenly going to become the good father? My responsibilities to you ended fifteen years ago in Weaverbrook, when you chose to keep your pregnancy a secret.'

Hana stiffened. She closed her eyes. In a voice no louder than a whisper she said, 'You wouldn't have stayed with me.'

'I was an *Imperial soldier.*'

Ianthe had paled. 'Lies,' she said. 'You were never *in* Weaverbrook.'

'Inny . . .' Hana reached for her.

'No!' She snatched her hand away. 'Don't you dare touch me. You told me you met him years before Dad died, you said . . .' She let out a small shriek of frustration, then shook her head fiercely. 'He can't have been in Weaverbrook.'

'Inny, please.'

'He's not my father.'

'I'm sorry.'

Granger stared in astonishment as Ianthe began to wail.

CHAPTER 4

TREASURE-HUNTERS

To Sister Briana Marks:

My name is not important. I am a jailer in Ethugra who has recently, and legally, been granted incarceration rights to a powerful psychic. Given this person's value to your Guild, I would be glad to hand them over in return for a finder's fee of two hundred thousand gilders. If this is agreeable, please have a Guild representative (yellow-grade only) meet me at Averley Plaza on the 30th HR. I will find her.

> *Faithfully,*
> *A Friend*

Granger stared at the letter. How could he send it now? Ianthe was more of a mystery to him than ever before. She knew things she couldn't possibly have known: the slop drawer, the four hundred gilders. And yet she seemed blind to the most crucial information of all: the poisoned water, *her own parentage*. Every one of his instincts told him that her reaction to that last revelation was genuine. She hadn't known he was her father.

Had Hana been telling the truth all along?

Or had they outwitted him again?

He cradled his head in his hands. She couldn't have *seen* him put the money into his pocket. She couldn't have *known* about

Duka's condition from hearing his sobs. So why hadn't she known he was her father? Nothing made sense – not least her supposed ability to find trove. Psychics didn't find treasure. The sea had no mind to read.

Granger folded up the letter and slid it down inside his sock. If Ianthe turned out to be valuable, he would send it, and if she didn't, well, it might at least stop Creedy's damn whaleskin galoshes from chaffing his ankle so much.

Ianthe ignored him for four days. Granger went about his duties in a workmanlike fashion, bringing his captives food and water and emptying the slop drawer. Ianthe kicked all their food into the brine before her mother had a chance to protest or even to thank Granger. But she drank the water and she allowed her mother to drink it too.

On the fifth day she said, 'If you want me to find trove, you'll have to let me out of here.'

'Who says I want to find trove?' Granger replied.

She threw the water jug at him.

Two more days passed.

On the seventh day of their incarceration he found Ianthe in an edgy, restless mood. She sat with her chin pressed against her knees, gripping the soles of her boots as though making a conscious effort to stop her coiled muscles from lashing out again. They had, at last, eaten their breakfasts and left the empty bowls for Granger to collect. He took this to be a small victory.

'She wants to work with you,' Hana said.

'Does she? Was this her idea, or yours?'

Ianthe stared at the wall.

'Take her out in your boat, she'll find treasure.'

Granger shook his head. 'I could lose my licence if anyone sees me.'

'Then go at night,' Hana said. 'Her sight is good enough.'

It was bad enough being on the brine in daylight, but the thought of trawling Ethugra's canal's at night felt like a lead weight in his gut. 'My boat leaks.'

'Your friend's boat doesn't.'

Creedy scratched at the Gravediggers tattoo behind his thumb. 'I don't get it,' he said. 'She's either psychic or she isn't.'

Granger sat in the bow of the sergeant's launch beside a tarpaulin that hid their dredging equipment – the lamps, ropes, nets and iron hooks Creedy had borrowed from another of his cousins. Stone façades and barred windows slipped by on either side, both above and below water. The seabed was about seven fathoms down here, and the honey-coloured water unusually clear, but Granger couldn't see anything of worth in the flooded street below. Rubble. A torn net. Bones and paint cans. 'Maybe it's instinctual,' he said.

'Meaning?'

'Meaning, birds once used to migrate across the oceans. How did they navigate? What guided them across the endless wastes to the same roosting spots year after year? Or dragons . . . You've seen the way berserker dragons hunt the Drowned off the Losotan coast. They know where to dive and where to avoid.'

'I once saw a dragon taken by an erokin samal,' Creedy said. 'Man, that was nasty.'

Granger shrugged. Maybe that wasn't such a good example. 'I don't know,' he said. 'I can't explain Ianthe's talents yet. She might not be psychic, but she has *something*.'

Creedy shook his head in disapproval. 'I know a con when I smell one, Colonel.'

A passenger boat puttered by, almost identical to the vessel Granger had taken out to Creedy's place. This one was full of jailers' wives back from the Averley Day Market, their wares piled between their knees, but it was as overcrowded as any other. Ethugran captains liked to pack them in. Long rays of sunlight slanted into the city from the west, turning the top stories of the buildings to gold.

Gloom had filled Halcine Canal by the time they reached Granger's wharf. Creedy tied up, and then the two men climbed up the ramshackle stairs into Granger's garret.

To keep Ianthe hidden, Granger looked out a spare whale-skin cloak from the storeroom: a sour old garment, hardened by long exposure to rain and brine spray. He felt sure she would complain.

She complained and raged and threw it on the floor. But when he made it clear she'd wear the cloak or remain inside, she snatched it back up and swept it fiercely about her shoulders. Creedy said nothing but he stared at Ianthe in a way that made Granger feel uncomfortable.

Shortly after sunset, the three treasure-hunters departed in Creedy's launch. High cloud had drifted in from the south and veiled the dusk. There were no stars, but a half moon shone through the clouds like a faint illusion. Creedy manned the wheel while Granger swung a lantern from the bow to light their way. Ianthe told them to head to Francialle, and then she yanked her foul-smelling cloak over her face and buried her head in her knees. They left Halcine Canal and turned into Elm Canal and then Broughton Canal, before finally nudging the boat into the old Unmer district via the Rat Passage. Night deepened around them. Creedy cut the engine and took up his boat hook. 'What now?'

'She starts looking.'

They waited.

'Ianthe?'

She gave a snort of irritation, then crawled over to the side of the boat and peered down into the water.

Granger exchanged a glance with his former sergeant. Creedy shook his head. It was impossible to see anything down there.

It began to rain, softly at first, and then harder. Water lanced down from the darkness, pulverizing the black brine and turning the reflections from Granger's lantern into millions of flashing gilders. All around the old Ethugran prisons bore the onslaught. Water drummed their roofs and gargled down through gutter pipes. Drip after drip fell from the eaves and spattered bridges and stone pontoons, exploded against window ledges and door-steps, trickled down through cracks and into the sodden heart of the old Unmer district. Rain beat the tarpaulin and crept down Granger's neck and across his back. The air filled with the scent of wet earth, as though each droplet had carried with it the fabric of another land. Granger inhaled it deeply.

Creedy manoeuvred them through a sodden labyrinth of deep defiles, grunting softly as he pushed at the walls with his boat hook. Ianthe hung over the side, wrapped in silence under her cloak. Granger held up the lamp and swung it around him, revealing the massive walls that pinned them in on every side, the barred windows half submerged in brine, their ironwork scuffed by innumerable boat hooks. Occasionally they heard sobbing from the cells around them, but those noises were indistinct, drowned by the constant percussion of the rain.

Finally, Ianthe said, 'Here.'

Creedy brought the boat to a stop.

'Something metal,' she replied. 'Six fathoms down. Two yards that way.' She pointed near the bow.

'Trove?' Granger peered into the water. He could see nothing but the reflection from his own lantern dancing in that blackness.

Ianthe turned away from the gunwale and sat down fiercely, jerking the cloak over her head like a cowl. 'What do *you* think?'

Granger pulled on his gloves, mask and goggles. He picked

up a dredging line – a long rope with a cluster of hooks at the end – and tossed it into the canal. The rope slid out through his fingers as the barbed anchor dropped into the depths. Four fathoms, five, six. Finally it settled on the bottom, and Granger pulled it towards him. He felt the hooks bump and scrape across the seabed, but they snagged nothing. He dragged the line in again, and repeated the process.

The rain came down.

On the third throw, Granger felt the line bite. He gave it a tug. Something heavy freed itself from the bottom. A noticeable weight. Carefully, he drew it up towards him.

It was a small clockwork machine about the size of a naval concussion shell – an engine, perhaps, or part of one. The device was roughly cuboid, fashioned from a peculiar green-blue alloy, and much heavier than it looked. Through several holes in the outer casing, Granger could see some complex mechanism inside: gears, tightly wound metal coils and bulbs of red glass. Four short, rubber-sheathed wires dangled from metal stubs welded to one of the object's facets. Brine sluiced out as he turned it over.

'What is it?' Creedy asked.

Granger didn't know.

'Definitely Unmer.' Creedy held out his hands. 'Let's have a look.'

The queer device made Granger feel uncomfortable, although he couldn't say precisely why. Its weight seemed to change as he turned it over, and he thought he detected a faint hum coming from the glass bulbs, a resonance that he felt in his teeth. Did it retain a trace of Unmer sorcery? He emptied it of seawater and then passed it over to Creedy. Then he turned to Ianthe, who remained wrapped in the shadows of her cloak. 'How did you know it was there?' he asked.

She shrugged.

'You can't see anything in that murk.'

'*You* can't,' she retorted.

Creedy adjusted the lens in his eye socket and examined the object. 'I can get you a buyer for this,' he said. 'The metal itself might be worth a couple of hundred. If it does anything weird once it's dried out, you can double that figure.' He put it down. 'Not exactly a gem lantern, but not a bad start.'

They searched the canals for hours. It rained constantly. Ianthe peered into the black water in silence. But was she actually using those vacant eyes to hunt for treasure, or was she using the mind behind them? Granger didn't know. She couldn't steer them; she could only gaze into that bitter void and hope to detect the glimmer of metal amidst the silt and rubble. Yet to Granger's sight the canal water was as impenetrable as the grave. It frightened him because he did not know what they might discover. Not all Unmer artefacts were harmless.

On the outskirts of Francialle they pulled up a star-shaped pendant fastened to a long flat, razor-sharp chain. It would have cut into the skin of anyone who wore it, and yet Creedy insisted it had value. Handling it in his tough gloves, Granger felt the same uneasiness as before. It seemed to resist the movements of his hand, as though attracted or repulsed by some minute and invisible geography of the air. These queer sensations began to turn his stomach, so he flipped the thing to Creedy, who played with it and laughed. After that, the finds came more quickly. In Cannonade Canal they found a pair of metal goggles that allowed the wearer to see the waters as a virulent blue glow awash with threads of silver. By twisting the lenses one could change the colours of the illusion to yellow, black and green. Interesting, Granger conceded, but ultimately pointless. Shortly afterwards they dragged up a tangle of golden fibres that left him with a ringing sensation in his ears, although he heard no actual noise at all.

94

The canals continued to reveal their secrets: an old Unmer dragon harness brimming with needles; three hot glass spheres connected by wooden rods; a paint tin.

They threw the tin back, and moved on.

The rain stopped at dawn. The fresh smell of metal crept into the air with the first morning light. Overhead the sky began to fill with the subtle shades of yellow and purple. Tea-coloured vapour rose from the canals and hung between buildings in a soft ethereal scum. Only the brine itself stayed dark. Granger wanted to head back, but Creedy kept insisting they stay. 'One more find and then we'll go. Just one.'

In the heart of Francialle they manoeuvred the launch into a small square basin tucked in behind a massive prison block belonging to the Bower family, where Ianthe told them to stop again.

Granger rubbed his eyes. 'What is it?'

Ianthe looked up from the water. 'A sea-bottle.'

The two men exchanged a glance. The empire paid three thousand gilders for each ichusae removed from the ocean, but they were worth even more on the black market. Certain warlords had been known to use them as weapons.

This last treasure seemed determined to elude them. After a dozen attempts with the hooked line, Granger still hadn't snagged the thing. He couldn't see anything in the dark water but his own hideous face, the grey, paper-creased cheeks, the goggles like cavities in his skull. He abandoned the hooked line in favour of a claw, a tool more suitable for grabbing smooth objects. By manipulating two cords he could open and close the tool's jaws like a pincer. It was tricky, but on his second try, he thought that the line became a little heavier.

Gently, he began to draw the line in. It snagged on something. He pulled harder.

Something underwater wrenched it back.

Granger reacted instinctively, dropping the line. Two yards of it whizzed across the bow wale, then came to a rest.

Creedy stood up. 'Dragon?'

'In *Ethugra*?' Granger replied. There wasn't space between these buildings to harbour such a monster. Whatever had taken the line was more likely to be much smaller: an Eellen, a Lux shark or thresher-fish, perhaps even one of the Drowned. 'What do you see, Ianthe?'

The girl did not reply.

'Ianthe?'

'A Drowned boy,' she replied. 'He's playing with you.'

Creedy lifted his boat hook. He walked over to the side of the boat and picked up the loose line in his other hand. 'Little shit,' he said, wrapping the rope around his gloved fist. 'I'm going to make you breathe air.' He gave the line a sudden, powerful, yank.

It didn't budge.

Creedy let the line go slack. 'Bastard's snagged it on something.'

The line snapped taut, almost pulling Creedy into the canal. His unusually quick reactions saved him. With his feet planted square under the port strake, he dropped to a crouch, allowing the weight of the vessel itself to resist the force. The launch skimmed sideways across the pool, pushing a wave of black seawater before it, before thumping into the prison façade. Brine sloshed over the gunwales, over the tarpaulin, over Ianthe.

She cried out.

'*Hu-shan*,' Granger hissed the old Imperial curse. 'Are you burned?'

Ianthe was flapping water from her whaleskin cloak.

'*Did it touch your skin?*'

'No.'

Creedy got to his feet, cursing, the line still wrapped around his fist. He untangled himself and then spun the line around one of the steel oarlocks on that side of the boat. Then he turned to Ianthe. 'Drowned fucking boy?' he snarled. 'What was it? Shark? Rock-caster? Eellen?' When she didn't answer he raised the boat hook as if to strike her.

'Sergeant,' Granger said quietly.

Creedy halted, and lowered the weapon.

'We're going back,' Granger said. 'It's getting lighter, and we have enough trove for now.' He looked at the pile of artefacts heaped next to the wheel console: the engine, the pendant, the tangled wire, the dragon harness and the spheres. A thousand gilders' worth of unfathomable rubbish. Even with Creedy's half deducted, it was enough to feed his captives for several months. *Or a down payment on a new boat.* That had been his original plan, after all, and he shouldn't forget it.

Creedy took the treasure away with him to find a buyer. Before he left, Granger offered to let him have the Unmer doll too. 'No sense in keeping it here,' he pointed out. But Creedy was strangely reluctant to accept.

'Sell it later if you need to,' he said. 'I'm tired, I'm going home.' He didn't want to come up to Granger's jail, and he didn't want to wait at the jetty.

Granger returned Ianthe to her cell.

Hana looked up sleepily. 'How did it go?'

'She did well,' Granger said.

'She always does.'

Granger just nodded. He went back upstairs and opened the box in which he kept the doll. But the doll was missing. He wasn't particularly surprised. He stood there for a long moment, wondering why he didn't feel angrier at Creedy.

The sun was up by the time he went to bed, and the garret was already becoming uncomfortably hot. As he lay in his bunk, he thought about the treasure hunt. Granger himself had stared into those lightless canals and seen nothing at all. How had Ianthe done it? Uncanny vision did not explain how she'd known about Duka, the drawer and the four hundred gilders. No matter how many different possibilities went through his head, he couldn't figure out the answer. His gut told him that his captives were lying.

She can't read minds.

If that was so, then why did Hana want to keep her daughter from the Haurstaf?

The Haurstaf will murder her.

Granger frowned. If Ianthe *was* psychic, the Guild would embrace her. And *if* she truly possessed nothing more than heightened physical senses, she posed no threat to them. They might or might not use her, but they had no reason to harm her.

He stared at the ceiling, watching sunlight ripple across the joists. At this hour of the morning the mists would have burned off Halcine Canal, and the water would be shining like a vein of gold.

Perhaps he was approaching this from the wrong direction?

What if she was completely normal – not psychic or special in any way? Granger's own grandmother – Ianthe's great-grandmother – had come from Awl without a glimmer of the telepathic ability so entrenched in her race. There had been nothing there for Ianthe to inherit. Could an ordinary fifteen-year-old girl have found a way to beat the Haurstaf at their own game? What if her strange powers were not merely a quirk of nature, that one-in-a-million mutation that appeared in the blood of western women, but rather the result of something that could be attained by *anyone*? Something sorcerous?

An Unmer artefact.

Granger sat upright in his cot. That made a lot of sense. Suppose Ianthe *had* unearthed some rare treasure – a pendant, ring or pin that granted her these inhuman abilities? The Haurstaf would certainly not flinch from murder to keep it a secret. Emperor Hu could use such an object to challenge the Guild of Psychics and break their monopoly of power. The Haurstaf's very existence would be threatened. If such an object existed, it would be worth more to the empire than a fleet of battleships.

A magic pendant, ring or pin?

Was Ianthe hiding it somewhere on her body even now?

He jumped out of bed, threw on his galoshes and stormed downstairs.

Ianthe was already asleep, curled up on her pallet, but Hana lifted her head, looked up at him and smiled. That smile disarmed him now, as it had all those years ago. She became the same young woman he'd known in Weaverbrook, and for an awful moment he didn't know if he could do what he'd come down here to do. But then he understood the purpose behind her smile. She was tricking him, making a fool of a brine-rotten old jailer. His anger stirred again.

'Wake her,' he said.

Hana frowned.

'I said, wake her.'

For a moment Hana looked uncertain, but then she shook her daughter awake.

'Where is it?' Granger asked the girl.

'Where is what?' Hana replied.

'I'm not going to play any more games with you. Show it to me.'

Mother and daughter looked at each other. 'I don't know what you're talking about,' Hana said.

'All right.' Granger let out a sigh. 'Strip.'

'What?' Hana said. Ianthe looked suddenly fearful.

'Strip,' Granger repeated to Ianthe. 'Take off your clothes and hand them over.'

Hana moved between Granger and their daughter. 'Why are you doing this?'

Granger felt his face fill with blood. 'I'm not going to harm you,' he said through a clenched jaw. 'But if you don't give me the artefact right now, I'll find it myself. Even if that means stripping you naked here and now.'

Ianthe let out a sob. 'I told you what he's like,' she cried. 'He's no better than the others.'

'Don't do this, Tom. Please.'

'Then tell her to do as I say.'

Hana shook her head incredulously. 'You think she *stole* something?'

He said nothing.

'I have no idea what you think she's taken, but you are *not* laying one finger on her.'

Granger grabbed Hana by the arm and dragged her away from the girl. Ianthe gasped and scrambled away from him, her eyes wide with fear. He reached for her, but she shrieked and kicked out wildly. Her boot caught his shoulder, causing his old wound to flare in pain. He grunted and surged forward, grabbing her arms to pin her up against the wall. She spat in his face.

'Stop it,' Hana yelled.

Granger was shaking the girl. 'What is it?' he said. 'A ring? A pendant? Show it to me.'

Hana seized him by the neck and head. She was clinging to his back, trying to pull him away, her fingers scrabbling across his sweating face. Ianthe screamed. Granger turned and slammed himself, and Hana, against the wall, again and again until he felt her grip relax. His chest tightened with pain, but he ignored it. He tore her arms loose and pushed her away from him.

Now he was furious. 'Where is it?'

'She doesn't have anything like that,' Hana sobbed.

'Then what is it? How does she know the things she does?'

'She can see through the eyes of others.'

Granger stopped. He was breathing heavily, his lungs straining to suck in air. His shoulder throbbed where the girl had kicked it.

Hana was sobbing. 'She knew about your money because you *saw* it,' she said, 'and she knew what your friend said because you *heard* him say it. Inny was born with a . . .' For a moment she seemed to struggle to find the right word. 'I suppose it's a gift,' she said at last. 'She can only see and hear things that other people see and hear. It's the same with smell and touch – she tunes into their senses. But she can't read their thoughts any more than you or I can.'

A brine *mutation?* Granger considered this. *She didn't see me fill the jug with poison because it was* dark?

'What about the trove?' he demanded

'The Drowned have eyes too,' Hana retorted, 'and their vision is attuned to the gloom. They can see better than any human can. You never notice them, but they're down there. Thousands of them. Tens of thousands.'

Disassociated perception? Given the right heritage, one in a million conceptions might produce a psychic child, but Granger had never heard of a condition like this – not in Awl, not anywhere. His anger egged him to argue with her, to beat the truth from her. He was sick of being lied to. And yet Hana's comment explained everything. 'She can see through *my* eyes,' he said, 'listen through *my* ears? Even when I'm somewhere else?'

'You could be on the other side of the world.'

'And she can do this trick with *anyone?*'

'Almost any living thing.'

'Haurstaf?'

Hana nodded.

Now Granger understood why she was such a threat to the Guild of Psychics. The Haurstaf openly sold their powers to every warlord who could afford them. In battles it was not uncommon to find telepaths on both sides, each reporting on the other's position. Emperor Hu might rage at Sister Marks, cursing both their expense and their infuriating neutrality, but he was helpless to act against the Guild. If his enemies used their services then so must he.

But if Ianthe could sneak behind the eyes and ears of anyone she chose to, she would be the perfect spy. There could be no secrets while she lived, not even among the Haurstaf themselves. She was worth more to the empire than a hundred psychics. Surveillance was an essential expedient of control. And Ianthe's talents could be turned against anyone.

'*Almost* any living thing,' Hana repeated. 'But there is one person whose eyes she cannot see through and whose ears she can't hear through.'

'Who?'

'Herself,' Hana said. 'Your daughter is deaf and blind.'

CHAPTER 5

BETRAYAL

Dear Margaret,

Thank you. Mr Swinekicker paid off Maskelyne's Hookman, at least for the time being. Mr Swinekicker says I shouldn't worry about the future. He'll sort something out. Some new prisoners arrived the other day – an Evensraum woman and her teenage daughter. It's going to take them time to adjust. It's hard to come to terms with the idea of staying here for the rest of your life. I survive because the money you send makes my life bearable. Without your help, I don't think I could go on.

> *Love,*
> *Alfred*

Granger woke late in the afternoon to the smell of fried eels. Hot sunshine poured into the garret through open windows, throwing ripples across the ceiling. He rubbed his eyes.

Creedy was busy at the stove. 'Six hundred gilders,' he said, turning so that his clockwork eye flashed in the sun.

'Each?'

'Between us,' Creedy replied, returning his attention to the frying pan. 'The pendant wasn't worth shit, and that engine wouldn't even bark. Your share's on that crate.'

Granger got up and stretched. He noted the stack of coins and bills piled on the munitions crate; it was far less than he would have believed possible for a haul like that. He thought about challenging Creedy, but then decided against it. Right now, he needed him. And if the sergeant's help came at a price, at least it was one he could afford. 'What time did you get here?' he asked.

'About an hour ago.'

'Do you ever sleep?'

'I thought we might try for that sea-bottle again.'

Granger shook the fog of sleep from his head. 'Give me a minute.' He went over to the window and took a piss, then put a pot of water on the stove to boil. His shoulder still ached from this morning's confrontation. He ran a hand over the tough grey skin. It felt as hard and cracked as a dry riverbed.

Creedy scooped the eels onto a plate and sat down. He didn't offer Granger any. 'I've been thinking,' he said, 'about what we talked about before – about deepwater salvage.'

'There's nothing more to discuss. We don't have the resources.'

'Not now,' Creedy admitted. 'But a few more hauls like last night, and we could start attracting some real investment. There are people in Ethugra with deep enough pockets. We'd make a hundred thousand in the first year.'

Granger shook his head. 'You're talking about going up against Maskelyne.' He didn't want to tell Creedy his real concerns about expanding the operation. Deepwater salvage wasn't something you could go into quietly. You needed a large ocean-class vessel, cranes, power winches, deep-sea nets and a good-sized crew to keep everything running. It would be difficult to hide an operation like that. People would notice, and talk. He couldn't risk exposing Ianthe to that level of attention. Her talents were far too valuable to put on display.

His deaf-blind daughter. He thought about her walking down the wharf, stopping whenever he looked away. She had not been able to see the ground in front of her, except when he looked in her direction. He tried to imagine her growing up in Evensraum, unable to hear the wind in the trees unless someone else was there to hear it too. What kind of life was that for a child? The implications of all this were too intricate for him to unravel at once. He needed to think them through.

'We don't need to *compete* with him,' Creedy said. 'He has all the deepwater gear we'd need.'

Granger looked up. 'A *partnership*?'

The other man shrugged. 'Maskelyne's a businessman.'

'He's a criminal,' Granger said, 'and a murderer.'

Creedy chewed his food slowly.

Granger picked up the money from the crate. With these gilders and the four hundred from yesterday, he could pay off his debts at the boatyard and maybe convince Maddigan to order in some new planking for his boat's hull. Once the old girl was fixed up, he could trade her in against a storm-sealed deepwater cruiser, hopefully a tug or even an ex-naval vessel. About thirty or forty thousand would buy him something sturdy enough to cross the open ocean.

He poured two mugs of tea, then joined Creedy. 'Somebody stole that Unmer doll.'

Creedy scraped eel jelly from his plate and spooned it into his mouth. 'Lot of thieves about.'

'So it seems.'

'It's no big deal,' Creedy said. 'Now we have the girl.'

'Assuming she agrees to keep working with us.'

Creedy grunted. '*She* doesn't have shit to say about that.' He finished his meal and stood up. 'Are we going, or what?'

The two men took Creedy's launch back to the basin behind the Bower family prison in Francialle, leaving Ianthe behind. Creedy switched off the engine and stared into the brine with open hostility, as though he expected resistance from whatever lay below, and was fully prepared to counter it with force. They began to dredge the gloomy waters with a claw.

But again the bottle eluded them.

Shadows gathered in the basin and the canal beyond as evening approached. The sky between the buildings turned golden with the setting sun. Creedy grew irritable and then angry. His clockwork eye ticked and whirred as though struggling to focus. In his long whaleskin gloves, cloak and goggles he looked like some infernal golem. He hauled in the rope for the hundredth time, examined at the empty claw and then smashed it down on the deck. 'She's messing with us,' he said. 'There's nothing down there. You said yourself the Unmer only dumped ichusae in deep water.'

'Francialle used to be full of Unmer forges,' Granger replied. 'Conceivably, they could have made thousands of ichusae here. Changed ordinary glass phials and copper stoppers into something else.'

'How did they get all the brine inside them?'

'I don't think they did.'

A voice from above called down: 'You changed your mind about the map yet?'

Granger looked up to see an old man peering down at them from one of the barred windows above. His face was gaunt, his cheeks hollow from malnutrition, lending emphasis to his wildly protruding eyes. He gripped the bars of his cell with skeletal hands.

'Shut your damn mouth,' Creedy replied.

'I told you there was no trove down there,' the old man said. 'Maskelyne's men cleaned it all out years ago. You want to be looking near the Glot Madera, but I ain't telling you where unless you buy my map.'

Creedy must have returned to this spot sometime after dawn, Granger realized. No doubt he had tried to look for the bottle on his own. This bothered him less than he would have expected. It wasn't against the law.

'Madman,' Creedy muttered.

'The original map was drawn by the Unmer,' the old man retorted. 'I saw it in a collection in Maggog, copied it exact from memory.'

Creedy snatched up his baling tin, scooped it full of brine and then hurled it up at the barred window. The old man yelped and disappeared as seawater splashed across the prison façade. Some of the brine must have splashed him, for he began to howl in pain.

'Sun's almost down,' Creedy said. 'We'd best go get the girl.'

'Not tonight,' Granger said.

'What do you mean?'

'I mean exactly that, Sergeant,' Granger replied in a tone that implied the conversation was over.

Creedy looked at him for a moment, then shrugged. 'Whatever you say, Tom.'

They returned in silence. As Granger alighted on his wharf, Creedy looked up at him with malice in his eye. 'Tomorrow night, then?'

'Maybe. I'll send you a message.'

The sergeant spat into the canal, then gunned his launch away, spewing muddy foam in his wake.

Granger looked at his own boat. She was a common skiff, sixteen feet long from bow to stern, and built here in Ethugra three decades ago from sea-forest wood. Most of her hull spars and seats had been replaced by dragon-bones, but her hull was entirely original, and thus rotting. He ought to make some temporary repairs while he was still wearing his brine gear, and while it was still light enough to see what he was doing. Carefully, he climbed aboard, easing his whaleskin boots into the partially flooded bilge. The old wooden planks creaked under his boots.

From the bow storage compartment he took out his foot-pump, tools, storm lantern and an open tin of resin. The resin had hardened, leaving the brush jammed upright like a handle, so he placed the lantern on the wharf, lit it and balanced the tin on the lantern's metal hood. While the resin was warming, he pumped water out of the bilge. Ideally, he should have raised her out of the water, but he didn't need a perfect repair. Just enough to get her to the boatyard.

He spent an hour applying the sticky resin into the caulking between the hull planks. It was fully dark when the job was finally done, and his oil lantern glowed like a lonely beacon among the glooming prison buildings. A cloud of moths flitted around the flame, while scores more drifted past like grey confetti on the black water.

Granger spied another light moving down there in the depths. He snuffed his own lantern.

Several fathoms down, the Drowned man Granger had seen earlier emerged from a submerged doorway under Dan Cutter's jail. He was heading south, hurrying across the uneven canal bed, swinging his gem-lantern to and fro as if searching for something amidst the rubble. The child who had accompanied him previously was nowhere to be seen.

A sense of unease crept over Granger, although he couldn't say why. He suddenly felt very cold. As he turned to go back inside, he happened to glance up. The sky was moonless and clear, crammed with stars that sparkled like fragments of mica. He spotted the constellations of Ulcis Proxa and Iril, and part of Ayen's Wheel glimmering low in the north. A tiny cluster of lights was travelling across the sky there. It stopped abruptly, then altered course, moving off in a westerly direction. Granger paused to watch it go. He'd not seen Ortho's Chariot for five or six years, and as he stood there he couldn't help but wonder what it might be. The last Unmer airbarque, travelling forever beyond the reach of the Haurstaf and Emperor Hu's raging indignation? The occupants must surely be dead by now. Or was it just a star that had lost its way?

He went back inside.

He'd been gone longer than he intended to, and his prisoners would be hungry. He went downstairs to check on them.

Ianthe watched him moodily from under her hair. Hana looked drawn and weary. 'Inny tells me it's a beautiful night,' she said. 'You saw Ortho's Chariot?'

Granger nodded. 'It's supposed to be a bad omen.'

'Evensraumers don't think so,' she replied. 'Inny told me about your argument with Creedy.'

'She's been spying on me?'

Hana raised her eyebrows. 'Don't blame her for that, Tom. What would you do in her position?'

Granger glanced at his daughter. Of course her mother was right. He was Ianthe's jailer before he was her father. Still, he didn't like her prying into his affairs. 'Then you'll know I didn't get to the market today,' he said, 'and there's not much left in the cupboard. Supper is porridge.'

'I hate porridge,' Ianthe said.

'Eat it or go hungry,' Granger replied. 'Decide which one of those two you hate the most.'

'There are fish in the canal,' she said. 'You could catch us some supper.'

'Forget it.'

'Please,' she wailed. 'Just for an hour. It's so dark and smelly in here. I can tell you where to cast.'

Granger found himself considering this, despite himself. He hadn't gone fishing for months, and it was a nice night. His prisoners weren't likely to go anywhere. 'It's too risky,' he said. 'If someone sees us . . .'

'They won't,' Ianthe insisted. 'I'll be able to sense them long before they can see us. Please, please, please.'

'No,' he said. 'That's final.'

An hour later he was standing on his jetty with his fishing rod, casting a line out across the canal waters.

'Not there,' Ianthe said. 'There!' She pointed in the direction of Cuttle's jail. 'There's a shoal of angel fish around that pontoon.'

'That's where I cast,' Granger insisted.

'No you didn't.'

Granger reeled in the line again, grumbling. He'd been at this for half an hour already.

Hana was lying on her back, stretched out on the jetty planks, breathing deeply of the fresh night air as she gazed up at the stars.

Ianthe let out a moan of frustration. 'Mother! I need you to watch me.'

Hana's gaze flicked to her daughter. 'I'm sorry, Inny.'

Granger flicked out the line again. This time, his bait plopped into the water a yard beyond Cuttle's pontoon. Ianthe scrunched her eyes up and seemed to be concentrating. After a moment she said, 'You scared them away.'

'*You* told me to cast there.'

'Not right on top of—' She paused. 'Wait, there's something else coming. Something . . . it's swimming straight for the bait.'

Granger stared into the canal, but could see nothing in the black depths. 'A fish?'

'I don't know what it is!' Ianthe exclaimed. 'It isn't looking at itself, is it? It's going for the bait . . . now.'

A splash disturbed the waters out by the pontoon. Granger saw something large and silvery flash in the gloom, and then his line gave a sudden jerk, bending the fishing rod near double. This was a good-sized fish.

CHAPTER 6

THE OLEA

Dear Margaret,

Last night I dreamed I escaped this cell. I was heading across open water in a strong steel boat, with the sun rising before me and the whole sea shimmering like copper. And then I woke and found myself trapped in this damn cell again. The same four walls every day, the same lousy food. And now there's a dead man in the next cell. He died during the night, and Mr Swinekicker has just left him there. What kind of life is this? What kind of man leaves a corpse to rot?

Love,
Alfred

Granger let Creedy stew for three more days. He set up the washbasin for his two captives, running a tube down from the purifier on his roof, and he improved the floor in their cell as best he could. He used his own boat to travel to Averley Market, but it leaked so badly he dared not risk the long trip out to the boatyards yet. He bought food, wine and resin, and spent a whole afternoon patching up the hull. It grew hot and humid, and the grey skies pinned the air down over the city as thoroughly as the roof of a bread oven. On the third night he dragged Duka's body out of the cell and dumped it in one of the narrow nameless

Hana gave him a girlish clap. 'Are they good to eat?'

Granger sat down on the jetty beside the netted fish. He turned to her and grinned. 'I don't know about good,' he said.

Some Ethugrans only bothered to boil brinelife twice, claiming it was safe to eat thereafter, but it was common to see mutations in those families. Granger played it safe. He wore gloves for gutting, and then boiled his catch three times, emptying the pan of ochre scum and refilling it with purified water each time. The fish turned from grey to white. It was after midnight by the time he'd dished it out into bowls and sat down with Hana and Ianthe.

This small, strange family sat on old munitions crates in Granger's attic, eating by the light of an oil lamp. He'd opened his best bottle of wine, sweetened it with sugar to make it drinkable and dug out some blankets for Hana and Ianthe to use as cushions. The women were silent for once. Granger couldn't stop himself from glancing over at them. Their clothes were ragged and filthy. He would have to see about getting them some new ones now that he had a bit of money. Mrs Pursewearer might sell him some. She'd know the sort of things they'd need. He'd have to buy planking for their cell, too, to raise the floor properly. Maybe he could stretch to a washbasin, run a hose down from the purifier. Watching Hana eat reminded him of the first night he'd met her at the farm in Evensraum. She been more curious about him than afraid. He suddenly realized he was staring, and she was looking at him.

'How did you end up here?' she said.

'Long story.'

'I never imagined you'd become a jailer.'

'It's only temporary, until I can get my boat fixed.'

She took a sip of wine, and grimaced. 'Where will you go?'

He shrugged.

Hana sat up. 'You got one?'

'Of course he got one,' Ianthe snapped.

Granger grunted and pulled back on the fishing rod. He began to wind in the slack. Out in the canal, the fish exploded out of the water and then thrashed across the surface. The creature was about three feet of solid muscle, with a blunt, fist-like head crammed with teeth.

'A grappler,' Granger growled. 'Get back, both of you – it's likely to splash brine everywhere.'

The woman and her daughter retreated away from him along the jetty.

Granger fought hard against the line, his rod bending under the strain. He lowered the rod, reeling in as he did so, then heaved it back again. The fish burst out of the water a second time, flashing white and silver in the starlight, spraying foam everywhere. Again Granger lowered the rod, working the reel. Again he pulled back. His pulse was racing. With weary arms he dragged his catch inch by inch closer to the jetty.

The fish stopped suddenly. It felt like a dead weight. Cautiously, Granger pulled back on the rod and reeled in another yard of line. The waters settled. Granger could feel his palms sweating inside his gloves. He reclaimed another yard. Still no reaction from the canal. The line vanished into the black water twelve feet beyond the edge of the jetty. Granger paused, breathing heavily, and eased his goggles down over his eyes. He nudged the landing net closer with his foot. This was the dangerous part.

The fish bolted again, but Granger was ready to take the strain. He leaned back. When he felt the line slacken, he dipped the rod and reeled in once more. Twelve feet became eight, then six, then he could see the creature's fat silvery form under the inky surface. He lowered his landing net into the water, eased it around the exhausted fish and hauled it in.

canals behind his prison. And then he flagged down Ned and paid him to deliver a message to Creedy.

The sergeant arrived that same evening, with two bottles of beer and a broad grin on his grizzled jaw, as if the two of them had never argued. 'Enjoying the family life, Colonel?'

Granger sat down and pulled on his galoshes.

Creedy's grin widened. 'It was only a matter of time.'

For the next four nights they dredged Ethugra's canals for trove. Creedy grunted with approval at each new treasure they discovered, before packing them carefully away in his huge canvas satchel. Ianthe's abrasiveness waned as she relaxed into the task and let the fresh air start to relieve the stress of confinement. She seemed happy to be in the two men's company. Clearly she enjoyed the work.

For Creedy's benefit she kept up the pretence of staring into the black waters, as though she was able to perceive details in that murk with her useless eyes. Whenever they found trove, Granger knew that there must be Drowned nearby, that Ianthe had spotted the treasure only because they themselves had seen it. He imagined multitudes of them moving about down there while the surface world remained oblivious. It was like the way the empire viewed the liberated territories: one did not observe the under-classes unless one was obliged to. In Granger's experience such an attitude was inherently dangerous. When the under-classes occupied the foundations of a society, it was all too easy for them to undermine it.

Creedy and the girl showed genuine interest in the objects they retrieved. But Granger couldn't shake his dark mood or bring himself to enthuse about their finds. Relatively common items made up the bulk of their discoveries: bright shards of pottery, rusted clasps and hinges, parts of old Unmer sailing vessels. Few were worth more than a handful of gilders. But every so often they found something rarer.

In Malver Basin they pulled up a trepanned skull. After they had emptied it of brine something could be heard rattling around inside, and when Granger listened closely he could swear he heard the sound of flutes coming from the unknown object. It was tuneless and ethereal, and he sensed it served no good purpose. But they would sell it to one of Creedy's buyers, and it would end up god knows where, and the responsibility for returning it to the world would remain on Granger's shoulders. He needed the money.

From a tar-black sink on the outskirts of Francialle they retrieved a phial of blood-red crystals, which Creedy tried to open.

'Best leave it be, Sergeant,' Granger said.

Creedy held the phial close to his eye lens. 'They could be rubies,' he muttered.

'Maybe,' Granger replied. 'Maybe not. Let the buyer take the risk.'

This was their problem. Neither of them really knew what most of this stuff *did*, or, for that matter, what it was truly worth. There were a few Unmer experts in Ethugra, but no one they could trust. What looked like treasure to them them might be worthless in the marketplace, while what appeared to be common might actually be priceless. They were at the mercy of their own ignorance.

But late on the fourth night, Ianthe led them to a discovery that Creedy recognized at once.

On a hunch Creedy had steered the launch deep into the Helt, where the canals formed a precise grid and the massive iron-stitched prison blocks rose sheer above them for more than ten storeys. Finds were sparse here, but Creedy insisted they keep searching. They must have traversed the same intersection four times before Ianthe raised her hand for them to stop.

'An amphora,' she said.

It was heavy. If Granger had known beforehand just how

much effort would be required to pull it up, he might just have left it on the seabed. And when he saw its dreary bulk resting in the hull, he almost pitched it back in to save himself the trouble of carrying it further.

Creedy stopped him. 'I know what that is,' he said excitedly. 'Hell's balls, man, I know what that is.'

Granger peered down at the object. It was a clay amphora sealed by a wax stopper. He'd seen hundreds of them for sale in Losoto. 'Wine,' he said. 'Or whale oil. Either way, it's not worth much more than twenty gilders.'

Creedy shook his head. 'It's an olea,' he said. 'These markings on the front show a record of its battles.'

Granger frowned at the indecipherable writing scrawled across the container. 'A fish?'

'Jellyfish,' Creedy said. 'The Unmer used to breed them for sport.'

'That's an old amphora,' Granger said.

'Doesn't matter,' the other man replied. 'Olea are sorcerous.'

'It's still alive?'

He nodded. 'And seriously pissed off. Imagine how you'd feel being cooped up in a jar for two hundred years.' He grinned, and his eye-lens glittered in the lantern light. 'Might get eight hundred for it at market, but a collector would pay more. Up to four thousand for a good specimen.'

Granger stared at the amphora. With his half share, he'd manage a down payment on a deepwater vessel. It was more than he'd dared hope for in such a short space of time. He could be out of Ethugra by the end of the year. 'Do you know any collectors with that kind of money?' he asked.

The sergeant was silent for a moment. Then he shrugged. 'The only one in Ethugra who collects them,' he said, 'is Ethan Maskelyne.'

A hollow feeling crept into Granger's gut. *Ethan Maskelyne*. Maskelyne the Metaphysicist, Maskelyne the Unappointed, the Wizard of Scythe Island – Ethugra's unofficial boss had more so-briquets than the tides. He was an amateur scientist, and an avid collector of Unmer esoterica. But to Granger, the title of Maskelyne the Extortionist seemed most fitting. His Hookmen supposedly protected the city from the Drowned, but they took in payment nine out of every hundred gilders earned by the land-living. Once in a while they'd drag a few sharkskin men or women up from the depths and chain them out in Averley Plaza to die in the sun.

'Eight hundred in the market?' Granger said.

Creedy looked up. 'But five times that from Maskelyne himself.'

Granger didn't like it. Maskelyne would want to know exactly where the olea had come from. Were there any more? How did two jailers come to be in the trove business in the first place? What else had they found? Granger did not want to be scrutinized by a man like Maskelyne. But something else bothered him even more. Finding this treasure had been too . . . *convenient*. Creedy had wanted to bring Maskelyne in as a partner and now he had a perfect excuse to approach him. And why had Creedy been so insistent that they come here at all? Granger peered down at the amphora again. It remained as unremarkable as any he'd seen, covered with scratches that might be some ancient Unmer script, or not. Anyone might have scrawled them. A fighting jellyfish? Or a jar of vinegar?

'No,' he said. 'We'll sell it through the market.'

'Aye, sir,' Creedy said evenly, although the darkness in his expression said otherwise.

Towards dawn, Granger sat with Ianthe and Hana on the roof of his jail, eating thrice-boiled fish baked in sugar and cinnamon that Hana had prepared while they'd been away. A small oil lantern rested on the brine purifier nearby. Ianthe was telling her mother about the amphora.

'What did it perceive?' Hana asked.

Ianthe snorted. 'I don't know! Jellyfish don't have any eyes or ears, do they?'

'You saw nothing inside?' Granger asked.

'I don't *see* at all,' Ianthe said.

Granger noted that her tone had become less cynical and hostile. She was beginning to accept her situation, and that troubled him more than he cared to admit. She didn't belong here, nor anywhere with him. He couldn't take them with him.

He sighed and rubbed his temples. Once he bought his new boat, he might as well return them to Evensraum. Or even Lionsport, at the edge of the empire. They'd probably be safer there.

'Can you see what Creedy's doing?' he asked.

Ianthe's spoon halted halfway to her mouth. She appeared to smile slightly, although it was so brief it may have been Granger's imagination. And then her blank eyes gazed at the ground for a moment. 'He must be sleeping,' she said, then went back to her meal.

'How do you know? How can you find him?'

She spoke with her mouth full. 'It's like flying through darkness. You can see little islands of light everywhere, but the islands are really someone's perception, and you can drift down inside them if you concentrate.' She swallowed her food and took another bite. 'Then the darkness goes away and you hear and see exactly what they do. But when there's nobody about, it's just black, empty of anything. I can see this roof because you and Mother do. And I can see a room in that building,' she pointed to Cuttle's jail, 'because somebody is moving about over there. But the area between is just dead space, like your friend Creedy's house.'

'You know where he lives.'

She shrugged. 'Only because I sat in his head and watched him go there.'

'But if he's somewhere else? Could you still find him?'

She shrugged. 'Maybe,' she said. 'But I'd have to look inside all the different lights, and that would take all night. How do *I* know where he is?'

Granger thought about this. Ianthe could follow someone, spy on them, by putting herself inside that person's mind. But once out of their head, it was difficult for her to relocate them amongst the millions of other people – unless she knew exactly where to look. 'Can you tell who is who?' he asked. 'When you move into these islands in the darkness, these perceptions, do you know whose eyes you are looking through?'

Ianthe finished her meal and set down the bowl. 'Not at first,' she admitted. 'You can see your own arms and legs, but you can't see your own face, can you? Sometimes the only way I can know for sure is to look at the person through someone else's eyes, unless they happen to look in a mirror, I suppose. Women look in mirrors a lot . . . so does Emperor Hu. I don't think Creedy owns a mirror, though.'

'You shouldn't be spying on the emperor,' Granger said.

She gave him a sarcastic smile. 'Only on your friends?'

Granger grunted. He got up and strolled to the edge of the roof. His garret sloped darkly behind him, and down in the canal the brine was as black as sin. No green and gold lights. He couldn't see his own boat. There was only the constant slap of water in the darkness and the sour metal stench of the sea. The great shadowy masses of the surrounding jails loomed over him, now silhouetted against the lightening sky. Steam rose from the funnels of Dan Cuttle's place. He was probably boiling up a vat of bones. He searched the skies for Ortho's Chariot but couldn't spot it. Scores of stars still sparkled ahead of the coming sunrise. The day looked like it would be another fine one. Granger felt the time was right.

He turned to the girls. 'Wait here.'

He went back into his garret and took out the large paper parcel he'd hidden under his cot, then carried it back up to the roof and gave it to Hana.

'What's this?' she asked.

'Just something I picked up.'

Hana unwrapped the parcel. It contained two ankle-length satin frocks, each adorned with all sorts of fancy lace frills. One was mostly peach-coloured, with silvery sparkles across the front, while the other boasted pink and yellow stripes and puffy arms. Hana held up the peach dress and blinked at it. 'You bought these for us?'

'The other one's for Ianthe. It's got ruffles.'

Ianthe's face remained expressionless. 'Ruffles,' she said in a flat voice. 'Yes, it does, doesn't it?'

Hana appeared to suppress a smile. She moved more of the crumpled paper aside. 'And what's this? Undergarments?' She lifted out a pair of the knee-length white pantaloons Mrs Pursewearer had sold Granger and held them out at arm's length. 'These look . . . well made.'

'I'm told they're good quality,' Granger said.

Ianthe gave a little squawk, then covered her mouth with her hand.

Hana looked up at him with bright eyes. She gave him a huge smile, then stood up and kissed him on the cheek. 'I don't know what to say. Thank you. Thank you from both of us.'

Granger looked at his feet. He nodded awkwardly. 'Your old

clothes were pretty rotten,' he said. 'I didn't want you both getting fleas.'

Creedy was shaking him. 'Colonel, I found a buyer.'

Granger blinked and raised his hands against harsh sunlight. 'What time is it?'

'Afternoon.'

'What day?'

'I dunno. Today.'

'Gods, man, do you never go to bed?'

'Not when there's money to be made,' Creedy replied. 'I found us a buyer for the olea. A collector, here in Ethugra.'

Granger sat up in his cot and stretched his neck. The roof of his garret wavered with copper-coloured reflections. He remembered putting Ianthe and Hana in their cell, but not much after that. He must have been exhausted. 'The jellyfish? I thought Maskelyne was the only collector in Ethugra.'

'That's what I thought,' Creedy replied. 'But then I started asking around, sly like, so nobody—'

'How much did you get for it?'

Creedy frowned. 'I said I've found us a buyer. I didn't say I'd sold the bloody thing. He wants to meet you.'

'Me?'

'The brains of the operation.'

Granger got up. 'What do I know about jellyfish?'

'About as much as me,' Creedy said. 'But you're prettier than me, and the buyer's some titled Evensraum merchant. All airs and graces. Wipes his arse with squares of silk. I don't know if I could speak to him without murdering him.'

Granger frowned. What was an Evensraumer was doing in Ethugra? *Unless* . . .

'He's a prisoner?'

Creedy nodded. 'A rich prisoner. Holed up in one of the Imperial jails on Averley. Special privileges and all that. The bastard used to own more land than Hu. He's got gilders coming out of his pores.'

Granger knew the type. Wealth bought luxury and status even in Ethugran prisons, even if it couldn't always purchase freedom. There were captives in this city who ate better than their jailers did. They were always pre-assigned to Imperial jails, thus avoiding the allocation system used for regular inmates. Emperor Hu made a good profit from such prisons, although it was rumoured that Maskelyne's men actually ran them.

Maskelyne again, Granger thought miserably. *Why does it always come back to him?*

'What is it?' Creedy said.

'Nothing.' Granger sighed. Maybe he was just being paranoid. 'When can I meet him?'

'Whenever you like. He ain't going anywhere.'

'Now?'

The other man shrugged. 'The olea's in the boat. I'll drop you off there.'

Shortly afterwards he found himself hunched beside Creedy in his launch as it thundered along. He'd left fresh water and soap for Hana and Ianthe. Creedy gunned the engines without regard for other canal traffic, pushing them quickly through Franciallc and into Averley Plaza. They discussed money. How much should Granger ask for the olea? Creedy waved his arms and talked about thousands, but Granger wasn't convinced. If he got more than eight hundred, he'd be happy. The sun was still above the rooftops when they reached the marketplace embankment, bathing the Imperial jails and administration buildings in soft, golden light. Creedy wrenched the tiller to port and cut the engines, expertly berthing the metal vessel between a fishing barque and a clutch of coracles. Once he'd tied up, he dug out a bulky whaleskin parcel from a hidden compartment under the port strakes and beckoned Granger up the stone steps to the embankment.

The market had finished hours ago. Only a few beer sellers stayed open, serving those stallholders who had remained after their morning's work. Groups of Asakchi and Valcinder merchants lounged against the stony figures of the Drowned, drinking and talking, while a group of children raced around the empty stalls, shrieking with delight at some game. Creedy led Granger to one of the many huge brass doors lining the westernmost façade and then banged on it repeatedly. A great booming sound echoed within.

'Ask for Truan,' Creedy said, handing Granger the wrapped amphora. 'I'll be yonder, drinking my share on credit.' He gave a short salute and then wandered off towards the beer sellers.

The amphora felt as heavy as a boulder. Granger was about to put it down, when the door opened and a hard-faced little man peered out and blinked. 'I'm the jailer,' he said. 'You the guy with the thing?' He glanced at Granger's parcel, then waved him in without waiting for an answer and swung the door shut behind them both.

They were standing in a grand stone hallway. A sweeping staircase rose to a second-floor gallery. Down here on the ground level, two arched doorways led to administration offices on either side, wherein Granger could see scribes working at their desks amidst stacks of paper. One of the seated young men glanced up from his quill and frowned through his spectacles, before returning his attention to his ledger. The building contained a weighty silence that seemed several degrees more substantial than the air itself.

Given the solemn majesty of his surroundings, the jailer who had admitted Granger could not have looked more out of place. He was as small and tough as a street dog, with a naval haircut and a brawler's skewed nose. He wore a perpetual scowl, giving his face the same creased, weather-worn appearance as his salt-stained leather tunic and his sailcloth breeches. Ink crosses and sigils tattooed across the back of his hands suggested he'd spent some time in a less imposing prison than this one, albeit on the other side of the bars.

One of Maskelyne's men? Granger's unease deepened.

The jailer stared at the parcel in Granger's arms for a moment, then beckoned him to follow up the staircase. On the right side of the upper gallery he unlocked a stout iron-banded door, which looked a hundred years older than the stonework around it. Granger realized that it must originally have been fitted to a series of identical doors in the flooded levels below, only to be moved up floor by floor as the building grew higher to escape the rising seawater. Imperial builders often followed this pattern, constructing identical floor plans one above the other in order to strip out and reuse every possible fixture and fitting before filling the drowned levels with rubble.

The man waved Granger through. 'Truan's wing,' he said.

His wing?

Granger stepped through the door and into a large, opulent lounge in which velvet chairs, sofas and polished hardwood tables had been artfully arranged on Valcinder rugs. Carved bone chandeliers depended from the high ceilings, while the tall windows on his left overlooked one of Ethugra's grander canals and the façade of another Imperial jail on the opposite bank. Latticeworks of iron covered those windows, yet even these were ornate and painted white. As surprising as all this was to Granger, his attention was nevertheless grabbed by the opposite, innermost wall of the room. He'd never seen anything like it before.

A score of alcoves lined this wall, each sealed by a massive plate of glass and filled with a different type of brine. Granger recognized the tea-coloured water of the Mare Lux, the dark red Mare Regis brine and that painful green ichor that composed so much of the seas around Valcinder. But there were other colours too – the blues and purples and the soft golds of those weird and distant oceans that he had only heard mentioned in tales.

Within all of these alcoves were oleas.

Each species had been segregated from the others. There were wondrous, ghostly things with tendrils like wisps of fog, and fat brown jellies that looked like pickled brains. In one alcove, schools of tiny quick-moving motes gave off a queer electric luminance, while in the next hung an enormous bloated crimson shape among whose folds Granger thought he could discern an eye. He had an odd sensation that it was watching him.

'Marvellous, aren't they?'

Truan, for it must have been he, had entered the chamber through another door. He was a tall, lean man with a long, cadaverous face. He wore a padded gold tunic embroidered with steel wire in the latest Losotan fashion, and white hose that only served to exaggerate his skeletal appearance. Brine spots stippled the backs of his hands. His green eyes regarded Granger with vigour and intelligence. He dismissed Granger's companion with a wave and waited until the man had closed the door behind him.

'Would that I could have them fight each other,' he said, indicating the creatures in the flooded alcoves. 'But olea are far too valuable to waste in sport. That hexen midurai is one of only three known specimens in existence.' He pointed at the large crimson jelly. 'From its size, I estimate it to be over sixteen hundred years old. And these,' he waved a hand at several unremarkable ochre lumps floating in a tank of yellow brine, 'are hexen parasitae from the Sea of Dragons. They way they breed is as remarkable as it is hideous. Even the Drowned avoid them.'

'You know why I'm here,' Granger said.

The Evensraumer nodded, then gestured for his guest to sit on one of the sofas. 'Would you care for some wine, Mr Swinekicker?'

Granger looked at the sofa with distaste. He shook his head.

'Tea, then? I don't often get the chance to converse with outsiders.'

'No.'

Truan smiled. 'I can see from your expression that you disapprove of my lifestyle.'

'You're supposed to be a prisoner here.'

Truan's eyes narrowed. 'I *am* a prisoner here, sir,' he said. 'It's true that my wealth affords me certain luxuries and allows me to pursue my interests, but walls are walls. I will remain here until the emperor decrees otherwise, while you are free to leave the city whenever you choose.'

Granger thought about his waterlogged boat, but said nothing. He set his parcel down on a nearby table and began to unwrap it. He was surprised to find that his heart was racing.

Truan hovered nearby, eyeing the amphora with interest as it was revealed. Finally he strolled over, leaned across the table and squinted at the markings etched into the clay. He turned the jar a little to one side, frowning. 'Is this a joke, sir?' he said.

Granger felt his heart grow cold. 'What do you mean?'

'It's a wine amphora.'

A sudden awful realization gripped Granger as he stared down at the lump of pottery they'd dredged up. *Creedy.* Creedy had decided which canals to search. Creedy had identified the find. Creedy had found the buyer. And Creedy had brought him here, away from his home. Anger coiled inside him. He was about to turn and leave when his pragmatic side urged him to stop. Might the Evensraumer not simply be lying to lower the price? He swallowed his rage. 'If it's of no value,' he said, 'I'll take it elsewhere.'

Truan continued to study the object. 'Unmer wine is of *some* value,' he said, 'provided it has not been exposed to the air. I suppose I could offer you twenty gilders. But not a coin more. Frankly, I'd be doing you a favour.'

'Forget it.' Granger picked up the amphora.

'Thirty, then,' Truan said. 'That's five more than the market price.'

Granger began walking towards the door.

'Thirty-five,' Truan called after him. 'My final offer.'

Granger reached the door, and turned the handle. It was locked. He hammered his fist against the iron barred wood.

'Very well,' Truan said. 'My jailers charge me exorbitant commission on anything I order. I'll give you fifty for the wine if you don't tell a soul. You are robbing me blind, after all, and I won't have my other suppliers hear of it.'

Granger turned to look at the other man. Fifty? For a jug of wine? Truan seemed unusually keen to get his hands on such a worthless artefact. And yet his instincts continued to gnaw at him. *Something is wrong here.* The amphora, the buyer, it was all too *convenient* for Creedy. And there was something else, something about Truan that bothered him. This man was no trader, that much was clear. He had raised his price three times before Granger had even reached the door. After all, they had both been captive in that room. Granger wasn't going anywhere until the jailer came to release him, and Truan would have been well aware of that. Not even the poorest Losotan merchant, much less one as rich and successful as Truan purported to be, would have made such a mistake. But if he wasn't who he said he was, then who was he?

Granger had his suspicions. 'Perhaps I'll have that tea after all,' he said.

Truan smiled again and waved Granger back to the sofa. Then he strolled across the room and pulled a bell chord. Chimes sounded in the hall outside. Granger took a seat and waited with the sealed amphora in his arms. A fortune or a pittance waited within.

'Which part of Evensraum are you from?' Granger asked.

'Deslorn,' Truan replied.

'A shame what happened there. The typhoid, I mean.'

'I believe it was cholera,' Truan said. 'We left the place long before the city filled with refugees. One of the benefits of being in shipping is that one owns ships.'

Air bubbled up through one of the jellyfish tanks. The pale blue creatures inside shivered.

'I had family in Weaverbrook,' Granger said.

Truan raised his eyebrows. 'I had no idea you hailed from that part of the world, Mr Swinekicker.'

A key clicked in the lock. The jailer came in carrying a tray of tea.

'Haven't been back to see them in a while,' Granger said.

'I can sympathize,' Truan said. 'Nothing is more important than family.'

The jailer set the tea down on the table. 'Anything else, sir?'

'That will be all,' Truan replied.

Granger looked at the jailer's tattoos. 'This can't be easy for you,' he said. 'A man with a history like yours, running around like a boot boy after his master?'

The jailer glanced at Truan and back at Granger, and in that moment Granger finally understood Truan's real identity.

He grabbed the amphora and leaped to his feet, barging past the jailer and knocking him off his feet. He raced down the stairs and was halfway towards the front door before he heard angry shouts and footfalls coming from behind. Evidently the jailer had recovered enough to come after him. Granger ran on, his chest cramping at the sudden exertion. His scarred lungs were not used to such exercise. The air seemed full of acid, but he ignored it. The bitter taste in his throat was worse. Creedy had lied to him, tricked him into coming here.

Ethan Maskelyne's accent had been good, but it hadn't been perfect. Granger had spent enough time in Evensraum to know the difference. But he hadn't been sure of his suspicions until the jailer had confirmed them. An Ethugran jailer might be paid enough to treat an Evensraum captive as his master, but he would never believe it to be true. Granger's comment should have humiliated and angered the man. And yet the only emotion in the jailer's eyes had been fear. Fear of what Maskelyne would do to him.

He reached the front doors and burst through them. Glancing over his shoulder, he saw a blizzard of paper whirling around the scribes' desks. Maskelyne's man had already reached the bottom of the steps and showed no sign of slowing down. Granger plunged out into the sunlight of Averley Plaza.

The beer drinkers lounged about in groups. A few turned to glance his way as he came storming out of the Imperial jail with the heavy amphora still clutched in his arms. Children shrieked happily as they played about the empty market stalls. The Drowned observed it all with their dead stone eyes, their faces frozen in eternal grimaces of agony. But Creedy was nowhere to be seen, and his launch was no longer moored at the dock.

Bastard.

Creedy had managed to get him away from Hana and Ianthe.

Granger stood in the centre of the plaza, wheezing. He needed a boat, any boat, to take him home.

Someone seized his arm.

Snarling, the Imperial jailer looked more like a street dog than ever before. His face was flushed, his eyes narrowed. 'Where do you think you're going?' he said through his teeth. 'Nobody runs out on my boss.'

Granger smashed the amphora across his head.

The jailer dropped to the ground, his head and shoulders drenched in oil.

Granger hardly gave him a second a glance. He was already running along the dockside, looking for a boat.

There were few to choose from, and no passenger ferry boats at all. Almost all of the market traders had already gone home, and none of their customers remained. A score of unguarded whaleskin coracles bobbed against the steps, but they would be too slow. Two fishermen sat repairing their nets on the wharf side above an old closed-deck barque, but their deepwater hull was too wide to negotiate Ethugra's narrower channels. Such a vessel would be forced to head out of the Glot Madera and circle around almost a quarter of the city before heading back in through Halcine Canal. Granger passed three more barques before he finally came upon a suitable craft.

She was a Valcinder sloop – a true canal boat, as sleek, quick and narrow as any in Ethugra. Her captain lay snoozing on the open deck, with his boots propped on the gunwale and a Losotan newspaper draped over his head. He woke with a start when Granger jumped down beside him.

'What? Who the hell—' He was young and dark, dressed up in one of those smart black uniforms they sold in the Losotan markets – all braid and buttons.

Granger took him for a hire captain or a smuggler. No one else bothered to look so neat. 'Take me to Halcine Canal,' he said. 'I'll pay.' He began unravelling the bow line.

The Losotan blinked. 'I'm waiting for a fare.'

'You got a fare,' Granger replied.

'Not you! I'm supposed to take an Imperial administrator to Chandel.'

Granger threw the bow line at him and kicked off from the wharf. 'I'm in a hurry,' he said, 'and I'm taking this boat to Halcine Canal, with or without you at the helm. You'd better choose quickly' – he inclined his head towards the retreating dock – 'because you're running out of time to jump.'

'You're not stealing this boat!'

'Then I'm a paying passenger. Less trouble for both of us.'

The Losotan glanced between Granger and rapidly increasing gulf between his boat and dry land. Then he shook his head and climbed back to the helm. 'We've got to do this fast,' he said, 'or I'm going to lose a whole bunch of gilders.'

Granger grunted. 'Fast suits me just fine.'

Even before they reached his jail, Granger knew he was too late. The flap giving access to his rooms had been torn off and now lay floating on the oily surface of the canal. He leaped onto his wharf, leaving the Losotan hire captain to tie up, and ran up the steps to his garret.

The place was a mess. His cot, furniture and clothes lay strewn across the floor. Even the kitchen cupboards had been torn off the walls and smashed.

But they didn't have enough time.

They had been looking . . . for what? Trove? His savings? It didn't matter. A quick glance was enough to tell him that this had been a rush job. They had started to search the place but had been interrupted. A few floorboards lay ripped up, but the rest were untouched. Piles of tools and junk remained undisturbed where they'd always lain.

Granger didn't dare to let himself hope. He ran downstairs to the cells.

Their cell door had been forced open, torn partially off its hinges. A feeling of dread gripped him as he waded along the corridor towards it.

He expected their cell to be empty. Every bone in his body told him that he'd find his prisoners missing. And so he wasn't prepared for what he did find when he heaved the broken door aside and staggered through.

They had taken Ianthe, of course.

But not Hana.

She was lying on her back in the shallow brine, wearing the fancy dress he'd bought for her, a faint wheezing sound coming from her mouth. Almost her entire body had been submerged. Grey blisters covered her arms and legs, and patches of sharkskin had already begun to creep across her face. Her eyes stared at the ceiling from underneath an inch of seawater. Evidently she had swallowed some of it, for her breathing sounded painfully thin and ragged. And yet even now she was still trying to stay alive, forcing her mouth above the waterline to suck in air that her ruined lungs could barely absorb.

Granger approached, careful not to make waves in the brine around her, and squatted down beside her. He was still wearing his whaleskin gloves, and he reached one hand underneath her head to support it and his other hand under her chin. Her eyes moved under the water. She saw him and took a sharp intake of breath.

'Don't try to speak,' he said. 'Try not to make any sudden movements. Most of your body has already changed, and you need to keep the sharkskin wet. If I lift you out, it's only going to hurt you even more.'

She took a gulp of air, but didn't move.

'Was it Creedy?' he asked.

She tried to nod, but he held her chin firmly.

'Don't nod,' he said. 'Can you move your hands? Make a fist for me.'

Under the water, her hand moved away from her side. She clenched it.

'How many others were with him?'

She held out two fingers.

'Two other men? Make a fist for yes.'

She clenched her hand again and then relaxed it.

'Did you recognize them?'

Her hand didn't move.

'Do you know where they took her?'

A look of distress came into her eyes, she tried to shake her head, but Granger restrained her. 'It's all right,' he said. 'You need to keep still.' She was neither one thing nor the other. Part human, part Drowned. In this condition her lungs wouldn't last much longer. He could hardly hear her breaths now.

'You can't survive like this,' he said gently. 'Your lungs have been contaminated. They're failing. Soon you won't be able to breathe air. If you keep your mouth above water, you'll die.' He kept his gaze fixed firmly on hers. 'I'm going to push you under.'

She panicked and struggled against him.

He held her firmly. 'You'll feel like you're dying,' he said. 'But you won't. The toxic shock will knock you unconscious, but there's a decent chance you'll wake up again. You'll go on living.' He could see the terror in her eyes. They both knew she might never regain consciousness – not everyone did – but Granger had no other option. 'I'll find Ianthe,' he said. 'And I'll kill the men who took her.'

Her hand shot out of the water and gripped his glove. Her

throat bobbed and she let out a gurgling, choking sound. She was trying to speak. 'Hhhhhh . . . guuuuuh.'

'You don't have to say anything.'

'Maaaaahhh . . . Awwwwd.' She tried to lift her face up out of the brine, but he stopped her again. 'Maaasss.'

'Maskelyne? They mentioned Maskelyne?'

She nodded.

'You let me worry about him,' he said. 'Ianthe's in no danger. They want her to find trove.'

She relaxed her grip on his glove. For a long moment she just looked up at him from under the water. Finally she nodded.

Granger pushed her head under and held her there until she stopped moving.

Back upstairs, Granger peeled off the heavy whaleskin gloves and laid them on the top stair banister. If Hana was going to wake from her toxic shock, she'd do so some time within the next few hours. He'd need to carry her body to the opposite cell then lower her through the hole in the floorboards into deeper brine. But he'd wait until she was aware of what was happening. He didn't want her to wake up alone.

Creedy would have taken Ianthe straight to Maskelyne, which meant she must have arrived at his island keep by now. A direct assault on Maskelyne's fortress would be impossible without the assistance of the Imperial Navy, and Granger wasn't in a position to arrange that. Stealth might get him to the fortress walls, but he would be unlikely to find a way inside. He'd have to wait until Maskelyne took Ianthe out onto the open seas to dredge for trove and then attack Maskelyne's ship directly. He'd need a deepwater vessel, a crew and weapons.

And Granger had none of them.

He heard a boat's engine thrumming in the canal outside.

Something about it disturbed him. In the six years he'd lived in Ethugra, he'd grown accustomed to such noises: the post boat, his neighbours' vessels, the passenger taxis. He didn't recognize the sound of this one.

Quickly he ran to the window and peered out.

She was an old iron straight-sided coastal barge of the sort that used to bring whale oil into the city from the depots and shell keeps out by the Ethugran Reef. A fat bow wave surged before her as she sped along Halcine Canal. Granger spat a curse when he saw the crew waiting aboard.

Hookmen.

Six of them stood on the barge's deck, wrapped in bulky whalers' oilskins. Half of them clutched harpoons, flensing poles or head-spades, but the rest carried knives. The helmsman wore a brine mask and goggles, but the rest were naked-faced, scarred and bearded – hard men from the former gutting stations along Dunvale Point. They were looking Granger's way.

He grabbed his whaleskin gloves and pulled them on. Then he ran downstairs and waded along the corridor to Hana's cell.

She was as he'd left her – lying unconscious in the shallow brine.

Granger scooped her into his arms. As he half-dragged, half-carried her out to the corridor, he could hear through the open cell window the barge cut her engines, followed by the sound of boots pounding across his wooden jetty.

In the opposite cell, he pulled her over to the hole in the floorboards. His chest was tight with agony again, and his breaths seemed to whistle in his throat. Now he could hear raised voices coming from upstairs.

'I'm sorry, Hana.' he whispered into her ear. And then he eased her body down through the hole.

Most of the air had already gone from her lungs, and so she slipped away into the brine and crumpled gently onto the floor of the flooded room below. A cloud of sediment rose around her, muddying the tea-coloured waters.

Granger dragged one of the broken pallets across the opening to hide it, and turned as the first of Maskelyne's Hookmen came through the door.

From their appearance they might have been Drowned men themselves. Their leader stood half a foot shorter than Granger, but he was far stouter and more heavily muscled. Sharkskin covered most of his naked forearms like a skin of cracked cement. He had daubed the wounded flesh with some greasy white tincture. Five gutting knives with wooden handles and blades of varying curvature and length hung from loops on the front his padded oilskin. He grinned, displaying wide brown teeth, as the others filled the doorway behind him.

'Hello, Tom,' he said. 'How are you doing, Tom?'

Granger scowled at him. 'I know you?'

'Don't think so, but I know you.'

'What do you want?'

'I don't like that tone of voice, Tom,' the other man replied. 'Why are you taking that tone of voice with me?' He stepped forward, pushing out his chest as though challenging Granger to reach for one the knives hanging there. 'I mean, you're a fucking Drowned lover, aren't you, Tom? You shouldn't be speaking to me like that.'

Granger had seen his type in a hundred bars and back alleys. He had no patience with this fool.

'Get out of my house,' he said.

The Hookman grinned. 'That's not nice, Tom. We're only doing a job here.' He looked down at the pallet covering the hole.

'I mean, you sound like someone who wants their face shoved in the fucking brine. Why would you want that, Tom?'

There were four others blocking the doorway behind, but they couldn't all push through the door at once. Since he wasn't getting out of here without a fight, Granger thought it best to have the fight on his own terms. No sense in waiting.

He slugged the Hookman in the face.

Granger's blow was as hard as any he'd ever given. The Hookman grunted in surprise, but he didn't go down. The bastard had a neck like a girder. Granger brought his other fist up in an uppercut, striking the other man under the chin. He heard the blow connect. It should have broken the Hookman's jawbone.

But it didn't.

The shorter man came at him in a rage, pummelling his stony fists under Granger's ribs.

Granger didn't want to allow him any space to let the others in, so he drew in his elbows and suffered the punches. They felt like hammer blows. He brought his elbow up into the other man's armpit to halt one angle of attack, while trying to force him back towards the door.

But the Hookman was too strong for him. He shoved back, one fist continuing to pound Granger's ribs, the other arm trying to reach over Granger's elbow, scrabbling to grab his hair. With his free left hand Granger fish-hooked the man's cheek, jerking that fat snarling face to one side. He grunted and heaved, but couldn't find the strength to break the other man's neck. The pair wrestled in the shallow brine, the Hookman's teeth gnashing Granger's fingers, dribbling spit down his wrist. Behind him, the others were pushing forward, trying to get past their leader.

Granger's right hand was pinned against his opponent's chest. He reached around until he felt the handle of one of the Hookman's knives. He grabbed the weapon and yanked at it, but it wouldn't budge. Instead he forced the handle down, trying to turn the blade upwards into the other man's guts.

Out of nowhere, something cracked against his skull.

The room reeled. He tasted blood.

He wrenched the knife handle down, heard a grunt.

Another blow struck his ear.

Specks of white light flashed at the edges of his vision.

A third blow sent him staggering back against the wall.

'Fucker cut me.'

The lead Hookman stood ankle deep in brine, clutching a wound in his side. From the small amount of blood evident, Granger could tell that the knife hadn't gone in very deep. Beside the wounded man, another, taller, fellow gripped a long pole with a curved iron tip. This, then, had to be the weapon that had struck Granger. The pole-wielder stepped aside to let a third, bearded, man into the cell.

'He's going to take a swim, Bartle,' said the beard.

'Not now,' said the leader. 'I want him to see what's coming.'

Granger's head still smarted from the blow, and his chest had now begun to ache. He doubted he could get past all three of them without a weapon. He managed a grim smile. It occurred to him that he'd now blown his chance for diplomacy.

The Hookmen's leader – Bartle, he'd been called – used his boot to slide the pallet away from the hole the in floor. He peered down into the brine, and grinned. 'Sleeping like a lamb,' he said to the beard. 'Go get the nets.' Then he looked up at Granger. 'Harbouring the Drowned's worth twenty years, if you've got the cash to pay Maskelyne's fees. How you stacked for cash, Tom?'

CHAPTER 7

ANOTHER MAN'S PRISON

Two Hookmen remained in Granger's place while the others took him back to the same jail he'd just come from on Averley Plaza. They frisked him thoroughly for weapons, then marched him up the stairs to the room where he'd met Creedy's supposed buyer.

Ethan Maskelyne was standing beside one of the windows, his face inclined toward the late-afternoon sun. He didn't turn around when Granger arrived, but he said, 'You weren't supposed to leave here quite so soon.'

Movement caught Granger's eye. He glanced over at the olea tanks. The body of the man who had chased him outside was floating in the third chamber. Hundreds of tiny blue jellyfish clung to his skin, pulsing softly.

Maskelyne turned round. 'You should have brought her straight to me, Mr Granger,' he said. 'I would have given you a fair price, and we could have avoided all this hostility.'

'She wasn't for sale.' Granger judged the distance between himself and the other man. If he bolted, he could probably reach Maskelyne before his Hookmen took him down, but that wouldn't be doing Ianthe any favours.

'Actually, that wasn't for you to decide.' Maskelyne studied Granger for a moment. 'You're a military man, you understand hierarchy. Whether you like it or not, Mr Granger, our society is structured in a way that the rights of its wealthiest and most powerful citizens take precedence over the rights of others. Considering everything I have given back to the empire over many years, I think this is only fair. I had infinitely more right to decide the girl's fate than you ever did.'

'What about Ianthe? Does she have a say?'

Maskelyne smiled. 'I understand your disappointment. But you needn't worry about her. If her talents are half of what Mr Creedy tells me they are, she'll be well rewarded – she'll certainly have a better life in my care than you could ever have given her.'

How much had Creedy told him? The sergeant was a fool if he thought Maskelyne was going to cut him in on his operation. His body would end up in a tank of seawater before the week was through. 'Where is Creedy now?'

'Mr Creedy is working for me,' Maskelyne said.

'And Hana? What do you intend to do with her?'

Maskelyne frowned.

'The girl's mother, the woman you left to die in my jail.'

Realization dawned on Maskelyne's face. 'You can't blame my men for defending themselves,' he said. 'They have families too, after all.'

'Just let her go.'

Maskelyne shook his head. 'I'm sorry, Mr Granger, but I can't allow the Drowned to simply wander around the city. I have a duty to uphold the emperor's laws.' He sighed. 'I don't suppose a traitor like yourself can understand that. She'll be taken to Averley Plaza and put with the others.'

Granger couldn't help himself. He ran at Maskelyne with the intention of breaking his bloody neck.

But the Hookmen must have been waiting for this, for they stopped him before he covered three yards. A hooked pole snagged Granger's foot and he toppled forward and slammed

141

into the floor. Suddenly there were two men kneeling on his spine, twisting his arms back, shoving his face down into one of the plush rugs.

'Emperor Hu has been looking for you for a long time,' Maskelyne said. 'We'll give you a trial, of course, and a cell with a view of the square in which to await your execution. I think you should use this time to reflect on everything you've done.'

True to his word, Maskelyne had Granger placed in a cell overlooking Averley Plaza. It was a small vaulted chamber with a concrete floor, located on the fourth storey of the jail. The bed frame was all welded metal and had been bolted to the floor, but the dusty old mattress looked soft enough. There was even a blanket. To remove the need for a cistern in the cell, the commode could only be flushed from a central pipe room. They'd use brine for that. But the steel sink had real taps providing as much purified water as Granger required – a luxury in Ethugra. All in all, the place was cleaner than most provincial hotel rooms. Only the window bars and the heavy metal door betrayed the room's true purpose. This was a place of confinement, even if it was of a standard normally reserved for the wealthiest of prisoners. Chalk dashes covered one entire wall. Evidently the previous occupant had been here for a long time.

The window offered him a view of Ethugra's central harbour, where administration buildings crowded around the docks and the market stalls. The stony figures of the Drowned stood in silent rows along the waterfront, their contorted bodies granting shade to small groups of fishermen, old women, costermongers and trove sellers. An eclectic mix of boats, mostly fishing vessels, ferry boats and canal traders, churned trails of spume across the tea-coloured seawater. The wharf itself lay directly below his window, some sixty feet down.

Granger spied a vessel approaching.

Two of Maskelyne's Hookmen had Hana in their flat-sided canal barge. She was trapped in a net, over which they'd thrown a brine-soaked blanket. They berthed among fishing boats, hurling orders at Ethugra's civilian captains and throwing out their bow and stern lines like insults. Hana couldn't walk unaided, and so they carried her up the steps to the esplanade.

The Drowned died more quickly in direct sunshine, but the Hookmen chose a place for her under the shade of Maskelyne's own prison façade. Whether this was to allow him a better view, or simply to prolong her suffering, Granger didn't know. Her death, it seemed, was going to be a lengthy affair.

Wearing whaleskin gloves, the two men peeled the blanket away from Hana and unravelled the net. They used knives to cut her frock away, leaving her naked. And then they fitted manacles to her ankles and wrists, running the chains through eyelets set into the flagstones. She managed to stand, and even stagger a few feet towards the harbour's edge, before she began to scream.

The sound was odd, coarser and deeper than Granger would have expected. Exposure to brine had already changed her larynx, thickening the tissues and cartilage in her throat. Here on dry land she sounded like a man. Her cries drove him to urgency.

He glanced at the chalk marks again. *Waste of time.* He paced the cell. *Walls, floor, bars, commode, washbasin, bed.* The water pipes had been fused securely to the taps. Hana's screaming harried him like a fire siren. *Walls, floor, bars, pipes* . . . He covered his ears, but it didn't help. *Stop.*

Think.

The floor. The bed.

Granger examined the bolts fixing the bed to the floor. They had been ground smooth and then welded to their surrounds. He couldn't free them without tools. He ripped open the mattress with his bare hands, and rifled through its innards. Nothing inside but hair and dust. *Useless*. He felt his way around the walls, testing the mortar between the stones with his fingers, but he found no weakness. Too much care had gone into building this place. Too much money. He tried to kick the water pipes away from the sink, but they wouldn't budge. He examined the metal door, hunting for a flaw in the design. The hinges were outside. A floor-level hatch allowed food to be passed through, but even if it had been open he doubted he could have squeezed his arm through.

Hana's screams continued.

Slowly, slowly.

He was breathing too rapidly. He had to think. He checked the bars in the window. Solid iron. This was one part of the building they hadn't salvaged from cells below the waterline. He couldn't bend them without leverage. The ends were buried into holes bored deep in the surrounding stones. No way to prise them loose. He paced the cell, looking closely at everything again. *Floor, walls, bars, ceiling.* A length of chain hung from a hook at the apex of the room. It must have once have been used to support a lantern, but there was no lantern there now. Granger might be able to reach it by standing on the commode, but he couldn't see how he could get it loose. Everything looked as tough as anything that could be made by man. No way out without explosives. If old Swinekicker had had the resources, he might have built a prison like this.

But not *quite* like this. The old man had talked at length about the art of confinement: the escapes, the little oversights that could let your income slip away from you, the changes he'd make to his own place if he only had the money. And now Granger examined his own cell with the same cold cynicism. To look into the room from the corridor outside required the guard to kneel on the floor and peer through that narrow food hatch in the bottom of the door. Wealthy prisoners, it seemed, were granted a peculiar degree of privacy. It was the only flaw Granger could discern. How could he use it to his advantage?

Hana's cries filled the air.

Granger returned to the torn mattress. He scooped out the rest of the hair stuffing and then set to work tearing the blanket into thin strips. He plaited the strips together until he had fashioned two short lengths of rope, one longer than the other. He tied a knot in the end of the shorter.

Then he stripped to his underwear.

He pushed the legs of his breeches down into his galoshes, then stuffed the breeches full of mattress hair. He chewed holes in the hem of his shirt and used his bootlaces to tie the shirt to the belt loops in his breeches. Then he began packing the shirt too. When he'd emptied the mattress of stuffing, he used the remains the mattress itself and then pieces of blanket, keeping only a fistful of scraps aside. Finally, he slid his whaleskin gloves on to the padded-out arms of his shirt and stood back to inspect his creation. He had made a mannequin, a stuffed figure dressed in his own clothes. It wouldn't suffer a close inspection, but it didn't have to. He didn't even bother to furnish it with a head.

Granger climbed up onto the cistern, from where he could just reach the lantern chain hanging from the ceiling. He fed the longer of his two makeshift ropes through the bottom link, until it snagged on the knot at its end. He gave it a gentle tug. It held well enough. He hopped down again, then hoisted up the mannequin and tied it to the rope.

From the food hatch at the bottom of the door, one could see a pair of boots dangling before the window. By pressing his face against the floor, Granger could make out the hanging dummy's legs and the lower part of its torso and arms. *Good enough.*

Now he had to get the jailer's attention. He couldn't afford to wait until meal-time, whenever that was. He grabbed the last few scraps of blanket and stuffed them down into the washbasin plughole. Then he turned on the taps.

The basin filled and soon began to overflow. Water spilled over the floor, gradually reaching the corners of the cell. As it began to leak out of the gap under the door, Granger wrapped the shorter length or rope around each of his hands and waited.

Less than a quarter of an hour later he heard noises in the corridor outside. A key clunked in a lock. A door slammed. He heard the jailer cursing, his boots sloshing along the flooded corridor.

Two bolts snapped back, and the hatch at the bottom of the cell door clanged open.

Outside, the jailer gave an angry hiss. 'If you've broken that bloody sink, we'll beat . . .' he began. And then he must have seen the hanging mannequin, for he said, 'Shit. Shit, shit, shit, shit, shit.'

Keys rattled.

The door opened.

Granger stepped from his hiding place into the open doorway and kicked the jailer in the stomach. Before the other man had time to register surprise or pain, Granger looped the short rope around his neck and dragged him down. He twisted the rope.

The jailer made a choking sound.

'We're walking out of here,' Granger said.

The jailer opened his mouth to object, but Granger twisted the rope tighter around his neck. 'Don't speak,' he said. 'Or I'll crush your larynx.'

A corridor stretched in both directions, with numbered cell doors lining both walls and an iron-banded wooden door at the end of the passage. Granger marched his captive towards this last door. From his initial trip here he knew that the guards' office lay beyond. 'How many guards?' he whispered into the man's ear. 'Hold out your fingers.'

The jailer made no move.

Granger tightened the rope.

'One.'

'I said don't speak.' They had reached the door by now. 'Unlock it.'

The other man obeyed, fumbling with his keys.

'Quickly.'

The door swung open to reveal a small windowless chamber, a watch station for the cell corridor – little more than an airlock to separate free men from their captives. Racks of keys hung from pegs along the back wall, each labelled with a cell number. A single guard reclined in a chair, his feet propped on the desk before him. He had been half asleep, but now snapped alert as the two men bustled in: one dressed in underwear, the other turning blue. He looked at Granger and then he reached for his blackjack lying on the desk between them.

'Leave it,' Granger said.

The guard hesitated.

'Throw me your keys or I'll break his neck.'

'Break it,' the guard said. 'They'll give me his job.'

Granger pitched his captive across the table and into the seated man. The guard's chair toppled backwards and he went down, pinned under the thrown man's weight. Granger stepped around the desk and kicked the guard hard in the groin. Then he dropped to a crouch, slamming his elbow down into the back of the jailer's head, knocking him out cold.

The guard groaned through his teeth, still trapped under the unconscious man.

Granger spied a bunch of keys hooked to the man's belt and tore them loose. He picked up the jailer's keys from the floor. His chest had begun to cramp again. He staggered upright, wincing at the pain, and locked the door to the cell corridor. Then he tried the opposite door, the exterior one. It was unlocked. He opened it a fraction and peered out.

A broad staircase descended several flights to the main foyer. On the opposite side of the landing stood another door, but this was not reinforced. A tall window looked out on the gloomy façade of another building. There was nobody about. Granger glanced back at the fallen guard. Then he stepped out, shut the watch station door and locked it behind him.

He hurried down the staircase, clutching his chest.

When he reached the foyer he stopped. An open doorway to his right led to the prison offices, from where he could hear the susurration of scribes at work. To get to the front door he'd have to walk straight past them, in his underwear. The front door would undoubtedly be locked, and he didn't know which one of the keys he had stolen would open it. He rifled through the bunch, selecting a couple that looked to be around the right size.

Then he took a deep breath and crossed the foyer to the door.

A shout came from the office. Granger pushed the door, but found it to be locked. He tried the first key, but it wouldn't turn. Over his shoulder he heard a scribe shouting for the guards. He tried the second key.

The lock turned.

Granger burst out into bright sunlight.

The marketplace was mostly empty. Rows of stalls stood like canvas colonnades. A few costermongers milled around behind them, chatting or stacking crates to be moved to the wharf side, sitting on the steps of the Imperial Administration Buildings. Fishermen and ferrymen lounged in the shadows of the Drowned. A old man sat mending his net. The Hookmen had gone, leaving Hana alone. She was crouching on the ground with her arms wrapped around her knees, wailing in a thick broken voice. Not a damn soul paid any attention to her.

Granger locked the door behind him, then ran over to her.

The Hookmen had soaked her in brine to prolong her life, but her stony flesh had already begun to crack across her arms and shoulders. It looked like paving slabs. Most of her hair had turned from black to grey. Her face appeared scorched. Brine crystals frosted the corners of her mouth. Her ankles and shins glistened redly where the manacles had bitten in.

'Hana?'

She looked up, but her eyes were clouded by cataracts and he doubted she could see him. Others were looking over at them now. A few men stood up. The net-mender stopped his work. Someone whistled. From the direction of the prison, Granger heard a door rattling.

He placed a hand on her shoulder, ignoring the sting of the brine. 'It's Tom.'

She just wailed. If she recognized him, or even understood his words, Granger didn't know. He examined her manacles and chains, then glanced around for something with which to break them. The fishermen would have tools in their boats. He stood up.

The door to Maskelyne's prison opened, and a group of men filed out – five, six, eight of them. Granger recognized Bartle and two of his crew from Swinekicker's place. A scribe stood beside them holding a bunch of keys. The other four were jailers and carried blackjacks looped around their wrists. Bartle saw Granger and grinned. 'What do you think you're doing, Tom?'

Granger crouched down beside Hana again. 'I'm sorry,' he said. He wrapped his arms around her and hugged her tightly to his chest. He kissed her ear and stroked her hair. The metal salt taste of brine lingered on his lips, and then began to burn. Granger crooked his arm around her neck and squeezed.

She gasped, but she didn't struggle.

Her tough, leathery flesh barely yielded under his grip. He gripped her neck harder, squeezing the muscles of his forearm into her windpipe, trying to drive the last pitiful breaths from her. But then Maskelyne's men reached him and it was too late.

One of the jailers swung his blackjack, striking Granger across the temple. Granger's vision swam, but he held on to Hana with all of his strength. He heard her choke.

They struck him again, and the world went dark.

'Forty-six minutes,' Maskelyne said. 'That's how long it took him to break out of the best and most expensive prison in Ethugra.'

The jailer hung his head.

'Where do *you* think the fault lies?' Maskelyne said.

'The fault?' The man glanced at the body in the olea tank. 'I don't know, sir.'

'You don't know?' Maskelyne sat up. He studied the man for a moment, trying to judge the fellow's level of retardation. 'Well let me ask you this: Did he spend those forty-six minutes tunnelling through the walls?'

The jailer was growing paler with every passing moment. 'We thought he'd killed himself.'

'We?'

'I thought he'd killed himself.'

Maskelyne stood up and wandered over to the brine-filled alcoves. He pressed his hands against the glass and watched the jellyfish drift past like tiny luminous globes. They had absorbed almost all of their meal by now. Only the corpse's skull and part of its spine remained in the tank. 'Men like that don't kill themselves,' he said. 'They keep on going, and going, and going until somebody like me stops them. That's why men like me are so valuable to the empire.'

'Yes, sir.'

'You stripped his new cell?'

'Completely, sir. Basin, bed, mattress and commode. He's got nothing but his clothes.'

'Nothing?'

The jailer shook his head, then nodded. 'A blanket, sir.'

Maskelyne thought for a moment. He glanced at his pocket watch. It was approaching forty-five minutes since his men had hosed the colonel down and placed his unconscious body into the new cell. 'I'd like to see him myself,' he said.

'Yes, sir. Thank you, sir.'

Maskelyne wandered over to one of the tables. He opened an ornate box and took out a tangle of red wires like a small bird's nest, which he placed in his jacket pocket. 'Bring a chair,' he said to the jailer.

'A chair, sir?'

'Any one of these will do.'

They walked over to the prison wing, with the jailer carrying a chair from the lounge. He set this down to unlock the watch station and then carried it inside. The duty guard rose to attention and admitted them into the cell corridor.

Maskelyne ordered the jailer to place the chair outside Granger's cell. He took a seat, while the other man opened the hatch at the bottom of the door.

There was a moment's pause.

And then the jailer let out a hiss and said, 'He's trying the same damn thing again, sir.'

Maskelyne looked at his pocket watch again, and smiled. 'What could he have used to stuff the mannequin with this time?'

The jailer frowned. 'Nothing, sir.' He looked puzzled, and then realization slowly dawned in his eyes. He peered back through the hatch again.

'Open the door,' Maskelyne said.

This time it was no mannequin hanging from the lantern chain, but the body of Thomas Granger himself. He had fashioned a second rope from the blanket they'd left with him. To this one he had added a noose. His eyes were closed, his neck crooked, and his tongue protruded from his mouth. His boots dangled a foot from the floor.

Maskelyne looked up at the hanging figure in utter disbelief. Brine scars now covered Granger's lips and one side of his face. From the plaza outside could be heard the wailing of the Drowned woman.

'Cut him down,' he said. And then he turned and left the room.

Granger's eyes opened the moment he felt the jailer grab his legs. He reached inside his shirt and tugged at the knot he'd tied across his chest. The whole of his makeshift harness immediately came undone, and he dropped down from the rope into the arms of the startled jailer.

He slammed his head into the other man's nose, shattering it, then slugged him hard across the side of his head.

The jailer slumped to the ground.

'You're very good at exposing my employees' inadequacies, Mr Granger.'

Maskelyne was standing in the cell doorway.

'If the circumstances had been different, I might actually have hired you to vet them for me,' he went on. He slipped a hand into his tunic pocket and withdrew an object that looked like tangle of red wires. As Granger watched, Maskelyne's hand began to bleed. A faint humming sound came from the wire device. He let out a shuddering breath. 'Do you know what this is?' he said.

It was assuredly Unmer, but Granger knew nothing beyond

152

that. The humming noise intensified, and yet it did not appear to emanate from the device. Rather, it felt as if Granger's own bones were reverberating, as though his body had been plucked like a harp string. His legs felt suddenly weak. His jaw tightened, making it difficult to speak. He managed to say, 'Cut Hana loose.'

'The siren-wire is a hideous little weapon,' Maskelyne said. 'Ill suited to humans.' The strain was evident in his eyes. Droplets of blood fell from his fingers to the floor. 'It can kill a man unaccustomed to handling it.' He grinned, revealing bloody teeth. 'As with so much of Unmer sorcery, one must build up a tolerance.'

All the strength left Granger's legs. His knees trembled and then buckled and he found himself lying on the ground. The ceiling reeled over him drunkenly. He tried to rise, but his nerves just screamed, and his limbs would not function. 'Her chains,' he said.

Maskelyne's face loomed over Granger, long and cadaverous, his expression taut with concentration. He was bleeding from his eyes now, but he continued to clutch the Unmer artefact in his fist. The hum from the siren-wire seemed to infuse his words. 'It's important for people to watch her die,' he said. 'Understanding the horror of the seas keeps them safe from harm.' He crouched over Granger, his jaw locked, his whole body trembling. 'Try to get some rest, Mr Granger, for both our sakes.'

That night he didn't sleep at all. The world turned, carrying Granger and his prison under the stars. Hana's voice grew steadily weaker. She uttered no words that he could understand. Whether she was no longer capable of human speech, or whether her pain had pushed her beyond words, he did not know. He prayed that someone – a fisherman or market trader – would show her mercy, silence her. But no one did.

They had removed everything from the cell but his clothes.

By dawn she was struggling to breathe and quite incapable of screaming. From his cell window Granger watched the Hookmen return. They took buckets of brine from the harbour and used them to soak her drying body. They forced seawater down her windpipe, softening up her lungs for another day. She gasped and choked, and then the pitiful cries began again. Granger gripped the bars of his window.

Around mid morning a jailer brought Granger a wooden pitcher of fresh water and a bowl of fish-gut soup. He tested the food by placing a strip of it under his tongue. When, after a few minutes, it began to burn, he spat it out and rinsed his mouth. The remainder of the meal he placed on the window ledge, where he hoped it might attract a rat.

Hana didn't die until late afternoon that day. The Hookmen continued to soak her blistered grey flesh with brine, using a funnel to pour it down her throat, but they could not prolong her torture any longer. Two of the men began to argue, each loudly apportioning blame on the other for the woman's demise. Clearly Maskelyne had not intended for her to depart so quickly. After all their attempts to revive her failed, they began the Positioning before her corpse dried out.

Three men erected a dragon-bone tripod over her body. Ropes and splints were laid out nearby. Using the stoutest length of rope they hoisted her to a standing position. They bound her arms and legs in splints and then arranged them in their chosen posture. They raised her head and lashed her hair to the small of her back to keep her chin high. A man wearing whaleskin gloves opened her eyes, then jammed his thumb between her lips and prised them apart. His companion shoved something small in her mouth and laughed uproariously, but his colleague removed it quickly. Granger couldn't see what it was.

When they'd finished with the corpse, it was standing, facing

Granger's cell window with its arms upraised in a pleading gesture.

Granger sat on the edge of the bed and closed his eyes. Ianthe would have been taken to Maskelyne's deepwater salvage head-quarters on Scythe Island, to be assigned to one of his vessels. As long as she found trove for him, she'd be safe enough. Safe, but never free of him. And it would only be a matter of time before Maskelyne discovered the true extent of her talents.

Granger picked up one of his galoshes and reached his arm down inside it. The letter he'd once intended to send to the Haurstaf was still there, tucked into a flap in the whaleskin.

He looked at it for a long time. The date he'd chosen for the appointment was still three days hence. Using a strip of fish gut, he scrawled another message across the bottom of the letter, watching as the grease burned his words into the paper.

He strode over to the cell window and peered out. Down below, Averley Plaza teemed with people. Shouts, laughs and cat-calls filled the air. The market traders had already set up their stalls for the day ahead, their canopies shining in the sunlight. Foul-smelling clouds lingered above the fishmongers' braziers. Canal boats ferried jailers' wives to and from the docks, where fishermen, crabbers and dredgers unloaded their wares. Piles of reclaimed stone and wood steamed on the wharf side as they dried, while half a hundred vessels ploughed the amber waters of the harbour.

Granger folded the letter into a tight wad and threw it. It arced across the harbour waters, and landed on the wharf side four storeys below.

He watched, waiting for someone to pick it up.

An old woman and her daughter passed by. The young girl glanced at it but didn't stop. Shortly afterwards, a young man, barely older than a boy, stopped, and picked up the letter. He was dressed like a deckhand. He opened it up and read it. Then he looked about. Nobody else had noticed.

Granger watched silently from his high window as the deckhand shoved the letter into his pocket and wandered off. When he reached the wharf, he called out to an older fisherman sitting on the dockside. His father? This man rubbed his hands on his breaches before accepting the letter. He was too far away to see his expression clearly, but he took a long time reading it. Some discussion passed between the two. The young man pointed back towards the wall of the jail where he'd found the letter. The older man shrugged, then shoved the paper into his own pocket.

And then he did nothing.

Granger cursed under his breath. Couldn't they see how valuable the letter was? The Haurstaf would gladly pay to receive news of one of their own, an undiscovered talent rotting in an Ethugran prison.

But the fisherman just sat there, watching the boats in the harbour.

Granger's fate, his daughter's fate – hell, perhaps even the future of the empire – now lay in the hands of a stranger.

CHAPTER 8

IANTHE

Ianthe found herself inside a hollow metal ball. Aqueous yellow light danced across curves of pitted steel, across thick gloves resting on the knees of whaleskin breeches. Not her gloves; the hands inside them belonged to the sailor whose perceptions she had borrowed. She could not move this body, merely occupy it. From all around came a deep and regular hissing and rushing sound, like the breathing of some strange consumptive monster. *Haaaa . . . Shuuu . . . Haaaa . . . Shuuu . . .* Tiny portholes on all sides looked out into golden brine as thick as honey and illuminated by gem lanterns.

She was inside a man, and the man was inside a metal vessel, and the vessel was being lowered down through the sea.

The submariner peered through a porthole. Golden motes drifted past, like flecks of hay. Some form of sea life, perhaps? Ianthe could see nothing in the gloom beyond the lantern light.

Haaaa . . . Shuuu . . . Haaaa . . . Shuuu . . .

The sound seemed to come from overhead. There must be a pipe up there, an air supply. Frustratingly, her host did not look up to verify this. He had no interest in that particular aspect of the machine, Ianthe could sense. She could also sense his fear. He didn't want to be down here.

Now through the brine she discerned vague shapes and pools

157

of darkness. The machine was nearing the sea floor. Her host reached up and rang a bell three times. Ianthe smelled his perspiration. He looked through one window after another. A grid of ancient, tumble-down walls criss-crossed the ground – the footprints of roofless dwellings now buried under silt. This place, then, had once been a city. Now fish glided through doorways and windows. A hacker crab ambled backwards along a soft grey street, its claws raised as a warning to the rapidly descending craft.

They were dropping fast.

The submariner must have been aware of this too, for he rang the bell another three times.

Then he looked down, and Ianthe realized that the floor of this craft was not solid. A circle of brine waited under the submariner's seat. Grapples, hooked rods and coils of cables filled the floor space around the hole. Evidently this craft was intended to retrieve trove.

The mechanical breathing continued – *Haaaa . . . Shuuu . . . Haa . . . Shuuu . . .* – and now the submariner's own breaths sounded laboured. He rubbed sweat from his eyes, then slid off his seat and crouched over the hole.

How did this man's handlers expect him to find treasure in such a crude manner? He could see nothing but a yard of seabed through that open portal, and not much more beyond those thick glass windows.

A bell rang overhead.

The craft slowed until it was barely a fathom above the sea bed – then stopped.

The submariner looked up to where a huge brass helmet hung under a fat spool of rubber piping fixed to the ceiling. He manoeuvred himself up past the seat, until he was almost standing upright in the confined space. Then he pushed his head inside the helmet.

Now Ianthe found herself looking out through the edge of

an even smaller window, this one in the helmet itself. *Haaaa . . . Shuu . . . Haaaa . . . Shuuu . . .* The rasp and suck of air grew loud in her ears. She realized that the breathing pipe had been in the helmet all along. Sweat trickled down her neck – his neck. *His neck.* He gave a grunt, then wrenched the helmet round so that its tiny window lined up with his face. Ianthe heard four clamps, one after the other, snap into place.

He crouched down over the hole again. His heart was racing, his lungs straining in his chest. He picked up a spade. Then he lowered himself down into the brine.

Ianthe felt icy cold water close around her host's knees, then his waist, and then he was gliding down through that toxic murk. His boots sank into grey silt, raising clouds as fine as pollen. She could see even less than before now. Gem lanterns glimmered on the exterior of the diving craft, but they were centuries old, and their radiance had long since lost its vigour. The man unhitched one of them and held it out.

A few yards ahead of him lay the ragged outline of a low wall. An anchor chain rose up beyond this, the links rimed with brine crystals. The submariner began to walk towards the chain, inclining his head in his direction of travel to keep the heavy helmet balanced as he dragged his feet through the sucking earth. That short walk seemed to take an age, but finally he reached his goal. He ran a gloved hand along the rough surface of the wall, disturbing a cloud of silt. Then he regarded the chain and looked up.

He was barely six fathoms down, yet the brown weight of the seawater above made it appear much deeper. Dusk glimmered on the surface of the waters like a peat fire. The anchor chain terminated at a buoy, close to which lay the silhouette of a ship's hull.

The submariner found a gap in the wall and stepped through into the street Ianthe had seen from the diving craft. She spotted the trail of the hacker crab she'd noticed earlier, but the creature itself was nowhere in sight. Something dark wriggled at the edge of her vision.

The man's heart quickened. He swung round.

An eel darted away into the gloom.

'Give me grace.'

His voice startled Ianthe. She had assumed he'd be unable to speak down here. But there was air here, of course – a frighteningly small pocket, certainly, but air nonetheless. Her host's heart slowed, and he resumed his trek.

'Sixteen gilders a dive,' he muttered. 'Bastard wouldn't buy a night in 'thugra.'

She was used to hearing people speak to themselves, but this man's voice sounded odd down here, huge and metallic. Yet it was strangely comforting, like a light in an immense void. *You wouldn't want a night in Ethugra*, she thought.

His eyes filled with perspiration, and he blinked. 'Still better than here,' he said.

Ianthe smiled inwardly. Wasn't it funny how people sometimes seemed to respond to her thoughts? She tried again. *What are you looking for down here?*

This time he didn't give any indication that he'd heard her.

He trudged on down the street.

But then something horrible happened.

Ianthe felt brine seep into her boot. The chill sensation came as such a shock that it took her a moment to remember that she wasn't actually here. *It's his boot, his foot, his . . . flesh.* The seawater was dribbling down behind his ankle, scalding him. Yet he paid no attention to it whatsoever. His breathing continued steadily. If anything, he actually picked up his pace.

For Ianthe, the feeling was so intolerable that she almost fled his mind. She imagined blisters appearing on her own ankle, the skin bubbling, then turning grey and leathery. She wanted to lift her foot, but she couldn't. The man was merely a vessel, and she his passenger. It wasn't even her pain. If he could bear it, then so would she.

There were other tracks on the seabed now. By the golden light of the gem lantern, Ianthe could see scores of bootprints criss-crossing the street. They converged on one massive roofless house. Slowly the submariner made his way over to the doorway of that drowned building and stepped through.

A wide pit stretched before him, strewn with the bones of a dragon. It appeared to be an excavation, for many of the smaller bones and much of the silt had been scraped back towards the walls of the dwelling. The size of the dragon's skeleton indicated that it had been a mature adult, perhaps as much as a thousand years old. A man could walk easily between the bars of its ribcage. Every morsel of its flesh had been picked clean. Its skull rested against the far wall, where it seemed to gaze blindly at the heavens. Ianthe's host paused and took three long breaths. The encroaching brine had by now filled the lower half of one suit leg. She could feel the pressure of it pushing against his knee binding.

'Another day,' he muttered.

He strode forward into the garden of bones. Then he drove his spade into the ground below the dragon's ribs and began heaving heaps of silt aside. Grey clouds muddied the waters. After a few minutes effort, something glinted under his spade. The man knelt down and began rummaging through the silt with his gloved hands.

He pulled something out.

Ianthe breathed a sigh of relief. She had seen enough sea-bottles to recognize this one at once. The tiny Unmer artefact was missing its stopper, and a blur of liquid could be seen pouring forth into the surrounding seawater, as vaporous and agitated as the air above a hot vent. Such bottles were often found amidst the remains of dragons. Serpents had an insatiable – and ultimately deadly – desire for them.

The submariner slipped the bottle into a net bag at his hip and then stooped to clear away more silt. An original stopper was worth as much as the bottle itself. Something golden flashed under his hands. He waved away clouds of suspension.

At first Ianthe thought she was looking at a gilded shield. A clearing in the sediment revealed a metalled surface embossed with sigils. It was unmistakably Unmer. There was the stamp of Ursula Dragon Mother, the constellation of Coreollis, the Fist of Armitage and the Precept, and a wheat sheaf and sickle that could only signify some powerful noble house. Interspersed with these devices were words written in the runic language of the First Alchemists – a spell, or possibly a ward against human men.

The submariner paused, panting heavily, then hurriedly brushed away more silt. More of the surface came into view, then more still. The man pushed his gloves into the yielding dust, looking for an edge. But wherever he dug, he simply revealed more of that flat gold plane. Whatever this treasure was, it was much larger than a shield.

Finally, he stopped. The brine had begun to leach through the bindings around his knee and irritate the skin on his thigh. What was more, his other boot was now leaking, too. Both his feet had begun to feel like hot lead.

Ianthe could stand no more of it.

Quietly and smoothly as a memory, she slipped out of his mind.

The world went dark. She found herself adrift in a void. In the distance she could see pools of electric-blue radiance – the perceptions of the Drowned nearby. Other marine life revealed itself as shoals of pink or yellow lights that wandered through the darkness like fireflies. Ten yards from her human host, a dull brown sphere betrayed the hacker crab's hiding place. Such creatures perceived their environments through rude eyes. So much life in the seas! Its variance and abundance never ceased to amaze her.

By comparison, the human world above her seemed dull. The perceptions of Ianthe's own kind filled the dark with a million blue stars, tending to red where dusk and dawn tinged the fringes of the day. She slipped up through the void to where the deck of the ship waited for her in a cloud of disparate images.

'He found something,' Ianthe finally said.

She could feel the cold steel passenger rail in her hand, and the deck of Maskelyne's dredger *Mistress* thrumming vaguely underfoot as she leaned over the side, pretending to peer down into the depths. Returning her mind to her own body was like stepping out of the world into a dark and silent cell. Her ears heard nothing and her eyes looked out into an impenetrable void. It frightened her. And so she set her thoughts adrift again, flitting effortlessly from one sailor to the next as she sketched a perspective of her surroundings.

Ethan Maskelyne was standing beside the port crane, from where he had been overseeing the whole winching operation. He was dressed in whaleskins just as soiled and battered as those worn by his crew. His white hair had yellowed from long exposure to brine. Every inch the sailor. 'You can see him?' he asked.

'He's almost back at the machine now.'

'Bathysphere,' Maskelyne said. 'It's a bathysphere. Did he find more ichusae?'

Ichusae was the word he gave to sea-bottles; perhaps it had been the Unmer word – Ianthe did not know. Out of habit she turned her head to face him, a gesture that came naturally to her. She had long ago grown used to imitating the behaviour of the sighted. 'One sea-bottle, but he uncovered something else too. Something large buried under the silt.'

'Cannon large or hull large?'

'I don't know. It's made of gold.'

Maskelyne gave a smirk that seemed halfway between pleasure and derision. 'You're leading me astray,' he said.

Moments later a bell rang somewhere, and the sailors rushed to winch up the bathysphere.

'That *is* uncanny,' Maskelyne said.

They heaved the bathysphere up out of the depths, then swung the crane so that its load hung over a shallow depression in the deck. Brine streamed from the metal sphere, swirling away into the deck drains. The submariner clambered out, unhitched the net bag from his hip and took out the sea-bottle. Brine poured out from it, sluicing over his heavy gloves. One of the sailors handed him a copper stopper, which he jammed into the neck of the bottle before handing his prize to another man. This sailor wiped the glass surface clean and gave it to Maskelyne, who held it up and squinted through it.

'Perfect,' he said.

The submariner crouched and unscrewed a winged brass cap in the heel of his boot, allowing the trapped brine to drain out of his suit leg. Then he raised his arms while another crew member hosed him down with fresh water. Finally he unhitched his helmet.

'Looks like a chariot,' he said. Pain creased his faced as he began unstrapping his suit buckles. Most of the other sailors stood well back, but the man with the hose continued to wash him down. 'We'll need to crane out the larger bones,' he went on, smoothing back his wet hair, 'and clear a few tons of sediment before we can get a line around it.'

Ianthe's mind flitted between the crew members until she found someone looking at Maskelyne. For a long moment he stared at the bottle, seemingly deep in thought. Then he said, 'Find me more like this, Ianthe, and I'll let you see your mother.'

Maskelyne the Executioner. Ianthe's heart clenched. She wanted to scream at him: *She's dead! I saw what your men did to her after they carried me away. I saw it all.* But she couldn't let him know the extent of her knowledge. She glared at him through the eyes of one of his subordinates, wishing only that she had the power to raise her host's hands to seize his scrawny neck.

By now the submariner had stripped naked. He raised his arms again and turned around slowly, allowing the crewman with the hose to wash away all trace of the poisonous brine. But Mare Lux waters had already scorched one of his legs up to the thigh, and the other up to the calf. His flesh looked blotchy, red, inflamed and lined with darker veins. Maskelyne produced a jar of ointment and handed it to the submariner, who began applying it liberally to his wounds. To Ianthe's astonishment, this seemed to reduce the inflammation.

'Save some for the others,' Maskelyne said.

The submariner handed back the jar. 'Thank you, sir.'

Maskelyne smiled at Ianthe's expression of befuddlement. 'It is a very rare and expensive balm,' he explained. 'Unmer, of course. I only wish we had more of it.' He smacked his hands together and turned to address a small man in an officer's stripes standing nearby. 'I want this thing raised quickly, Mellor. Put the crew on dragon watch and have all of our divers suited up and ready. Double pay and hand-over shifts until it's up on deck. Work through the night if you can do so without risking men. I want them out of there at the first sign of trouble.'

'Aye, sir.' The officer replied in a breezy, whistling voice.

'You,' Maskelyne said, pointing at Ianthe, 'come with me.'

He ushered her through a metal hatch and down a twist of stairs into the operations room. A map of this quarter of the Mare Lux lay spread out across a table in the centre of the broad, wood-panelled chamber. Gem lanterns clung to the walls between the portholes like poisonous jellies, throbbing with clusters of yellow-, blue- and rose-coloured light. There were booths and chairs enough to seat twenty down here, and a long bar of polished dragon-bone curving along one wall where hundreds of crystal glasses glinted in racks. Sweetmeats and hundred island fruits had been set out on platters on a small table nearby, while numerous pedestals displayed a baffling array of Unmer artefacts: machines, masks, crystal wands and knots of spell-wire, all bolted down securely to the wooden tops. Glass-fronted cabinets boasted yet more treasures: labyrinths of golden metal, tiny mannequins with ruby eyes, countless phials of every shape and size. One enormous cabinet gleamed with weapons: dragon-bone matchlocks and flintlocks and steel carbines, pistols fashioned from silver and glass, runic knives, liquid knives, rat knives and scimitars. An old blunderbuss occupied a prominent position. It was a singular piece, wrought from some strange white metal heavily embossed with Unmer runes and covered in fungi-like protrusions around the stock. The ends of its barrels protruded through the jaw of a human skull.

Maskelyne turned his gaze away from the cabinet and helped himself to a drink of honey-coloured spirit. Then he filled a glass with wine from a carafe on the bar and handed it to Ianthe.

'Your vision seems entirely unlikely,' he said. Through his perception she watched herself accept the glass of wine. Darkness was gathering in her own eyes. She forced herself to look away from him. 'And yet here we are,' he went on. 'An unmolested dragon's cadaver, just as you said. One ichusae recovered, and a skybarque to boot.'

'A skybarque?'

'An Unmer vessel,' Maskelyne replied. 'You've seen Ortho's Chariot at night?'

She nodded.

'Same thing. When the Unmer realized they couldn't defeat the Haurstaf, they used airbarques to distribute their hideous little bottles across our oceans.' He made a sound somewhere between a snort and laugh. 'If *we* can't have the world, then *you* can't have it either. My two-year-old son has already developed a more mature attitude, and *he* has a psychopath for a father.' He chuckled at his own joke, and took another drink. 'Anyway, an airbarque is a rare find. With any luck we might find a thousand ichusae inside it' – he sounded like he was smiling – 'and so remove another source of pollution from the oceans.' He held up the tiny bottle they had recovered from the seabed for Ianthe to see. 'Puzzling little things,' he remarked. 'Where does the poison come from? Why does liquid flow out of the bottle and not back into it at higher pressures? And why does copper stem the flow?' He glanced at her again. 'All this matter must come from *somewhere*, after all, don't you think?'

He moved behind the bar and began hunting around, looking for something. 'If I removed this stopper,' he said, 'this room would eventually fill with brine. We'd sink.' He located a heavy brass corkscrew. 'And yet when we break the container . . .' He placed the tiny bottle on the bar and raised the corkscrew over it.

Before Ianthe could yell at him to stop, Maskelyne struck the ichusae hard with the blunt end of the corkscrew. Instinctively, she raised her hands to protect her eyes . . .

But something unexpected happened. The bottle smashed, leaving only a small pool of brine on the surface of the bar. Maskelyne looked down at it. 'Magic,' he muttered. 'There's nothing inside, nothing that I can find. No portal, no trick, no . . .' She sensed his jaw clench. 'How can I hope to understand such lunacy? And yet this is the way I must save the world.'

'What do you care for the world?'

'I like the world,' he said. 'I live there.' He took a swig of his drink, and Ianthe felt the raw spirit burn his throat. 'And I, unlike so many others, am in a position to do something. What sort of man would I be if I didn't at least *try*?' He sounded angry. 'What sort of *father* would I be?'

Murderer! Tears welled in Ianthe's eyes, and she fought to keep them back. Her thoughts tumbled over themselves, backwards to the moment when Maskelyne's men burst into the cell. They were seizing her, Creedy shouting: *Get the girl out. Hold the mother till Granger gets back. Maskelyne wants them brought to Scythe together.* All these lies for her benefit! And then they were carrying her along the corridor and up the stairs, and she was kicking and spitting, and Granger wasn't there. Her jailer. Her protector. She cast her mind out, searching for him, but there were too many people in Ethugra. Boots thumping on the stairs. Sunlight. And then she looked out through her mother's eyes—

'How large were the dragon-bones?' Maskelyne asked.

'What?'

'Fallen chariots, airbarques, they're like catnip to dragons. Like gold, or . . .' He raised his glass and gazed into the swirling amber liquor. 'You should see how they fight over them. One usually finds that the larger the resident beast, the larger the hoard.' He downed his drink and poured himself another. 'Either we were lucky enough to find a deserted site, or the bones down there are trophies and our resident dragon is off hunting somewhere nearby. Unfortunately the latter is more likely. Even the most deranged addict must occasionally leave his hoard of drugs to feed.'

'He's not boring you with his dragon stories?'

Ianthe turned to face the voice out of habit, but she saw the new arrival through Maskelyne's eyes – a slender woman in a simple white dress, she had come into the chamber through a door in the back. Her auburn hair gleamed under the gem lanterns like brandy. Her bright blue eyes sparkled with humour. In her pale arms she cradled a toddler, who gaped at Ianthe for a moment before burrowing its face in its mother's hair.

'Tell me that's not troche she's drinking,' the woman said.

'It's my best Evensraum red,' Maskelyne protested. 'Four hundred gilders a cask.'

The woman came close to Ianthe and smiled. 'He can be so stingy with his guests.' She extended her hand. 'I'm Lucille.'

'My wife,' Maskelyne added.

For a brief moment Ianthe found herself holding the woman's fingers.

Lucille bounced the baby in her arms. 'And this little tyke is Jontney.' The boy looked at Ianthe again, then hid his face. 'Oh don't be so shy,' his mother said. She passed Jontney to Maskelyne, who started fussing over him at once.

'Ming,' Jontney exclaimed.

'Have you fed him?' Maskelyne asked.

'He's just being greedy,' Lucille replied. She turned to Ianthe. 'Ming is milk.'

'Agon want ming.'

'Agon had his ming too,' his mother said.

Jontney peered shyly at Ianthe from his father's arms.

All this time, Ianthe's ego had been darting between the minds of Maskelyne and Lucille, unconsciously weaving the gamut of their perceptions into an ever-changing tapestry of light and sound inside her own head. She herself was part of that creation – the wild-haired, blank-eyed girl in a whaleskin cloak standing between the man and his wife. There was something horribly inhuman about her – something, she felt, that deserved to be hated. Suddenly angry, she bulled her consciousness into Jontney's mind and heard him bawl suddenly in response.

Children were more sensitive that way. Their own egos had not yet fully developed, leaving room for influence.

Maskelyne frowned kindly at the child. 'Hey, hey, hey. What's the matter with you?'

The child's distress filled Ianthe. She could hear his screaming through his own ears, feel the warmth of tears on his cheek, the snot bubbling in his nose, the after-taste of his mother's milk. He was hot, flustered, annoyed. But he was receptive. She *pushed* a single thought into the boy's mind, and he lifted his hand and struck Maskelyne across the face.

'Hey you.' Maskelyne tried to soothe his son to no avail.

'Let me take him,' Lucille said.

Maskelyne passed the screaming boy to his wife. 'He's not usually like this,' he explained to Ianthe. 'I don't know what's wrong with him today.'

Ianthe withdrew her consciousness from the child, pulling it back out into the void. She was about to settle back into Maskelyne's mind, when she sensed something nearby – a great sphere of perception moving quickly through the darkness between the living. It was underwater and it was coming at them fast.

At that same moment, alarms sounded on the deck above.

'That will be our dragon,' Maskelyne said. He strolled over to the weapons cabinet and took out his blunderbuss. Then he opened a nearby hatch in the floor, revealing an insulated compartment packed with ice. Freezing vapours swirled within the open hatch. He scraped away at the frost until he had uncovered several black glass globes. He examined each carefully, before selecting one and putting it in his pocket. He grinned at Ianthe's puzzled frown. 'Ammunition,' he said.

Upon opening the hatch, Maskelyne found his men scrambling and slipping across the deck amidst the clamour of bells. He did

not approve of this chaotic urgency. He looked for Mellor, finding the first officer standing by the port-side bow gun.

One of the crew shouted, 'Captain on deck.'

Mellor turned.

Maskelyne grinned. He strolled forward and called out in a
cheerful voice, 'Am I the bravest man you men have ever known?'

The crew replied as one: 'Aye, sir.'

'Am I the smartest man you men have ever known?'

'Aye, sir.'

'Am I the man to slay the beast we see before us now?'

'Aye, sir.'

'Then let's bloody the sea.'

The crew cheered.

Maskelyne reached Mellor and gazed out past the deck rail.

There the dragon flew above the sea. It was an enormous
female, a great brown drunken monster with a meat-swollen
belly and teeth as old and black as fossils. Its scales were dull and
crusted with rime from centuries of brine. Its claws were as yellow
as a smoker's teeth. The tips of its mighty wings thrashed the tops
of the waves, flinging up spume. As it drew nearer they could see
that it carried the corpse of a Drowned man in its jaws.

Mellor said, 'Takes a hellish cunning for them to reach such
a size.'

'Don't forget yourself, Mr Mellor,' Maskelyne replied.

'She's coming into cannon range now.'

'Let her dive.'

Mellor looked like he was about to protest, but then he said,
'Aye, sir.'

The serpent had seen the boat and would know its purpose.
But Maskelyne had no doubt that the creature's own addiction
would drive it under the sea before it attacked. Fearing that its
hoard of ichusae had been plundered, it would dive down to

check. Once there it would discover the theft and resurface enraged. And anger could unbalance the wisest of foes.

Sure enough, as the beast drew nearer, it plunged beneath the waves.

Marksmen and feeder crews stood silently by the six batteries of guns. Maskelyne took a black glass bulb from his pocket and fitted it into one of the protrusions on the stock of his blunderbuss, twisting it secure with a click. He checked the weapon's mechanism, then raised it and sighted along its length. The white metal felt unpleasantly cold to the touch. Several of the runes carved into stock had razor-sharp edges, and seemed all too keen to pluck blood from the wielder. The skull fused to the barrel ends made the gun feel unbalanced and clumsy, as though it had not been designed for human sensibilities.

He pulled his whaleskin cloak more tightly around him and lowered his goggles over his eyes.

The crew did likewise.

The sea to port erupted in an explosion of brine as the dragon burst forth from the depths in a great brown storm of wings and scales. Its eyes burned as yellow as molten rock, full of old rage, and something else . . . *Madness,* Maskelyne realized. The creature was insane. It loomed above the deck rail in a haze of rainbows as seawater steamed from its body. A wet gale blew Maskelyne backwards. He aimed along his gun.

'Fire to port!' Mellor cried.

The ship's three port cannon batteries fired in rapid sequence. *Thud, thud, thud.* Maskelyne had been counting on the barrage to drive the serpent back from the ship, but the panicked crew had been in too much of a hurry. Even at this close range, two of the shells missed their targets and flew harmlessly out to sea. The third one tore through the dragon's left wing.

The beast roared and then dived straight at the midships gun.

Claws clacked and skittered on steel. Maskelyne felt the ship tilt under the dragon's weight, heard the slap and suck of the sea against the hull. Metal groaned. The serpent's great brown neck lunged across the deck and knocked the bathysphere aside, its black teeth snapping at the fleeing crew. And then it lashed its head skywards, dragging a screaming man from a knot of his comrades and hurling him high into the air. Men hollered and slipped and scrambled away in every direction. The bow and stern gun crews ratcheted their cannons inwards as far as they would reach, but the barrels could not be brought to bear upon such a close target.

Maskelyne cursed and lowered his blunderbuss. To shoot the weapon down at such an angle would endanger his vessel. He ran his hand across the glass bulb. It was beginning to warm up dangerously. He leaped down to the midships deck.

The serpent crouched in the centre of the ship, snapping its jaws and lashing its tail back and forth. It turned its golden eyes upon Maskelyne and spoke in Unmer, 'Return what you have stolen or I will crush this ship and send you all to the deep.' It raised its head as if about to strike down at Maskelyne.

Maskelyne lifted the blunderbuss under the beast's chin. 'You'd do that anyway,' he replied in the dragon's own language. Then he squeezed the trigger.

The weapon clicked gently, and then became suddenly hot as a ball of flame swirled inside the glass bulb he had fitted to the stock. Vibrations ran though his hands, accompanied by a faint whining sound from inside the gun's mechanism. And from the skull-topped barrel erupted a swarm of void flies.

The tiny black insects came pouring out of the blunderbuss, steered by the runic spells etched into in its barrel and unravelling into an ever-broadening spiral. Crackling wildly as they reduced the air around them to vacuum, these Unmer creations would remove every particle of matter with which they came into contact, whether it be stone, steel or dragon flesh. In a heartbeat a cloud of them had engulfed the great brown serpent . . .

. . . and passed straight through it. Like ten thousand tiny blades, they ripped the dragon's body to shreds as they forged unstoppable trails through scales, bone and flesh. Scraps of meat fell like rain. Only the dragon's lower body and tail remained mostly unscathed. It slumped heavily to the deck amidst a haze of blood.

The void flies continued onwards, a crackling stream that spiralled up towards the distant clouds and the heavens beyond.

Maskelyne wiped gore from his goggles and lowered the gun. 'Clean up,' he said.

CHAPTER 9

THE HAURSTAF

'Here,' Torturer Mara said, 'is where we made the leucotomy, and here . . .' he used a glass rod to push a section of the patient's brain tissue aside '. . . is the cavity I told you about.' The patient gave an involuntary twitch. His hands clenched at his sides, and he made an odd yowling sound.

Sister Briana Marks breathed through her fingers. 'Well that settles it once and for all,' she said. 'The Unmer actually do posses a hole in their heads.' She squinted at the exposed brain and frowned. 'It looks like the inside of a chicken.'

Torturer Mara withdrew the rod and plunked it into a beaker, then wiped his hands on his apron. His stained garment was the only thing less than pristine in this operating room. Sunlight poured in through tall windows, gleaming on the white-tiled floor and steel tables. 'A very different animal to modern man,' he said. 'The cavity would have acted like an echo chamber, amplifying telepathic thought. It's probably a vestigial organ from an earlier stage in the development of their species. It became redundant as soon as the lobular bridges formed.'

'The Unmer traded their telepathic ability for the power to dispatch matter?'

Mara shook his head. 'I wouldn't say *traded*. That word has uncomfortable implications. Besides, there's nothing to suggest

175

they were ever telepathic. Empathic, perhaps. The cavity is a rudimentary structure, like the worm-fish lung or the nomio's spinal ganglion. We think early humans possessed a similar type of brain, but then developed in a different way.'

The patient began to bang the flat of his hands on the table.

'Must he do that?' Briana said.

Mara picked up a scalpel and made a small incision in the brain. The patient became still.

'Thank you,' Briana said. 'You're very deft with that thing.'

The torturer's smile rearranged every wrinkle on his face. 'Practice,' he said.

'You know what this discovery means?'

'Well, it explains why they're vulnerable . . .' Mara began.

'No, no, it means I've lost ten thousand gilders,' Briana retorted. 'Hu is going to parade this in front of his whole empire. He'll use it to embarrass us.' She gave a long sigh. 'How can we possibly be related to these oiks? It sends shivers down my spine.'

The patient suddenly spoke in a loud, clear voice: 'Kurese, I will not stand. Replace it to me.' His fingers reached out in the direction of the table next to him, where Mara had placed the sawed-off top section of his skull, still resplendent with its white mane of hair.

Briana made a face. 'You see that? Half his head off, and he's still vain.'

'Shall I patch him back up again?'

'I suppose you'd better,' Briana said. 'Sister Ulla's girls can still use him as a pin cushion. Staple him up and put him back in the maze.'

The man on the table said, 'Replace it to me. We will war the Haurstaf.'

'You'll sit in a corner and dribble,' Briana said. 'Do you think we should give him a haircut while the skull's off? I suppose he could cut it himself—' She stopped as she sensed the presence of a third person in the room and turned to see a pretty young girl standing in the doorway with a look of horror on her face.

What do you want?

The girl started. 'Eh? I'm sorry, I . . .'

We have company, Briana said, driving the words into the young witch's mind like nails into wood. *Torturer Mara is Hu's own physician. So, under the circumstances, which do you think is the proper form of communication –* thinking *your words?* 'Or squawking them out like a fat little crow?'

'Thinking?' the girl said.

'You're not the brightest thing, are you?'

Mara paid them no heed. He picked up the staple punch and the scalp and calmly went to work on the Unmer patient's head. The girl in the doorway looked positively sick, and it took a moment before she regained enough composure to form a mental reply.

This letter arrived for you, she said, holding out a soiled scrap of folded paper. *An Ethugran fisherman brought it here. He's waiting outside the palace. I think he expects some sort of payment for it.*

Briana cast her mind out, but failed to sense the fisherman at all. He was no more psychic than a sewer rat, and therefore just as invisible to her from here. She took the letter and opened it.

To Sister Briana Marks:

My name is not important. I am a jailer in Ethugra who has recently, and legally, been granted incarceration rights to a powerful psychic. Given this person's value to your Guild, I would be glad to hand them over in return for a finder's fee of two hundred thousand gilders. If this is agreeable, please have a Guild representative (yellow-grade only) meet me at Averley Plaza on the 30th HR. I will find her.

Faithfully,
A Friend

'Oh, this is extortion,' she said. 'Two hundred thousand gilders!' She looked up at the girl. 'How much did we pay for you?'

'Nothing, Sister.'

'Nothing,' Briana confirmed. 'You see how good we are at putting a precise value on talent?'

'My parents thought it a great honour—'

'Oh shut up,' Briana said. 'Your parents were lucky we didn't have them executed for foisting you upon us. But this Ethugran *jailer* . . .' she shook the letter in Mara's face '. . . . has the audacity to demand a fortune for a potential.'

'Such is the world we live in,' Mara said wearily.

'We will war upon the Haurstaf,' the Unmer patient added.

Briana growled. 'Snip something, Torturer, please.' Did they have any representatives in Ethugra? She broadcast the question to every psychic in the palace, and they answer came back at once: *No.*

She'd have to send someone.

But who?

As she gazed at the letter, thinking, she noticed something else. Somebody had scrawled something, very faintly, across the bottom margin. At first she'd taken the scribble to be a stain, but now that she looked closer she could definitely make out the words. They looked like they had been written in brine. There was a date, and a name. And she recognized the name.

Briana smiled. Hu would recognize that name too and pay the Guild a considerable sum to learn of its owner's whereabouts. *Prepare a carriage for me*, she said to the girl. *I'm leaving the palace at once.*

'Yes, sister.'

'Wait,' Briana added. 'On second thoughts, I'll arrange it myself.' She gave the girl a long, clinical look and then turned to Mara. 'Torturer, I was just thinking. Is it really necessary to let the emperor know the results of this anatomical exploration?

I mean, aren't we just fuelling his prejudices? Wouldn't he be *happier*, deep down, if he believed that the Haurstaf – and by extension *all* humans – are completely unrelated to the Unmer?'

The Torturer made a gesture of non-committal. 'He's not convinced the Haurstaf *are* human. I believe his favoured term is *brine mutants*, although he has been known to use the phrase *inhuman parasites*. Of course, when he's really angry he—'

'Yes, yes,' Briana said. 'But look at that pretty little creature at the door. Does she look like a mutant to you?'

'Of course not,' Mara replied.

'Then you agree. Keeping Hu in the dark would be beneficial for all concerned. Think of it as propagating peace and harmony between our communities.'

Mara grunted. 'I'd be risking my position in his court.'

'We'd compensate you for that.' Briana inclined her head towards the young girl in the doorway. 'I could offer you the opportunity to do a little more anatomical research?'

The girl glanced from the torturer to Briana. 'Sister?'

Mara looked the young witch up and down, stroking his chin.

'In more comfortable surroundings,' Briana added. 'You must stay as our guest for a few more nights. I insist.'

'Hu's gone to Lorimare for the summer,' Mara said. 'I could actually delay my return by several weeks.'

'Take months if you like.'

The girl was turning red. 'I will not,' she said.

'You absolutely will,' Briana said.

The girl burst into tears and ran from the room, slamming the door behind her.

A moment of silence passed before Briana said, 'So ungrateful. We take them from the fields and slums, train them up and offer them a life of luxury and ease, and this is how they repay us. I blame the parents.'

'Such is the world,' Mara muttered. 'Shall we just say five thousand then?'

Briana took his arm and led him away. 'Let's not discuss money,' she said. 'It's so vulgar.'

The steel motor launch moved between the ships in the bay. Maskelyne followed her progress from a high window in his castle. He lost sight of her as she passed behind the older of his two Valcinder dredgers, the *Lamp*, and then spotted her again rounding the vessel's bow. She was battered and rusty. From up here he could not make out her name or the name of her port painted on the hull, but he heard her engine rattling. He guessed she was from Ethugra. She looked like a jailer's boat.

'Is it Hu?' his wife Lucille asked.

'No.'

'But it's heading for our house dock.'

Maskelyne smiled. 'The emperor would rather submit to torture than be seen aboard a tub like that,' he said. 'I suspect this is our Mr Creedy, come to negotiate his partnership share.'

She wilted against his shoulder and murmured in his ear: 'Or maybe it's your secret lover.'

Maskelyne raised his eyebrows. 'Mr Creedy is not my secret lover.'

'I don't like him.'

'That seems like an appropriate and reasonable reaction.'

'Will you kill him?'

Maskelyne turned to face her. 'Why would I do that?'

'To save money.'

'I'm married to a sociopath.'

She turned away, drawing his arm after her before letting it go. 'Aren't men of your reputation supposed to murder on a whim? What do they call you now? Maskelyne the Butcher?'

'The Executioner,' her husband replied. 'I don't think Mr Creedy's death would do much to enhance my standing among the city jailers. He is innocent of any crime, after all.'

'He sold his friend's daughter into slavery.'

'Like I said,' Maskelyne remarked, 'innocent.'

The launch docked at the stone pier on the westernmost end of Key Beach. A large man wearing a grey whaleskin cloak alighted. The blue lens of his clockwork eye flashed in the sunlight. He was carrying an enormous kitbag over his shoulder. He tied up, then stood alone for a long moment, apparently watching the deepwater wharfs, where Maskelyne's stevedores were unloading the Unmer chariot from the hold of the *Mistress*. Then he looked directly up at the the very window in which Maskelyne stood and waved.

'It *is* him,' Lucille said. 'I'd recognize that eye anywhere.'

'I'm afraid so.'

'I wonder what he has in his bag.'

'Some sort of bomb, I imagine.'

Mr Creedy began strolling up the pier, but then he stopped again and stared down at the crescent beach to his right. Evidently he had noticed its unusual composition. A few of Maskelyne's men were wandering across that strange silver shoreline, stopping every now and then to pick up likely keys from the tens of millions deposited there and trying them in the locks of boxes they carried.

Maskelyne smiled. 'Now that will have him wondering.'

'I'm going to check on Jontney,' Lucille said. 'I'm worried that he's coming down with something. It's not like him to behave this way.'

'Have you spoken to the doctor?'

She shook her head.

'Call for him anyway,' Maskelyne said.

His wife looked at him sadly. 'What will you do about the bomb?'
Maskelyne kissed her on the cheek. 'Take our son for a walk.'

Maskelyne decided to receive Mr Creedy in his laboratory. He
rang for his manservant, Garstone, ordered him to prepare lunch
for one and to throw open the laboratory terrace doors to dispel
the monstrous odours in there. Then he told him to direct the
Ethugran jailer to the anteroom and ask him politely to wait.

By the time Maskelyne had lunched and dressed in his laboratory overalls, his visitor had been waiting for almost an hour.

The laboratory boasted four enormous glass tanks, each
flooded with brine from a different sea and connected to the ceiling by a wide glass tube. Daylight filtered through the vessels from
tall windows on either side of the laboratory and was changed by
the waters into hues of red, brown, yellow and green. The two
Drowned men in the Mare Regis tank were turning cards, but
looked up from their table when Maskelyne ushered Mr Creedy
in. In the gloomy red seawater their faces appeared dim and
monstrous. The girl who had formerly occupied the Mare Lux
tank had been removed for dissection – but her twin sister peered
out through the glass of the Mare Sepsis tank opposite. She had
acclimatized well to the change in seawater. The sores on her face
had all but disappeared, although her hair and eyes had changed
colour. It seemed that Mare Sepsis brine was not as toxic to
the Drowned as sailors claimed. When she saw Maskelyne, she
became suddenly excited. She scribbled something on her slate,
then turned it round to show him.

OJUJH WAW.

Maskelyne had no idea what it meant, and he doubted the
girl did either. She'd been submerged in that brine for nearly two
months now, quite long enough for her mind to have become
pickled.

In the last tank, the remains of an old man sat on a stool and brooded. The green seawater gave him the pallor of a decayed corpse and, indeed, the Mare Verdant brine had already dissolved a great deal of his muscle mass and flesh, leaving naked bones visible at the clavicle, hip and both thighs. In time he would vanish entirely, but not before his skeleton paced for many days behind that glass wall.

Such was the queerness of the Mare Verdant. The waters consumed the flesh while acting as a body surrogate to harbour and propagate life's energies beyond death. Maskelyne's instruments detected no significant currents within that water, and yet there must be some subtle manipulation of pressure. How else could a man's bones continue to move without muscle and tendon? It was, like so much of the Unmer legacy, an enigma. Because neither the corpse nor the card players had attempted to use their own slates for over a year, the truth remained elusive.

Mr Creedy took it all in with open eyes, or rather, one eye and one aperture. He seemed ill at ease in the proximity of so many Drowned, which was of course why Maskelyne had chosen this place to meet him.

'I hope you do not intend to betray me, Mr Creedy,' Maskelyne remarked.

'Sir?'

'For harbouring the Drowned?'

The big man grunted. 'Betray you to yourself? Don't think that would get me far.'

'Well, quite.' Maskelyne took a seat at his desk and gestured for the jailer to sit opposite. An infinity device, consisting of a marble in a sealed glass tube, sat upon the desk between them. Maskelyne wound it out of habit and then watched the glass tube slickly revolve. The marble rolled from one end to the other. 'Remind me,' he said. 'what our agreement was.'

Mr Creedy lowered his kitbag to the floor and sat down. 'A hundredth lay, sir.'

'A hundredth lay is fine if we find something, Mr Creedy. But what happens if we don't? You'll think I'm trying to deceive you.'

Creedy's clockwork eye made a shuttering sound. 'I noticed you unloading a chariot from the *Mistress*.'

'Yes, and what is such an object worth?' He spread his hands on the table. 'Let us say . . . four or five million gilders to a collector. You would agree?' Creedy nodded, so Maskelyne continued, 'In order to raise that artefact, I was forced to dispatch a particularly foul-tempered old dragon, which, I am afraid to say, entailed the use of a phial of void flies. Unmer void flies, Mr Creedy, sealed in their *original jar*. Do you have any idea how much I could have sold that container for?'

The other man said nothing.

'A hundred million,' Maskelyne said. 'Conservatively. Void flies have been known to destroy cities, decimate populations, ruin whole countries. You know the Unmer make their arrows from them?'

Mr Creedy touched his clockwork eye. Then he leaned forward and spoke in a threatening tone. 'You wasted them on a *dragon*?'

Maskelyne leaned back. 'I wasted nothing, Mr Creedy. Void flies, by their very nature, cannot be studied in depth. But there are other mysteries that can. And that, for me, determines an object's true worth.' He paused to watch the infinity device on the desk as the marble rolled from one end of the tube to the other. 'Do you have a family, Mr Creedy? Any children?'

The jailer shook his head.

'Then perhaps it is more difficult for you to understand,' Maskelyne said. 'As a father, I have a duty to preserve my son's future. Now, I can only succeed if I fully understand the processes by which the Unmer have threatened that future. Wealth, power, everything else is simply insulation.' He paused again to watch the marble roll back and forward in the revolving tube. 'If I gave you a chest of gilders, what would you spend it on? Women? Whisky? Guns? A fine apartment with a view?' He shook his head. 'All insulation. None of it has any importance. None of it has any true worth.'

Creedy lifted his kitbag and placed it on the table before them. 'You're telling me I'm not going to get paid?'

Maskelyne sighed. 'I'm trying to make you understand the real value of trove, Mr Creedy. Because if you don't, then our business relationship is doomed to fail. Does it please you to learn that I have personally destroyed over ninety thousand ichusae? I would happily give you one-hundredth of the satisfaction and pride I feel when I destroy the next ninety thousand, if it were possible to do so.'

Creedy's jaw tightened.

'Or that I have no intention of selling the chariot we salvaged two days ago?'

The other man stared at the kitbag on the table for a long moment. Finally he said, 'I want the girl back.'

Maskelyne leaned back in his chair. 'That is no longer possible. But let me make you an alternative offer.'

The aperture in Creedy's clockwork eye whirred as it narrowed.

'You saw the beach of keys when you first arrived?'

Creedy nodded.

'Do you know where they come from?'

Creedy said nothing.

'The Drowned leave them there,' Maskelyne explained. 'They crawl ashore during the night, enduring considerable pain, and deposit the keys on that shore.' The infinity device continued to make its revolutions. 'Why?' He shrugged. 'The long-term Drowned do not communicate with us in any meaningful fashion. Brine alters the mind by some slow, subtle process. The sea consumes them, takes them over, until eventually they become limbo people, ghosts, repeating human actions that they do not appear to fully understand. Look there.' He gestured towards the card players in the Mare Regis tank. 'Those men turn cards all day long. In the beginning they played the game of Forentz, but as the months passed by, rules began to mean less and less to them. Now they simply turn the cards over, and then gather them up again. There is no longer any discernible purpose to their actions, no competition between them. They are simply parroting actions they remember but no longer understand. Three months of submersion irreversibly alters the mind, just as three hours is enough to permanently alter the body.' He made a dismissive gesture. 'But I believe the Drowned gain some other form of intelligence, some deep instinctual feeling that the brine itself instils within them. I believe that they are looking for the key to some unique Unmer treasure, some locked container or tomb or room or vessel. Something they wish me to find and open.'

Creedy looked at him blankly.

Maskelyne indicated the infinity device on the desk. 'Observe this machine,' he said. 'As the tube revolves, the marble falls from one end to the other.' He waited until the marble had done just that. 'Of course, gravity causes it to fall. But Unmer devices do not suffer from such constraints. They are not bound by our physical laws. Their very existence suggests that our universe is infinite, that anything that *can* happen, happens somewhere . . . or somewhen. If this little desktop machine is maintained indefinitely, then the marble should – one day – refuse to fall. And yet I don't instinctively feel that that will happen. Something is missing from the device, something the Unmer discovered.'

'Sorcery,' Creedy said.

'We *call* it sorcery,' Maskelyne admitted. 'But that's just a word. You might as well describe it as an act of god. I prefer to think of it as *the essence of infinity*, a force that the Unmer utilized when they forged their treasures. They were able to unlock the gates of infinity and reach inside. Their treasures are of little worth to me in any real practical sense. I am more interested in what they represent, in the details of their manufacture, for therein lies the key to their mystery. Don't you see? Solve that mystery and you save the world.'

The big man was silent a moment. 'What do you propose?'

Maskelyne smiled. 'I propose to set you up, Mr Creedy. I will outfit you with a ship of your own, a crew and a generous salary. You will also have a captain's lay of any saleable trove you find – which is one-fifteenth – on the condition that you return any locked containers to me unopened. I need men such as yourself, sir: men with wits and ambition, training, an eye for treachery and a firm hand to quell it, and of course a certain moral flexibility. These are dangerous seas and turbulent times. Only the ruthless survive, Mr Creedy.'

'A fifteenth lay?'

'Of such trove as has no intellectual value to me.'

'My own ship?'

'You agree, then?'

The jailer grinned. 'Where do I sign?'

Maskelyne rummaged in the desk drawer for some papers, then inclined his head towards a pen protruding from a brass holder in front of Creedy.

'I always knew you were a fair man,' Creedy said. He plucked the pen from its holder.

There was a *click*.

And the hidden trapdoor under Creedy's chair opened.

The jailer, chair and all, disappeared down a shaft in the floor. From below came the sound of an enormous splash, followed by a cry cut short. And then the pumps began to work. The floor of Maskelyne's laboratory trembled. A gurgling, rushing sound came from the huge pipes below, and then behind the wall and, a moment later, Creedy's writhing body dropped down into in the Mare Lux tank amidst a swarm of bubbles.

He was gagging, clutching at his throat as he drowned.

Maskelyne looked at the struggling figure behind the glass, then looked down at the empty pen holder and sighed. 'They *always* take the pen with them.'

The Guild man-o'-war *Irillian Herald* was gliding along the Glot Madera, her tall masts and yards rising above the buildings on either side. Briana Marks stood at the prow, as pale and slender as a dragon-bone figurehead. Her long coat tails flapped in the breeze as she stared out at the godforsaken dump that was Ethugra. A red sun burned low in the west, blurred by the haze of smoke that lingered over the city. The buildings themselves spread out before her in a filthy maze of yellow stone and chimneypots, eaves and gables aflame in the sunset, rooftops cluttered with cranes and piles of seabed rubble. Construction never stopped here. She could hear the sound of masons' hammers coming from a dozen places in the city, like some irregular heartbeat.

The ship's old Unmer engines thrummed under Briana's feet as she watched the greasy brown waters flow past the *Herald*'s red dragon-scale hull. The channel was full of dead rats, newspapers and milk cartons. Indeed, the whole city reeked of brine and death. She could smell occasional wafts of spoiled food on the breeze, the earthen scent of mortar and the ever-present metal stink of the sea. There were no birds, she noted. Not one bird in Ethugra.

A whistle shrilled and the engines dropped to a low rumble. On the open deck below, Guild mariners began taking up their positions at the docking lines. Beyond the ship's bow Briana could now see the pillars of a great gate, and a wide harbour beyond. The womb of the city. On a promenade at the far end of the harbour waited a welcome committee of Ethugran administrators – men in black cloaks and white wigs, standing grimly in the heat. Thankfully, the general populace had been banished from this reception.

The engines dropped to an even lower tone as the great ship passed the gate and began to turn, lining her port side up with the deepwater berth at the promenade. Briana reached out towards the waiting men with her mind, and sensed . . . nothing at all. Not a spark of ability among the lot of them. She was alone here.

And yet she was never truly alone. She could hear her Guild sisters chattering in the back of her mind, like the ever-present murmur of a city. Even after all of these years she had never grown used to it. In the palace at Awl the Haurstaf voices could feel like a nest of wasps trapped deep in her subconscious, but even here, two hundred leagues away, there was scarcely any respite. Try as she might, she couldn't shut it out. The most powerful psychics could always reach their queen. Briana took a draught of poppy water from the tiny bottle in her coat pocket, but she feared it would not dull the sounds for long. She had become too dependent on the drug. It affected her less each time she took it.

Ropes groaned as the *Herald* eased alongside the dock. The ship's metal gangway clanged against the edge of the plaza. Briana pocketed her poppy water and went down to meet her hosts.

The administrator who greeted her had a deformed spine and walked like a man forced to drag an invisible burden around with him. He moved by sliding one foot forward and then dragging his other foot along the ground after it. He had a prominent nose like a great knuckle of bone, and eyebrows like clods of wool under his white horsehair wig. He seemed so much older and mustier than the others, if such a thing was possible. 'Sister Briana Marks,' he said. 'Such a pleasure – indeed, an honour – to welcome you to our proud city.' He spoke infuriatingly slowly, crawling over his syllables in a singsong voice. 'My name is Administrator Grech, and I am wholly at your service. If there is anything I can do for you, anything at all, it will be my. . . er . . . pleasure and honour.'

Briana detested his manner at once. 'I've no intention of staying in this ghastly place a moment longer than is absolutely necessary,' she said. 'I'm here to see a prisoner, one Thomas Granger – former colonel of the Gravediggers.'

'Ah yes,' Grech muttered. 'Oh dear.'

Briana glared at him with impatience. Verbal exchanges could be so tedious.

'We responded to your message immediately,' he added. 'But I fear your man-o'-war had already departed Losoto.'

The other officials stood around in silence, waiting in the baking heat. Averley Plaza was so quiet Briana fancied she could hear the roar of distant fires within the sun.

'Alas,' Grech said. 'Fate has been cruel to both of us. Had we known of your wishes earlier, we would have striven to accommodate them. *Striven*, Sister Marks, for you know that Ethugra has always been a loyal friend to the Haurstaf, and one must—'

'Get to the point, you hideous little man.'

'His execution is scheduled for three days hence.'

'His trial, you mean?'

'Trial, yes. As you say.'

She shrugged. 'I'm well aware of that. The verdict means little enough to me. Colonel Granger has information I require. I'll see him now.'

Grech cringed. 'Alas, alas. But we have had word from the

Imperial Palace. When Emperor Hu learned that the leader of the Gravediggers had been captured, he decided in his great wisdom to sit in judgement on the case himself.'

'Hu is coming *here*?'

'He has cut short his stay at the summer palace and is sailing from Losoto as we speak. We are deeply honoured.' Grech wrung his hands. 'But, and forgive me if I say alas again, but he has ordered that no one be permitted to see the prisoner until the trial.'

Briana looked at him coolly. 'Did he know *I* was coming here?'

Grech bowed so low he seemed to fold in on himself. 'Assuredly not, your graciousness, but—'

'Then obviously the orders don't apply to me.'

The administrator cringed. 'His instructions were *very* clear. My life would be forfeit if I failed to carry them out.'

'That's fine with me. We'll see the colonel after lunch.'

Grech's lips quivered. 'I beg you to wait, madame. Two or three days more, and Hu will be here himself.' He reached toward the sleeve of her dress then stopped himself and wrung his hands again. 'Please accept my hospitality in the meantime. My wife's mother is from Awl, she'll cook for you herself.'

'God, how awful.'

He stood there with a pleading look in his eyes. Briana sighed. She would have had it out with Hu right now if the emperor kept a telepath on his ship. She looked at Grech again. 'Your hospitality had better be exceptional.'

'Everything I have is yours.'

'You'd better hope that it's enough.'

'He looks at me strangely,' Maskelyne said. 'It's almost as if there's someone else in there.'

The moment he said this, Jontney lowered his eyes and went back to his toys. Maskelyne found this all the more disconcerting.

His son looked like a normal two-year-old, but his perception of his environment seemed altogether more *mature*. Maskelyne had the distinct impression that the little boy was very much aware of what his father had just said and had tried to disguise that knowledge. Jontney banged his toy dragon against the floor.

Doctor Shaw frowned.

'Those bruises are self-inflicted,' Maskelyne said. 'We found him twisting his arms through the bars of his cot, howling with pain.'

'I see.'

'You don't believe me?'

'No, I mean, of course.'

The doctor rummaged through his satchel, avoiding eye-contact with Maskelyne. He appeared to be looking for something, but then changed his mind. He reached down and pressed a hand against the boy's forehead. 'No fever.'

Jontney bit his hand.

Shaw cursed and jerked away, knocking his satchel over. Phials, bandages, clamps and pincers spilled out across the floor. 'And no lack of vitality,' he added, scooping everything back into the case.

The playroom was evidence of that. Great mounds of toys of every shape and colour covered the floor: manatees and cloth jelly-fish and boats carved from real wood, soldier dolls and brightly lacquered houses and wagons, clatter-clatters and sponge throws, pyramids, stack-rings, thrumwhistles, bricklets, woof-woofs, huckle-henrys, twistees, wibble-wobbles and a hundred other objects still known by the idiot names the Losotan shopkeepers had given them. The bastardized vernacular irked Maskelyne, but he bought the toys – mountains of them – for Jontney. He could not refuse his son anything.

And dragons of course. Most of all Jontney loved his dragons.

'I have a tincture we might try,' Doctor Shaw said, although he looked as doubtful now as he did when he came in. Evidently he could see nothing wrong with the child. 'To calm his riotous airs,' he added with a nod.

'What is in the tincture?' Maskelyne inquired.

The doctor waved his hand. 'Oh, the usual. Kelp and leech-blend and such.'

Maskelyne sighed. 'Very well.'

Doctor Shaw produced a spoon and a medicine bottle from his satchel. He filled the spoon with dark green liquid and, with surprising deftness, manhandled it into the child's mouth. Jontney looked startled. He coughed, and his eyes welled with tears. Then he lifted his small fist. He was holding something shiny.

In that awful moment, Maskelyne saw that it was a scalpel.

Jontney plunged the blade into the doctor's thigh.

The doctor cried out and struck the child with the back of his hand. Jontney reddened and began to wail. Blood was stream-ing from the doctor's leg, covering the rug, the toys. His face whitened with shock. He clamped his hands over the wound and exclaimed, 'He cut me, he *cut* me.'

Maskelyne just scooped his son up into his arms and carried him out, leaving the doctor fumbling in his satchel for bandages and alcohol.

He found Lucille in the morning parlour. She glanced up at him and smiled, then she saw Jontney, and her smile withered. She stood up.

'Take him,' Maskelyne said.

'What happened?'

'He's fine,' Maskelyne replied. 'Just frightened. I need to take care of the doctor.' He dumped his son into Lucille's arms.

'He's covered in blood.'

'It's not his blood!'

'Ethan!'

But he was already hurrying away. 'I'll be back in a minute,' he called, and slammed the door after him.

On his way back to the playroom he stopped at the armoury.

Racks and cabinets packed with Unmer weapons filled every wall. There were swords of blue and yellow poison-glass and burning-glass with wicked amber edges, seeing knives of the type used by Emperor Hu's blind bodyguards, carbine weapons and hand-cannons for launching sorcerous or cursed missiles, devices that drank blood and whispered or screamed spells and Unmer war songs, jewelled dragon harnesses and mirrored armour, black stone armour and platinum runic plate, death vision helmets and torcs and rings of every conceivable warrior's nightmare. Ten score objects sparkled in the gloom, treasures salvaged from drowned battlefields across the world. And every single piece of it exacted some horrible price from the wielder or wearer, what the Unmer would refer to as *Balance*.

Maskelyne opened a mahogany box full of silver pins, each with a crystal head of a different colour. He shifted through them carefully, selected one and held it up. A faint blue light shone from the tiny translucent sphere. He listened to the crystal for a moment and shivered.

Suitable payment.

Doctor Shaw was still in the playroom. He had bound his thigh with bandages and was in the process of easing his breeches back on over his wound. He looked up nervously when Maskelyne entered. 'A high-spirited lad,' he said. 'I'm afraid I should have kept a more careful eye on my satchel.'

'Indeed, you should have,' Maskelyne said.

The doctor's throat bobbed. He moistened his lips. 'Give him a spoonful of medicine a day for seven days. That ought to sort him out.'

Maskelyne produced the pin with a flourish. 'Your payment, sir.'

'No payment necessary,' the doctor said.

'But I insist,' Maskelyne replied. 'Do you know what this is?'

'I'm not much of a collector, Mr Maskelyne.'

'It's an alchemist's pin. Would you like to see how it works?'

The doctor looked uncertain.

Maskelyne approached him and held the pin over the doctor's wounded thigh. It began to thrum in his hand. The crystal head changed from blue to gold and then finally began to glow white. 'The Unmer used these to sterilize wounds,' he explained.

The doctor frowned. He gazed at his wound for a long moment, then touched the bandages tentatively. 'That's . . . extraordinary,' he said. 'The pain has gone.'

'Now watch.' Maskelyne pushed the pin straight into the doctor's leg.

Doctor Shaw flinched and began to protest, but then he stopped. 'I feel nothing at all,' he said.

Maskelyne nodded. 'That's because the nerves are dead.'

'What do you mean?'

'Can't you feel the numbness spreading along your leg?'

The doctor looked suddenly worried. He pinched the pin between his thumb and forefinger and tried to pull it out, but it wouldn't budge. A look of desperation came into his eyes. 'What is it doing to me?'

Maskelyne smiled. 'These pins were the precursors to ichusae sorcery,' he said. 'They change one substance into another substance. Brine changes flesh into sharkskin. An alchemist's pin is far less subtle. It alters the minerals in your blood.'

'What?' The doctor seized the pin head and pulled with all his strength, but it remained firmly embedded in place. A strange cracking sound came from his leg. He gave a short yelp. 'What substance? What's happening to me?'

'Are you familiar with starfish, Doctor?'

The doctor's eyes were wild.

'When one severs the limb of a starfish,' Maskelyne said, 'it simply grows a new one. But the interesting thing is that the severed limb grows into a new starfish. Now, are those two starfish different organisms, or are they actually the same creature?'

'What?'

'The Unmer believe that mankind is a single organism,' Maskelyne went on, 'that every man and woman is merely a part of the same creature. And when we breed, we create new parts of that same creature, like branches on a tree. So sex is actually asexual – it's simply the method by which the whole . . . *human entity* grows. Do you understand?'

'Help me,' the doctor said, 'please.'

'If you believe that – and there are days when I *do* believe it,' Maskelyne explained, 'then an assault on a child is an assault on the father and the mother, and on every other living person. It's an attack against *mankind* itself.'

The doctor stared at him in fear and disbelief. 'Assault?'

'You struck my child.'

'But I meant no harm.'

Maskelyne shrugged. 'You *caused* harm.'

Now the doctor's gaze searched the ground. He was trying to comprehend this. 'But now *you're* hurting *me*,' he said. 'It's the same thing.'

'You're probably right,' Maskelyne admitted. 'But it's too late now.' He thought for a moment. 'I wonder if we could justify your death if we assume that mankind isn't a single organism, but is actually *two* organisms. That way, I could be part of one . . . and you could be part of the other.' He nodded. 'Yes, that works. You die, while I maintain the moral high ground.'

'What? You're completely insane.'

196

Maskelyne sat down beside him. 'You're not a psychiatrist are you, doctor?'

Shaw shook his head.

'No, I didn't think you were.'

'Please . . .' The doctor was gasping now, trying to move his rapidly stiffening leg. 'Stop this.'

'Can't be done,' Maskelyne said. 'Your blood is changing.'

The doctor grabbed his trouser leg and pulled it up. Green crystals had already begun to form on his skin. He let out a wail. 'Changing into *what*?'

'Exactly what it looks like,' Maskelyne said. 'Your widow is going to be a very rich woman.'

Ianthe withdrew her consciousness from the whirlwind of terror in the doctor's mind. She lay in darkness and focused on the rising and falling of her chest as she breathed. Maskelyne's wife, Lucille, had put her in a small bright room in the west wing of the fortress. The views she'd seen through the other woman's eyes had been of a sickle-shaped island with deepwater docks and industrial buildings down by the shore. *Heavy iron ships waiting in their moorings in the bay. A metallic beach flashing in the sunshine, lapped by the tea-coloured sea. The scent of brine of the breeze.* They were three leagues east of Ethugra, but she hadn't been able to see the city from Lucille's perspective.

She could feel silk cushions under her. She knew they were blue.

For a long while she lay there, thinking. Should she try to reach her father again? She hadn't been able to locate him since Maskclyne's men had captured her. Had he even returned to the prison on Halcine Canal? Had she simply missed him, or had he abandoned her again? She didn't even know if he was alive or dead. And with a million people living in Ethugra, a million perspectives to explore, she might never know the answer to that question. Her frustration quickly turned to anger. Nothing really mattered but punishing Maskelyne for what he'd done. And she had the means to accomplish that.

She slipped into Jontney's mind, but found him cuddling his mother, and so she quickly departed again. She didn't want to feel Lucille's arms around her. Maskelyne was in a storeroom next to his armoury, where he was busy rummaging through a box of tools and humming to himself. He had already looked out a hammer and a stone chisel.

Ianthe let her mind fly through the abyss between minds like a comet racing through the heavens. The inhabitants of Scythe Island formed a small but intense constellation beneath her, surrounded by a plain of countless lights burning under the sea. To the west she perceived Ethugra as a great conflagration of dusty spots, a galaxy formed by tens of thousands of people. As she neared the city, she became aware of a fine ship berthed in Averley Harbour. A group of people had gathered on the plaza before the Administration Buildings. And all of them were looking at one woman.

CHAPTER 10

THE TRIAL OF TOM GRANGER

The emperor's dragon-hunter-class steam yacht rolled into Ethugra like a circus. The triple-funnel, single-masted *Excelsior* was far sleeker than Briana's man-o'-war. Indeed, if Hu's claims were to be believed, she was looking at the fastest and most luxurious human-built vessel in the world. She slid out of the Glot Madera and into Averley Plaza under steam power alone, accompanied by a fanfare of trumpets from the heralds on her deck. The sails furled along her yards were as crisp and white as marzipan. Her three funnels sat behind the wheelhouse and in front of the mast, disgorging torrents of steam and vaporous whale-oil smoke into the heavens. Her bow sliced through the muddy waters, the copper-clad hull ripple-blown and flashing in the sunlight, her cannons agleam like admirals' buttons. Half a hundred Imperial pennants hung from her rigging in a riot of red and gold. A massive harpoon gun protruded from her prow, its stanchion gripped in the raised hands of the ship's iron figurehead. Briana thought that the cast figure was a representation of some thunderbolt-wielding sea god, but as the ship drew nearer to the dockside she realized that its face had been moulded into the likeness of Hu himself. The sculptor had been somewhat liberal in his interpretation of the emperor's physique.

Trumpets blared again, now joined by the marching crackle of snare drums.

The crowd around Briana cheered.

'Oh, for heaven's sake.' Briana reached for her poppy water, but someone bumped into her, and she lost the tiny bottle amidst the scuffling feet. It clattered away before she could reclaim it. She fired out a mental warning as powerful as a cannon blast and heard cries of protest from Haurstaf halfway around the world. But not one of the shrieking imbeciles around her paid her any notice. These jailers had skulls as thick as iron, as insensitive as the corpses of the Drowned along the waterfront.

Administrator Grech turned to her and grinned. 'Heavenly, isn't it?'

'A ship like that says a lot about the man who commissions it,' Briana retorted.

'Indeed, indeed,' Grech replied with good humour. 'Marvellous.'

'Crass.'

Her reply was lost amidst the general bustle. Grech nodded feverishly.

The emperor's dragon-hunter docked alongside the Haurstaf man-o'-war. Briana could see Hu's Samarol bodyguard lining the forecastle, their silver wolf helmets grinning like tribal totems. Now trombones and whale horns joined the chorus of trumpets and drums. The crowd applauded, whistled, waved in response. Bugles shrilled and bass drums began a booming roll as the whole cacophony reached its raucous climax.

And then the ship's guns fired.

Briana almost dropped to the ground in panic, before she realized that the crowd was cheering even more frantically.

And as her heart calmed, she realized that the *Excelsior*'s cannons had not been loaded with shells after all. The air was full of silver and gold sparkles. The ship had fired a barrage of foil confetti.

The music ceased abruptly. As the last of the confetti settled over the plaza, the emperor's Samarol bodyguard began moving down the gangplank. Blind to a man, each of the twenty assassin slaves clutched Unmer seeing knives in their mailed fists, using these uncanny weapons to find their way. Some claimed those blades could see intent and give their owners unnatural reflexes, but Briana had never been able to verify this. No Haurstaf had been able to wield one without lapsing into madness.

When the Samarol had formed a semi-circle around the gang-plank, the emperor himself appeared.

Hu was dressed in golden battle-armour. Upon his head he wore a crown of crystallized dragon eyes set in copper. His long red cape was Unmer-made, woven from the silk of Mare Regis spiders, and it fluttered strangely behind his shoulders in the dead air, lifted by a breeze that did not seem to be present. At his side he wore the Transient Sword, a Valcinder copy of the legendary lost Unmer weapon, but striking nonetheless. Its lacquered steel blade was tangerine in colour and festooned with holes supposedly made by void flies, although Briana suspected *that* particular flaw was merely an affectation engineered by the smiths.

The emperor strolled down the gangplank. 'Sister Marks,' he said brightly. 'Whatever are you doing here?'

She smiled flatly. 'I've been a guest of the Administration for the last three days,' she said, 'I want to see Tom Granger.'

'Of course,' he said, 'you'll see him at the trial.'

'I want to see him *before* the trial.'

'Quite impossible,' the emperor replied. 'Colonel Granger is a dangerous man. I could never allow myself to put one of the Haurstaf at risk.'

Briana looked at him coolly. 'If you do not wish to use our services, there are simpler ways of letting us know.'

Hu made a dismissive gesture. 'Come now, there's no need for unpleasantness on such a beautiful day. If it's really so important to you, I'll grant you an audience.' He even managed to look magnanimous. 'May I ask what the interview is about?'

'No,' Briana said. 'You may not.' She had all but lost patience with him. Hu had pushed her as far as he could, but even a fool such as him could not risk endangering his campaigns or his empire by removing Haurstaf psychics from his armies and cities. Nevertheless she felt inclined to end his contract with the Guild there and then. But she stopped herself from speaking. Hu's pride might irk her, but it was still better to have him as a client than a foe.

Administrator Grech chose this moment to slide forward. He gave a low bow. 'Your Majesty,' he said in his sing-song voice. 'We are so deeply, deeply honoured.' He beckoned towards the waiting crowds of his peers. 'You will be pleased to know that the, eh, corral has been constructed to your specifications. Might I presume that the . . . eh . . .'

'Aboard the *Excelsior*.' Emperor Hu followed him without so much as another glance at Briana.

Granger watched the celebrations from his cell window. The Haurstaf vessel had been in port for three days now, and yet, for all his pacing and hand-wringing, the visit he'd been hoping for had not materialized. What exactly was the Guild playing at?

The emperor's ship had arrived with all the pomp and ceremony typical of Hu, although Granger had not been able to see their glorious leader himself from this vantage point. The flags in the rigging blocked his view. However, it seemed that the crowds down there were finally dissipating. Silver and gold sparkles floated in the harbour, slowly turning brown. Would the emperor come to his cell to gloat?

Granger hoped so. Hu was notorious for underestimating his enemies.

When he heard footsteps in the corridor outside, he stood up, his heart thumping.

A man's voice came from outside the cell. 'The corridor door is locked, Colonel, and I don't have the key to it. It ain't opening for nobody who they can't see first. And it certainly ain't opening to save my old skin, or hers. You stand well back now.'

A key clinked in the lock. The door opened.

Sister Briana Marks stood there, accompanied by an old jailer Granger had not seen before.

'Five minutes,' the jailer said.

She glared at him. 'I'll take as long as I please.'

The old man sighed. 'Aye, I suppose you will.' He let her into the cell and closed the door behind her, muttering to himself all the while.

Sister Marks had aged noticeably in the six years since Granger had last seen her. Her face and hair had lost their youthful shine, and frown lines now etched her brow. She regarded him with weary, cynical eyes. 'The jailer wasn't lying, Colonel,' she said. 'I'm afraid I wouldn't make a very good hostage. The emperor would love nothing more than to see me killed, especially by you.'

Granger grunted. 'I'm not going to hurt you.'

The witch glanced around the cell. 'My men checked your home,' she said. 'We didn't find anyone alive.'

'She was taken.'

'Taken? By whom? Where?'

Granger said nothing.

'Gilders aren't going to be much use to you now, Mr Granger,' she said. 'But I might be able to get you out of here, if you help me find this woman.'

Granger shook his head. 'Get me out first.'

'You're not in a position to make demands. I'll find her eventually, even without your help.'

'No you won't.'

'A sensitive can't go undetected forever. She's bound to give herself away.'

He wasn't sure how much he should tell her. Too much might risk Ianthe's life. Too little, and he didn't have much to bargain with. The witch was right – any normal psychic would eventually give herself away. But he didn't trust this woman. If she found out what she needed to know, she'd leave him to the emperor. *Politics*.

'She's in danger,' he said.

The witch raised her eyebrows. 'Then your silence is risking her life. That doesn't sound like the man I've heard so much about.' Her expression softened. 'You embarrassed Emperor Hu in his own court, Mr Granger – in front of his enemies' representatives, in front of *me*. You made him look like a blundering fool.'

'He is a blundering fool.'

'Of course he is, but he's also the pettiest and most vindictive man I've ever met. You must have known that. How did you think he was going to respond to your comments?'

Granger shook his head. He'd been angry, irritated and suffering from brine burns, but that was no excuse. He'd acted rashly.

'Hu took it all personally,' Marks said. 'Now he plans to execute you in front of the whole city tomorrow morning. A trial by combat, if you can believe it.' She walked over to the window and peered out at the preparations. 'The Guild cannot intervene to save you, of course. We must maintain a position of neutrality.' Now she turned around and smiled. 'But if it turns out that you *have* discovered a sensitive, and I can verify her existence, I'll see to it that you're charged with her imprisonment and with attempted extortion.'

'Charged?'

Her smiled broadened. 'The trial would take place at the Guild Palace in Awl. Not even Hu would dare to interfere with our justice. We'd be compelled to take you out of the empire to await your hearing, Mr Granger.'

Granger thought about this. 'You'd simply move me from one hangman's noose to another.'

'Not necessarily. The Guild would decide a fitting punishment after we have deliberated. I can't promise anything except that you will still be alive tomorrow evening, and for several weeks afterwards. Much depends on what the woman you imprisoned has to say in your defence.'

'Girl,' Granger muttered. 'She's fifteen. Her name is Ianthe.'

'And who has her now?'

Granger didn't sleep that night, and when dawn came he watched the red sun rise through rags of cloud as brown as brine until it stood fuming above the Ethugran rooftops like a dragon's eye. He looked down at the plaza for a long time. A dragon-bone corral had been erected on the wharf side. Three walls of teeth and bone formed an enclosure abutting the water's edge. They had even moved the emperor's steam yacht back to allow a man – him, to allow *him* – to leap from the corral down into the poisonous brine if he so chose. But that way lay a more lingering and painful death. Hookmen would soon drag him back from those depths to fight again.

When the crowds began to assemble he turned away from the window and sat down in a corner, naked to the waist and shivering despite the building heat.

They came for him shortly afterwards. Four of Maskelyne's Hookmen unlocked the cell and seized him and beat the wind from his lungs with blackjacks. They fastened an Unmer slave collar around his neck, riveting it shut with an iron tool like a set of callipers. A wire connected the collar to a small metal box covered in dials and glyphs. The smallest and leanest of the Hookmen lifted the box and said, 'This is what happens when I turn this dial.' He turned the dial.

Granger collapsed. His head struck the floor. He could taste blood on his lips, but he felt nothing at all beneath his neck, as though his head had been severed from his body. Whorls of shadow, blacks and browns, gathered at the edges of his vision, squeezing his view of the floor into a tunnel. He smelled something like burning horse hair.

'Mucks up your nerves,' the man said.

Abruptly Granger felt his limbs spasm. His senses returned.

'Get up.'

He got to his feet, and they marched him out of the cell and down the corridor, and down the steps to Averley Plaza. Before they reached the door of the jail, the Hookman with the box twisted the dial again. Granger's head cracked against something solid, and he found himself lying on the floor again.

'Quit it,' said one of the other Hookmen. 'You fry him too often, he won't get up.'

'Ah, lighten up,' the first man replied. 'Don't make much difference now anyway.'

'You break that, it's your head.'

'Get up, you.'

A boot slammed into Granger's ribs, just as his senses returned with a jolt. He coughed and spat blood across the floor.

'Up, I said. Hu's got something special planned for you.'

Groggily, Granger crawled to his knees, then staggered upright.

The door opened to bright sunlight. Granger shielded his eyes against the glare. Crowds filled the plaza from wall to wall. Men and women jeered and hurled insults at him as the Hookmen led him through towards the dragon-bone corral at the water's edge. Several large military supply tents had been erected in front of the Imperial Administration Buildings, while a podium in the centre of the quadrangle allowed the emperor and his guests a view of the trial. Hu sat on a throne up there, surrounded by administrators in their dusty white wigs, while his Samarol bodyguards formed a barrier between his Imperial Majesty and the Ethugran populace. There was no sign of Briana Marks.

The Hookmen brought Granger before the emperor, who rose from his throne and raised his arms to silence the crowd. He had dressed for the occasion in platinum mail that shimmered like starlight. On his head he wore the crown of dragon-eye gems. His lobster cape fluttered behind him, lifted by non-existent winds. The cheers dropped to an expectant murmur. Hu looked down on Granger and said, 'Kneel.'

Granger stood exactly where he was . . .

. . . and then slammed into the ground again, as the Hookman activated his Unmer slave collar. All sensation left his body. He could feel the warm flagstones against his cheek and smell the sweat of the crowd, the emperor's perfume and something else – a pungent, almost feral odour that did not belong here in the city. Darkness swelled at the limits of his vision, and he fought to remain conscious. *Where* was the Haurstaf witch?

The voice of Administrator Grech echoed across the plaza, 'In accordance with the laws defined in section 412, amendment 11 to the Military Operations Mandate, his Imperial Majesty Jilak Hu has found Thomas Granger to be in breach of the said Military Code of Conduct, as per articles 118, 119 and 173, and has therefore, legally and without prejudice, instituted his Imperial right, as described in the so-called Post-Awl Texts, to subject the prisoner to trial by combat.'

A great cheer went up from the crowd.

Granger tried to breathe, but his paralysed lungs would not draw in air. His head began to throb. He felt as if he was about to pass out.

'For each malfeasance, the prisoner will face an opponent or opponents selected by a committee chaired by his Imperial Majesty, so judged to lawfully represent the severity of the crime. The selection process—'

'Get on with it,' Hu growled.

'The, ah . . .' Grech's throat bobbed. 'The selection process in no way infringes upon the prisoner's rights as defined in the so-called Post-Awl Texts. A funeral will be provided at a cost to the empire of no more than fourteen gilders. May he rest in . . . Is he quite all right?'

Sensation returned to Granger's body in a rush. He sucked in a desperate breath, trying to shake the dizziness and confusion from his head. The world swam around him, a hot whirlpool of sweating faces and fists.

Strong arms wrenched him to his feet, dragged him backwards and pitched him roughly into the corral. Granger staggered, but remained upright. He felt for the wire at his collar, but it had been removed. The corral gate closed in front of him, leaving him trapped on three sides by an unbroken wicker of dragon bones and teeth. Behind him lay open water, and the shining hull of the *Excelsior* at anchor thirty yards out from the harbour edge. He scanned the crowd in desperation. Where was that damned witch?

'Bring forth the first opponent,' Grech called out.

The crowd moved back as two Imperial Army soldiers threw back the flap from one of the military tents. Granger could sense the uneasiness and excitement of the people nearby. Men pushed and shoved each other to get a look at the thing they dragged from that tent, while others, closer to the tent, pushed back.

It was a hound, one of the emperor's own hunting stock, judging by its enormous size. The great black beast growled and snapped at the handler, who was struggling to hold it at the end of a long leash-threaded pole. Evidently it had been starved and beaten, for its eyes were wild with hunger and rage.

'All the way from the emperor's own Summer Palace,' Grech announced. 'Mauler of four wolves and three score Evensraum warriors. Devourer of devourers. Dragon bane. The only war hound to have survived four full seasons in the Contest Pits with nary a scratch. Long of tooth and wild of temper. The emperor gives you . . . the *Beast Arun*!'

The handler alternately pushed and dragged the hound towards the bone enclosure, whereupon Maskelyne's Hookmen reopened the gate. By shoves and kicks they forced the snapping animal into the pen and loosed it from its leash.

It crouched before Granger, drooling and snarling through its bared teeth, and regarding him with baleful eyes. Granger backed away towards the water's edge.

The hound rushed at him.

The crowd roared with anticipation.

The hound leaped.

Granger stepped sideways.

The hound disappeared over the edge of the dock and splashed into the brine below. It managed one pitiful yelp, before the burning waters closed over its body.

Silence. All eyes turned from Granger to Emperor Hu.

Hu could not contain his rage. He jerked to his feet and roared at the soldiers waiting beside the tents, 'The next one! Bring the next one!' Administrator Grech cowered at his side, speaking hurriedly in a voice Granger could not hear, but the emperor just batted him away, returned to his seat and glared at Granger.

Granger took a deep breath. He looked for Briana Marks again, but she was still nowhere to be seen. By now the sun had risen high above the Administration Buildings and beat down mercilessly on him. He wiped sweat from his brow and turned to see who or what his next opponent would be.

Administrator Grech stood up. 'For your amusement,' he said, 'brought to Ethugra from the emperor's own dungeons . . . despised by all who hear of their deeds . . . petty thieves, arsonists, traitors, and defilers of women . . .'

Three soldiers stepped out of the tent. They wore Imperial steel hauberks over boiled leathers and plain cap helmets with nose- and cheek-guards, and each carried a standard-issue short sword in his left hand and a light buckler strapped to his right forearm. Two were tall but stooped, somewhat hesitant and shambling in the way they moved, but the third, shorter man walked with a litheness that implied youth.

'The cunning behind Imperial Infiltration Unit Seven . . . the most *bloodthirsty* and the most *notorious* men in all of *history* . . . responsible for three thousand allied deaths at Weaverbrook . . . Emperor Hu gives you . . . the last of the infamous Grave-diggers.' Grech took a breath. 'Gerhard "The Rook" Tummel, Swan "The . . . eh . . . Swan" Tummel, and Merrad "Grave-digger" Banks!'

Swan? Tummel? Banks?

The corral gate opened, and the three men walked in. The younger man took off his helmet, blinked up at the sky and then smiled meekly. 'Bastard of a day for it, Colonel, if you don't mind me saying.'

Banks looked as if he had been wandering the borderlands

of death. His cheeks were hollow, his skin anaemic but bruised under his eyes, his hair lank and uneven. But his eyes still brimmed with the same quick humour Granger had known him for. After a moment, his two companions also removed their helmets, and Granger recognized them for who they were.

Swan and Tummel had appeared old and wretched when Granger had last seen them six years ago, and yet now they looked like they had lived their lives all over again since then. Swan was toothless with a sagging, stubbled face and rheumy eyes – the sort of visage one expected to find in a coffin. His brother, Tummel, looked ten years older.

'Petty thieves?' Granger said. 'Arsonists?' He paused. *'Defilers of women?'*

'That last one's pretty good,' Swan said. 'I quite like it.'

'That's because it's the only one you haven't done,' Tummel said.

'I could have if I'd wanted to.'

Tummel grunted. 'You couldn't run fast enough.' He turned to Granger. 'He did, however, burn down a grog shop.'

'One grog shop,' Swan muttered. 'What is it with you and that? You never even liked the place.'

Banks glanced back as the corral gate closed behind him. 'They picked up Swan and Tummel in a card den last year,' he said. 'Somebody turned them in over bad debts.'

'What about you?' Granger said.

Banks shrugged. 'I was sending money home,' he said. 'I don't know how they traced it, but they came for me a couple of months ago. It was either this or death.'

'You stayed in Losoto?'

Tummel nodded. 'Right up until three days ago. We had a half-arsed plan to overrun the emperor's guards and capture the *Excelsior*,' he said. 'But we couldn't wake up Swan.'

'What do you intend to do now?' Granger asked.

Banks sighed. 'We were hoping you might have a plan, sir.'

Granger looked out into the crowd. They had begun to chant: *death, death, death.*

'We'll drag it out,' he said, 'and hope for intervention.'

'*That's* the plan?'

'Do you have a better one, Banks?'

The other man shrugged. 'Have at you, then,' he muttered.

The three Gravediggers took up a fighting stance around Granger, who backed away and readied himself to dodge. Swan made a hesitant jab, but the tip of his sword fell deliberately short of Granger. Banks cried out and leaped into the fray, swinging wildly, allowing his opponent to sidestep easily.

The crowd began to jeer with disapproval.

'You'll need to do better than that,' Granger said.

'You're unarmed, sir,' Banks replied. 'And I'm rather good at this. Barracks champion three years on the trot.'

'Don't underestimate me.'

Banks sighed again, and this time came at Granger hard. But he opted for another down-cut, giving Granger more than enough time to avoid the blow. His sword sparked against the flagstones. Swan and Tummel moved to flank his rear, just as they would have done in a real fight.

Banks should have pressed forward, but he chose not to. 'How'd you get past the dog?' he said, backing away again. 'That bastard spent the whole journey from Losoto chewing through the bars between our cages.' He shrugged. 'Didn't help that Swan kept teasing it.'

'I didn't tease it,' Swan said.

'You made faces at it,' Banks replied.

'What faces?'

'That face you're making now.'

'I can't help that. I was born like this.'

Granger didn't say anything; he was waiting for a pincer movement from his flanking opponents. But even *that* manoeuvre never came. Swan and Tummel made more pitiful swings and jabs with their blades. Whether through weakness, or a reluctance to injure their opponent, Granger didn't know. Either way the fight was rapidly becoming a farce.

The crowd began to boo and shout abuse.

Emperor Hu stood up on the podium, and inclined his head.

One of his Samarol bodyguards slotted his seeing knife into the bracket atop a carbine rifle. Then he raised the barrel.

'Banks,' Granger growled.

Banks turned just as the rifle fired.

Granger heard the lead ball zing past his ear. It struck Swan in the side of his head and knocked him down. He lay there unmoving, blood leaking from a hole above his ear. Banks stood dead still, a look of horror on his face.

Tummel was silent for a moment. Then he roared and rushed at the corral wall, shouting, 'Come in here, you bastard, come in here.' He smashed his sword repeatedly against the mesh of dragon-bones, hacking fragments from it. 'Come in here and fight me you blind bastard. Fight an old man, you coward. Fight an old man.'

Hu merely looked impatient. 'Get on with it,' he said. 'And try to make it entertaining. I don't want to waste another rifle-ball.'

Granger picked up Swan's sword. 'Banks?'

The private continued to stare at his companion's corpse.

'Banks!'

His eyes met Granger's.

'Fight me for real, Banks.'

'Sir?'

213

Granger rushed at him, pushing him back with a solid flurry of blows that forced the other man to raise his buckler and block. Banks began to parry, almost reluctantly at first, and then with more urgency as the strikes continued to come down on his left side.

Tummel sat on the ground and lay down his sword.

Granger broke away from Banks and whispered, 'You're going to have to try and kill me.'

Banks just shook his head.

'Keep their attention away from Tummel,' Granger urged. 'Make it real. Make it entertaining.' He saw an opening and thrust his sword at Banks's undefended left. The private responded instinctively with his own blade, but not before Granger raked the younger man's hauberk, the edge of his weapon rasping across the steel links.

From the podium he heard Emperor Hu laugh. 'They're getting into it now, aren't they?' he called out with delight.

Granger kept the pressure on Banks, forcing him back towards the corral wall, towards Tummel. The old Gravedigger merely sat on the ground and stared back at the body of his brother. It seemed that all life had deserted him.

'On your feet, seaman,' Granger growled.

But Tummel wouldn't respond.

Banks, meanwhile, must have realized Granger's real intentions, for he broke suddenly from the fight, turning his back on Granger even as the colonel's blade was raised to strike. He grabbed Tummel by his armpits. 'Get up, you old fool. Get up and fight.'

Granger cursed at Banks's manoeuvre. The private left himself open to a killing blow. In what he hoped would look like a desperate mistake, he swung the blade furiously at Banks's right side, striking the top of the buckler hard. The sword skimmed off and stuck into an enormous dragon-bone bar above Banks's head.

'It's a charade,' the emperor said. 'Shoot the other one.'

Banks screamed at Tummel. 'Get up, you old fool!' He started to drag him upright.

A shot rang out.

Tummel's head jerked forward. Blood spattered across Bank's face.

Banks released Tummel's body and looked up at the Samarol bodyguard, who was now lowering his carbine rifle for the second time. The huge blind warrior detached his seeing knife from the weapon's barrel and turned it slowly in his fingers. His silver wolf-head helmet grinned blankly.

Banks turned to Granger, a pained expression on his face.

Granger freed his sword from the corral wall and backed away from the other man, assuming a fighting stance.

'You'd kill me?' Banks said.

'If you let me.'

'Forgive me for saying so, Colonel, but this is the *shittiest* plan you've ever had.'

Granger had no answer for his friend. He glanced over at the the crowd again, but there was still no sign of Briana Marks. Sudden movement caught his attention.

Banks came at him in a desperate fury, now wielding his sword with all the skill Granger knew the younger man possessed. And Granger was hard pressed to parry these blows. Steel clashed and clashed. The plaza seemed quiet but for the crack of swords and the scuffs and grunts of each opponent. And then Banks slammed his buckler into Granger's face.

Granger recoiled, shaking his head.

A great roar went up from the crowd.

Banks was breathing heavily, his eyes full of pain and fear.

He rushed at Granger a second time, that quick mind of his composing a flurry of feints and blows that tested Granger's own skill to the limits. He seemed detached from his actions, indeed possessed of a strange sort of madness. Only when the two men clashed and wrestled did Banks finally break away. Now Granger could feel pain rising in his chest as the strain of exertion began to take its toll. He doubted he could beat his opponent.

And then he saw Briana Marks.

He realized he had heard the launch's engine somewhere in the back of his mind, but had not registered it until now. The Haurstaf witch alighted from the slender deepwater craft, and hurried up the dock steps to the plaza. She was wrapped in whale-skins and wore goggles on her forehead. Ianthe was not with her.

Banks turned his sword over and made to move at Granger again.

'Wait,' Granger said.

But the young man was already lost to whatever madness or battle lust gripped him. The look in his eyes suggested that per-haps he no longer even recognized his opponent. Everything was about the fight, about survival. He launched a vicious attack with sword and buckler both, thrusting and punching with consum-mate skill.

Granger parried, but not fast enough. Banks's sword sliced through his right shoulder.

Banks lunged forward for the killing strike, but Granger managed to break away, more by luck than design. He jogged backwards. Briana Marks had by now reached the podium. The emperor bowed and then waved away one of the administrators to offer her a seat. She glanced over at Granger and shook her head.

What did *that* mean?

Granger ran towards the corral wall. 'Sister Marks?'

She lowered her gaze.

'Sister Marks?'

Still she refused to acknowledge him. Emperor Hu glanced between Granger and the witch and then frowned. He spoke quietly to Marks, but she ignored him completely and simply continued to stare at her hands.

Granger heard Banks approaching from behind and turned to find the private with his sword already raised to strike. In that moment he saw the pain and despair in his young opponent's eyes. Granger lifted his own blade in a desperate attempt to fend off the blow, but he already knew it was too late. Banks had the advantage.

But he didn't take it.

He stopped, and just stood there for a heartbeat with his sword raised, staring down at Granger. Then he threw his weapon away. It clattered off the flagstones and came to rest several yards away, gleaming like a mirror. Silence settled over the plaza.

A third shot rang out.

Private Merrad Banks remained standing for a moment longer as his life blood surged from a hole in the centre of his forehead. He started to lift a hand up towards the wound and then he paused and sat down on the ground. His body slumped forward.

Granger rushed to him and held him. He could smell Banks's sweat and blood, feel the heat from the other man's sun-warmed steel epaulettes, but there was no life left in that body. Everything Banks had been had come to an end here in this rotten corner of the empire. He heard the corral gate scrape open behind him.

'Finish him off,' Hu said. 'But do it slowly. No less than fifty cuts.'

Grech took to the podium again. 'Ladies and gentlemen,' he began, 'jailers of Ethugra, protectors of the Imperial law. For the final trial, our gracious ruler has chosen, for *your pleasure,* to pit against the traitor the strongest, the fastest, and the most *merciless* of all combatants!' He raised his hand to quell the excited chatter from the crowd. 'Three score years in the training! His mortal flesh empowered by Unmer sorcery, his eyes scorched from his own skull from gazing into the furious reaches of infinity. Ladies and gentlemen . . . the emperor presents to you, his very own . . . *Samarol!*'

The crowd went wild.

The bodyguard who had fired the shots now detached his seeing knife from his rifle for the final time and held it lightly in one mailed fist. Despite his great size he moved with the grace of a wolf. His helmet grinned fiercely, but its silver eyes evinced a rage that did not belong to its wearer. It was the fury of the empire carried by a surrogate. It was an executioner's mask. And was it possible to think of the Samarol in any other way? What mortal man could hope to prevail in a fight against one?

The Samarol stepped into the corral, and the gate closed behind him.

Granger glanced at Briana Marks, and, for an instant, their eyes met.

She stood up and called out to the emperor, 'Wait.' And then she hurried over to the corral gate and beckoned Granger to approach.

'Maskelyne wasn't at Scythe Island,' she said. 'He's out at sea somewhere. I couldn't reach him.'

'So that's it? You're leaving me here to die.'

'I've no evidence he has a hostage with him at all, Mr Granger, let alone a psychic one. I can't sense another seer within three hundred miles of here. And I cannot interfere with an Imperial trial on your word alone.'

'You could,' he replied. 'But you choose not to.'

He could see from her expression that he'd struck upon the truth. The Haurstaf had the power to ostracize and thus bring down empires at their whim, and yet that that power could only be maintained through strict impartiality and honesty. Those emperors and warlords who paid so much for psychic communications in wartime needed to know that the information they received was not influenced by others – that all parties were paying for the truth. Briana Marks could stop Hu if she desired, but she wouldn't risk Haurstaf honour to do it. His life wasn't worth that much to her.

As she turned to go, he said, 'Look for her again, after the trial.'

She nodded and walked away.

'Proceed,' the emperor said.

The Samarol came at him running, astonishingly quickly for a man of his size. His leather boots made no sound on the flagstones. His seeing knife flashed. Granger feinted left, but then pushed himself away from the corral wall in the opposite direction. The bodyguard turned like a dancer and passed by in a blur.

Searing pain ran up Granger's arm.

He stared in astonishment at blood welling from a knife cut across the back of his right wrist. It was deep. He hadn't even seen the bodyguard's attack.

The crowd shouted, 'One!'

The Samarol relaxed into a jog, and made a circuit of the corral. Granger turned with him, following the other man's progress with the tip of his sword. Blood flowed freely over his right hand, spattering the flagstones at his feet. As the bodyguard drew near, he picked up his speed, flipping the knife from one hand to the other and back again.

Granger thrust his blade up at the man's head.

The Samarol ducked and pivoted, and spun away.

'Two,' roared the crowd.

Granger felt warm blood spilling down his leg. A second cut had sliced through his breeches and split the skin on his thigh. He clamped his hand across the wound and turned again to follow the bodyguard's progress.

The Samarol made a second leisurely circuit of the arena, and as he ran he wiped his knife against a leather patch sewn across his belt. He closed on Granger a third time, the seeing knife now clenched in one back-turned fist, his wolf helmet gleaming.

Granger swiped his blade in a wide arc, hoping to drive his attacker back. After all, he had the advantage of reach.

But the bodyguard caught the sword on the edge of his knife, and turned the blow up, over his own head. Granger had never seen reflexes like it. The man was inhuman. Within a heartbeat he had ducked again, moving inside Granger's reach. And then came that same strange pirouette, and Granger felt something scrape his rib.

'Three.'

Granger's chest had been punctured on his left side. A third stream of blood now flowed from his flesh. He staggered back a few steps, gaping at his own lacerated body. His muscles were starting to ache and soon they would fail him altogether. The Samarol meanwhile continued his performance for the crowd, cleaning his seeing knife again as he jogged away. He had been deliberately inflicting shallow, non-lethal wounds. He was carving Granger up for the emperor's amusement.

Granger watched his opponent wiping the edge of that unholy knife against the leather patch on his belt. The Unmer metal was conveying its surroundings to the blind warrior, while granting him unnatural swiftness. In this battle the blade was Granger's real enemy.

The Samarol turned inwards for a fourth attack.

And Granger let him come. He feinted an uppercut with his sword, leaving his right shoulder vulnerable to attack. The bodyguard spotted the opening and struck out with the knife, but Granger was ready for him.

As the attack came, Granger dropped his sword and grabbed his opponent's wrist. And then he plunged the knife even deeper into his own shoulder. A grunt of surprise came from behind the wolf helmet. The Samarol tried to withdraw the knife, but Granger now seized the other man's wrist in both hands and held it fast. He had momentarily denied the bodyguard his sight.

Still fiercely gripping the other man's wrist, he swung him around, and around again in a circle, hoping to further disorientate his opponent, hoping to break his grip on the Unmer blade. But the Samarol folded his knees and buckled in one fluid movement, dragging Granger down to the ground with him.

Granger landed heavily against the man. For several heartbeats they wrestled, the Samarol trying to wrench the knife from Granger's flesh, while Granger tried to stop him. The pain was intolerable. He felt the edge of the blade raking against his clavicle. He felt his grip loosened by his own blood. He couldn't hold on. He was going to lose this struggle.

But then he thought about Swan and Tummel and Banks, their dead eyes staring lifelessly at the ground, the blood leaking from the holes in their skull as the emperor applauded. He imagined Creedy's brute face looking on as the Hookmen threw Hana into the brine, and he let the sound of her screams fill his heart. He pictured Ianthe in the hands of that bastard Maskelyne, using the girl to enrich his wretched little empire. *Hu, Creedy, Maskelyne* – Granger saw each of their faces behind that shining wolf's mask before him now. And it filled him with rage.

He seized the brim of the warrior's helmet and wrenched it

backwards with all of his strength. He felt the chinstrap stretch and then suddenly snap as the helmet came away and flew across the arena.

The Samarol cried out. He released his hold of the knife and clamped his hands across his face. That face had only been exposed to the light for a heartbeat, but that was long enough for the horror of it to be burned in Granger's mind.

No flesh clung to the man's skull. It was as if the Unmer sorcery had consumed his living tissues, leaving nothing behind but raw bone. The eye sockets and nasal opening were covered by a smooth brass plate, utterly featureless and without ornamentation, and yet the bodyguard groped at it as if the light was searing his very nerves. He scrambled away from Granger on his hands and knees, howling like a child as he sought to reclaim his helmet. But without the knife in his hand and the helmet to cover his metal visage he could not find it.

Granger plucked the seeing knife from his shoulder and tucked it into the band of his breeches. He was weak and giddy and struggling to breathe against the pressure mounting in his chest. His hands and torso streamed with blood. But he thought he might now survive today after all. He stared at the corpses of his friends, Swan, Tummel and Banks, and a terrible grief came over him. That he should survive this trial at their expense. He could not forgive Hu for this.

All the crowd were silent as he turned to face the emperor. 'I survived your trials,' he said. 'Will you honour the law and release me?'

Briana Marks's face looked ashen, but the emperor's own was red with rage. 'How dare you speak to me?' he cried. 'Look at what you've done here! Do you have any idea how much Samarol cost? How many years it takes for the absorption to hold?' His thin chest rose and fell rapidly beneath his golden mail. He turned to the crowd. 'This man has shown himself to be a cheat. This is a mockery of justice!'

The crowd remained silent.

Administrator Grech came alongside the emperor and tried to speak, but Hu just slapped the old man across the face. He raised his Imperial hand again and pointed at Granger. 'Shoot him,' he said. 'Shoot him now.'

Outside the corral, the remaining Samarol reached for their carbine rifles. Nineteen knives slotted into nineteen barrels.

Granger looked to the Haurstaf witch for help, but she simply buried her head in her hands.

'Kill him!' the emperor roared.

There was nowhere for Granger to go, and nowhere to hide. Walls of dragon-bone caged him on three sides. The gate remained sealed.

The Samarol lifted their weapons.

Granger glanced at his fallen comrades one last time. And then he ran, away from the emperor and his Samarol. And as the bodyguards' fingers closed on the triggers of their rifles, Granger reached the harbour's edge and dived headlong into the brine.

CHAPTER 11

THE DEADSHIP

16th Hu-Rain, 1457
25 degrees 17 minutes north
5 degrees 37 minutes west

Scythe Island is forty leagues SSW of our current position,
but feels more distant yet. Have made good progress across the
Candlelight Straits. Expect to reach the fringes of the Mare Regis
by noon tomorrow. No dragon sightings. Chronograph stopped
three times by dead airs. Have opted to use Sanderson Device in
interim. Mellor feels there might be an Unmer deadship nearby.
The men are uneasy about this.

The girl remains an enigma. How is she able to perceive what
lies in the depths of the ocean? I cannot imagine any scientific
answer. Her ability seems more akin to the Haurstaf's own
metaphysical powers. Indeed, Ianthe may herald a new bloom in
mankind's evolutionary tree: a unique flower indeed – and, if so,
then needful of pollination. More careful observation is required.

Word from Carl before we sailed – the Unmer chariot is
in excellent condition, but the power source has, alas, suffered
from the inevitable rot. Brine has eroded almost all of her
whisperglass. Close to ten thousand ichusae recovered, which I
am told is a record for a single haul in marine salvage. It seems
to me that every one represents another lungful of air for Jontney.

224

*I maintain high hopes for our current expedition. Our hold is
already one-tenth full, and all this from the Star Crab Bromera
alone! Notable among our treasures is a fine suit of clamshell mail
and six metal pyramids that, if separated, unerringly find their
way back to each other at night. No physical obstacle or locked
container is able to prevent this mysterious reunion. Because the
pyramids display evidence of electrical fluids, Mellor, as always,
has claimed this as proof of the Vitalist argument. I was too
weary to argue with him. Boy assigned to watch the artefacts has
died of unknown causes, and so the pyramids continue to keep
their secret for now.*

*Sea mist encroaching from the south. Have ordered the usual
precautions. The sun is burning a dark, dark red, although it is
not yet noon. Its evil light seems to hang amidst the vapours like
some dismal gas lamp.*

Ethan Maskelyne, aboard the Mistress

Jontney was screaming. Maskelyne dropped his logbook and
rose from the writing desk. He stepped out of the cabin into the
adjoining corridor and almost collided with his wife, who was
hurrying past.

'What is it?' he said.

'I don't know!' She looked dishevelled, her hair and frock all
in disarray.

'You were supposed to be watching him!'

'I had to use the commode!'

The pair of them rushed to the end of the corridor and
opened the door to the map room.

Jontney sat on the floor beside the map table, red-faced and
bawling. Beside him, ice vapour rose from the open hatch to
Maskelyne's void fly repository. The child had evidently been

rummaging in there, for white deposits of crespic salts lay scattered across the floor around him.

Maskelyne ran over and scooped up his son. 'Gods in hell,' he exclaimed. 'Have you eaten any?' He forced his fingers into the little boy's mouth and peered inside. 'Have you eaten any?' Jontney's howling became all the more insistent. Maskelyne turned to Lucille and cried, 'Hot water! Fetch me hot water now!'

His wife just stood there, her face drained.

'Hot water!' Maskelyne demanded. 'The galley, go to the galley.' He studied the child again. 'Gods, he's got the stuff all over his mouth.' He began wiping away the toxic powder from the boy's lips and gums.

Lucille hurried away.

'Hush now, baby,' Maskelyne said to his child. He hugged him close to his chest and smoothed the boy's hair. 'Hush, hush, it's going to be fine.' He gazed down at the open hatch and noticed a scalpel lying among the salt nearby. Someone had used it to carve away at the floorboards around both hinges of the hatch. Where had he seen that tiny blade before? After a moment, he realized.

Doctor Shaw.

Could Jontney have picked it up? Possibly. But surely the child could not have used it to free the hatch?

Lucille returned with pot of steaming water. Maskelyne handed the child over to her and tested the water with the back of his hand. *Too hot.* Cursing, he carried the pot over to the bar, where he emptied a half a quart of wine into it. When the liquid was just cool enough to swallow safely, he forced the boy to drink.

Jontney coughed and sputtered and wailed. He snorted watered wine out of his nose. But Maskelyne managed to get a fair amount of it down his throat. 'Now shake him,' he said to Lucille. 'Make him sick it up again.'

Lucille complied, and soon the child had brought back up the solution.

'Again.' Maskelyne lifted the pot to the boy's lips.

Lucille looked terrified. 'Is he going to be all right?'

'Crespic salts react with acid to produce an endothermic reaction,' Maskelyne said. 'If he's swallowed any, it could have frozen his stomach. We need to wash it out, warm him up. Now, there, make him bring it up again.'

The child was sick a second time, spattering wine across the rugs and the map table.

Maskelyne studied him intently. 'I don't know,' he said. 'He seems . . . fine. I think we've been lucky.'

Lucille cradled the little boy and tried to soothe him. She spoke softly, but with venom in her voice: 'How could you let this happen?'

'Me?' Maskelyne regarded her with amazement. '*You* were supposed to be watching him.'

'That hatch should have been locked!' she retorted. 'What if he'd got to the void flies?'

'It *was* locked. Evidently *someone* got it open for him. Where did you say you were?'

She looked at the floor. 'I've not been feeling well. The sea air . . .'

Maskelyne looked at her for a long moment. And then he sighed. 'I'm sorry, I shouldn't have snapped at you.' He took her and the child in his arms. 'Gods, Lucille, I've never been so frightened.'

She began to sob. 'What's happening, Ethan? Is someone trying to hurt us?'

Maskelyne didn't say anything, but he had his own suspicions.

★

Granger hit the brine and plunged under it, and for an instant the world became a haze of brown and gold: sunlight rippling across the rooftops of the old Unmer dwellings down below; the *Excelsior*'s anchor chain; a shoal of marionette fish hanging in the deep like harvest festival baubles. His ears resounded with *gloop* and *clang* of sudden pressure change.

And then the pain hit him.

His whole body burned. He felt as if his corneas were shrinking, his salted flesh crackling over an open flame. He ignored it and swam on towards the stern of the emperor's ship. Samarol bullets streaked by him, leaving short trails of bubbles before their own velocity tore them to shreds.

After a dozen strokes he realized that he was going into shock. A sense of panic and confusion overcame him. He fought against it, desperate to keep his muscles moving, desperate to reach that anchor chain now twenty paces ahead. Now fifteen. Ten.

Every nerve in his body cried out to him to stop. Strange thoughts whirled through his consciousness: *The seawater was roasting him alive. He was swimming through the sun and it was not composed of fire but of molten glass. And now he could see that the glass formed the medium through which all thoughts and dreams passed. A lens at the heart of the universe; it was the source and destination of all things. The eye of Creation. He realized that he could die here in peace, and that all would be well. The pain was leaving him now. All he had to do was accept the brine's embrace.*

Yet some internal spark would not let him give up. He saw a vision of Ianthe, her face blurred by the waters, her black hair aflame, and it spurred him on. And suddenly the pain returned with horrific vigour, as if the lapse had been nothing but a sorcerous whisper, a Siren's call, and the Mare Lux had chosen to bare her teeth once more. He swam and swam through the gnawing brine and, as he crashed onwards through the limits of his own endurance, he bared his own teeth and grinned madly at the agony of it all.

He reached the anchor chain and pulled himself up, fist over fist, until he broke the surface of the waters and drew in a great shuddering breath.

The *Excelsior*'s copper-clad hull loomed over him, her port lifeboat snug against the bulwark, while higher still her yards cut across the Ethugran sky like lines of cirrus cloud. Hand over fist he pulled himself up the chain, teeth set, muscles screaming, his eyes burning like hot coals in his skull.

He reached the capstan hatch and slipped inside the ship.

Granger found himself in a dim corridor above the gun deck. A line of interior doors each bore Hu's Imperial crest: the dragon slain by a heavenly bolt of light. These looked like guest quarters. The bulk of Hu's crew had been ashore to watch the trial, and there was nobody about. But he could not rest here. The brine on his skin felt like fire. It was changing him with every breath he took, steaming from his hands and forearms. If he was to survive he must first purge himself with fresh water. He opened the nearest door.

It was a small cabin with a neat bunk, a gem lantern and a washbasin. Granger turned on the taps and bent over the washbasin. There was barely a trickle of water. He scooped the water into his eyes and face several times, until the stinging sensation faded. Then he blinked and looked down at his torso. His blood had already begun to crystallize in his wounds. He fought the urge to wash it away immediately lest he reopen those wounds. Instead, he washed the naked skin around them as best he could.

He didn't want to take too much time over this. The emperor's men might arrive any moment.

He located the anchor in the winch room three decks below the forecastle. It was too heavy to be raised by one man alone, so Granger lifted the brake and then turned the huge steel spool in the opposite direction, lowering the chain further into the sea. As the spool unwound, the weight of the chain itself began to drag the whole pulley mechanism around on its own. He kicked it to give it impetus, forcing the heavy line to unwind faster and faster. Finally it jarred to a halt. The end of the chain remained connected to the spool by a securing pin as thick as his thumb. Granger tried to kick it out, but it was welded in place and would not budge. He left it alone. The torque of the ship's engines should be more than enough to shear it when the time came.

His skin started to burn again.

Granger left the winch room and headed aft in the direction of the wheelhouse. He followed a companionway under the gun deck, passing sail rooms, storerooms and a gunnery workshop. All were empty. The corridor opened into the crew quarters, a low chamber packed with rows of triple bunks. The pain in his flesh was starting to become intolerable again. He could feel his limbs begin to stiffen. When he spotted the door to the wash room, he hesitated, then ducked inside.

It was as large as four of the guest cabins back to back, but windowless and sour-smelling. A metalled floor sloped to a gutter channel along one end. The wooden walls were rotten and warped. An enormous barrel to which a ladle pan had been connected by a length of cord stood against the back wall under a dripping tap. Granger ran over and vaulted into the barrel itself.

Cold water immersed him. He submerged his head and then stood up again and washed his face, neck, torso, groin and finally his arms and legs. He shook his eyes clear of water, and then repeated the whole process. Even in this dim light he could see his skin had already been damaged by the Mare Lux seawater. Grey, leathery patches of sharkskin covered his arms like cracked paving, leaving raw red flesh between. Crystals had already formed over most of his wounds. They had staunched the flow of blood, but itched terribly and felt painful to the touch.

He climbed out of the barrel and stood there in the dark for a long moment, contemplating his disfigured flesh. He'd been too late to save himself completely, and the chances were good he might die yet. The flesh would either heal or harden further, restricting his movement. He sat down on the floor, trembling with exhaustion and fear, and felt something prod him in the side. It was the Unmer seeing knife, still tucked into the band of his breeches. He took it out and turned it over, but his sharkskin fingers could hardly feel it at all.

Sea mist rolled in from the south, blotting the sun until the skies around the *Mistress* turned from ochre to orange to a deep and angry red. Maskelyne ordered his sharpest lookout to the bow and ordered his engineers to set the dredger's engines to one-quarter speed. He climbed the ladder to the wheelhouse and took control of the vessel himself. Yet even from this high vantage point he could see little in the fiery gloom but the dim pink glow of the lookout's gem lantern and the red-brown slush of seawater coursing past to port and stern. The thin iron skeletons of the deck cranes drifted in and out of mist, while the *Mistress*'s bathysphere squatted in its cradle in the centre of the deck like an enormous brass egg.

They were in the Border Waters, the confluence of the Mare Lux and Mare Regis. It was an area of unpredictable weather and vicious currents. Ships were apt to drift leagues away from their assumed positions. He'd heard rumours of reefs, too, shoals of copper sharks and wisp lights, and even great deepwater erokin samal capable of claiming entire crews with their searching tentacles. But the stories that troubled him the most were those of wandering deadships.

He pulled a cord and blew the ship's foghorn. A deep, low blast reverberated through the mist. He did not expect to find another ship out here, but the sound reassured him nevertheless. It filled the sepulchral air with a sense of life.

He hadn't heard Lucille come in but turned at the sound of her voice.

'He's asleep,' she said. 'At least he was until a second ago.' She inclined her head towards the foghorn cord. She was dressed, like him, in deepwater gear. In her bulky whaleskins she looked pitifully small and fragile. She removed her goggles and took a moment to unwrap the silk scarf from her face. 'I asked one of Mellor's boys to watch over Jontney.'

'That scarf's not really necessary,' he said. 'These mists don't do much damage.'

'It's the word "much" that concerns me in that sentence, Ethan.'

He smiled. 'Mist blisters heal. I'd still love you, even if you looked liked a sea monster.'

'And you'd love me no less if I didn't.' She stared ahead into the mist. 'Where are you taking us?'

'Losotans called it the Whispering Valley,' he said. 'Before the flood, I mean. Lots of old Unmer settlements down there.'

'So lots of treasure?'

'That's the idea.'

She shook her head. 'It's as thick as soup out there. Do you think Ianthe would be able to see through this?'

He said nothing, but kept his gaze on the crimson fog.

She nuzzled against him. 'This reminds me of Hattering.'

'The mists?'

'Well, apart from the mists,' she replied. 'And the boat. We were both dressed in whaleskins. I thought you looked quite dashing.'

He smiled 'Dashing? In whaleskins?'

'What was the name of that friend you were with? The naval officer?'

'William Temping.'

She nodded slowly. 'That's him. Whatever became of him?'

Maskelyne sniffed. 'I cut his throat.'

He felt her tense, just slightly. And then she moved away. 'I'd better go check on Jontney,' she said.

'He was a terrible fraud,' Maskelyne said. 'Did you know he even cheated on his wife? Some woman he kept in Losoto, apparently.'

'Was that why you killed him?'

'No.' He was silent for a heartbeat, thinking, but he couldn't recall. Finally he said, 'I must have had a good reason.'

She looked at him for a long while, then shrugged. 'I'm sure you did what you thought you had to do, Ethan.'

A bell began to ring on the deck below. Maskelyne peered out through the window and saw the bow lookout's gem lantern swinging madly in the mist. He reached for the engine throttle but then changed his mind. One of his crew was rushing across the deck from the lookout's position, but he couldn't yet make out who it was.

'What is it?' Lucille asked.

Maskelyne opened the wheelhouse door and looked out. The crewman on the deck shouted up to him, 'Deadship, Captain.'

'Bearing?'

'Straight for us. Like she knows.'

Maskelyne closed the door again and spun the wheel hard to

ALAN CAMPBELL

starboard. And now through the red fog he could make out the dim black shape of a ship. She was a huge, ancient ironclad, bereft of masts, yards or sails. Upon her midships deck stood a solitary tower – a latticework of metal struts supporting a rusted toroid. She was one of the old electrical ships that had once carried whale oil across the Northern Wastes. *An icebreaker?* Maskelyne looked more closely at the prow and saw that it had been massively reinforced. He hissed through his teeth. The *Mistress* was now turning to starboard, while the Unmer vessel maintained its course. The two ships would pass within yards of each other.

Eight of the crew had gathered on the port side, while one of the officers – probably Mellor – was handing out carbine rifles to them.

The deadship drew closer. There did not appear to be any crewman aboard. Her hull and sterncastle had been forged from iron, but now Maskelyne could see that she had been damaged by intense fire. Yard-long sections of the bulwark had been scorched black and warped out of shape. Cables slumped around her tower like worn shrouds. He counted the remains of six guns mounted along her port side, strange metal weapons, each with a conical arrangement of circular plates fixed to the end of its barrel. They looked charred, melted, inoperable. An iron figurehead in the likeness of an Unmer maiden remained upon her prow, now stripped of paint and partially reduced to slag. The corruption gave her a ghoulish grin. *Dragonfire did this*, Maskelyne thought. *Dragonfire.*

Every crewman had his rifle trained on the Unmer ship, following her as she slid by mere yards from the *Mistress*. Under the steady thump of the dredger's engines Maskelyne fancied he could hear the groan of the old ironclad's buckled hull and the rush of seawater caught between their two keels, and then something else – a faint, high-pitched humming sound, almost at the limits of his hearing, seemed to emanate from that tower.

A heartbeat later, the Unmer ship had passed by. Maskelyne watched her dissolve into the fog.

He let out a long breath.

'Is it true what they say about deadships?' Lucille asked.

'I wouldn't bet on it.'

'Mellor thinks the dead crews still steer them.'

Maskelyne frowned. 'Something steers them, but it isn't ghosts. Their engines draw electrical fluid from the air.' He rubbed his eyes and then rested both his hands on the wheel again. 'I don't know . . . the energy is probably transmitted from somewhere, a station or a bunker, somewhere the Haurstaf and their allies didn't penetrate.'

'You think there could still be a free Unmer community out there?'

'It's possible.'

She shivered. 'I'm going to check on Jontney.'

She left Maskelyne alone in the wheelhouse. For a long while he peered into the gloom, watchful for anything unusual. The rumble of the *Mistress*'s engines failed to calm his nerves as much as it usually did. An Unmer ironclad, still sailing these waters after god only knew how many hundreds of years? The souls of her sorcerous crew burned into her very metal at the Battle of Awl? He couldn't accept that. The Unmer captains were long dead. The Brutalists and operators were long dead. The ship was still receiving its power from a distant station, which meant it might also be possible to steer it from afar. A free Unmer community? Maskelyne knew of only one Unmer warrior still at large. He tried to remember the line from the old children's rhyme he'd learned at school.

> *And to the storm Conquillas brought,*
> *A dragon clad in armour wrought,*
> *By Hessimar of Anderlaine.*

There was more, but the rest wouldn't come to him. Those great serpents, led by Argusto Conquillas, had allied with the Haurstaf and risen up against their Unmer masters. Conquillas had decimated the Unmer fleet at Awl and thus betrayed his own kind for the love of a Haurstaf witch.

The lookout's bell rang out again.

A sense of dread crept up Maskelyne's spine, for through that red and turbulent air beyond the window he spied the dim hulk of the deadship bearing down on them once more. There could be no mistaking that hideous rusted tower, that weird droning sound. Evidently it had come about in the fog. He spun the *Mistress*'s wheel full lock to starboard, then flung open the wheelhouse door and called down to the foredeck. 'Get Ianthe up here, I need her sight.'

The deadship drew nearer, and for a heartbeat Maskelyne thought he could see a group of figures standing motionless upon her fog-shrouded deck. But then the vision faded, and the ship appeared deserted once more. Nothing but burned iron, a mess of cable. The mists were playing tricks on his eyes.

The two vessels were on a collision course. Maskelyne gunned the *Mistress*'s engines and attempted to take her past the Unmer ship once again. It would be close. Down on the foredeck his crew rushed forward to the bow, training their rifles on the approaching threat.

Sixty yards now.

The *Mistress* began to turn to starboard. The Unmer ironclad maintained her course.

Thirty yards.

Ahead, the great dark vessel loomed large. Now Maskelyne could see her figurehead with its melted grin. It seemed to know it was going to collide with them.

The deadship struck the *Mistress* a glancing blow on her port side. Even from up here in the wheelhouse Maskelyne felt the force of the impact. Abruptly his vessel lurched to one side. He heard the other ship's hull boom, and then a hideous groaning and scraping sound as the icebreaker's reinforced prow scraped along the *Mistress*'s side. That blow would have crushed a lesser ship, but Maskelyne's dredger was a tough old girl. Engines thumping, she thundered on, pushing the schooner aside.

Slowly, the two ships separated. The Unmer vessel drifted off into the fog.

Maskelyne's heart was thumping. He cut power to the engines, then opened the wheelhouse door and called down. 'What damage?'

The crew were picking themselves up from the deck. One by one they began to peer down over the port side, sweeping gem lanterns back and forth across the hull. Mellor sent a man running towards the midships hatch, presumably to check for internal damage.

'There's no obvious breach, Captain,' Mellor called back. 'But she's taken a hell of a pounding. I've sent Broomhouse to check the bulkheads from fore to aft.'

At that moment the midships companionway hatch opened, and another crewman appeared with Ianthe. He led the girl by the arm to the wheelhouse ladder and bade her climb. She looked nervous and shaken and had been hurriedly wrapped in an old whaleskin cloak.

Maskelyne took her hand and helped her into the wheelhouse. 'We've been hit by another vessel,' he said. 'An Unmer deadship.'

She said nothing.

'It's still out there somewhere,' Maskelyne said. 'I need you to watch out for it.'

'There's no one aboard it,' she replied.

It struck him as an odd thing to say. 'I'm not one to pander to superstitions myself,' he said. 'But that vessel has already come straight at us twice. Someone has to be steering it.' He thought about the figures he'd glimpsed momentarily upon the deadship's deck, but chose not to mention them.

Ianthe merely shrugged.

The door swung open, and Mellor's head appeared at knee level. He was clinging to the ladder outside. 'Four of the engine room bulkheads have been buckled, Captain, but it's not too grim. Our hull is intact, engine sound, and we're still tight as a drum. Repair crews are working on it now.'

'Tell them to go easy,' Maskelyne ordered. 'I don't want them putting the bulkheads under any more stress. We'll refit back in dry dock at Scythe. No cross-braces. Have them raise props from the motor housings only and weld the plates in the meantime.'

'Aye, Captain.' Mellor reached up and shut the door.

Maskelyne gently increased power to the engines and spun the wheel to port again, keeping an eye on the ship's compass as he brought the *Mistress* back on her original course. Red-brown fumes drifted over the foredeck and the dim figures of his crew. Through the starboard window he could see the dun lantern of the sun, almost directly to the south. It was almost noon, although it felt like dusk. *Like the seas are burning.* With any luck they would be out of the border waters and into the Mare Regis proper by mid afternoon.

For a long while Maskelyne kept his gaze on the mists ahead. Neither he nor Ianthe spoke. The lookout's lantern on the prow burned like a solitary star. The old dredger rocked gently back and forth as she ploughed on through the poisonous waters, her engines maintaining a steady rhythm. Maskelyne could sense the uneasiness of his crew in the way they moved about the deck and in the fashion in which they clutched their rifles. He noted how each man kept himself apart from his companions. The fog drew denser and bloodier until it coiled around the cranes like dragon's breath. Maskelyne had the impression that they were moving into some strange borderland that was not a part of this world.

The lookout's lantern began to swing for the third time.

'Where is it?' he asked Ianthe.

She was clearly terrified. 'I don't know.'

'The lookout can see it,' he growled.

She pointed straight ahead. 'There!'

And then Maskelyne spotted it. The deadship reared suddenly out of the thick fog like a cliff. It was almost upon them. Maskelyne cursed and spun the wheel hard to port. He wrenched the engine throttle into reverse. But he already knew that it was too late. The Unmer ironclad was going to crash straight into their starboard side, and there was no way Maskelyne could avoid it.

Granger crept along the crew deck companionway until he found a hatch leading down to the gun deck. He listened, and, hearing nothing, slipped down.

A low space ran the width of the ship, divided here and there by mast-collars and monstrous steel-reinforced ribs of dragonbone. The firing hatches on either side were open, and the emperor's ranks of bronze cannons gleamed dully in their tackles and breech ropes. The guns were antiques, Imperial Ferredales, forged in Valcinder at least three centuries ago – extraordinarily old and rare, and yet crafted with such skill and precision that their power and range could match many modern shell weapons. Granger almost choked to see that the lanyards now connected to retrofitted flintlock mechanisms in each breech. Each gun must have been worth three million gilders before Hu had ordered them vandalized in this way. Rams, swab buckets and powder rods lay upon the floor beside each gun, while stacks of various missiles – sacks of grapeshot, chain shot and troughs of heavy iron balls – filled the central space between the opposing bulwarks. The powder would be held in the deck below, accessed via a series of smaller hatches he could see in the floor. There was not a crewman in sight.

Granger's skin itched and burned, but the pain had diminished somewhat. His eyes still felt hot and raw. He paced the gun deck, marvelling at the size of these reinforced dragon-bone arches. Sixty mature serpents had been slaughtered to construct this ship, among them Garamae the Betrayer, who was said to have devoured Lord Marquetta's baby son during the armistice in 1403. He crouched down and pulled up one of the powder hatches and sniffed. A sulphurous odour filled his nostrils. A faint green glow illuminated an iron floor.

Granger walked over to one of the port gun hatches and peered out. He could see the bone corral upon the dockside, the emperor's podium, and the Administration Buildings rising up beyond. Most of the crowd had spread along the water's edge and were staring into the brine, along with many of the emperor's crewmen. Hu himself stood by the harbour steps beside his launch, guarded by his Samarol bodyguards. He appeared to be having an animated discussion with Administrator Grech and Briana Marks.

Granger padded back to the powder hatch and dropped down. He found himself in a small iron cell. Parchment cartridges of powder stood in neat stacks against the walls. Shelves held boxes of flints, coils of cambric fuse, shredded sailcloth and sealed jars of phosphorous that gave off a dim green luminance. He grabbed an armload of cartridges, then stuffed a handful of flints into his pocket along with a few yards of fuse and climbed back up to the gun deck.

One of the forward hatches offered him the best angle of fire. He sighted along the cannon's barrel, and, satisfied, winched the heavy gun carriage back on its wheels using the rear tackle. He swabbed the barrel interior, then shoved the powder cartridge down inside it, followed by a cloth wad. Then he picked up a ram and tamped the powder home. From the centre of the deck he took one of the grapeshot sacks and rammed that down the barrel after the charge. Lastly, he forced in another wad of cloth to keep the shot in place, and then heaved the gun carriage back up against the bulwark by alternating between each of the side tackles.

Granger took a moment to catch his breath. His arms ached from the exertion. His own sweat stung his altered skin like vinegar poured into a wound. He felt sore all over, irritable, impatient. His every instinct screamed at him to get away now. *Find the bridge, fight your way in if need be – lock the doors, gun the ship's engines and get out of here.* He could turn the *Excelsior* back into the Glot Madera, run as far as he could before the skeleton crew broke the door down, use a powder bomb to bluff his way out, or just blow himself to hell and take as many of them down with him as he could. But his need for revenge wouldn't let him leave yet. He took hold of the lanyard behind the gun's breech and peered out of the hatch again, letting his gaze roam over the milling crowd of jailers, administrators and soldiers. He couldn't see the emperor anywhere.

A sudden roar came from the launch's engines. Had Hu already boarded his pilot vessel? Granger couldn't see him on the deck. He must already be inside. Granger cursed and rubbed madly at his burning eyes. The launch was too low in the water. The grapeshot wouldn't hit it from this angle. The cannon's barrel was aimed firmly at the crowd.

But then he spotted the emperor emerging from amidst the

241

group of administrators at the top of the steps. He was still within range.

Granger stepped back from the cannon and pulled the lanyard.

An enormous concussion sounded. The gun carriage slammed backwards against its breech rope. Grapeshot burst out of the barrel, scattering in the air, and tore through the dockside crowds. Through drifting smoke Granger saw dozens of men and women drop, their flesh torn open by the tiny missiles. He glimpsed bloody clothes, scores of wounds. Someone screamed.

Emperor Hu remained standing exactly where he was, clutching his face. And then his bodyguards closed around him and bustled him roughly down the steps towards the waiting launch.

Granger had missed his target.

He cursed again. Then he snatched up the remaining powder cartridges, and ran with them to the nearest ladder. He climbed up and hurried through the crew quarters, his heart thumping wildly. Near the rear of the ship he found a stairwell that looked likely to take him up to the bridge. But as he started to climb, he came face to face with another man who had been rushing in the opposite direction.

The insignia on the man's white uniform marked him as the first officer. When he saw Granger he halted abruptly and his eyes widened with alarm. 'You . . .' he began. But he couldn't find the words to finish his sentence. Granger, with his scorched flesh and howling red eyes, must have made a terrifying spectacle.

The officer suddenly reached for the pistol at his belt.

Granger kicked the man's legs out from under him.

He fell back heavily onto the stairs. He fumbled for his pistol again.

Granger snatched the seeing knife from the band of his breeches and plunged it upwards into the other man's neck. He pinned the officer's arms with his knees, holding the dying man down while he choked and gurgled on his own lifeblood. It was over in a moment.

Granger wiped the seeing knife clean on the officer's uniform and carried on up the stairwell.

He reached the top of the stairwell without further incident, clutched the powder cartridges close to his chest, and flung open the door to the bridge. It was empty. Three outward-sloping glass windows composed of innumerable tiny panes offered views to port and starboard, and ahead across the *Excelsior*'s foredeck to the Haurstaf warship berthed further out from the quayside. A sweeping control bank of lacquered wood and gold piping curved around the silver and bone ship's wheel. The rear wall had been exquisitely carved with dragon motifs, hunting scenes and Imperial seals. An enormous steel harpoon hung there like a trophy, over a brass plaque that read: *Garamae's Thorn*. No fewer than ten gem lanterns adorned the ceiling, all shining in hues of pink, gold, orange and green. *Not a man in sight.* Granger could scarcely believe his luck. Evidently Hu had deemed it unnecessary to keep even a skeleton crew in charge of his own yacht's bridge.

He closed the door behind him. Through the port window he spied the emperor's launch scudding across the harbour towards the ship's boarding ladder. There was no time to spare. He scanned the engine gauges and controls. *Boiler pressure, good. Water level, good. Engine oil. Fuel oil. Feed cocks. Decomp. Hydraulics. Pressure valves. Primer shunts.* Everything was in order. A separate bank under the forward window contained an array of meteorological and navigational instruments – barometers, chronographs, compasses and the like – but he ignored those for now. Likewise the comspool. He had to hope the engine room crew had been lax enough to keep the main whale-oil feed line open, or he'd be running on reserve.

He primed the engine and opened the oil feed cocks, then pumped the decompression lever until the gauge levelled. Then he pressed down firmly on the first of the three copper shunts.

Far below he heard the engine grumble into life.

'Let's see what you can do,' he muttered.

Granger opened half the air shunts, spun the wheel hard to starboard and twisted open the main-line feed-through cock. Steam hissed behind the control panel. Hydraulic power valves snapped open. The great ship gave a slight tremble and then began to slide forward.

A hail of rifle shots burst through the port window, showering Granger with shards of glass. He grinned maniacally and then pumped the main-line primer and opened the rest of the air shunts. The bridge juddered heavily in response.

The ship began to pick up speed.

Granger watched the bow of the Haurstaf man-o'-war slide by as he took the *Excelsior* out into the harbour. Ahead, he could now see the gates of the Glot Madera heave into view. A fishing boat and two canal ferries made sudden course changes to move out of his way.

From the control deck came a steady clacking sound, as the ship's comspool began disgorging a message it had printed onto a thin strip of paper. Evidently there *were* crewmen aboard somewhere. They would probably be down in the engine room, which meant they might not yet be aware that the emperor was not aboard. Granger tore the tape loose and read it.

ER – NO/REC – ORDERS/TO – OPEN MAINFEED – AI

Awaiting instructions. The *ER* glyph meant the message had indeed come from the engine room. Granger clicked open the pressure cap, turned the destination-wheel round to its *ER* setting, and then dialled and punched in a reply using five of the seventy-three commands available on the command wheel.

BR – CONFIRM – REQ/OPEN MAINFEED –
EJH/DANGER – REQ/ALL HASTE

He depressed the release valve and heard a series of *phuts* as his reply disappeared into the ship's warren of steam messaging pipes. A comspool in the engine room would begin typing it out almost at once. The *Excelsior* meanwhile was now building up speed as she passed through the gates of the Glot Madera. The great Ethugran Administration Buildings loomed to port and starboard. Granger locked down the wheel and hurried over the port window.

Unable to match the yacht's pace, the emperor's launch had turned around and was heading back to the dockside. Hu himself was now standing on the smaller boat's deck, shouting and waving his hands up at his crewmen and soldiers on dry land. As Granger watched, the emperor's men began to commandeer vessels all along the quayside. They were coming after him.

The comspool on the control deck began its rhythmic clacking again. The briny smell of octopus ink came from its innards as tiny metal elements rattled away behind the printing wheel. It sounded out of sorts. Granger checked the device's oil reservoir, and then adjusted the steam inlet valve and feeder gearing. The tape began to spool out more smoothly.

ER – CONFIRM – REQ/VERIFY – FLAG/YELLOW – AI

He cursed. Someone in the ER crew wanted a verification code, and Granger didn't know the correct response. There were nine flag glyphs around the command wheel he could choose from. But which one? If he lucked upon the correct response, the engine room crew would open the main fuel feed line. If not, they'd shut down the engines immediately, thereby foiling his escape. Granger peered ahead along the Glot Madera. The deep-water channel ran straight for a thousand yards or so, before curving gently to the south-west. The *Excelsior* would reach the corner in two or three minutes. An eight-to-one chance of choosing the correct coded reply? It wasn't good enough. He couldn't allow the crew to stop him here. He dialled in a different response.

BR – NO CONFIRM/TAPE FOUL –
REQ/REPEAT LAST MESSAGE

With the wheel still locked in place and the *Excelsior* firmly fixed on her current heading, Granger picked up the last of his powder cartridges and left the bridge. He had minutes to reach the engine room and then get back to the wheel. And less time yet to murder the crew.

The deadship struck them on the starboard side with enough force to send Maskelyne staggering sideways. He lost his grip on the wheel. A terrible metal groaning reverberated through the *Mistress*'s bulkheads as the ironclad's reinforced prow crushed a deep trench in the dredging ship's hull. The *Mistress* lurched sickeningly, her deck cranes tilting closer to the roiling red-brown waters as the crew hung on for their lives. The bathysphere clanked against its mountings, then broke free and smashed against the port bulwark.

Ianthe cried out in alarm.

The grinding and moaning of stressed metals continued for a tortuously long time, before finally subsiding. Maskelyne gazed down at the wreckage in disbelief and horror. The bow of the Unmer ship remained embedded in one side of his own vessel.

246

That heavy iron prow had crumpled the *Mistress*'s hull like paper. Had it holed them? He couldn't see how it could possibly *not* have holed them.

He flung open the wheelhouse door and called down. 'Mellor! Have someone fetch my family. Round up everyone but the repair teams. I want them top deck, now. And I want a time-frame here.'

'Aye, Captain.' The first officer relayed Maskelyne's orders to several crewmen, who took off at a run.

'Are we going to sink?' Ianthe asked.

'Very likely,' Maskelyne replied. 'Come with me.' Without looking back to see if she was following, he climbed down the wheelhouse ladder and hurried along the deck to the point of impact.

Most of the crew from the lower decks had already appeared, and their gem lanterns moved about in the gloom around Maskelyne as they began to assemble into ranks. Someone was taking a head count, calling out names. The deadship's figure-head leaned over the starboard bulwark amidst a mess of twisted metal, and it seemed to Maskelyne that that maiden's grimace evinced a hint of cruel satisfaction. He could smell burned iron, rust and ash, and the bitter salts of the ocean, but something else . . .

Fuel oil. The dredger's whale-oil tanks had been ruptured.

Maskelyne leaned over the side and peered down at his stricken hull. The ship's skin had been crumpled almost to the waterline and ruptured in at least four places. Clear fluid was seeping from the fore rents, leaving the surrounding brine with a nacreous sheen.

Mellor arrived at his side. 'We're pumping out all the ballast tanks,' he said. 'Those that haven't been damaged, anyway. Two midships pumps were shorn from their outlets, and we can't get to the fore ones. Abernathy will try to keep us afloat a while longer, but he's not confident. Secondary repair crew can't get access to the engine room. Flooding sounds like it's above the hatches.'

'What about the men already in there?' Maskelyne asked.

'Not a sound from them, Captain.'

'Cut down through the crew quarters.'

'That'll shorten the time we have, sir.'

'Do it.'

'Aye, sir.' He turned to go.

Maskelyne stopped him. 'Where are my wife and son, Mr Mellor?'

His question was answered by a different voice. 'Ethan!' Lucille was with Ianthe, and now ran over, carrying Jontney in one arm and Maskelyne's blunderbuss in the other. She had already fitted a frozen void-fly cartridge to the stock. She gazed up in wonder and horror at the dark hulk of the Unmer ship, before evidently remembering the gun.

'I thought you could use this,' she said, handing the weapon to him.

He took the gun and examined the mechanism. 'Where did you learn how to load it?'

'It's not that difficult, Ethan.'

He arched his eyebrows. 'I suppose you're right.' Then he reached over and fussed with Jontney's hair. The boy looked up at him and smiled – the sort of open, trouble-free smile that Maskelyne hadn't seen in the child for a long time. 'Keep him safe,' he said to his wife. 'Mellor will look after you both. Do whatever he says.'

'What are you going to do?'

'I'm going to board that ship,' Maskelyne replied. 'It looks like it's our only way out of here.'

★

Granger tried the engine-room hatch, but found it to be locked from the inside. He placed the powder cartridges on the floor against the hatch and took out his knife, flint and fuse. But he stopped. The metal hatch opened towards him, its rim resting against the metal bulkhead. He wasn't sure the explosives he'd brought were enough for the job. He stood there for a moment longer, while his mind ran through the naval ballistic tables for this thickness and grade of steel as it compared it to the sort of brisance he could expect from high-grade cannon-powder. It couldn't be done without shaping the charge, and he had no time for that.

He hammered his fist upon the hatch.

After a moment, a voice came from the other side. 'Who's there?'

'Who am I speaking to?' Granger demanded.

'Able Seaman Fletcher, sir.'

'Don't open this hatch to anyone, Able Seaman,' Granger said. 'That's an order. Not to me, not to anyone. And *do not* under any circumstances take orders from the bridge. Do you understand?'

'Yes, sir. What's going on?'

'Revolutionary militia have taken control of the *Excelsior*. They're holding the first officer hostage on the bridge.'

'Revolutionaries?' Granger then heard a second voice behind the hatch, conversing with Fletcher, but he couldn't make out what was said between them. Fletcher said, 'We can shut the engines down from here, sir.'

'You'll do no such thing,' Granger replied. 'Let them burn through the reserves. That'll give us some time to get the emperor's Samarol aboard. Do you have pistols with you?'

'No, sir.'

'Swords?'

'No, sir.'

'How the hell do you expect to protect the engines without arms?' Granger yelled. 'You can have my own pistol for the time being. Open up a minute.'

He heard the locking lever clunk back, and the hatch opened.

Granger – still clutching his knife in one fist – stepped through.

Maskelyne climbed across a boarding plank onto the Unmer dead-ship, closely followed by two of his most stolid crewmen. Kitchener was an old soldier who had watched Maskelyne's back during the Poppy Wars – a good man to have at your side whenever swords were drawn. Roberts was younger, but sharp and quick-witted and less superstitious than most. *A good head on his shoulders.* The rest of the crew held back to make whatever repairs they could, and to try to cut down to the men trapped in the *Mistress*'s flooded engine room. Many of them had baulked at the very idea of setting foot aboard the Unmer vessel. Maskelyne did not take this to be a good sign.

Bloody vapours drifted through tangled cables. A layer of ash covered the warped iron deck, filling the air with an odour like that of an old, damp fire-pit. Booming sounds came from the metal under their boots as the three men approached the ship's huge electrical tower.

'You hear that?' Roberts asked.

'Hear what?' Kitchener said.

'That whine.' He pointed up at the toroid atop the tower. 'It's coming from that thing.'

'It's still receiving power from somewhere,' Maskelyne said.

The men fell silent. Maskelyne placed his hand against the tower's lattice of struts, and felt a slight vibration. His skin tingled as the invisible electrical fluid passed into him, and it seemed to him that the whining sound intensified. He could feel it in his teeth. He withdrew his hand quickly. Tiny pink aether flames danced across his fingertips for a moment and then disappeared. *Still operational after three hundred years? Where is the power coming from?*

He walked over to examine one of the queer guns bolted to the deck. The cone of circular plates over its barrel prevented any type of shot from passing through the weapon. Perhaps it had also once utilized electrical fluids? It seemed unlikely that he could repair the device, for it looked utterly destroyed. Its metal surfaces had been heated to the point where they had actually flowed downwards, leaving tallow-like trails of iron. Maskelyne leaned closer and smelled burned copper. Nothing salvageable.

The three men made their way across groaning deck towards the sterncastle.

'Look at this,' Kitchener said. He indicated an area of deck where a black scorch mark formed the shape of a sprawled human body. It looked as if the corpse had been removed, leaving a perfect shadow behind.

'There's more over here,' Roberts said. 'Four, five of them.'

Maskelyne gazed down at the twisted shapes. 'The remains of the crew,' he said. 'They were sorcerers, all of them.' *And not as much as a fragment of their bone left behind.* Dragonfire had consumed them utterly. Maskelyne bent down to examine the shadow more closely—

—and abruptly recoiled. For an instant he'd felt searing heat, and it had seemed that he *himself* was lying there amidst the smoke and flames, with the stink of burning flesh in his nostrils and the cries of the dying all around. *Burned alive. They were burned alive almost three hundred years ago.* The sensation left him shaking, and it took a moment to clear the echoes of that terrible screaming from his head. Had the ship itself absorbed the essence of the men who'd died here? All Unmer creations contained a

251

spark of the infinite. Was it possible that the crew had somehow contrived to find refuge there?

'Let's not linger,' he said.

They found the door to the captain's quarters in the sterncastle.

There was little evidence of fire damage inside. A short wood-panelled corridor opened into a small, sour-smelling wash room on the left. It contained a beaten copper sink and a wooden commode, a stack of rotten books on the floor. Roberts gagged and turned away at the stink, but Maskelyne pushed past him and picked up one of the books. It was a volume on surgical sorcery written in Unmer and packed with illustrations of opened human cadavers beside wire-wound rods and spheres. He translated the title as *Venal Tissues of Man*.

To the right an open doorway led to a larger dressing room wherein the remains of the captain's clothes still hung in musty wardrobes. The garments were covered in tiny spiders. Webs cocooned them completely, and yet not one strand of silk reached beyond the wardrobe itself. On the dressing table lay a copper egg and a small flute carved from a human finger. Maskelyne picked up the egg, but sensed nothing unusual about it.

At the end of the corridor a third door gave them access to the captain's cabin.

Here Maskelyne stopped and stared in astonishment. Every corner of the cabin was filled with Unmer treasure. An entire rack of brightly lacquered swords, surgical swords, knives, daggers and stilettos hung upon the wall beside the bed, their steel blades agleam. A glass cabinet held chronographs, sextants, anemometers, compasses and astrolabes, all exquisitely wrought from a strange green alloy. There were shelves upon shelves of scientific instruments and small, boxed machines whose purpose could only be guessed at. An open chest at the foot of the bed contained a glittering hoard of gold coins. Maskelyne retrieved a coin with the intention of examining it, but it made him feel suddenly nauseous, and he dropped it back among the others. His skin prickled for a moment afterwards, and his hand began to tremble uncontrollably.

'Captain?' Roberts said.

Maskelyne ignore him. His attention had already turned to a wide workbench under the stern windows, where a shining gem lantern stood amidst what appeared to be a number of optical and magnetic experiments.

Kitchener whistled through his teeth. 'Never seen the like,' he said.

'Fair bit of money here, Captain.' Roberts added.

Maskelyne turned his blunderbuss over and pressed two fingers against the glass void-fly phial. It still felt ice cold. He leaned the weapon against the table and then let his gaze travel across the room. Several of the experiments looked familiar. A sealed bell jar contained a tiny copper vane, like a miniature version of the anemometers in the cabinet. Each of the vane's four thin, square fins had been painted black on one side and polished on the other. They were turning slowly, even in the sealed environment within the jar. Beside this mechanism a brilliant white gem lantern illuminated a diffraction box, wherein the rays of light passed through a pair of closely spaced vertical slits in the centre of the container and made patterns of interference across a rear screen. In addition to these finds he noted a large array of kaleidoscopes, reflecting telescopes, boxes of magnets, wires and prisms, and even a pair of Unmer spectacles. Runic inscriptions covered the silver frames, the decorations whirling around a tiny wheel fixed to one side of the rightmost lens. A triangle had been impressed into the wheel, within which was etched several digits, almost too small to see. Maskelyne picked up the spectacles and squinted at them. The number in the triangle was *1.618*.

The golden ratio.

'Looks like our captain was an amateur opticist,' Maskelyne said. 'Spectacles like this were once worn by archivists, but I've not seen a pair quite so fine before.'

'Nothing amateur about anything the Unmer do,' Kitchener growled. 'And nothing normal about it either. There's a reason this ship came after us. Mark my words, sir. There's an evil will behind this. Someone wanted us aboard this vessel.'

Maskelyne examined the table. 'The captain was studying the properties of light,' he remarked. 'The diffraction box illustrates that light exhibits the properties of waves, while this vane suggests that it is actually composed of particles. And yet if light travels in a straight line through a vacuum, can a single ray still be a wave?' He found himself musing about each speck of starlight oscillating at a particular frequency. Had our brains developed to interpret those frequencies? How did light particles interact? There had be some *association* between them – perhaps analogous to the association that existed between the fragments of mankind? Looking at the experiments, Maskelyne suddenly felt that he was on the verge of finding something important, a key to the mystery behind all Unmer artefacts.

He picked up the spectacles and studied them closely. They were more intricate than any he'd seen before. The lenses were not solid, but actually composed of a number of incredibly thin optical elements sandwiched together. When he turned the tiny wheel fixed to the frame, these inner circles of glass rotated around each other, but not in any commonsensical alignment. He could perceive nothing strange or magical about the set-up.

He put the spectacles on.

The cabin looked normal.

He turned the wheel beside his right eye and heard the almost imperceptible murmur of the glass discs revolving inside the lenses. This sound was followed by a sudden crackling buzz. The legs of the silver frame felt warm against his head.

And something odd happened. The cabin now appeared to be much darker than before, and yet everything around him was awash with a low, flickering silver luminance, as if each object – the bed, the cabinets, the artefacts – possessed a strange and intermittent aura. The workbench experiments shuddered in the dim light. He watched ghostlike wisps of light tremble across the diffraction box, the kaleidoscopes and the telescopes. It looked like some sort of interference pattern. No doubt the artefact was broken, and had been brought here to be repaired. The spectral radiance, however, did not extend beyond the cabin, for the mists beyond the window now appeared as black as night. White dots shifted in the gloom outside – like stars. Kitchener and Roberts emitted no discernible luminance at all . . .

Indeed, both crewmen were now missing from the scene entirely.

Maskelyne removed the spectacles. Kitchener and Roberts reappeared, standing there regarding him as if nothing had happened. He put the spectacles back on. The two men simply vanished before his eyes, leaving the surroundings intact, but stammering in that darkly uncertain light. Suddenly he thought he detected movement at the corner of his vision, and turned abruptly. But there was nothing there, just the cabin walls and the door.

Had that door just closed?

Remarkable. Was he witnessing some previously hidden property inherent in the objects themselves? The very essence of sorcery? Could that explain both the consistency of the cabin and the sudden disappearance of his two crewmen? The ship was sorcerous, but his comrades were not? Was it possible that these spectacles could perceive one and not the other? Maskelyne could not imagine another solution. He wondered if he could tune the spectacles to eliminate the interference and produce a clearer picture.

He turned the wheel back to its original position.

This time a searing white light blinded him, as if a magnesium powder flash had been set off directly in front of his eyes. Images crashed into his retina: the cabin, a ship, the sky, cabin, ship, sky, all accompanied by a terrible stuttering roar. Maskelyne tore the spectacles from his face, overcome with agony, and pinched his eyes.

'Captain?' Kitchener said.

After-images remained burned into Maskelyne's retinas. He'd glimpsed something he recognized . . . But what was it? Now he couldn't see a thing. 'I'm blinded,' he cried, and realized that he couldn't even hear his own words. The roaring sound still drummed in his ears. Yet even as he spoke, he realized that this sensory storm was already beginning to fade. Slowly, his vision began to return to normal. He heard himself breathing once more.

'Some water,' Kitchener said to Roberts. 'Fetch clean water.'

'No,' Maskelyne replied. 'I'm all right. I can see again. I can hear.' He set down the strange spectacles and then took a deep breath. His nerves felt utterly shredded. He was shaking. What was it he'd glimpsed during that terrible glare? A face? The more he thought about it, the more he felt sure that was it. *A hideous iron visage, scorched and blackened by fire.* 'Blame my own foolishness,' he said at last. 'I should have known better than to make assumptions. You are quite right, Kitchener. Normalcy is not a quality one should ever associate with the Unmer.' He shook his head clear of the last vestiges of the vision. 'Start bringing the crew over now. Leave the trove, but bring the gas welders and grab as much water, food, rope, tools and sailcloth as you can carry.'

'Sailcloth, captain?' Kitchener inquired.

'I want to put a spinnaker up on that tower,' Maskelyne replied. 'If there is a will at work here, we ought to give ourselves the opportunity to thwart it.'

Ianthe retreated into the darkness of her own mind. She found that she was breathing rapidly. What had happened? She'd been looking out at the cabin through Maskelyne's eyes. She saw the optical experiments and watched her host pick up the spectacles. She had looked out of his eyes in awe at the change in luminance when Maskelyne had first turned the wheel and then gasped at the abrupt disappearance of the two crewmen. And then . . .

Suddenly Ianthe had no longer been able to perceive the cabin at all. She had been standing right here, on the deck of Maskelyne's dredger, gazing up at the figurehead upon the Unmer ship. She had been looking at the scene *through her own eyes*.

When the *Excelsior* began to shudder violently, Granger knew he'd been away from the wheel too long. He vaulted up the final few steps and burst into the bridge to see the westernmost edge of the Glot Madera looming large to port. One side of the emperor's dragon-hunter was scraping along the prison façades, gouging deep scars into the stonework.

He swung the wheel hard to starboard and reversed the engine throttle, hoping to turn out the *Excelsior*'s bow, but the yacht's momentum continued to carry her along on her destructive path. Rubble crumbled and pattered across the deck. Metal groaned and shrieked as the ship's port bulwark crumpled. Granger cursed and slammed the throttle forward again. He didn't have time to worry about the hull.

The ship turned slowly. With a final screech of metal, she broke away from the bank and began steaming out into the centre of the canal. Golden sunlight reflected off the ship's copper-plated hull, illuminating the prison façades on either side of the channel as if by the radiance of some great golden lantern. Ahead of him, Granger could see the seaward opening of the Glot Madera with nothing beyond but the distant shimmering horizon.

CHAPTER 12

A VOICE FROM THE ASHES

18th Hu-Rain, 1457
24 degrees 16 minutes north
5 degrees 43 minutes west

*Aboard the deadship for two days now. Fog lifted yesterday
morning, and yet its bitter gloom remains in the hearts of all
aboard. This ironclad vessel seems determined to confound our
attempts to return to Scythe Island. Her engines sputter to a halt
whenever we deviate from a narrow range between 342° and
354°, as though the supply of electrical fluid to the tower
is suddenly quenched. We are being interfered with from afar.*

But by whom? And where are they trying to take us?

*Heading west nor'-west would bring us into the Haurstaf-
controlled waters around Awl and the Irillian Islands, leaving
us at the mercy of the Guild. The northern fringes of the empire
lie due east of here, from where we could easily secure passage to
Losoto. This margin between 342° and 354° leads nowhere but
the frozen wastes of Pertica, where we would surely perish among
the poisonous ice fields. In an attempt to regain some control, we
have raised a makeshift spinnaker on the ship's tower, yet it can
barely hold enough wind to maintain our current position against
these southerlies. It is as if nature herself is conspiring against us.
Abernathy removed the engine housing, but we have been unable*

to understand its workings. Amidst the myriad cables and glass lozenges he discovered a woman's pelvis.

These events and others have led the crew to believe that this is a haunted vessel. But how can that be? Can any consciousness survive death? If an answer to this question exists, then it must surely lie in Unmer lore, being so interwoven with infinity itself. An object viewed outside of Time must encompass every one of its states of being, from the nothingness before creation to the nothingness afterwards. And yet what if that object – a ship, for example – encompasses the essence of something that is larger than the physical universe, larger even than Time itself?

Is infinity woven into the fabric of this miserable ship?

Might it not then continue to act as a vessel for its dead crew?

Whatever the cause or the crucible turns out to be, there seems little doubt that a malign will is at work here. The chronographs and compasses we salvaged from the Mistress refuse to work here, and yet many of the Unmer trove artefacts we carried over have suddenly sprung to life, each glowing, chattering, or screeching as its dormant electrical fluids are reanimated. Most of the fresh produce we managed – in our great haste – to bring aboard has already rotted. It is as if the deadship's own corruption has flowed from its pores. Lucille suggested I delay the rot by freezing the stores in crespic salts, but I required every ounce of those chemicals to keep my last phial of void flies from thawing.

Everyone aboard has been troubled by nightmares.

I myself am haunted by visions of the Mistress's demise. Her loss has affected me deeply. She remained afloat for nearly two hours before the sea finally swallowed her. We stood upon the ironclad's deck and watched her disappear into the red-green brine. Mellor's second repair team had by then succeeded in cutting through into the engine room – but, alas, we could do nothing for the men trapped in that flooded compartment. The seawater had altered them beyond all hope of recovery.

Lucille has nightmares in which our son is dying, although these are undoubtedly caused by her fears over his persistently strange behaviour. Last night she awoke to discover that Jontney was missing from his cot, although our cabin door had been bolted. After a frantic search we found him crawling across the top deck towards the open sea. Lucille has now sworn to remain awake until we are safely home, but her exhaustion is evident.

The men avoid my gaze and say little to each other. Morale is fading, with anger swelling to fill the spaces. It is only a matter of time before violence breaks out. I must find a way to channel it before then. I fear someone will have to be sacrificed to save the others.

Objects have gone missing from my cabin, including two cans of water, a gem lantern, some coins and the Unmer spectacles. We have a thief aboard, a thief who seems intent on endangering the life of my son. Who here has the motive to do such a thing?

Someone knocked on the door. Maskelyne set down his pen and got up from the workbench. He opened the door to find Kitchener standing in the passageway. The sailor was standing over an open crate.

'We found these in a hidden compartment under the hold,' he said. 'We were about to throw them overboard, but I thought I'd better check with you first.'

Maskelyne looked down at the open box. It was almost completely full of dust, but he could see the edges of artefacts partially buried in there: heavy iron rings, wrapped with wires. He brushed away the dust and picked one up. The windings felt hot to the touch. A foul, burned metal odour came from them. 'How many are there altogether?' he asked.

'Twelve in each crate,' Kitchener said. 'And we pulled five crates out of the compartment. We stored our supplies down there first, but they rotted so fast you wouldn't believe. I had a few of the men start carrying what was left up into one of the bow cabins, while Roberts and me went looking for the source of the problem. We found the compartment quickly enough.' He hesitated. 'It wasn't just the rot, you see? The supplies had been moving about too.'

'Moving?'

'Our own boxes wouldn't stay in one place. We'd leave them alone for an hour, and come back to find that they'd slid right across the floor, like somebody had been moving them when nobody was looking. The men . . . well, you know how things go, sir. Talk of hearing whispers when no one was around, that sort of thing.'

Maskelyne touched his dust-smeared fingers to his tongue. 'Tastes like . . .'

'Bone marrow,' Kitchener said.

'It's an amplifier,' Maskelyne said. 'Unmer Brutalists used the consumption of human tissue to increase their energy.' He turned the ring over in his hand. It looked quite dead now. What else, he wondered, could it amplify? 'The effects you witnessed are just residual, amplification of decay, inertia, voices.'

'Then they go overboard, sir?'

'All of them.'

The crewman looked relieved.

'Except this one,' Maskelyne added. 'I'll keep it for study.' He placed the device on his desk. 'Is there anything else?'

Kitchener hesitated. 'It's the wheel console, sir,' he said. 'Abernathy got the inner sleeve open.' He rubbed his eyes and then took a deep breath. 'It's full of bones. We think maybe five or six infants.'

Maskelyne nodded. 'Human sacrifices. Tell Abernathy to close it up again before it unsettles the crew. What's our situation with water?'

'The purifier's still acting strangely, captain. The stuff coming out of it looks like urine and tastes about as good. Most of us are drinking it anyway. Got no choice.'

'Who's *not* drinking it?'

'Duncan, Abernathy, a few of the others. They say they'd rather die.'

Their situation was deteriorating far more quickly than Maskelyne had expected. At his rate, most of his crew would be dead before the ship made it back to Scythe Island. He sighed. 'I'll see what I can do. We need Abernathy with his wits intact. In the meantime, report anything else unusual to me.'

When Kitchener left, he returned to his journal and added a few final words.

> *Whoever our thief is, I will make a martyr of him.*
> *Ethan Maskelyne, Unnamed Unmer Icebreaker.*

Ianthe's heart was racing as she returned to the quiet darkness of her own body. Maskelyne's thief was closer to him than he could possibly imagine. But how could he ever suspect his own child?

She reached under her bunk and grabbed the children's blanket she'd hidden there and then unfolded it on her lap. There lay the spectacles Jontney had stolen for her, the lenses and engraved silver frames gleaming like treasure. Ianthe looked down at them for a long moment. Then, carefully, she slipped them over her eyes.

The cabin blossomed into existence before her, an explosion of light in the darkness. It was accompanied by a strange crackling sound that quickly faded. There was barely room to stand up and turn around, and yet there now seemed to be more crammed into this tiny space than in the whole of the outside world: the grain of the ancient timber panelling, the warped floor, her bunk, the black iron door handle and its keyhole. Moreover, she could hear the slosh of the waves against the hull, the ship booming and groaning all around her – hear them with her own useless ears!

Ianthe drank deeply of these new sensations, hardly able to control her excitement. Everything here appeared normal, bright and clear, without the flickering silver auras she had witnessed through Maskelyne's eyes. The spectacles, she supposed, had not been designed to be worn by two people at once.

But then she noticed something strange. Her bunk was no longer made up with the fresh sheets Lucille had given her, and her clothes were no longer piled in the corner where she'd dumped them. The cabin was entirely empty of everything she'd brought in here. Nothing remained but the dismal old walls. Whatever had happened to Maskelyne in the captain's quarters was happening to her, too. Objects were vanishing.

Could the goggles only perceive Unmer items?

Ianthe raised her hand in front of her face. There was nothing there at all, not even a trace. She looked down at her own body. Nothing. She was invisible, a ghost in her own cabin.

She slumped down on her bunk again, now gripped by despair. Why, when she'd finally been given the means by which to see, should her vision be so fatally flawed? What use were these lenses if they turned everything important into air?

Perhaps one could adjust the lenses?

Slowly, she turned the little wheel on the side of the frames. The cabin flickered violently, and that same crackling sound harried her ears. For a moment everything became blurred and indistinct. Her pile of clothes did not reappear. She spun the wheel around further now, tears now welling in her eyes. The cabin glowed with a phosphorous yellow light, and then abruptly became quite dark. She gasped with fright. Had she broken the blasted things? But then she realized she could still perceive variations in the deep shadows. For a moment it looked as if she was standing in a *woodland*. Was that the sound of wind rushing through the trees? The image flickered again and abruptly dissolved to complete black.

Frustrated now, Ianthe twisted the wheel all the way forward until it stopped.

The cabin became a shuddering blur again and then came into sharp focus. She thought she had glimpsed something moving quickly around her, like a passing shadow, but now that the lenses had settled she couldn't see anything like that now.

She could, however, see her clothes. They had appeared in the corner. Ianthe raised her hand in front of her eyes again, and this time she could perceive it quite clearly. She sprang up from the bunk and clapped her hands and laughed out loud. Everything around her was finally as it should be: the clothes, the sheets on the bunk, Jontney's blanket. The spectacles worked!

Now she was curious.

Ianthe twisted the little wheel backwards again. Her surroundings flickered, and the clothes vanished from the corner once more. She turned the wheel forward, and the clothes reappeared. She tried it several times, rocking the wheel backwards and forwards, watching everything she owned slip in and out of existence. Whatever was happening?

She spun the wheel back as far as it would go.

The cabin erupted in a blaze of light. A kaleidoscope of images clattered across her vision with the sound of bells and shrieks and angry wasps. Colours burst before her eyes like naval shells. And then as quickly as it had started, it stopped. Her surroundings resolved themselves once more. She was back in her cabin.

Only it was not the *same* cabin. Its proportions were identical, but the panelling looked new, agleam with varnish. Everything now seemed fresh and untarnished. A padded quilt of blue and gold diamonds lay across the bunk, while a silver watch and a miniature enamelled portrait hung from hooks above the pillow. The portrait was of a robust lady with orange hair and piercing violet eyes. A shelf had materialized beside the door, on which rested a bright copper gem lantern and an open book.

Ianthe heard men shouting somewhere above. They were speaking Unmer.

She got up and opened the door.

The corridor outside looked different from before. All the ash and decay had been swept away, leaving a neat passageway of polished dark wood. The shouting was louder here. It was definitely coming from above deck. Ianthe paused for a moment, then, nervously, crept along the corridor.

She recognized the wooden steps up to the main deck, even if she could not account for their miraculously rejuvenated condition. The whole ship now looked as if it might have been built yesterday. She climbed the steps and rested a hand on the hatch above her. Then she pushed it open.

A cacophony of shouting, roaring and strange whirrs and droning sounds filled the air. Black and yellow smoke engulfed the skies, shrouding the entire ship in deep and unnatural gloom. Ianthe's eyes widened. The sea itself was ablaze, with fires raging across the slate-grey waters as far as she could see. There were hundreds of ships out there, all Unmer vessels: men-o'-war and old electrical warships, wooden schooners, dragon-bone yachts, merchantmen and smaller pickets. Every one of them was burning.

As Ianthe turned, she realized with horror that her own vessel had not escaped the devastation. Her surroundings bustled with activity. A score of crewmen were pulling up buckets of seawater and emptying them across the deck in a desperate attempt to quench fires raging across the stern and starboard side. These men looked like no race of sailors Ianthe had ever seen. They were unusually tall and fine-featured, with long faces and narrow eyes. They wore brigandines and pauldrons of stiff black canvas, heavily ornamented with ciphers and numerals, and all had adorned themselves with rings, earrings and amulets wrought from silvery metals. Many had shorn their hair completely and bore Unmer glyphs, circles and strings of numbers tattooed across their naked skulls, while others had teased their hair and beards into thin tails wrapped with wire. Not one of them turned to look at Ianthe. She realized that she was a ghost among them.

Unmer sailors beat the sterncastle with sodden blankets, while their companions continued to drag up buckets of water. Smoke boiled through the struts of the ship's tower. Metal groaned. Embers darned the air like red flies. Meanwhile, two-man teams operated a number of strange bronze cannons fixed at regular intervals inside the bulwarks. The whirrs and droning sounds were coming from these devices. Ianthe watched as three of the teams on the starboard side fired together. Crackling circles of blue energy burst from the conical ends of the barrels and shot away into the fuming sky with a shrieking hum.

And there she saw the dragons.

Three of the great serpents bore down on the Unmer ship, their black wings thrashing the air, their long bodies clad in flashing silver armour. Each seemed as big as the ship itself, and on the back of the central, and largest, beast rode a man.

He was wearing golden armour and held aloft a spear to which he had attached a fluttering red pennant. Ianthe could not see him clearly from down here, but she fancied that he was as lean and tall as the sailors around her.

A bell began to ring somewhere aft. Men shouted:

'Kabash raka. Nol.'

'Sere, sere.'

Ianthe could not translate their cries, but she recognized the urgency in their voices.

Shrieks came from the ship's electrical weapons, as their Unmer operators let loose a further barrage. Blue circles of flame made vortexes through the tumbling smoke as they shot skywards. The dragons split formation, the outermost two peeling away as the central and largest of the three dropped low underneath the onslaught and dived towards the ship. Its armoured belly gleamed red by the light of the burning sea; its rider's long white hair blew behind his head.

Ianthe heard a cry from somewhere very close: 'Brutalist!'

She sensed movement nearby and shrank back as a hugely muscled man stepped past her, without as much as a glance in her direction. He was naked to the waist, his skin inked with hundreds of numerals and concentric circles, all stitched together with copper wire. He stood motionless, his fists resting on his hips and his teeth set as he glared up at the approaching serpent. One of those fists held a massive iron ring. *An Unmer Brutalist. A combat sorcerer.*

'Conquillas,' he yelled.

The dragon opened its maw and vented a spume of liquid fire.

The Brutalist abruptly dropped to one knee and raised the ring above his head. A sphere of green light bloomed from this object, encircling him instantly in a tremulous haze. Black sparks raced across the shimmering surface, accompanied by a series of frantic snapping sounds and the steadily building howl of gales as smoke rushed inwards towards the globe. The air itself was being consumed, driven out of existence. Ianthe realized that the iron ring was amplifying the sorcerer's own innate ability. And then came sounds, like the clattering of iron-shod hooves. Through the shifting curtains of radiance and shadow Ianthe caught a glimpse of the

Brutalist's face – grim and determined, his eyes fixed in concentration. His lips moved as he chanted words she could not hear.

Dragonfire burst across the ship, exploding through the struts of the tower and cascading down over the deck in blazing streams and drips. Incredibly, for a moment the Unmer sailors withstood the onslaught. Black fire erupted from their own flesh as they struggled to banish the heat and flames to non-existence. But the vacuums they were creating around themselves merely served to suck in more fire. It was too much. They were quickly overwhelmed, and man after man began to fall all around Ianthe, their screams filling the air. Ianthe cried out in terror as the liquid fire engulfed her – and it took twenty rapid heartbeats before she realized she felt no heat at all. She wasn't really here. *A ghost, a ghost, a ghost.* The fire washed up against the bulwark and broke and surged in waves to aft and stern. She found herself chanting the words over and over in her head, but it didn't lessen her fear.

The whole ship was burning. The tower crackled and spat and roared like an enormous pyre. Unmer sailors howled and rolled on the deck, consumed by fire, white-toothed grimaces visible in their scorched, bloody faces. The dragon rushed by overhead, a massive silver shape that whipped the flames in its wake.

The big man stood up.

Incredibly, the fire had not touched him at all. A circle of deck around him remained unblemished.

'Conquillas!' he yelled. 'Nash, nagir seen awar, Conquillas!'

And then he turned and looked directly at Ianthe.

Darkness.

Ianthe struggled against some unseen force. Someone was holding her tightly. She let her mind slip into the void and saw lights of people all around her. She was still surrounded, but she could no longer see by whom. She chose the nearest mind and hurled her consciousness into it.

She was still on the ship, but now it had returned to its former decrepit state. *Warped iron, ash, the blackened, rusted tower. But these men . . . ?* She had returned to the present, and these sailors standing around her were not Unmer, but Maskelyne's own crew. From this borrowed viewpoint she spied the first officer, Mellor, gripping her in his arms, while another sailor passed her spectacles over to Maskelyne himself. Four other men looked on.

Maskelyne put the spectacles on and stood for a long moment, gazing around him. Finally he took them off again and stared down at them grimly. 'Unmer memories,' he said. 'How long have you been wearing these? Do you even understand the danger?'

'Give them back,' she yelled.

Maskelyne just looked at her. 'They don't belong to you, young lady.'

Ianthe held her tongue.

Maskelyne studied her for a while longer, as if weighing something up in his mind. At last he said, 'You've been trying to harm my son.'

Ianthe snorted. 'What?'

'Scheming,' he went on. 'Ever since you've been aboard, you've been scheming, planning the murder of a child.'

'You killed my mother!'

Maskelyne's brow's rose. And then he frowned. 'Who told you that, Ianthe? It's not true.'

'Liar.'

Maskelyne glanced at Officer Mellor, who just shrugged. 'What do you want me to do?' he sighed. 'Over the side with her, I suppose?'

'She's too valuable,' Maskelyne replied. He sighed and

tapped the spectacles against his leg. 'Do you suppose Roberts could fashion some stocks from the packing crates?'

'Stocks, sir?'

'Head and wrists. You know the sort of thing.'

Mellor nodded.

'Strip her,' Maskelyne said. 'Put her in the stocks, and let each of the men have their way with her. God knows, we could all use something to lighten the mood a bit round here.' He looked wearily at the spectacles in his hand. 'Clean her up once they're done and lock her in her cabin.'

Mellor hesitated. 'Sir?'

Maskelyne's expression darkened. 'I gave you an order, First Officer.'

Ianthe's heart was thumping. Her limbs felt numb. She wanted to cry, but no tears came. Mellor started to drag her away, and for a moment she lost sight of herself.

Not one of Maskelyne's men was looking at her.

Granger looked out of the port window. The Ethugran pursuit ships were little more than a smudge of smoke on the western horizon. None of them had been able to match the *Excelsior*'s speed across open water. Granger himself had scarcely been able to believe the rate of knots she'd accomplished. He turned his attention to the shimmering sea ahead. Maskelyne's fortress sat atop Scythe Island's quartz cliffs like a crown. A faint mauve aura surrounded it, as though it had been built from whisperglass. Below the sheer rocky drop at its base, a private wharf extended from a sparkling crescent of beach. The industrial harbour and dredging operation would be tucked into the shadows just around the headland, momentarily out of sight.

Air exposure had dried out and toughened Granger's skin. His hair had fallen out, and his eyes smouldered like embers in the grey wasteland of his face. Occasionally he'd catch a glimpse of himself in the chromic sheen of a chronograph or some other ship's instrument, and it seemed to him that he looked like a man clad entirely in old leather armour. At other times he perceived himself as some hideous golem, a thing spawned from the depths of the earth itself. His own flesh creaked when he moved. His joints continued to throb dully and remained stiff enough to impede his movement. But he didn't care. He was alive. His muscles still worked. His brain still worked. And Maskelyne wasn't yet dead.

There was no way to approach the island without being seen, so Granger set a direct course. He slid he throttle forward again, and the emperor's yacht responded with a powerful surge of her engines.

As he took the *Excelsior* around the headland, the island's main deepwater docks, whale-oil factory and shipyard came into view. Two iron dredgers waited in their berths in the shadowy harbour. One of four dock cranes unloaded crates of goods from one, the operation managed by a team of stevedores. Gas welding torches flickered on the deck of the second ship, while another crane shifted enormous metal plates from the quayside over to the workers. Yellow-brown smoke rose from one of the whale-oil factory's three chimneys and bruised the sky above. Several labourers stopped to stare in Granger's direction, but none of them paused for long.

The *Excelsior* was an Imperial vessel, after all.

He took the yacht alongside the private quay and disengaged her engines. Without any crew present to fix the bow and stern lines, he'd have to do the work himself.

Securing the ship took longer than he'd hoped. He pitched out the fenders along the port side, then threw one of the heavy bow lines across a quayside cleat and used the forward steam winch to draw it tighter, but he was forced to return to the bridge and use the engines to counter stern drift. When everything was finally fast, he lowered the gangway and stepped onto the quayside.

The sun beat down on him from a clear blue sky. There was nobody about, no sign of life in the fortress up there on the cliffs, no sounds but the rush of waves on the beach and the distant banging from the shipyards. Granger walked up the quay.

When he drew near the beach, he stopped in surprise. This slender crescent that stretched away on both sides of the quay wasn't composed of sand or gravel as he'd expected, but rather of countless keys: iron keys, rusted keys, but mostly of keys that glinted in the sun like silver, forcing him to squint against the glare.

What were they doing here?

The question troubled him, although he couldn't say exactly why.

There must have been a thousand steps leading up the cliff to Maskelyne's fortress. By the time Granger reached the top, he was panting and dizzy with the heat. His dry grey skin felt as hot and dusty to the touch as the stones around the path. He paused for a minute and gazed out at the view. The Mare Lux stretched as far as he could see, the waves shining like chamfered copper. Ethugra crouched against the horizon in a watery haze, a single island of prison blocks rising from the curve of the earth. Four or five ships were approaching from that direction, but they wouldn't reach Scythe Island for several hours. Granger noted that the Haurstaf man-o'-war was not among them. He scanned the seas to the north and noticed a flash of white sail. Could that be her? Had Briana Marks abandoned her search for Ianthe? Or had she received some other intelligence?

Granger turned and surveyed the castle above him.

It had been constructed from blocks of amethyst quarried from the island's spine. Light bled through translucent purple edges and angles, so that the whole structure seemed to radiate an

273

internal glow, like a jellyfish. Two fluted pillars flanked an open doorway leading into the cool, plum-coloured interior of a barbican. Scalloped machicolations overhung the outer walls, but these were bereft of arrow loops and must surely have been designed for decoration. Private Banks would have been able to tell Granger more; it was the sort of place the young soldier had once enthused over. He looked up inside the barbican for murder holes, but saw none. The place appeared to be deserted.

Granger strolled inside.

The barbican inner door was closed, but there was a bell pull. Granger yanked the cord and heard a faint chime.

He waited.

A short while later, the door swung open to reveal a tidy courtyard walled and flagged with the same red-blue quartz. The air had a calm, floral quality. A stuffy little grey-haired man wearing servant's brocade stood there, blinking. He took one look at Granger and immediately tried to close the door again.

Granger booted it open, knocking the servant to the ground. 'Where's Maskelyne?' he demanded.

The man stared up at him in horror. 'What *are* you?'

'Where is your master?'

'Gone,' he replied. 'At sea.'

'Where's the girl?'

The man blinked. 'What girl?'

Granger stood on his neck.

'She's with him,' the servant gasped. 'They're . . . all . . . at . . . sea.'

'Where?'

'I don't know!'

Granger put more weight down on his boot.

The man sputtered something incomprehensible.

Granger removed his boot.

'They went . . . to find trove,' the servant said. 'I don't know where.'

Granger raised his boot again.

The servant lifted his hands in a pleading gesture. 'The Drowned will know,' he said. 'My master keeps a few specimens in his laboratory. They see and hear everything he does.' He stared at Granger. 'They look just like you.'

The servant – who gave his name as Garstone – led Granger through a series of plum-pink amethyst halls and corridors, and finally up a stairwell into a laboratory that occupied most of the southern half of the second floor. Dozens of Unmer machines in various stages of disassembly lay scattered about on workbenches, along with a number of old gem lanterns and tools. A writing desk occupied the centre of the chamber, upon which rested a pile of papers, a metal pen in its holder and a device consisting of a marble trapped in a pivoting tube of glass. Situated around the desk, four huge brine tanks – each containing a different colour of seawater – bubbled quietly. Wide tubes connected them to the ceiling. Two men sat in crimson Mare Regis brine, playing cards. A young girl looked out from the yellow brine Mare Sepsis tank, while a partially dissolved old man sat on a stool in the grass-green Mare Verdant tank. The final tank had been filled with Mare Lux brine. On the floor of this tank sat Creedy.

Granger's former sergeant and partner looked up, then stood up and stared out through the glass.

Garstone indicated Creedy's tank. 'That one still retains his senses,' he said. 'He's only been submerged a week or so. I'll go downstairs and fetch you some chalk and a slate.'

'Stay where you are,' Granger said. He walked over to Maskelyne's desk, snatched up some papers, then reached for the pen. But he stopped. Something was bothering him. He glanced back

275

at Creedy's tank and noticed three identical pens lying on the floor in there. Granger stepped back and studied the floor in front of the desk, where a slender gap betrayed the presence of a trapdoor. He grunted, then stepped to one side of the trapdoor before removing the pen. The trapdoor fell away, slamming against the inside of a shaft. From the darkness below came the smell of brine.

Granger started to write his message on a sheet of paper.

'Please,' Garstone said. 'Those are my master's private papers, his work, his experiments. He'll kill me if they are spoiled.' He came over to the desk, opened one of the drawers and took out a slate, which he handed to Granger.

Granger threw the slate aside and continued to scribble over Maskelyne's documents. Then he strolled over to the Mare Lux tank and held up his message to Creedy.

WHERE IS THE GIRL?

The brown seawater made Creedy seem huge and distorted. His eye lens dilated. He picked up a stub of chalk and a slate from the floor of the tank and wrote his reply.

FUCK YOU.

Granger scrawled another message on the back of the paper.

TELL ME, OR YOU DIE.

Creedy gave him an ugly grin. He wiped his slate clear and wrote:

COME GET ME.

Granger returned to the desk, where he gathered up all of Maskelyne's documents. He scrunched them up and piled them around the base of the tank, as Creedy looked on from his watery prison. Granger walked back to the desk and flipped it over. Maskelyne's glass device fell to the floor and shattered. A wire extending from the underside of the desk disappeared into a hole in the floor.

276

'What are you doing?' Garstone protested.

Granger ignored him. He hunted around the workbenches, searching through the tools, until he found a flat-headed screwdriver. He used this to disassemble the writing desk. In a short while he had a decent-sized pile of wood, which he piled around the documents at the base of Creedy's tank. Then he took out his knife and flint, and lit the paper. Flames blossomed.

Creedy thumped his fist against the inside of the glass. Garstone yelled at Granger to stop.

Granger held up his message again.

WHERE IS THE GIRL?

Creedy erased his slate and frantically scribbled a new message.

PUT OUT FIRE.

The flames had begun to take hold of the wood now, and were licking the walls of the tank, staining the glass black. Smoke began to fill the laboratory.

Creedy banged his slate against the tank.

PUT OUT FIRE.

Granger held his own sign higher.

WHERE IS THE GIRL?

Creedy scrubbed his slate clear again and wrote:

LOOKING FOR TROVE. WHISPRING VAL. M. REGIS.

The fabled treasure-hunting site. Dredgers had been scouring the Whispering Valley since its rediscovery three years ago. The valley held the ruins of an Unmer castle, destroyed and abandoned long before the rising seas had claimed it. The sheer number of weapons salvaged from the surrounding area led many captains to believe a great battle had taken place there.

Granger wrote another message.

HOW LONG?

But Garstone interjected. 'Ten days,' the servant said. 'He won't be back for months.'

Granger turned around and walked away from the tank. He left the fire burning.

'I won't let you do this,' Lucille said.

Maskelyne didn't look up from his work. He had snuffed the lights and opened the windows in order to examine the Pole Star through an unusually heavy refraction telescope. The device had been fitted with a lead plate over its larger lens, and yet, oddly, this did not obstruct his view. The Unmer archivist spectacles lay to one side. He had been too afraid to put them on again. 'Do what?' he muttered.

Her voice was low and cold in the darkness. 'You know exactly what I mean.'

Maskelyne peered through the telescope. Removing the lead plate caused the stars to blink out of existence. Only by replacing the plate could he observe the heavens. He assumed there must be some disguised hole or slit in the metal. Or the lead itself must somehow be acting as an optical element, which meant that it could not be lead. 'I had always intended for her conceive a child,' he said. 'Her talents ought to be passed on.'

'But not like this,' Lucille said.

'This ship has unmanned the crew—' he began.

'What does that have to do with anything?'

'The men are terrified,' Maskelyne said. 'Terrified of ghosts. Terrified of the dark. Terrified of their own shadows. Ianthe's punishment is necessary to strengthen the command hierarchy aboard this vessel. I'll go further, if I have to. If we are going to make it back home, I require my men to be more afraid of me than they are of the dead.'

'Half of them will refuse to do what you ask.'

Maskelyne set down the telescope and turned to face her.

He could hardly make her out in the gloom. 'You've spoken to them?' he asked. 'Or was your conversation just with Mellor?'

She was silent for a long moment. 'You never used to be so cruel, Ethan. What happened to you?'

He turned back to his experiments. 'Any man who refuses to carry out my orders will be thrown overboard.'

After a moment he heard the door shut softly behind him.

Maskelyne found himself gazing down at the Unmer spectacles, the other experiments abandoned. He had put this off too long. He picked up the lenses and examined them carefully, trying to see how the whisper-thin optical elements interacted, but he might as well have been staring into an insolvable labyrinth. He wrote in his journal:

> *The spectacles show an interpretation of the past. Does the device simply record perceptions, or did the Unmer discover a way to make a link between minds located elsewhere in Space/ Time? The Haurstaf command this talent, at least spatially. Is it possible that these spectacles are able to achieve the same feat, both spatially and temporally? Can I explain this in spatial and temporal terms?*

He thought for a moment, then added:

> *What if space was simply a measure of* variance, *where variance is the product of both the* distance *and the* difference *between any two things?*
>
> *If the* distance *between two particles is zero, the space between them must also be zero. Without space, attraction and repulsion forces cease to be.*
>
> *If the* difference *between two particles is zero, they are fundamentally identical. In such a case, the space between them*

must also be zero, regardless of the distance that separates them.
Effecting a change in one particle would therefore affect its twin,
even if that twin was a thousand miles distant.

It might explain how certain Unmer artefacts worked across vast distances. The jealous knife, the seeing knife and even the trio of small pyramids Maskelyne had dredged up at the start of this voyage. He put pen to paper again.

Time = A measure of the difference between one thing and itself.
For Time to exist in Space, there must be some sort of
change – some movement, spin, or oscillation. But if Space
is simply an ever-shifting sea of variance, then Time must
be relative. The Unmer's ability to manipulate Space might
conceivably be the very thing that allows them to manipulate
Time.

This made sense in terms of Brutalist magic, since various Unmer devices appeared to quicken or slow the speed of time. Food decayed rapidly in the presence of amplifiers. The Unmer themselves lived for hundreds of years. But even if their sorcerous devices could alter the flow of Time, or observe the past, they could not change the past. However, if – as he began to suspect – the spectacles actually exchanged the wearer's perceptions with those of a long-dead sorcerer, then that sorcerer would be able to peer out of the present owner's eyes, which implied that the past could be changed. And that was a paradox.

Maskelyne paced the cabin. He raised the spectacles to his face but then lowered them again. He stopped and sat down on the bed and gazed at the lenses for a long time, cursing his own fear. Then he took a deep breath and put them on again.

*

Dragonfires raged across the icebreaker's deck. Bodies lay everywhere. The Unmer Brutalist knelt among the flames, his flesh now scorched and blistered. He raised his fists as four great armoured serpents swept down from the skies. Conquillas rode the largest beast, his void bow now gripped in his gauntleted hands. He pulled back the bowstring and let an arrow fly.

Maskelyne turned the little wheel on the side of the frame, and the scene flickered backwards in time.

He was standing on the deck of the same ship. The electrical receiving tower loomed over him, its great torus shining in the midday sun. The black paint covering the iron deck and wheelhouse was old, revealing rust in places, but the vessel itself had not yet been damaged. There were as yet no energy weapons situated behind the bulwarks.

They were coming into a harbour full of Unmer warships. Maskelyne could hear the droning of the ironclad's engines, the rush of the sea against the hull and the pounding of metalworkers' hammers from the shore. The orange flames of welders' torches flickered on a score of docked vessels, while other – more sorcerous – lights danced here and there on ship and shore. They were refitting the fleet. After a moment, he recognized the city behind the water's edge. It was Losoto, but not as it existed now. The sea was blue, as yet untainted, and perhaps thirty yards lower than current levels. Tiers of fine white buildings covered a steep hill above the harbour, the streets curling around the rocky headland where Hu's City Palace now stood. The great winged shapes of dragons looped through the skies above, held in thrall by their Unmer masters.

The Unmer were preparing to meet the Haurstaf fleet at Awl, which meant Argusto Conquillas had already betrayed his kin. His lover, Queen Aria, would now break the Haurstaf's pledge of neutrality and bring her Guild to war against those who had enslaved the East. And yet Maskelyne suspected Conquillas hadn't given a damn about mankind. The legendary hunter loved nothing but himself and his precious dragons.

Maskelyne turned the wheel again, moving further back in time. The spectacles crackled as days and nights fluttered across his vision.

He found himself walking through an oak forest, most likely the Great Anean Forest to the north of Losoto. Emperor Hu had built his Summer Palace on a lake among these hills. The trail meandered down a slope towards a wooden shack with a stone chimney stack, from which Maskelyne could see smoke rising.

When he reached the porch, the door opened, and an old Unmer woman came out. She was wearing simple peasant clothes. She looked up at him and smiled. And then she hugged him fiercely.

'It's so good to see you,' she said in Unmer. 'Your father is down by the river, fishing, always fishing. Don't you dare go and join him until you've eaten something.'

She ushered him inside. The interior was simple, but tidy: a few stools around a table, a bed with a colourful woollen blanket, a kettle sitting on a iron wood stove. A collection of small glazed animals stood on a shelf under the window. The old woman opened a cupboard over the sink and took out two cups.

Maskelyne turned the wheel again, forwards this time. The image of the shack blurred into pulsing shadows and lights. He heard a sound like gunfire, followed by a gravelly roar. He turned the wheel all the way forwards, to the present.

Blinding white light assailed his eyes. The noise rose to an intolerable screech. Maskelyne cried out and tore the lenses from his face again.

Gods in Hell.

It was as if some universal force or barrier prevented the dead sorcerer from viewing the present through Maskelyne's eyes. Maskelyne could look back, but the sorcerer could not look forward beyond his own time. The cosmos would not allow a paradox. The spectacles were of little use to anyone but a historian.

Evidently Ianthe had never turned the wheel all the way forwards. Maskelyne thought about giving them back to her. She'd soon learn not to tamper with Unmer artefacts.

Later, perhaps later. He looked down at his notes, and added:

If Space is the distance and the difference between two objects,
what happens in places when Space is zero?

Maskelyne rummaged through the box on the workbench until he found a matched pair of magnets. He pulled them apart, then pushed the north poles towards each other, until he felt them repelling each other. Then he turned one magnet around and noted the attraction between unlike poles. It seemed to him that the material in one pole was identical to the other. He picked up his pen again.

Can Space be stretched and compressed? Are the forces of
attraction and repulsion witnessed between poles merely the
tendency for such stressed spaces to reach an equilibrium
determined by the mean variance of the surrounding universe?
As the variance between two points is reduced, the energy
required to further compress Space increases exponentially,
until that space is compressed to zero. The energy contained in
such minutiae must be considerable indeed. Is there a horizon
where forces of attraction and repulsion no longer apply?

Could our universe have once been a single invariant point, perhaps one of many such points, containing vast amounts of Space in ultra-compressed form? What if the expansion and contraction of Space continues? Do tiny knots of super-compressed Space still remain in the heart of everything? Such knots must contain identical particles, trapped together and yet unable to repel each other until variance is introduced. Opposing particles would gather at the horizon (or horizons – if space is truly waveform), and yet be unable to come any closer. Furthermore, if compressed Space has no physical quantity, then each of these knots would act like a vacuum pump, drawing a constant flow of uncompressed Space (created by variant particles) into itself. What if we called this force gravity?

Maskelyne set down his pen again and gazed out of the window. The old ship creaked and groaned around him, rocked by the sea. He thought of the ocean currents, and it seemed to him that Space might flow in a similar fashion. It was all degrees of variance. He lifted one of the magnets and let it drop. It hit the workbench with a *thud.*

One wonders if it is possible for enough knots of super-compressed Space to gather together and thus provide an overwhelmingly powerful force of attraction? Such an object would become progressively larger as it sucked more and more of the cosmos into itself – stabilizing only when it reached a point of true invariance.

Is it possible to release the energy within these knots – within the heart of matter itself? The sudden expansion of Space must surely be absorbed by the particles around it, radiating outwards over time until equilibrium is achieved once more. If this assumption is correct, then these radiation waves created by the birth of the universe itself must still be detectable. Indeed, the universe must continue to expand wherever knots of super-

284

compressed Space are split apart. To an observer at any point of expansion, it would seem that that point was itself the heart of the cosmos. Ultimately, variance might only exist between a few massive knots of ultra-compressed Space. Space will thin as the universe dies. But as long as a trace of variance remains between the last dark leviathans, then a breath of Space remains. Like massive ships sailing a vaporous and ever-diminishing sea, it is not inconceivable to imagine a collision between them. Were such a collision to occur, these ships might break apart, spilling their holds and thus creating a new sea through which the remaining vessels might continue to sail.

Maskelyne set down his pen and rubbed his temples. He was making too many assumptions, sailing down too many channels without stopping to look around him. How did any of this account for the electrical fluids used by the Unmer? Were they merely the propagation of variance? And what about the expansion of heated gas? Did adding energy to a system expand Space only when there *was* Space to expand? He lacked any mechanism aboard this vessel with which to test his theories. Such sorcery belonged only to the Unmer.

He gazed out of the window at the setting sun, marvelling at the ferocity of its fires, which now turned the sky and sea to blood. It was just one of countless stars in a cosmos he could not understand. The universe was so vast and unknowable, so far beyond imagination. Had the Unmer even fully understood what they were doing?

Lucille didn't come to bed that night. Maskelyne lay in his bed and could not sleep. Whenever he closed his eyes he saw Unmer warships in a harbour that no longer existed. The old wooden ship pitched and growled, as gales whipped rags of spume from the Mare Lux and flung them against the cabin windows. It was growing cold.

At some point he must have slept, because he woke in the dark before dawn, gasping and terrified, certain that someone had placed the Unmer spectacles over his eyes. He could not shake the feeling that someone had been watching him.

Had he been dreaming?

He recalled something . . .

Adrift in the vacuum, spheres of starlight expanding into dead vacuum. He had dreamed of an explosion in the darkness, a great fuming bubble of energy, its edges uncertain. It grew larger than imagination. He realized that the particles of light were separating as they flew apart, leaving waves of energy in their wake, leaving variance. There could be no space between them because it had not yet been created. Space and Time existed only in the great froth of energy they left behind. The shortest distance between different particles was a wave. Space itself was merely the potential between any two points. He saw the universe as ripples of energy expanding across a pond and bouncing back, but the pond did not really exist, only the ripples.

The dull glow of morning shone through the windows. Maskelyne sat up and shivered. He must have fallen asleep again. He got up and got dressed and then took a long draught of water from his personal supply. Then he glanced at his journal.

At the bottom of the page he spotted a paragraph that he didn't recognize. He sat down slowly, and picked up the journal. The passage was undoubtedly written in his handwriting, but he had no recollection of ever doing so. It was a riddle.

Two brothers were separated at birth. They lived in the same house, and often spoke to one another at the supper table, although they never met. Each married the same two women,

*who bore them the same two sons. The world perceived them
as mad, and yet they themselves perceived the world as quite
normal. What quality did the brothers lack?*

Maskelyne felt queasy and woolly-headed, as though the
lenses had given him a hangover. Was he now writing things in
his sleep? How on earth had Ianthe managed to wear them for so
long?

He called for Kitchener to inquire about their progress and
was told that the stocks had been built and bolted to the midships
deck. Maskelyne instructed him to assemble the crew. He did not
ask about his wife. He did not want to know where she was.

He went back to his journal.

*My experiences with the lenses lead me to believe that Unmer
sorcery is concerned with variance. If our universe is an
expanding sea of variance, and if it does indeed conglomerate
in places to form knots of ultra-compressed Space, thinning the
remaining cosmos, then might our universe be only one of such
spatial reactions? Should invariance not exist between separate
universes, even if it is nothing more than a slender thread? Have
the Unmer found one or more of these threads? Are they somehow
able to manipulate them, to transfer energy and matter between
them? Is there a network, a series of hidden tunnels that reach
beyond our own universe?*

*One wonders if a map of such paths exists. Is this the object
I have been looking for? Is this what the deranged Drowned wish
me to find? A human man with knowledge of such pathways
could wield the same terrifying powers as the Unmer, while
remaining immune to the Haurstaf.*

*Compared to Unmer sorcery, the Haurstaf's mental powers
seem crude and simple. And yet they are devastatingly effective.
If the Unmer are the wizards of a thousand wavelengths, the*

Haurstaf are the masters of one. That the latter should have so much power over the minds of the former cannot be a coincidence. The Unmer have disturbed the natural order of the cosmos, and the cosmos has reacted to restore equilibrium.

It occurs to me that the Unmer, so used to wandering the halls of infinity, perhaps perceive this tiny world with indifference. And yet, for Jontney's sake, I cannot afford to do the same.

Ianthe had been secured in the stocks. The men stood around in silence. Maskelyne closed the sterncastle hatch behind him and walked over. Ianthe was staring absently at the deck, breathing heavily. He looked around for Lucille, but she was nowhere in sight.

'Strip her,' he said to Mellor.

The first officer nodded.

'Wait.'

Maskelyne turned to see his wife, now pushing through the crowd of men. She was carrying Jontney in her arms.

'I thought your son could learn something from this,' she said.

Maskelyne just glared at her.

'He ought to know what sort of man his father is.'

'Take him inside,' Maskelyne said.

Lucille didn't move.

'Take him inside!'

She stared at him defiantly. Jontney began to cry, his sobs the only human sound upon that deck.

Maskelyne was losing respect with every passing moment. He couldn't allow himself to be humiliated like this, not now – when their very survival depended on it. Lucille was forcing him into a situation where he'd have to hurt her to protect her. Didn't she realize how self-destructive her actions were? And then in a flash of inspiration he saw the truth. She *wanted* to push him. She wanted him to hurt her. Nothing else made sense. She was trying to help him. He was almost overwhelmed with a feeling of love for her.

'Mellor,' he said breathlessly, 'Take my son inside.'

The first officer hesitated for a heartbeat, then stepped towards Lucille.

'No,' she said.

Mellor reached for the boy.

Jontney shrieked.

Lucille turned away, but Mellor already had a grip of the child's jumper.

'Don't,' she said.

She tried to get away. Mellor scuffled with her, trying to pull the child free from her arms. She struck out at him repeatedly with her free hand, scratching his face, but Mellor did not retaliate. Jontney howled.

And suddenly Mellor had the boy in his arms. He broke away, walking swiftly towards the sterncastle.

Lucille was sobbing now. 'Don't do this, Ethan, please. I know you think you have to, but you don't.'

She was playing her part perfectly. At that moment this poor sobbing wretch of a woman looked more beautiful to him than ever before. His heart swelled with love. He made a fist and swung it at her head, punching her across the temple. She staggered but didn't fall, and then looked up at him with wide, stunned eyes. He smiled and hit her again, much harder.

This time she went down. She clamped a hand to her nose and it came away bloody.

'You coward!' she cried.

He kicked her in the chest, and heard her gasp. He felt the weight of her body move against his boot. She began to wail. Snot and blood bubbled from her nose. She beat the palms of her hands against the rolling deck. 'You're a coward, Ethan,' she said again. 'That's why you do these things. You're afraid of your men, of me, of everyone you've ever met. You're afraid because you don't understand them. All these foolish *theories* you make up to justify everything . . . the truth is, you're just a coward.'

Maskelyne recognized every word she spoke for the sacrifice that it was. She was trying to make it easier for him to punish her. The thought made his heart shudder with pain and love. Each blow he administered hurt him more than it hurt her. He wanted to pick her up and carry her away, and yet by doing so he would be betraying her. He wavered for an instant. He didn't know if he could match her courage.

She spat at him.

He was about to respond when he heard Mellor shouting. 'Ships to port.'

The first officer stood by the sterncastle hatch, gazing out to sea. Maskelyne realized that every man of the crew was looking in the same direction or moving to the port side to get a better view.

'Men-o'-war,' someone shouted. 'Two of them.'

Maskelyne could see them now: two old, Irillian tall ships, their hulls clad in red dragon scale. They were three-masted, with foretops on their bowsprits and silver cutwaters. The fire-power from any one vessel's triple gun decks would be enough to reduce the Unmer icebreaker to toothpicks. They were running near to full sail, despite the gales, and they were headed this way.

'It's the Haurstaf,' Ianthe said.

CHAPTER 13

A CANNON BATTLE AT SEA

Granger had been standing at the wheel for most of the night, and yet he hadn't spotted the lights he'd been hoping to see. Dawn had come and gone, and still nothing. He was red-eyed and edgy with exhaustion, but nothing could tempt him to sleep now. The Whispering Valley lay nor'-nor'-west of Scythe Island, and Briana Marks's vessel, *Irillian Herald*, had been steaming out of Ethugra in that general direction when he'd had last seen it, which meant that it seemed likely the Haurstaf witch had received some intelligence about Ianthe's position. Granger's detour to Scythe Island had cost him valuable time. Now he wasn't just chasing Maskelyne, but Marks herself.

There were two sextants and two chronometers on the bridge. An elaborate gold- and platinum-plated sextant sat in a special mount on the navigation console beside a matching chronograph. Both bore the Imperial seal along with the engraving: *Excelsior, His Majesty Emperor Jilak Hu*. But Granger found an old brass Valcinder-made set of instruments in a metal box behind the pipe-housing hatch. He took noon sight with these latter devices. From the worn look of them, this particular set had been much favoured by the *Excelsior*'s own navigator.

Granger located the almanacs, sight tables and charts in a drawer under the console. He calculated his position. He drew a pencil line across the map, stared at it and then rechecked his figures. The *Excelsior* had covered more distance than he would have believed possible. At this rate of knots he certainly faced no danger from the pursuing Ethugran fleet. Furthermore, he would reach the Whispering Valley in another six days, half the time it would have taken Maskelyne in his heavy dredger. But was he moving fast enough to overtake the *Herald?*

Just how many ships would he encounter?

And how could he hope to meet them in battle?

Granger leaned back against the navigation console, thinking. He couldn't ram another vessel. The dragon-hunter's sleek, lightweight hull would not fare well against an iron dredger or a scale-plated man-o'-war. If he encountered his enemy at night, he might try a drift-and-jump or even a raft flank in order to board the other ship unseen. But then Maskelyne and Banks both maintained full crews, while Granger was alone. The *Excelsior* had enough broadside to represent a serious threat, but he couldn't effectively man her cannons single-handedly. That was the root of his problem. Hu's imperial yacht had not been designed to be sailed by a single man. She required forty-eight men on her gun deck to operate her cannons alone, with another twenty or so to carry up powder and shot.

There had to be a way.

He set his heading, and locked down the wheel before scanning the horizon with the navigator's telescope. Satisfied that he wasn't about to collide with anything, he set off for the gun deck.

The stairs down aggravated his joints, but the pain wasn't enough to worry him. He'd found that, by simply working his muscles from time to time, he could loosen up his limbs. A few moments of agony was better than seizing up altogether. Eventually the stiffness would diminish. The burning sensations had almost gone from his toughened flesh, although he hadn't yet become accustomed to the feel of his rough grey skin under his own fingers. It felt as if he'd been boiled in a suit of leathers. He wondered briefly if he was arrow-proof, before dismissing the thought. The important thing was that his wits remained intact, for he had a problem to solve.

Amber reflections played across the bone arches in the gun deck. The emperor's cannons gleamed as if they had been forged yesterday. Granger found the smell of warm metal relaxing. He'd spent many years on many such decks, if not on one as fine as this. *Twenty-four cannons: Imperial Ferredales retrofitted with flint-lock mechanisms.* He could load them all by hand, although it might take him a couple of hours to do so, and he could use the lanyards to fire them one after another, but if he was down here in the gun deck, then he couldn't be at the helm. And fire-power was nothing without tactics.

Granger paced the deck. Given the time available to him, it seemed unlikely that he could devise and build a mechanical method for pulling the lanyards from the bridge. What if he simply removed them altogether, replacing the ropes with fuse cord running directly into the flintlocks? He'd seen spools of cord down in the powder deck. That was certainly much simpler. Fuse cord could burn at up to ten feet a second, depending on its composition. It would be simple enough to run a length of it from the bridge, down through the pipe ducts, and use a cigar to light it.

Just like in Kol Gu, ''38.

He smiled at the memory of that campaign. *Three hundred enemy goldtooths coming up the hill towards our camp, a hundred fuse cords and three chemical matches.* Hu had sent them to eliminate a Kol Gu Archipelago warlord, just the latest in a line of pirates who had fought each other over that shrinking island group. Granger could no longer remember his name. Creedy had used two of the matches to light his cigar, before Banks pointed out that the enemy was still at least an hour away. That had been almost four years before Weaverbrook, before Imperial Infiltration Unit 7 became known as the Gravediggers. *Banks, Springer, Lombeck, Swan, Tummel, Longacre.* So many faces that existed only in his memories.

Fuse cord.

The spools in the powder deck turned out to be a disappointment. Most of the cord was the cheap, low-grade stuff used in mining, with a burn rate of perhaps half a foot per second. The distance from the bridge down through the pipe ducts to the gun deck had to be at least a hundred and twenty feet. One twenty feet at half a foot per second gave him four minutes between the time he ignited the fuse and the cannon's detonation, which was hardly ideal for a pitched battle. What's more, he'd have to figure out a way of insulating one cord from another within the pipe ducts, while allowing them each enough oxygen to burn.

Only three hundred feet of the fuse cord was of higher fast-burn grade, which would allow him to rig two cannons to fire with a twelve-second delay between ignition and detonation.

It wasn't good enough.

Granger carried the spools of quick cord back up to the gun room. There had to be better solution. He began the heavy work of loading and tamping each of the cannons. He had hours ahead to figure it out.

Briana Marks drew her hair out of the collar of her white woollen tunic, and let it fall over her shoulders. She was standing at the back of the *Irillian Herald*'s wheelhouse, quietly watching the crew at work. Her captain, Erasmus Howlish, was leaning over the map table, speaking quietly to the navigator about their course. A former Losotan privateer, Howlish still bore the raised white lines across the back of his hands where a Guild torturer had once applied his lash. He wore his black hair in a long plait in defiance of protocol, but Briana allowed him this small conceit. One had to be flexible when employing one's former enemies.

The helmsman stood rigidly at the wheel, his eyes fixed on the horizon beyond the *Herald*'s foredeck. She was an old Valcinder man-o'-war, refitted in Awl to provide the sort of luxury accommodation expected by the Guild, but Briana cared little for the silks and silver and teak down in the staterooms. She preferred the simple functionality of the wheelhouse. Its position high on the quarterdeck gave her an uninterrupted view of the surrounding sea. This hemisphere of Unmer duskglass contained nothing but the ship's wheel console, a navigation station and a curved steel bench, over which Briana had placed her whaleskin cloak. The Unmer glass served to filter out much of the late-afternoon sun, along with most of the fury of the wind and sea. Through the glass dome she could see the rise and plunge of copper-coloured waves as gales whipped across the Mare Lux, driving amber breakers. Spume battered the *Herald*'s bow, but here in the dome it remained warm and peaceful.

Two telepaths, one on each of the *Herald*'s sister men-o'-war, had been relaying information to her throughout their search for Maskelyne. Briana knew her distant compatriots only as Pascal and Windflower, both young Losotan yellow-grade psychics who had been attached to the Guild navy since completion of their training. She had probably seen them numerous times at the school in Awl, but for now they remained disembodied voices to her. She had no desire to learn more about them than their names and rank. En route to the Whispering Valley, they had happened upon a strange ironclad vessel a few minutes south of the Border Waters. It was an Unmer deadship of archaic design using a makeshift spinnaker to tack south – and it was being captained by the very man they had been looking for.

Briana's own ship was still three leagues to the south-east, and it frustrated her that she couldn't see the pair of red-hulled Haurstaf craft converging on the ironclad.

An Unmer deadship.

They informed her that it looked like an icebreaker – perhaps one of the very ships sent south from Pertica to join the Unmer fleet at the battle at Awl. If so, nobody had seen its type at sea for almost three hundred years. Briana reached out with her mind, feeling for the presence of Unmer consciousness.

She heard her companions psytalking in hushed tones, but she didn't bother to listen in. She felt for the ship, searching for any psychic presence aboard. And then she noticed something odd. An echo? Not quite. It was *almost* a reverberation, like the resonant silence an Unmer tuning fork makes when its tone is below human hearing.

Are either of you sensing this?

Sensing what? Windflower said.

There are no Unmer aboard, Pascal added. *I've already checked.*

Briana sent her thoughts back across the sea. *Follow the ironclad, but hold off until I arrive.*

Yes, sister, Windflower said.

She's not going anywhere against these winds, Pascal remarked impatiently. *How long will you be?*

Briana shot back her reply, *As long as it takes to get there.*

Driven forward by the same strong southerlies that were impeding the deadship's progress, the *Irillian Herald* sped across the Mare Lux. Her mainsail and spinnaker billowed; the rigging creaked. Fine metallic spray blew across her top deck. At noon the ship's navigator struggled to take sight on the pitching boards. The afternoon remained bright, but blustery. A pod of nomios broke the surface of the waters to port and followed the Haurstaf ship for over an hour, flashing through the waves like chrome shuttles. Briana stood on the foredeck, scanning the northern horizon. She remained in contact with her Guild sisters, but there was little more to report. Maskelyne had retreated below decks and seemed content to remain out of sight. The deadship continued her creeping zigzag progress south, while her crew made no attempt to contact their pursuers. Finally, as the sun sank towards the edge of the world and the western sea turned a coppery-red, the *Herald*'s lookout gave a shout.

At first, Briana could see nothing, and then in the distance she spotted the yellow-white glow of sailcloth bobbing in the slanting sunlight. The two Haurstaf ships were coming about, following the darker iron vessel as she tacked to the south-east. There was a sudden commotion around Briana as the *Herald*'s crew turned the ship to intercept.

They came upon the deadship at dusk. Briana stood on the bridge, coordinating between Howlish and the captains of the other two Haurstaf vessels. As the *Herald* ran from the south, the rearmost Guild vessel, *Trumpet*, passed Maskelyne's stern, on a broad reach that caused her to lift and crash through the wave tops, while her sister, *Radiant Song* beat hard to cover the western flank. At Briana's orders, *Trumpet* fired a warning shot down the ironclad's port side, but the deadship merely continued on her present course and speed.

'We'll have to turn about, ma'am,' Howlish said. 'Or run the length of her guns at close range.'

Are those guns likely to be operational?

He made no reply.

'Are those guns likely to be operational?' she repeated, aloud this time. 'That ship doesn't look like much.'

'I'd rather not find out, ma'am,' Howlish replied.

'What do you suggest?'

The captain thought for a moment. 'She can't outrun us.

With that spinnaker, it's amazing she's making any progress at all. So she'll need to barge a path between us. I imagine she'll probably snap tack to put her stern against the *Song* and her broadside to the *Trumpet*'s bow. That would keep two of the three cannon batteries out of line.' He scratched his nose. 'That's what I would do, ma'am.'

'And how should we respond?'

'The fact that Maskelyne is using that spinnaker suggests that his engines are dead. It might be advisable to have the *Song* haul off to starboard and chainshot the ironclad's sail. That will take away what little manoeuvrability she has left.' He nodded to himself. 'It would give the captain a good reason to cooperate with us.' He inclined his head towards the waves. 'Using the corvus will be risky in these seas.'

Briana nodded. 'All right.' She sent the orders to the psychics aboard the other two vessels.

After a moment, the *Song* began to turn, bringing her cannons to bear on Maskelyne's ironclad. A series of flashes ran along the side of the Haurstaf vessel, followed a heartbeat later by the crackling boom of artillery fire. The Haurstaf shot tore through the ironclad's sail, reducing it to ribbons.

Smoke drifted over the waters.

'She's trying to turn now,' Captain Howlish remarked. 'We'll see.'

The remains of the Unmer ship's spinnaker began to luff and snap. Briana could see Maskelyne's crew rushing about on deck, trying to pinch their rudely rigged sail, but it was hopeless. The ironclad had stalled mid-way through her turn.

'She's in irons,' Howlish said. 'Shall we haul close?'

'What about her guns?'

'She's dead in the water,' Howlish said. 'Maskelyne's only hope now is rescue.'

'Very well, let's board her.'

'He might try to board us,' the captain added. 'You might want to let the *Song* or the *Trumpet* approach first.'

'We have the largest force here, Captain,' Briana replied. 'Have them stand at arms.'

'As you say, ma'am.'

Howlish did as Briana ordered; he sailed the *Herald* around the stern of the deadship and then hauled her in close to the wind. He ordered her crew to lower their own spinnaker and then to ready themselves to repel boarders. The Unmer vessel did not fire her strange cannons. Indeed, as the distance between the two ships closed it became apparent that those weapons were little more than pillars of slag. Maskelyne's crew had no means with with to defend themselves against the Haurstaf men-o'-war. Howlish's long experience as a privateer became apparent, for he managed to heave to within three yards of the stricken ship.

The deadship did not appear to have sustained any additional damage from the attack, but Maskelyne's crew, under the shadow of that scorched metal tower, were nevertheless eager to secure the grapples thrown over by the Guild mariners. Briana joined Howlish amidships just as the Haurstaf vessel dropped her corvus, the iron spikes clanging against the derelict's metal-plated deck. No shots were fired; indeed, not one of Maskelyne's crew was even armed.

The metaphysicist himself appeared on deck. He took one look at the tattered sail, then turned to the Haurstaf vessel and vaulted up onto the boarding ramp. He strode over to the *Herald* without a care in the world, forcing the Guild mariners already on the ramp to retreat.

Briana had seen him once before, many years ago at Hu's court. Although they'd never spoken, back then she'd been struck by the confidence and vigour in his stride. He'd been a scholar of wide renown among the Losotan privileged classes, a man of considerable means and an Unmer expert who had advised the emperor himself on several occasions. Yet this creature standing before her now was a shade of that former man. He was dirty, unshaven, stooped and painfully gaunt. His dark eyes glanced everywhere, as though his former arrogance had been replaced by a nervous and unsettled energy.

'Thank you for coming to our aid,' he said. 'Please pass my regards on to your cannoneers.'

'You did not seem inclined to stop,' Briana remarked.

Maskelyne stepped aside as Kevin Lum, the *Irillian Herald*'s first officer, led a cohort of armed men across the corvus onto the stricken deadship. Most of the Guild sailors began rounding up Maskelyne's crew, while others threw open the fore, mid-ship and sterncastle hatches and began their search of the vessel. Maskelyne turned back to Briana. 'You evidently want something from us,' he said. 'If I'd offered to parley, you might have taken advantage of our unfortunate position. However, Guild maritime law prohibits you from abandoning us on a powerless ship. I believe that would be seen as murder.'

'He's right,' Howlish said. 'The moment we shredded their sail, we made them enemy combatants. As long as they don't resist our boarding party, we have to take them with us.'

Briana cursed under her breath. Ethan Maskelyne hadn't changed at all.

Just then there was a commotion on the deadship's deck, as two Guild sailors dragged a young woman through the sterncastle hatch. She was about fifteen, olive-skinned, with a mess of black hair. She kicked and screamed at them, 'Let me go, you idiots, I need to get back . . . you don't . . . understand.'

Briana smiled. 'Does that look like resistance to you, Captain Howlish?'

'Very much so, ma'am.'

Maskelyne's eyes narrowed. He looked at the girl with marked distaste. 'This young lady,' he said, 'is not part of my crew.'

Out of the hatch behind her stepped a woman with a small child in her arms. She was bruised and bleeding and walked with a limp. One of the Guild sailors helped her towards the corvus, but she hesitated before stepping aboard.

Maskelyne's expression softened. 'My wife and son,' he said. 'I'm afraid this voyage has been hard on them both.'

Briana turned to Howlish. 'Just get them all aboard.'

'Very good, ma'am.'

'May I ask where you're heading?' Maskelyne said.

'Awl,' Briana replied.

Maskelyne frowned. 'I don't suppose you could drop us off at Scythe Island? I'd make it worth your while.'

She gave him a thin smile.

'That's what I thought.'

Evacuation of the deadship continued until after dark. Three of the *Herald*'s crew escorted the metaphysicist and his family to a stateroom, where their needs were to be attended to under armed guard. Maskelyne's wife Lucille began to sob. Her relief at departing that derelict vessel was palpable. The boy, Jontney, simply watched everything with quiet wonder. Maskelyne's crewmen were herded into the brig, although they seemed much less dissatisfied with their new accommodation than any of its former occupants. Howlish ordered his mariners to strip the ironclad of anything valuable and stow it in their own hold.

Ianthe was a problem. The girl seemed determined to remain on the deadship. She struggled against her two captors, scratching and trying to bite them until they restrained her thoroughly. Even then she wouldn't stop screaming.

Briana fired a mental blast directly at the girl, a wordless surge of anger that should have stunned a trained psychic. It was enough to stress the entire Haurstaf telepathic network, eliciting moans of pain and fright from every corner of the empire. Ianthe, however, did not appear to notice it. Briana stood and watched the girl for a long moment, this furious crow-haired child. *Have I made a mistake?* She reached out with her mind again, more tentatively this time, hoping to sense the source of the girl's anguish. At first she perceived nothing at all, just the featureless plane of human consciousness around her – a place known to Guild witches as the Harmonic Reservoir, where ripples of Haurstaf thought could resonate undetected by the great mass of humanity in the depths below. And then she noticed a glitch, an almost imperceptible fracture in the surface of these perfect waters. The reservoir was cracked. Curious, Briana pushed her thoughts towards that tiny imperfection . . .

Suddenly she was on the brink of falling. There was nothing to grab hold of – no emotions, no thoughts at all, just a dark and bottomless void below the sea, a vacuum that seemed to want to drag the Haurstaf witch inside.

Briana recoiled.

She found herself standing on the *Herald*'s deck once more, clutching Howlish's arm to steady herself. She had never sensed anything like that before. It was like a force of nature, a storm, but without wind or substance – an abyss.

'Are you all right, ma'am?' Howlish asked.

Briana couldn't answer. She was still fumbling to locate her own wits. What had just happened? She raised her head to find Ianthe gazing at her with a curiously detached look in her eyes.

'Did you just do something?' the girl said.

Briana swallowed, then took a deep breath. Her thoughts still spun. That break in the reservoir had been so tiny she might easily have overlooked it, and yet it had contained a space so vast it had overwhelmed her. 'We're not trying to harm you,' she said.

'Then let me go,' Ianthe said. 'Get these idiots off me!'

Briana nodded to the Guild sailors, who released the girl.

Ianthe bolted immediately. She ran back across the boarding ramp onto the Unmer ship. Briana watched her go with mute incomprehension, before she realized what was happening. She cursed and raced after the girl.

'Ianthe, wait!'

The girl reached the sterncastle hatch, threw it open and plunged inside.

Moments behind, Briana hurried down the steps after the girl. She found herself in a narrow wooden space with doors leading off both sides. It took her eyes a moment to adjust to the gloom – and then she spotted Ianthe stumbling along the passageway ahead, her hands held out like those of a blind woman trying to feel her way. The girl reached a door at the end of the passageway and burst through it.

This door led to the captain's cabin, and here Briana found Ianthe fumbling about on her hands and knees, searching for something.

'You can't stay here,' Briana said quietly.

'Help me find them.'

'Find what?'

'The lenses, the spectacles.'

'What?'

Ianthe gave a shriek of frustration. 'Spectacles! Unmer spectacles!'

Briana glanced around her. There was a bed, a wardrobe, a chest and a large workbench under the stern windows that held an amazing assortment of telescopes, boxes, prisms, magnets and wires. Among all these objects she spotted a slender silver-frame pair of spectacles.

'That's them!' Ianthe cried. She got to her feet, snatched the spectacles from the table and put them on with shaking hands. Then she stared at Briana. 'There,' she said. 'Now we can go.'

Night was encroaching by the time they sailed away. Clouds covered the stars, and the Mare Lux glimmered faintly like old brass in last rays of dusk. Briana stood on the *Herald*'s sterncastle and watched the icebreaker recede into the distance. It seemed to her that the abandoned ship was turning in the wind, its melted figurehead coming about to watch them depart. She smelled rain and lifted her face to the skies. Banks of thundercloud moved overhead, as dense and massive as continents. Lightning pulsed soundlessly across the far northern horizon and again, dimly, in the west. When she lowered her gaze again, the deadship had disappeared.

A few of the *Herald*'s crew were busy setting out basins and pots to collect rainwater from the expected storm. As she crossed the deck, Briana acknowledged their greetings with a few sullen nods. She didn't stop to talk. What did she have to say to these people? She went below deck to the galley, where she filled a bowl with thrice-boiled shrimp and land kelp and poured two mugs of coffee. She put the lot on a tray and took it to Ianthe's cabin.

The girl was lying on her bunk, still wearing her spectacles. She turned round as Briana came in.

'Hungry?' Briana said.

Ianthe ignored her.

Briana set the tray down on a small table beside the bunk, then sat down on the stool opposite. Steam rose from the bowl of shrimp, filling the cabin with the vaguely unpleasant aroma of detoxified seafood. The room was large and airy with freshly painted white clapboarding and a floor of crushed pearl. On the wall beside the wardrobe hung a painting of the Guild Palace at Awl – its black and pyrite towers and minarets in striking contrast to the deep greens of the surrounding forest. In the background rose the mountains that formed the spine of Irillia, their layered peaks blurring into a gaseous blue haze. Briana looked at the girl. 'Must you wear those things?'

'What do you care?'

'Actually I *do* care. They're Unmer, so they're probably dangerous. I don't want you running to me when your brain starts trickling out through your nose.'

Ianthe grunted.

Briana took a sip of her coffee. Gently, she reached out with her mind again, gliding across the abstract plane of the Harmonic Reservoir until she found the same glitch she'd discovered earlier. This time she approached more cautiously, stopping when she felt the pull of the void beyond. It wasn't like touching the mind of another psychic, but more like exposing herself to a crack in the substance of perception itself. Beyond lay powerful forces, and yet they seemed raw and utterly mindless. It was like standing on the edge of an abyss with the wind howling at her back; another step and she'd lose herself completely. She backed away quickly, afraid to go further. Ianthe gave no sign that she'd even noticed Briana's presence in that other realm. But she had noticed before, Briana recalled. *Did you just do something?*

'Your father told me you're good at finding trove,' she said.

'He's not my father.'

'He seemed to think he was.'

'I don't care what he thinks.'

Briana set her coffee down again. 'Why don't you tell me about it?'

'You're wasting your time,' Ianthe said. 'I can't read minds.'

'Very few psychics are born with any demonstrable ability,' Briana said. 'It takes years of training to develop the skill. But we always find some indication of potential in raw recruits, some quirk of personality that gives them away.' She thought for a moment. 'Have you ever guessed what someone was going to say before they said it, or been thinking about someone you haven't seen in a while, and then suddenly bumped into them in the street?'

Ianthe turned away and folded her arms. 'No.'

'So finding trove is just a lucky guess?'

The girl continued to stare at the wall through those etched Unmer lenses.

'An odd little talent like that could be indicative of a greater sensitivity,' Briana said. 'I mean, I'm not mocking you. A gift for treasure-hunting is always going to make you useful to people like Maskelyne and your father. You might even make a good living from it yourself one day. But I think that with the proper training you could be capable of so much more. Wouldn't you like the opportunity to develop your abilities more thoroughly, in comfortable surroundings, with girls of your own age?'

Ianthe snorted. 'You don't know anything.'

'That's true,' Briana said. 'But what do you know about the Haurstaf?'

Ianthe shrugged.

'We provide various services,' Briana said, 'intelligence gathering, communications, containment and security. Our clients range from humble merchants to emperors.'

'Containment?' Ianthe said. 'You mean oppression?'

'We contain the Unmer humanely,' Briana said, 'without the need for walls. Our psychics simply monitor their movements and punish them if they step outside their allocated territory. We certainly don't kill them unless we have to.' She looked at Ianthe. 'Would you rather we allowed them to wander free?'

Ianthe's arms tightened around herself. 'You brought war to Evensraum.'

'Hu brought war to Evensraum—'

'But you helped him,' Ianthe retorted. 'You make it possible.'

'We facilitate the implementation of our clients' strategies, if that's what you mean,' Briana said. 'But we never start wars. In fact, our presence in a conflict situation usually saves lives. The bombardment at Weaverbrook happened because Hu chose *not* to use a Guild psychic. He didn't make that mistake a second time.'

The girl snorted. 'I didn't see any psychics on the Evensraum side.'

Briana was silent for a while. Finally she said, 'The Guild protects itself, first and foremost. If that means adopting a mercenary attitude at times, then that is what we must do. Any other race of people would do the same.' She finished her coffee and set down the cup. 'I'm not your enemy, Ianthe. I'm trying to help you.'

Ianthe gazed at the painting on the wall. 'We're going to Awl, aren't we?'

'That's right.'

'What about Maskelyne?'

'What do you mean?'

'I don't want him near me.'

'That can be arranged,' Briana said. 'If it turns out he held a psychic against her will, he'll be punished accordingly.'

Ianthe turned to face her. 'Executed?'

'Would you like that?'

Ianthe didn't answer. She looked at the painting again. 'But what if you discover I'm *not* psychic?'

Briana laid a hand on Ianthe's arm. 'Eat your supper before it gets cold.'

★

Briana woke to the sound of rain pattering against the windows and the ever-present chatter of Haurstaf conversation: . . . *warlord Pria Ramad seeks to advocate his rights in Chal over . . . six thousand nomio on the twenty-first . . . state that any aggressors will be dealt with using the utmost . . . seven units hiding in the Fryling Bay . . . bring to 254 degrees 20 minutes . . .* Briana tuned it out as best she could, then got out of bed and padded naked across the carpet to the window. The ship rolled heavily under her bare feet. It was a dull, blustery morning outside. Rain streaked the window panes. The sea bucked and frothed under a leaden ceiling of cloud.

Her stateroom stretched across the breadth of the ship's stern from port to starboard, with duskglass windows on three sides. Normally light and spacious, today the chamber seemed as gloomy as a cave. Briana opened the shutters of her gem lanterns, brightening the room. From her wardrobe she chose a pair of white linen breeches, a spider-silk blouse and her padded woollen jacket from Losoto. She looked at herself in the mirror for a long time, counting every tiny wrinkle and imperfection on her skin. With every year that passed she felt more and more compelled to chart the process of age. It was like watching an enemy's every manoeuvre: necessary, but depressing. She thought about Ianthe's perfect skin and deeply lustrous hair and allowed herself a single, luxurious moment of hate.

Then she sat down and poured herself a glass of water, sharpened with a drop of poppy oil and a pinch of anemone.

. . . *borakai nineteen six eleven passing through from . . . administer the final payments through an intermediary . . . would not be welcome . . . are you awake . . . ? mark two two four, listening . . . out with his jurisdiction on the first . . .*

Shut up!

The chatter stopped. Briana found herself shivering, suddenly afraid that her outburst would be recognized for what it was.

A reaction prompted by the anguish of too many foreign thoughts passing through her head. The others would think that she was breaking down. *Am I breaking down?* Briana kept that thought to herself. She counted to five, slowly, trying to relax her thumping heart. Communication across the entire empire had momentarily ceased, and Briana could feel the Haurstaf network trembling with uncertainty. She swallowed hard and sent out another message:

Keep all communication on a peer-to-peer basis until further notice. The next voice I hear is going to find herself cleaning Port Awl horses with her tongue. She could almost hear a thousand groans reverberating through the ensuing silence. Yellow- and amber-grade psychics would be unable to maintain such intense concentration for long.

The lookouts have spotted a ship to the south.

Briana was about to lash out in anger, when she recognized the voice in her head. It was Pascal, aboard her companion ship, *Trumpet.*

It's Hu's steam yacht, the young psychic added. *And it's following us.*

Granger?

Briana pulled on her boots, gloves and storm mask, wrapped her whaleskin cloak around her shoulders and hurried above deck. Freezing rain lashed her cloak, and the wind snapped at the sails above her. Howlish had trimmed the mainsail and taken down the spinnaker. Even so, the storm was forcing him to luff. The rigging thrummed like plucked wire; the masts groaned. Masked crewmen were busy tying down the spinnaker and securing the fore jib. Under the heavy clouds the Mare Lux looked as dark and angry as she had ever seen it, a great shuddering cauldron of brine. She could smell it through the filters of her mask. The *Herald*'s sister ships, *Trumpet* and *Radiant Song*, lay some distance off the starboard side, their red hulls rising and then crashing down through the waves. Briana grabbed a rail and scanned the southern horizon. *There! A single plume of smoke.*

Howlish was in a jovial mood. After Briana had removed her mask and dumped it on the wheelhouse bench, he said. 'Good morning, ma'am. Fine day for it, don't you think?'

Briana shucked off her cloak. 'A fine day for what?'

'For sinking the emperor's flagship, ma'am.' The captain exchanged a glance with the navigation officer.

'Don't tempt me,' she replied.

'We could always claim he attacked us.'

She smiled thinly. 'Not even Hu's going to believe that one man operated the *Excelsior*'s cannon arsenal. Are there any other vessels in sight?'

'The horizon's clear, ma'am.'

'Can we run ahead of her?'

Howlish shook his head. 'Not in this wind, ma'am,' he said. 'We'd only tear the *Herald* to pieces. The *Excelsior*'s engines give her a huge power advantage over us.' He glanced at his pocket watch. 'At her present speed she'll be alongside in about ninety minutes.'

Briana peeled off her gloves and threw them down on top of her cloak. Dealing with an angry father was the last thing she needed right now, especially one who didn't appear to be the sort to give up and go away quietly. How would Ianthe react? Briana sighed. Sinking her old man might be the best solution after all.

'Ready the ship for battle,' she said to Howlish. 'And signal the *Trumpet* and *Song* to do likewise.'

'Signal?' Howlish asked. 'You want us to use the signal lantern?'

Briana nodded. 'I don't want these orders passing through the Haurstaf network,' she said. 'Pascal and Windflower are to maintain telepathic silence. We need to be able to deny all knowledge. And not a word of this to Ianthe.'

310

'Very good, ma'am.'

Howlish ordered full munitions crews to the gun decks and the *Herald*'s sails trimmed further, sacrificing speed for increased manoeuvrability in these high winds. Guild riflemen took up positions fore and aft, while the rest of the crew battened down in readiness. Signal lanterns flashed between the three Haurstaf vessels.

They were ready long before the *Excelsior* drew near.

Briana watched the steam yacht approach through the stern-castle telescope. She was two-thirds the length of the Haurstaf men-o'-war, but much lower and sleeker, with a single mast and three funnels behind the bridge. Judging by the amount of smoke she was disgorging, Granger was driving her engines hard. Her copper-clad bow cut through the waves like a dagger. Her cannon hatches were open, and the breeches of those antique guns gleamed along both sides of her hull. The sight of those guns unsettled Briana, but she tried to dismiss her nerves. Granger couldn't possibly have found a crew to man them.

She returned to the hush of the wheelhouse to find Howlish in quiet conversation with the helmsman, signal officer and navigator. Howlish looked up at her arrival. 'The *Trumpet* and *Song* are about to engage,' he said. 'They'll fall back and signal a warning while we maintain our speed and heading. With any luck we can draw him between their guns. I don't expect the *Excelsior* to give us much trouble.'

Briana nodded, but the uneasy feeling remained in her gut.

'There they go now,' Howlish said.

The two Haurstaf men-o'-war dropped behind, the *Song* maintaining her present heading while the *Trumpet* close-hauled westward across the *Herald*'s stern. Granger's steam yacht did not deviate from its heading. It came thundering on, smoke pouring from its three funnels as it cleaved through the waves towards the waiting men-o'-war.

311

'The *Trumpet* will start to signal now,' Howlish said.

Briana saw the *Trumpet*'s signal lantern flashing repeatedly upon her quarterdeck. Granger made no reply but kept to his same steady course. He was going to pass between the two warships. 'Why would he do that?' Briana said. 'Why expose himself to danger?' She watched the steam yacht draw level with the *Trumpet*.

Howlish nodded to the signal officer. 'Tell them to open fire.'

Crack, crack, crack, crack, crack.

The sound of cannon blasts rattled the dome's duskglass panes. Flashes of firelight lit the waters between Granger's yacht and the Haurstaf man-o'-war. A heartbeat passed before Briana realized that the flashes had come from the *wrong* ship. Granger's vessel had opened fire on the warship.

'The *Excelsior* just fired on the *Trumpet*,' the signal officer said.

Howlish looked aghast. 'He has a crew aboard?'

'He's blown a hole in her gun deck.'

'Why isn't she responding?' Howlish said.

'I see fires, captain.'

Crack, crack, crack, crack.

The steam yacht fired on the *Trumpet* again. Through the drifting smoke, Briana glimpsed fires blooming amidst the warship's shattered gun deck. And then an explosion blew out the man-o'-war's entire port side, throwing a cloud of wood splinters and dragon scales across the dark waters.

Boom, boom, boom.

'The *Song* is responding, Captain.'

By now the second Haurstaf warship had closed on the yacht and opened fire. A score of artillery shells tore through the yacht's port bulwark and bowsprit, shredding her foredeck and the upper corner of her wheelhouse. Scraps of wood puffed skywards, but the shots had been too high to do any real damage.

Crack, crack, crack, crack . . .

'Port-side guns.'

The steam yacht's cannons fired with a series of yellow flashes. Six, eight, then ten Valcinder cannons pummelled the *Song*'s hull in a full broadside attack. And still the shots kept coming, twelve, fifteen guns, the cannonballs smashing the warship's armour to dust.

'The bastard has a full gun crew in there,' Howlish said.

The *Trumpet* was fully ablaze now and going down fast. Smoke engulfed the *Song*, but Briana thought she spied flames there too. The second warship was turning now, attempting to take herself out of the path of Granger's guns while bringing her remaining cannons to bear on the yacht's stern.

Briana heard Pascal's voice burst into her head: *We need assistance. I'm calling the Guild.*

Do not *contact the Guild*, Briana replied. *Maintain silence.*

We're on fire, Pascal exclaimed. *Going down fast.*

Maintain silence, Briana insisted. She broadcast the order to both women on the two men-o'-war. *We're coming to help.* She turned to Captain Howlish and said, 'Do something, help them.'

'Two seventy degrees,' Howlish growled to the helmsman. 'Guns to bear on the enemy's bow.'

'Aye, Captain.'

We're safe enough. Briana told herself. However mad Granger was, he wasn't likely to kill his own daughter.

GD – DENY – REQ/VERIFY – CONFIRM – REQ/ASSIST

Granger punched the commands into the comspool and depressed the release valve. The orders would be meaningless to any crewman, but Granger didn't have any crewmen aboard. What he did have was a comspool on the gun deck retrofitted with the flintlocks he'd removed from forty-eight Valcinder Ferredales and attached to the breech vents of those same cannons via a web of rapid-burning fuse cord. For good measure, he'd dipped the ends of each fuse in a concoction of sulphur, glue and yellow phosphorus.

It seemed to be doing the trick.

A few seconds later he heard the concussions from below deck as the cannons fired. Four more rounds of heavy iron shot smashed into the Haurstaf warship on his port side. She was trying to reach now, which was fine by Granger. Evidently the warship's captain did not know the state of his own gun deck.

Granger's real target lay ahead of him. The *Irillian Herald* was turning about now, bringing her guns to bear on his bow. And Granger had every intention of letting her do so. He picked up one of the maps lying on the console and wrote across it in big bold letters:

THIS IS YOUR FATHER, IANTHE. I'M TAKING YOU HOME.

'Ethan Maskelyne wishes to speak to you, ma'am.'

Briana turned to find one of the men she'd left guarding Maskelyne's stateroom standing in the wheelhouse doorway. 'What?'

'He says it is extremely important.'

'Not now.' She dismissed the guard with a wave of her hand. Everything seemed to be happening at once. Howlish was bringing the ship into battle. The signal officer was flashing the *Song*, trying to ascertain the extent of her damage.

The guard glanced around him, then spoke in a low voice. 'I beg your pardon, ma'am, but he says the captain is an idiot and is doing exactly what Colonel Granger wants him to.'

'How the hell does Maskelyne know what's going on?'

The guard shrugged. 'I don't know, ma'am. He was the one who told me.'

'And now you believe he knows how to get us out of this?'

'He's Ethan Maskelyne, ma'am.'

Briana sighed. She turned to Howlish. 'How long till we're in range?'

'Minutes, ma'am.'

'Then I don't have time,' she said to the guard. 'If it's so important, he can write me a note.' She sent the guard away.

By now Howlish had turned the Haurstaf warship into the wind. The deck pitched as the *Herald*'s sails took up the strain. Rain lashed the wheelhouse glass. Spume burst against the bulwark and showered the Guild mariners fighting to control the boom. To starboard, Granger's yacht bore down on them at tremendous speed, her funnels steaming, her bow rising and then crashing down through the dark and frothing waters.

'Range shot,' Howlish said.

First officer Lum rang the bell pipe, then waited for a heartbeat and rang it again. The comspool on the navigation console began to chatter in response. He scanned the tape. 'Confirmed. Ranging to starboard now, sir.'

Moments later, one of the *Herald*'s cannon fired. A single shell flew out across the sea, but landed short of Granger's yacht.

'Range is good,' Howlish said. 'One through twenty, red stations.'

The first officer rang the bell pipe again, then paused before making three more rings in rapid succession. The comspool began chattering almost immediately. 'Red stations one through twenty firing now, sir. Confirmed.'

This time twenty of the *Herald*'s cannons fired at once. The combined noise of the concussions rattled the duskglass panes. A great burst of smoke erupted from the side of the warship as

315

twenty artillery shells arced across the space between the two ships. Most of the missiles flew wide, but two of them found their target. The uppermost section of the steam yacht's bow imploded as the heavy shells tore through.

'Strike confirmed,' the first officer said. 'Upper bow.'

The bell pipe rang twice.

'Re-range for six knots and scatter,' Howlish said. 'Twenty through forty, red stations.'

'Twenty through forty. Re-range and scatter. Aye, sir.'

The second barrage tore part of the roof off the steam yacht's wheelhouse and blew a funnel cleat and cable away, but the Haurstaf gunners missed the bow entirely. The other ship came steaming straight towards them, faster than ever.

Howlish yawned. 'Bear away,' he said. 'Ready chasers. Port guns one through twenty, red stations. Fire crews to stand by.'

'She's not deviating, sir,' the first officer said.

'She'll deviate. Ring the commands, Officer Lum.'

Bells sounded outside. The helmsman spun the wheel. Out on the storm-blown deck Guild mariners began hauling in the mainsail. Slowly, the warship turned her stern towards the approaching yacht.

The first officer frowned. 'She's still not deviating, sir,' he said in a hushed voice. 'She going to hit us.'

Howlish's eyes narrowed. 'What is the madman doing? He'll sink us both. Fire the chasers.'

The first officer began madly ringing the bell pipe.

But Briana could see that it was too late. Granger's ship was going to crash into them.

'Broad reach,' Howlish cried.

The comspool began to chatter out tape.

'Chasers ready, sir.'

'Leave the chasers. Put us on a broad reach now.'

The helmsman spun the wheel back.

Through the driving rain Briana saw the steam yacht bearing down on them, waves crashing against its thunderbolt-wielding figurehead. A solitary figure stood at the wheel amidst the shattered bridge. The *Herald*'s stern was now inching away, but not fast enough. Briana tensed for the impact.

'He's turning,' Howlish said. 'Too late, too late.'

At the last instant, the other vessel began to turn aside, but it was a futile manoeuvre.

The yacht struck the stern of the warship with an impact that almost knocked Briana off her feet. From the rear came a great crash of timbers and groan of metal. Men stumbled and fell across the rain-swept deck. The Haurstaf ship yawed wildly, her hull actually rising a few feet out of the water. The yacht kept coming, her vast momentum carrying her along as she scraped along the side of the warship with a juddering shriek. For an instant the two vessels were almost side by side. They began to part.

And then a second concussion thudded through the warship's timbers. Granger's yacht broke away, turning downwind as the man-o'-war rocked heavily and righted itself. In the Haurstaf wheelhouse, the helmsman fought against the wheel. The first officer steadied himself and rushed over to the comspool.

'Port-side guns,' Howlish said. 'All of them.'

'We're still turning, sir.'

Howlish scowled at the helmsman. 'Close haul.'

The helmsman was still struggling with the wheel. 'I can't . . . I think we've lost our rudder, captain.'

The captain snorted. 'Then how can we *possibly* be turning *into* the wind?'

'I don't know, sir.'

But it was true. The man-o'-war continued to pivot, as some unseen force pushed it into the very face of the gale, turning their broadside away from the departing yacht. The mainsail and jib began to luff. They were losing control.

The whole warship gave a sudden, violent jerk.

Captain Howlish fell against the navigation console. Briana grabbed the first officer's arm to steady herself. From somewhere aft came a long, low groan.

The man-o'-war began to move backwards.

Shouts came from outside. Howlish threw open the wheelhouse door to better hear his crewmen, admitting a blast of rain and wind. Briana lifted the hood of her whaleskin cloak and moved over beside him. 'Trouble?' she asked.

Three crewmen clung to the poop deck, leaning over the taffarell as they examined the wrecked stern by the light of a gem lantern. One of them was shouting something, but the wind stole his voice.

Howlish waved a fourth crewman over. 'What is going on?'

The man looked up and said, 'We've been harpooned, sir.'

'What?'

'A dragon harpoon, captain. Biggest one I've ever seen. It's buried deep in the stern post, down at the waterline. She's using it to tow us.'

'Tow us?'

'Aye, Captain. The steam yacht is towing us behind her.'

CHAPTER 14

HOW TO SINK A SHIP

Granger turned off the gas torch, lifted his mask and examined the cable welds with eyes blurred by exhaustion. He had secured the heavy tow line by wrapping it around three of the gun deck's steel-reinforced dragon-bone arches before finally welding it fast. He glanced over at the rearmost cannon hatch, through which the cable disappeared. The bulkhead had buckled under the strain, but it would hold well enough. Raising the back of the gun carriage with a chain winch had allowed him to give the harpoon the required trajectory – down into the stern post where it met the waterline – but the recoil had badly damaged the old cannon itself.

Finding everything secure, he wondered if he ought to check on the engines. He was pushing them close to their design limits. But he felt too weary to venture down there right now. The helm was locked on course, the man-o'-war secured behind him, and he had fuel enough to drag the bastard for a hundred leagues – more than enough to take them where he needed to go. The thing about men-o'-war was that they had a deep draught. And the thing about the *Excelsior* was that she had much a shallower draught. And that was going to make her mightily easy to ground in coastal waters.

But now he badly needed sleep.

He wandered aft to the emperor's private suite.

Hu's living areas comprised a warren of deeply lustrous rosewood, hauled up from undersea forests. Some of the blood-coloured beams looked thousands of years old. Free-flowing partitions and arches made from the boughs of once-living trees divided the space between the hull into numerous nooks, each illuminated by a different-coloured gem lantern. It gave the impression of wandering through a woodland carnival. The furniture had been made in the same style, all rich dark curves lacquered to a high sheen – the sort of rustic elegance popular in Losoto that was neither rustic nor, Granger felt, particularly elegant.

In the largest of these convoluted wooded spaces Granger found an enormous circular bed set on eight gilt pedestals, each carved into the image of Hu himself. He frowned at it with disapproval but sat down anyway and took off his boots. He lay back into a mattress as soft as air and found himself staring up at his own grotesque reflection. The emperor had fitted a mirror to the ceiling. He sat up again and rubbed his eyes and went to find the head.

Hundreds of bottles, tins and jars packed the wooden shelves above the sink – a formidable collection of perfumes, lotions, medicines and creams. Granger picked up a jar of Potelemy's Canker Sore Solution, popped it open and sniffed the contents. The odour brought a brief smile to his face. Permanganate of potash. He'd once had Banks and Creedy mix this stuff with bottles of Doctor Cooper's Famous Sweetwater to make liquid fire. They'd poured the lot down the air shaft of an enemy bunker in Dunbar. With the right mixture of toiletries you could burn a man's skin clean off.

While he took a piss he let his gaze wander over the shelves – Butterflower Soap, Parafranio's Wonder Water, Sparkling Eye Drops, Face Polish, Silk Lustre Dust, Royal Lady

Skin Soft Cream, Fragrance of the Glade – mentally sorting the explosive components and combustibles from the useless stuff. Most of these powders and potions cost more than he'd made in a month's soldiering. Even the tins could be utilized by submerging them in lye and filling balloons with the explosive gas given off. It appalled him that any man could waste such potential by slapping it on his face.

He flushed the head, then went back to the bed chamber and eased his wounded body down into the sheets. That horrible, burning-eyed visage stared back at him from the mirror in the ceiling. It occurred to him that Ianthe might look through his eyes, so he closed them. He lay there for a long time, gazing into the darkness behind his eyelids, thinking about her. Then he got up again and went back to the head. He took the jar of Royal Lady Skin Soft Cream from the shelf and weighed it in his hand. Stupid thing. But he opened the jar anyway and scooped some out and rubbed it into the leathery folds of his face.

After he'd finished, he lay back down on the bed. That hideous face in the ceiling mirror, now daubed with white cream, mocked him. Granger grabbed the sheets and pillows from the bed and set off back to the bridge. It made more sense to sleep there, after all.

'What do you want?' Briana asked.

Maskelyne looked up from his writing desk. 'Sister Marks,' he said. He set down his pencil and stood up. 'Actually, I want to help you.'

Briana glanced around the stateroom. This luxurious accommodation was usually reserved for visiting clients, and no expense had been spared on the deep Evensraum rugs, gilt furniture and clamshell lantern shades. Lucille was reclining on a white leather carasole bench with a glass of wine in her hand. Her bruises

ALAN CAMPBELL

looked shocking in the bright white light. Painted toys lay scattered across the floor around Maskelyne's son, who took one look at Briana and then crawled over to hide behind his mother's legs.

'As I understand it,' Maskelyne said, 'Colonel Granger has sunk your escort ships and is now dragging this vessel to some unknown destination.'

Briana opened her mouth to speak, but Maskelyne held up his hand.

'The harpoon is lodged in the *Herald*'s stern post below the waterline,' he went on, 'making it impossible to reach without diving equipment – which, of course, you lack. Nevertheless, our kidnapper cannot board us, nor fire upon us without risking the life of his own dear child.'

'He's—' Briana tried to interject.

'Furthermore,' the metaphysicist added, 'Colonel Granger must assume that you have already summoned aid telepathically, and so he must act quickly. What, then, are his options?'

'Obviously,' Briana said, 'he's going to turn this kidnapping into a political statement.'

Maskelyne's eyes opened in mild surprise. 'Precisely,' he replied. 'How many cultures have found themselves *liberated* because they could not afford the psychic services their own enemies relied upon?' His dark eyes gleamed. 'What do you imagine would happen, for example, if our renegade colonel decided to run the Haurstaf flagship aground on the Evensraum coast?' He smiled. 'Have you ever seen an animal carcass lying across an ant trail? The bones are so clean they look like they've been polished.'

Briana smiled thinly.

'Would I be correct in assuming you haven't contacted Awl yet?'

'I'm perfectly capable of dealing with this situation myself, Mr Maskelyne.'

'Well, quite,' he said. 'We wouldn't want your sisters to think you incapable, would we?'

Briana felt her face redden. 'Be careful, Mr Maskelyne. You are in no position to lecture others.'

'I apologize,' Maskelyne said. 'I meant no disrespect.'

'Of course not,' Briana replied. She placed her hands on her hips and gazed around the room, thinking. Jontney peered out from behind his mother's legs, but Lucille avoided her eyes. Finally, she faced Maskelyne again. 'Well, what do you propose?'

He indicated the door. 'If I can just have access to my equipment?'

The Unmer artefacts salvaged from the deadship had been packed into crates and stacked across the breadth of the *Herald*'s hold, lashed down under oilcloth. Maskelyne immediately began untying cords and pulling the coverings aside. While Briana waited nearby, the metaphysicist uncovered boxes of telescopes and prisms, and nautical instruments taken from the Unmer ironclad, along with crates of brine-damaged goods that looked more like seabed trove. Finally, he gave a grunt of surprise and pulled something out. It was a heavy iron ring, wrapped in wire and covered in grey dust. He blew away some of the dust and held it up.

'What is that?' she asked.

'An amplifier,' Maskelyne replied. 'It uses one form of energy to amplify another.' He turned it over in his hands. 'I strongly recommend you throw it over the side before all the fresh produce aboard begins to rot.' He set the ring down again and continued rummaging around in the trove for a while longer. Eventually he gave a sigh. 'My blunderbuss,' he said. 'It isn't here.'

Briana shook her head. 'I've no idea where it is.'

'It was in a long, narrow box,' he said, 'packed with crespic salts to keep it cold.'

'They might have put it in the arms locker.'

Briana summoned the lieutenant at arms, who led them to the arms locker, where they did indeed locate a box fitting Maskelyne's description. The metaphysicist opened the lid and took out the weapon. It was made of brass and dragon-bone, with a dark glass phial fitted underneath the stock. Curls of ice smoke rose from its flared barrel.

Maskelyne grinned like someone who had encountered an old friend. 'Perfect,' he said. 'We'll have that line off in an instant.'

Briana frowned. 'You plan to shoot it?'

'I do.'

'With *that* old thing?'

He nodded.

She felt like she'd been swindled. 'That's your great plan?'

'This *old thing* is no ordinary weapon,' Maskelyne said, holding the gun towards her. 'This phial contains Unmer void flies.'

A moment of silence passed between them.

'Crespic salts are used to regulate the temperature of the ammunition,' Maskelyne said. 'Once frozen inside this phial, the flies remain quite inactive. The barrel is designed to act as a thermal gradient along which the flies are induced to pass once the phial is punctured, thus creating a directional vortex of considerable destructive force, while preserving both the weapon and its operator from harm.'

'You brought *void flies* aboard my vessel?'

'Your crew brought them aboard.'

'And you didn't think to *tell anyone* about it?' Briana lifted her hands in exasperation. 'What would have happened if they'd got loose?' She shuddered to imagine the bloodshed such an event would have caused – a ship riddled with tiny holes; a *crew* riddled with tiny holes.

Maskelyne grinned again. 'Now that we have established the

worth of such a weapon in our present circumstances,' he said, 'we can start to negotiate a price.'

'A *price*? For what exactly?'

'Void flies aren't exactly easy to come by, you know.'

The *Herald*'s engineers had constructed a wooden derrick overhanging her stern, allowing a man to be lowered down over the rear of the ship to the smashed rudder by way of a pulley system. First officer Lum looked on as two of the crew hauled their companion back up again.

The first officer snapped to attention as Briana and Maskelyne arrived. 'Ma'am.'

'What's the verdict, Mr Lum?' Briana asked.

'We've completed our first inspection now, Ma'am.'

The two sailors helped the man swinging from the derrick back onto the deck. He took off his brine goggles and gloves and faced Lum. 'The rudder's in bad shape, but it ought to give us *some* manoeuvrability,' he said. 'That harpoon's in a tricky place though. Buried in solid from what I can see, about a foot under the waterline. I can't even get close to it because of the waves. I don't know how he got it in there using one of those old Ferredales. It's either the luckiest shot or the finest piece of marksmanship I've ever seen.'

'Can you hook the line?' Lum said. 'Pull it up?'

The other man shrugged. 'You've got the full weight of the *Herald* pulling against it, sir. We might be able to rig something up, but we'd brisk tearing off the whole stern post. Then you'd be looking at a hull breach.'

Maskelyne leaned on his blunderbuss and peered down over the side of the ship. He lifted his head, following the line of cable across the waters to the steam yacht some distance away. Then he raised the gun to his shoulder and sighted on the yacht.

'Wait!' Briana said. 'What are you doing?'

'Two birds,' Maskelyne said. 'One stone. If I sever the cable at this end, Granger will merely lose his catch. But if I shoot it out at the other end, the flies will pass through the cable, the ship and anything *inside* the ship. We'll leave him with a thousand tiny holes in his hull and, with any, luck, one or two in his own skull.'

'That's got to be two hundred yards. Let one of my marksmen take the shot.'

'Accuracy is not required,' Maskelyne said. 'This weapon produces a vortex of flies.'

'You might miss the cable altogether.'

Maskelyne lowered the gun and turned to face her. 'You haven't seen one of these weapons discharge, Miss Banks. A stream of void flies is quite unstoppable. Were I to fire this straight down, the shot would pass straight through the world and out the other side. With the right trajectory, I could easily, from my present location, reduce any city on this planet to rubble.' He moistened his lips. 'Now, will you please stand aside and let me take the shot before the phial thaws out?'

The crewmen and their first officer looked at Briana for an explanation, but she didn't feel inclined to provide one. She stepped back as Maskelyne raised the gun to his shoulder again. Then she took another step back.

A *click* came from the blunderbuss.

And then a hazy jet of black particles erupted from its flared barrel, crackling like fat in a frying pan as it sped away across the sea. The wind howled suddenly in Briana's ears. She watched as the stream of flies widened into a spiralling, cone-shaped vortex that momentarily engulfed Granger's steam yacht and then abruptly disappeared into the sea with a furious popping sound. The deck under her feet pitched forward suddenly and then rocked backwards as the whole ship slowed to a halt. The towing cable had been severed.

Briana could smell ozone lingering in the air.

Maskelyne lowered his gun, then turned to her and smiled. 'Tell your captain to raise the sails,' he said.

Something woke Granger, although at first he could not say exactly what. He had been dreaming of Evensraum, finding himself pushing through the crowds of refugees fleeing Weaverbrook after the bombardment. They'd been shuffling across ashen fields, ragged figures heading away from the burning town. Granger had been trying to find Ianthe, although in reality she hadn't yet been born. He had felt compelled to search nevertheless, calling out her name, desperate to find this girl that he knew did not exist.

As his bleary eyes took in his surroundings – the navigation console, the helm, the tangle of red sheets around his legs – he perceived that something was wrong. The quality of light here in the bridge seemed different somehow. It felt colder than it should. He realized he could no longer hear the sound of the yacht's engines.

He sat up, aware of a dull stiffness in his joints and noticed blood on his right elbow. Tiny puncture marks had appeared on both sides of the joint, as though a needle had been pushed right through him. The wound began to nip at once. He felt a second prickling sensation in his right ear, and lifted a hand to examine it. His fingers came away bloody. The top of the ear was bleeding, too.

He got up and flexed his limbs and as he did so he noticed light shining through numerous perforations in the bridge walls and windows. It looked like someone had blasted the walls with buckshot. He strode over to the window and examined a number of the little holes closely. The edges were sharp, with no cracks in the glass at all. Behind the glass the cold brown sea heaved against a leaden horizon. Thunderclouds towered in the west and in places he could see sheets of rain pinned against the sky like grey gauze. He opened the window and looked aft.

The captured Haurstaf warship wasn't there.

Granger threw open the door and stepped out onto the weather deck surrounding the wheelhouse. Icy gales buffeted his face. His skin prickled with the electric presence of the approaching storm. He walked around the outside of the bridge, scanning the horizon in all directions. *There.* A sail moved across the sea to the south-west, heading directly across the wind. It could only be the *Irillian Herald*.

He was about to go back inside, when he noticed that the *Excelsior* was sitting lower in the water. Realization that she'd been holed crept into his pores like the sea itself.

He ran back inside and hurried down the main stairwell to the engine-room level. Seawater sloshed between the bulkheads at the bottom of the steps. Countless tiny holes peppered the hull, the interior bulkheads and even the stairwell itself. Granger cursed. He knew what had caused this.

He waded into the cold, dark brine, and pushed open the door to the engine room. The stink of whale oil filled the whole chamber. Void flies had passed through scores of pipes, seawater pump housings and even the main block of the engine itself, causing fuel to leak from innumerable places. Thin shafts of light shone through the hull, while seawater continued to bubble up through a thousand perforations in the floor. He had no way to fix the pumps and seal all these leaks. Nothing he could do would prevent the *Excelsior* from sinking.

The *Excelsior* had two lifeboats: sixteen-feet-long wood-built skiffs with seating for twenty men, four sets of oars and hooped rails to support a storm cover. Between them, they might have held a third of her original crew. Both had been damaged by void flies, so he chose the soundest of the two and began sealing the holes with marine gum. By the time he'd finished, the sea had begun to lap across the *Excelsior*'s bow, leaving him minutes to load the smaller craft with supplies.

He grabbed some rope and a pile of bad-weather gear from a midships locker, then hurried back to the bridge for the old Valcinder compass, sextant, almanacs and his water flask. The emperor's yacht was sloping down towards the bow, which meant the galley would be underwater already. He had no time to search the cabins or stores for food.

Waves broke across the bowsprit. The ship listed, then righted herself with a terrible groan, and then started to slide under the frothing brine. Seawater came surging up the main deck and lifted the lifeboat's keel just as Granger climbed aboard. He cut her loose with his seeing knife and pushed off with an oar. A second wave took hold of the small wooden vessel at once, carrying her away from the stricken steam yacht and out into open sea.

The *Excelsior* sank in seconds. Granger watched from the life-boat as the steam yacht's wheelhouse tilted forward into the dark brown water. Two fathoms down, the portholes of the emperor's suite burned a deep yellow, then grew dim. The stern lifted mo-mentarily, and the funnels behind the bridge seemed about to topple. And then the whole ship slid down into the depths with a final sucking rush. The waters crashed and foamed and seethed in its wake. A heartbeat later, there was no trace of her but an oily slick on the surface of the waters.

Granger pulled his cloak more tightly around himself. Waves rose ten feet or more around the lifeboat, tossing the small vessel around like a cork. The wind blew steadily from the south-east, driving storm clouds and sheets of rain before it. It would be dark in less than an hour. He clambered over to the lifeboat's stern and checked the storage locker. He found the whaleskin tarpaulin for the hoop rails, a tank of fresh water, a gem lantern and a sealed bag containing an officer's pistol, powder and shot, a compass, a knife, spare flints and a signal mirror. None of it looked as if it had ever been used. There was no food.

He stowed the gear away carefully again and then slid two oars into their rowlocks and took a seat facing aft. Then he began to row after the *Herald*.

The storm raged into the night. Rain battered the lifeboat like grapeshot. Lightning pulsed in the western skies. In those moments of clarity, the heaving seas around Granger's boat glittered like mounds of anthracite, massive and terrifying. Darkness returned, with thunder in its lungs. Water blurred the lenses of his storm goggles and sloshed against his boots in the bilge. By the light of his gem lantern he hauled the whaleskin tarpaulin over the hooped frame and fastened it down, forming a damp, salty tent over the open hull.

Six hours at the oars had left his muscles beaten. Granger crawled into the bow and tried to sleep, with only the thin wooden skin of the hull separating his body from a mile of brine below. He lay there for a long time, listened to the rain on the tarpaulin, the creaking planks and the furious concussions of the thunder. He wondered if Ianthe was listening too.

'I couldn't stop them from doing what they did to your mother,' he said. 'But I'm not going to let that happen to you.' He felt suddenly foolish, talking to himself like this in the middle of the ocean. Was Ianthe even listening to him? 'I'll find you in Awl,' he said, 'even if I have to walk across the seabed to get there.'

He must have slept, for although it was still dark his joints had seized again, and the rain had stopped. The sea felt calmer. He got up and stretched, and lifted the shutter from the gem lantern. The storm canopy sagged over his head. A few inches of rain had collected there. He pricked a hole in the oilcloth with his knife and raised his mouth to catch the water that trickled through. It was pure enough, so he slaked his thirst and topped up his flask.

Then he pulled back the tarpaulin and looked out.

The storm had moved on to the north, leaving the skies overhead clear. A thousand stars sparkled in the heavens among the pale pink and blue wisps of nebulae. The sea shone like dark glass. The lifeboat rocked gently back and forth in low swells. Granger stood up and scanned the horizons, but he could not spot any sails. His breath misted in the freezing air. He was the only one breathing it for leagues around.

He took his position from the stars. Awl would be almost a hundred leagues to the north-west. He was about to sit down when he spotted Ortho's Chariot racing overhead. The tiny light zigzagged erratically across the sky, then seemed to pause directly above him for an instant before shooting off again to the north.

An uneasy feeling crept into Granger's stomach. For an instant he thought he had sensed the presence of an unnatural force. It was like the time he'd almost fallen from the makeshift bridge in Losoto's Sunken Quarter. The cosmos had seemed to *shift* in some subtle way, although he couldn't say how or why he felt this. He returned to his seat, took up the oars and began to row.

Time passed with nothing to mark it but the sound of the oars splashing through the water and the occasional grumble of thunder in the north. But then Granger heard a different sound, like the distant drone of a ship's horn. He set down the oars and listened. After a moment he heard it again – a long, mournful bellow. It seemed nearer this time. He clambered over to the stern and took out the pistol, powder and shot from the storage locker. He loaded the pistol and tucked it into the belt of his breeches.

The sound resonated across the water again, louder now.

To starboard Granger spotted a faintly phosphorescent shape under the sea. As it drew nearer he saw that it was a whale, about three times the size of his boat, with an elongated body and a massive blunt head. He aimed the pistol at it, but did not fire. The creature glided under the lifeboat's keel, about a fathom down, its black eye looking up at him.

A sudden splash off the bow made him wheel round.

A second whale had surfaced nearby. Its back arced out of the water as it blew out a jet of seawater. And then the great blade of its tail broke the surface and crashed down again, showering the lifeboat in brine.

The whales stayed with him for about an hour, until the sky began to lighten in the east. And then they dived down into that dark and fathomless brine. He heard them lowing for a while afterwards, but he didn't see them again.

At dawn he found himself surrounded by a school of tiny silver fish, flashing like needles in the bromine waters. He might have made a net from his own shirt to catch them, but he had no means to boil them without spoiling his fresh water. So he sat there and watched them sparkling all around his hull, as bright and poisonous as drops of quicksilver.

He rowed until midday, when he stopped to take noon sight under a blazing sun. But the rocking boat frustrated his efforts. He threw the sextant into the jumbled pile of his storm-weather gear, too tired and too irritable to persist. The wind had turned easterly and slackened off to a stiff breeze, which did little to cool him. He set his course by dead reckoning instead, assuming he hadn't drifted too far since dark. But he couldn't be sure exactly where he was. A north-west course would bring him to Irillia eventually, if his water didn't run out first. He'd seen nothing of the *Herald* all morning.

On the evening of the third day he spotted an erokin samal drifting three hundred yards to the south. The jellyfish had captured at least three sharks in its tendrils, turned their corpses into the bloated grey masses of flesh that it used to catch the wind. Granger rowed his boat due north away from the creature until he could no longer see it. Even so, he did not sleep well that night, unsettled by the thought of tendrils reaching under the tarpaulin and into his boat.

The next morning he found himself enveloped in rust-coloured mist. He had travelled farther north than he'd intended, reaching the border waters where the Sea of Lights met the Sea of Kings. Here the oily red currents of the northern sea mingled with the brown waters of the southern one, whorling around the hull like spilled paint. Their interaction produced the haze of fumes through which the sun now glowered. Granger put his goggles and storm mask on and set his back to the oars again, now pushing due west. He did not wish to encounter any sea life here.

And then he thought he detected an unusual noise in the mist – a high-pitched hum almost beyond his range of hearing. His eyes strained to see through the haze. Was that a shadow? He took his goggles off again. There was definitely something out there in the fog, something huge and dark. It could almost be the outline of a ship. Granger turned his boat around and began to row towards it.

CHAPTER 15

THE FROG

Before the flooding, Irillia, Evensraum and Pertica had been parts of the same great landmass west of Anea. Now each remained as its own chain of islands, with Evensraum to the south and Pertica lying in the frozen north. While lower lands drowned, Irillia's mountainous backbone had remained defiant in the face of the rising seas. More than a hundred islands stretched across the Sea of Lights and the Emerald Sea, but the most magnificent of these, Ianthe decided, had to be Awl.

As the *Herald* approached her berth she could see the remains of Port Awl's three former harbours down under the crystal-clear green brine. Each had been constructed above the other upon a sunken slope. Only the main commercial jetty had been built up from the original foundations. It looked long enough to berth twenty warships and sank for at least fifty fathoms at its deepest end. Incredibly, Ianthe could see scores of Drowned going about their business down there, a whole community living in the flooded streets below the town.

'Personally,' Briana said, following the girl's gaze, 'they give me the shudders. But it annoys the emperor.' They were standing with Captain Howlish behind the port bulwark, while Guild mariners worked around them, preparing the damaged warship for dock. The broken rudder made progress slow.

'And annoying the emperor is one of life's little pleasures,' she added.

'We had Drowned off the coast in Evensraum,' Ianthe said, 'until Hu caught them all in nets. He tried using their corpses to fertilize the land, but it just poisoned everything. So he burned them instead.'

'What a lovely image,' Briana remarked.

Howlish grinned. 'Hu once offered the Guild a thousand hectares of Anean farmland for a single hectare in Awl,' he said to Ianthe. 'And the Guild refused him.'

Ianthe gazed at the island in wonder. Her new lenses made the scene seem all the more magical. Her heart felt full to bursting with the thrill of viewing all this beauty first-hand. The Irillian mountains rose up into the morning sky, crisp tiers of faintly blue and lavender rock with numerous white streams and waterfalls that fell thousands of feet into mist. Tails of green forest rooted the lower slopes to the foothills below, while the highest peaks wore paper hats of snow. Port Awl sprawled over a steep ridge above the water's edge, overlooking a rocky bay between two heavily wooded peninsulas. Stone buildings clung to the hillside, one above the other, in a pleasant jumble of yellow cubes. Six men-o'-war lay tied up at the main jetty, four with red dragon-scale hulls and two with green; their serpent figureheads glinted in the sunshine. Dock hands threw ropes across to the *Herald* and began to winch the warship closer to the wharf.

'You grow flowers here!' Ianthe exclaimed. She had spotted flower sellers at the town end of the dock, their stalls bursting with every imaginable colour of bloom. 'We never had the land for it in Evensraum. Even after we had our own garden, we used every corner for growing food. You have to, or the servants talk.'

Briana frowned. 'Why not just beat the servants?'

Ianthe felt her face redden.

Moments later the gangplank came down with a clunk, and Ianthe followed the Haurstaf witch and the captain off the ship. Briana Marks looked especially pretty in her flowing white gown and ruby necklace; the weariness just evaporated from her as she stepped onto the stone wharf. 'Hand Maskelyne and his men over to the port constable,' Briana said to Howlish. 'He can do what he likes with the men, but I want Maskelyne brought to the palace.'

'What about his wife and child, ma'am?'

'Put them up at the Nuwega,' Briana replied. 'Guests of the Guild.'

The captain nodded.

'A cheap room.'

'Very good, ma'am.'

The rising sweep of Port Awl's main street reminded Ianthe of Port Vassar in Evensraum. Here were the same bakers, grocers, fishmongers, weavers and oil sellers. Other shops sold books, gem lanterns, jewellery, paintings, pottery, medicines and even Unmer trove. The Hotel Nuwega occupied a position midway up the hill, its grand façades and clock tower overlooking the harbour. Ianthe counted six taverns, each with tables and benches outside, where people drank and smoked and chatted. A number of young women in Guild robes sat amidst the locals. As they passed them by, Ianthe drew curious glances.

'They're wondering why you're wearing Unmer spectacles,' Briana said.

Ianthe lowered her head.

Briana sighed. 'You should really let me take a look at them,' she added. 'God knows what sort of damage they could be doing to your mind.'

'There's nothing sorcerous about them,' Ianthe said.

'Then why wear them?'

She shrugged. 'They help me see better.'

The Haurstaf witch looked at her strangely but said nothing more about it. They walked to the top of the hill and into a leafy plaza where Briana said the morning farmers' market was held. Birds chattered and hopped across the cobbles. On the northern edge of the square a low stone rampart offered views out across the interior of the island. Between the town ridge and the Irillian mountains lay a broad patchwork of green and yellow fields bisected by a looping river. A warm breeze coming up from the valley carried with it the scent of cut hay.

In the shade of a nearby tree stood four open carriages, their glossy black cabs resting on dragon-bone springs. Four men, evidently their drivers, played dice on a stone bench nearby. As soon as they saw Briana, one of them abandoned his game and hurried over.

'Guild Palace, ma'am?' He opened the door, unfolded a set of steps from the undercarriage and then waited until the two women had taken their seats. Then he grabbed the horses' reins and took his own position in the front of the carriage.

Tackle clinking, they set off at a leisurely clop, down the shady side of the ridge. Here Port Awl's houses overlooked the farmland to the north and the shining mountain peaks. The streets were cooler and rang with the sound of blacksmiths and gunsmiths at work. Ianthe peered through doorways to see coal-blackened muscles and forges and anvils, racks of carbine rifles and hand-cannons.

Late morning found the carriage clattering across a stone bridge over the River Irya, which Briana explained was merely an ancient word for water. Farmsteads dotted the landscape on either side of the waters. Sparrows darted among hedgerows of rosehip and stowberries. Sheep and cattle grazed in green pastures, raising their heads to watch the travellers pass.

'What breed are those?' Ianthe asked, pointing to a herd of black cows.

Briana snorted. 'How should I know? I'm not a farmer.'

Ianthe asked nothing more about her surroundings, but she continued to drink it all in: the fields of barley and whittle-grass, the furrowed black earth bursting with every type of produce, the quince, plum and apple orchards, the clumps of gnarled old oak and elm. In one field men and women in wide-brimmed straw hats loaded golden hayricks onto a cart. Fishermen sat on the banks of the Irya. Bees buzzed across meadow-flowers. This land was a hundred times richer than Evensraum. She wanted to get out of the carriage and take off her boots and splash through the rushing river, but that would not have been seemly.

They stopped to water the horses at a roadside tavern. Ianthe stretched her legs in the field behind the stables, returning to the carriage to find that Briana had bought a basket of bread, cheese, apples and a bottle of honey-coloured wine. They ate their lunch and drank wine from clay cups by the side of the road with the sun on their faces and the sound of birdsong in the surrounding hedgerows.

'Do you have other girls from Evensraum?' she asked the witch.

'We had a girl from Whiterock Bay,' Briana replied. 'A frightful peasant. That would have been back in thirty-nine.'

'Is she a Guild psychic now?'

'Didn't complete the training.'

'Why not?'

Briana shook her head. 'I don't recall.'

'So where is she now?'

Briana stuffed the remains of their lunch into the basket. 'Why do you ask so many pointless questions?' she said. 'Come on, I want to get there before dark. There are wolves in those hills, you know.'

'We had wolves in—'

'In Evensraum, yes. Really, Ianthe, you have to stop wittering on about that muddy little island.'

Ianthe hung her head. 'I'm sorry.'

Briana laid a hand on her shoulder. 'It's not your fault, dear. As the Haurstaf like to say: It takes time for the dirt to fall from one's boots.' She smiled. 'I only have to look back four or five generations to find parts of my family that came from relatively humble stock.'

'They were farmers, too?'

'Tax collectors.'

Late in the afternoon the road began to climb into the Irillian foothills. It wound its way up through forests of thousand-year-old oaks, their great boughs forming cathedral-like spaces in the green gloom and their roots smothered by leafy hummocks. Mossy stones marked the trail, and here and there shafts of light picked out the tumbledown remains of cottages set back from the trail. Birds whistled and insects buzzed, and once Ianthe thought she heard the rustle of a larger animal moving through the undergrowth. A deer perhaps? She noticed that the carriage driver had a pistol on his lap, but the horses seemed calm enough, so she didn't mention it.

Shortly afterwards, they encountered their first checkpoint. Two soldiers in blue uniforms manned a barrier beside the road. A section of forest had been cut back, leaving a wide perimeter around a central concrete bunker. Spirals of razor-wire encircled the encampment. Smoke rose from one corner where six more men sat around an open fire. Each of them carried a carbine rifle slung over his shoulder. One of the two barrier guards raised a hand to stop the carriage but then waved them on when he spotted Briana.

'All quiet, Captain?' the witch asked.

'Nothing but birdsong, ma'am,' the man replied.

The military presence became more frequent after that. In places, acres of woodland had been burned to stubble to accommodate larger camps where hundreds of soldiers milled around gun emplacements and paced perimeters and trained in muddy meadows between the concrete buildings. Razor-wire enveloped everything. Great cannon batteries pointed at the skies. The sound of small-arms fire became more frequent.

Ianthe flinched as yet more gunfire crackled nearby. 'Are they training?' she asked.

'News of our arrival precedes us,' Briana said. 'Most of these units have telepaths attached.'

'They're Guild soldiers?'

'The finest war machine in the empire.'

'I thought the emperor's Samarol were the finest?'

Briana just snorted. 'I once saw one brought down by an unarmed man,' she said. 'How good can they be?'

At last, with the long light of evening sloping through the trees, they passed through a final checkpoint in the gates of a massive stone wall, where soldiers winched up an iron grate to allow the carriage to pass. Ahead of them lay the Guild Palace of Awl. The Irillian mountains framed tiers of dark, pyrite-veined towers that soared skywards, their windows ablaze in the last rays of sun. Flags of white and gold hung from a score of poles set into the barbican, while pots of meadow-flowers adorned the promenade before the walls. On all sides, paths and steps led off into the cool shade of the forest behind. Ianthe spied a gazebo down beside a brook, where a group of eight girls in white robes sat listening to an older woman. Other Haurstaf strolled among the trees, enjoying an evening that seemed infused with the aura of summer itself.

Four carts waited on the flagged promenade before the main

palace gate, while their drivers reclined on a grassy bank nearby. Ianthe's own carriage drew up beside the others, whereupon their driver opened the door and folded down the steps.

'What do you think?' Briana asked.

Ianthe smiled, thankful that her lenses hid her tears.

The palace interior was cool and quiet, with grand halls and cascades of dark marble stairs and airy corridors leading in every direction. Guild psychics passed by, their white robes whispering on the mirror-black floors. Briana led Ianthe along a corridor in one wing and pushed open a set of double doors.

They had reached an enormous library, where hundreds of girls sat at desks, reading books. The faintly musty scent of paper and old leather bindings lingered in the air. Heads turned to face Ianthe. A murmur passed through the room. Someone giggled.

'Sister Ulla,' Briana said.

An old woman came over, her arms full of books. She was no larger than a child and wore her hair in a grey knuckle behind her head. Her face had the texture of a rotten log, and her restless little eyes looked like they had burrowed in there to escape predators. She glared at Ianthe with open hostility, then opened her mouth to speak.

Briana held up a hand. 'This is Ianthe,' she said. 'I want her tested for the usual, then put in with the current class.'

Sister Ulla said nothing.

'I am aware of that,' Briana said, 'but—'

The old woman remained silent.

'Probably an affectation,' Briana said. 'You know what these—'

Sister Ulla continued to stare at the other woman in silence.

Briana wrung her hands in frustration. 'Obviously that depends on what you find,' she remarked. 'I want a full progress report on this one.' She glanced at Ianthe, before returning her attention to the old woman. A long moment of silence passed between them.

Sister Ulla then turned to Ianthe. She frowned and said, 'Ignorant peasant. Don't you have any inclination of what I just said to you?'

'I'm sorry, ma'am,' Ianthe replied.

A ripple of laughter spread among the girls seated nearby.

'You will address me as *Sister Ulla*,' the old woman said.

Ianthe swallowed.

'I do not approve of those lenses,' Sister Ulla said, 'regardless of any excuse Sister Marks might make for you. However, we will tolerate them if you show a spark of promise.' She set her books down on a desk, then grabbed Ianthe's chin and leaned close, peering into her eyes as though looking for something. Finally she sighed. 'You have the mind of a pebble,' she said. 'I don't expect you'll do well here at all. Few girls of your breeding ever do. But if—' She stopped abruptly and wheeled to face a group of girls nearby. 'Silence,' she said. 'Regina, Constance.'

A hush fell across the room. Two girls seated some distance apart stood up.

'This is a library,' Sister Ulla said. 'It is no place for thoughts like that. What do you have to say for yourselves? Constance?'

The nearest girl raised her chin defiantly. A tiny blonde imp of a thing, she nevertheless managed to maintain a demeanour of arrogance that Ianthe had seen in so many Losotan settlers. Her blue eyes burned with indignation. The other girl was just as fair, but long of face and hardly pretty. She looked across at the smaller girl for reassurance.

'I was merely stating an opinion,' Constance said.

'Your opinions aren't worth stating,' Sister Ulla said, 'I suggest you both go and get yourselves cleaned up.'

Both girls looked suddenly fearful. And then a strange

thing happened. As Ianthe watched, the smaller girl – Constance – clutched her nose. Blood trickled down between her fingers and spattered her desk. Across the room, the larger girl gave a soft cry and clasped her hands to her own face. Her nose was bleeding too.

'Go,' Sister Ulla cried, jabbing a finger at the door. 'To the nurse's office, before I sterilize the pair of you to spare the world your offspring.'

The two girls grabbed up their books and hurried away.

Briana smiled at Ianthe. 'There are various grades of psychic,' she said. 'At one end of the spectrum are the *sensitives* like myself, specializing in communication. Sister Ulla represents the other end of the spectrum. She will test you, and hopefully teach you, in psychic warfare.'

Sister Ulla took Ianthe to a storeroom, where she bundled robes, towels, sheets and blankets into her arms, before showing her to a dormitory on a lower floor at the back of the palace. The windows overlooked a gloomy forest. A small folding bed had been set up at the far end of the room between the two ranks of proper beds.

'You've caused me considerable inconvenience,' the old woman said. 'The term is halfway finished already, and I refuse to go over previous material for *your* benefit.' She watched as Ianthe made her temporary bed. 'Not that it matters much. I don't expect you'll pass even the most basic of tests.'

'What sort of tests?' Ianthe asked.

Sister Ulla grunted. 'Any psychic worth her salt wouldn't have to be told. Now stop fussing with that sheet and get yourself washed and dressed. Robes and underwear go in that chest. Supper is at nine.' She left the room, slamming the door behind her.

A door in the rear wall of the dorm led to a large bathroom, with rows of buckets and ladles set out on the chipped tile floor. Ianthe washed and then put on the Haurstaf robe. The shapeless cloth felt rough and heavy on her shoulders. She returned to the dorm and dumped her old clothes in the chest at the foot of her bed. Darkness was gathering among the trees outside the window. She hunted about for a gem lantern but didn't find one. Was it nine o'clock yet? Ianthe couldn't see any clocks, so she sat on the bed and waited.

Nobody came for her.

After a while she let her mind wander out into the void. The perceptions of the palace occupants glimmered like hundreds of lanterns suspended in darkness. By combining their disparate visions Ianthe was able to build up an impression of a truly vast building, extending as far underground as it did into the sky. There were thousands of people around her – from the highest tower to the lowest subterranean chambers. Guild members reclined in warmly lit lounges or sat reading in velvet-draped bedrooms, or looked out upon the dusk from high balconies. Cooks toiled in steaming kitchens. Servants brushed cobwebs from nooks and pantry corners. Ianthe allowed herself to float among the Haurstaf like a ghost, occasionally slipping into an unsuspecting mind to view one chamber or another with increased clarity. She saw black marble fireplaces and piles of blood-red cushions, silverware like white fire and jewelled dressers and long hallways hung with gilt-framed paintings – such a gathering of treasure as she had never seen. Snippets of conversation drifted through the aether:

'. . . *not a gilder between them. How do you think Jonah felt about that?*'

'*I can't imagine.*'

She heard laughter and music and the clink of glasses and

cutlery. And here she came upon a great hall awash with light and chatter, where hundreds of girls sat at long tables under flickering candelabra, feasting from platters of chicken, partridge, pastries and trenchers of steaming stew. A separate table at the top of the chamber accommodated a group of older psychics, all chatting and drinking wine from crystal glasses while servants cleared away the crockery. Among them Ianthe recognized Sister Marks and Sister Ulla, and she realized she was supposed to be there, in that hall, too.

Ianthe snapped back into the empty dormitory. She was late and hungry and . . . whatever would the others say? She got to her feet and bolted for the door.

Silence descended on the dining hall as Ianthe closed the door behind her. A hundred girls turned to face her, some of whom she recognized from the library. Their smiles were beautiful and cruel. They began to whisper among themselves as Ianthe walked between the feasting tables. She couldn't see any spaces on the benches so she kept going until she reached the head table. Twelve women in long white robes looked down at her, with Sister Marks and Sister Ulla in the centre. Ianthe found little sympathy in any of their eyes. Sister Ulla positively glared, while Briana Marks wore a smile of faint amusement.

Sister Ulla said, 'So you finally decided to turn up?'

A chorus of giggles swept through the room.

Ianthe felt her face redden. 'I'm sorry,' she said.

'She wouldn't have heard the summons,' Briana remarked.

'No doubt,' Sister Ulla said. 'Which is why I told her to be here at nine.'

Ianthe lowered her head.

A long moment of silence followed, in which Ianthe suspected the twelve psychics were conversing. For all she knew, the whole room could be talking about her.

Finally, Sister Ulla pointed to one of the tables at the edge of the room, 'Take a seat over there at the end,' she said, 'and fill your plate with whatever the other girls haven't eaten. And don't dilly dally. You'll make the others late for bed.'

Ianthe retreated to the corner, where she found a space beside a fat girl with auburn hair.

'And take those ghastly Unmer eyeglasses off,' Sister Ulla added. 'I won't have them at the table.'

Ianthe hesitated.

'You'll remove them now, or go straight to bed without supper.'

Still Ianthe didn't move. And then she got up and ran from the room, desperate to leave before anyone saw her tears.

The other girls burst into the dorm in a squall of breathless chatter, but Ianthe kept her head under the blanket and her mind firmly inside her own head. She heard whispering, followed by silence. And then someone said, 'I don't think she can read minds at all.'

'Must we vocalize everything for her benefit?'

'I don't even sense a glimmer of talent.'

'Why go to the trouble? It's so tedious.'

'Did you see her dress when she came in?'

'I was too busy looking at her spectacles.'

They laughed.

Ianthe closed her eyes and tried to concentrate on her own breathing. After a while she heard the creak of bedsprings, and then the dorm became deathly quiet. But the silence never really felt like silence at all. She couldn't know what taunts passed between the other girls, but she imagined the worst. Like a shuttered gem lantern, the light continued to burn even if you couldn't see it. The lack of sound was worse than anything.

Hours must have passed, and still Ianthe couldn't sleep. And then she heard a floorboard creak nearby. Someone shook her shoulder, and a voice whispered, 'Are you awake?'

Ianthe pulled back the blanket.

In the darkness she could just make out a dim figure crouching next to her bed. She realized it was the fat red-haired girl she'd briefly sat next to at supper. The girl leaned close and whispered, 'Don't let them get to you. They pick on everyone at first. And Sister Ulla is a monster.' She pressed something into Ianthe's hands.

It was a piece of chicken, wrapped in a napkin. Ianthe began to eat it at once.

'You're from Evensraum?'

Ianthe nodded.

'I'm from Harpool, about thirty miles north of Losoto. My family are farmers, too.'

'We're not farmers,' Ianthe said. 'I mean, I don't . . . what does it matter?'

'Regina and Constance are the worst,' the girl said. 'They think they're Losotan nobles or something. It's like they're always going on about Emperor Hu and how their families have arranged a special deal with him and they're going to be attached to his court. It doesn't even work like that. You don't get to choose where you're posted.'

'What's your name?'

'Aria. I'd better go.'

'Thank you,' Ianthe said.

Aria turned away, but Ianthe grabbed her and whispered, 'Are they talking now?'

'They're asleep.'

Ianthe lowered her head. 'I wasn't sure.'

'Silences are difficult here,' Aria said. 'But you'll soon start to miss them.'

Ianthe got up before dawn and sneaked into the bathroom to wash herself before the other girls woke up. She returned to her bed but didn't have to wait there for long. As the first glimmer of light crept into the forest outside, the dormitory door opened, and Sister Ulla marched in.

'Up,' she said, 'up, you lazy creatures. We've too much to do today.'

The girls rose, complaining groggily. Ianthe looked over at Aria, but the big, auburn-haired girl avoided her eye. Constance and Regina, the pair whom Sister Ulla had expelled from the library with bleeding noses, were not so coy. Constance offered Ianthe a cut-glass stare, then brushed her blonde curls from her shoulder in an exaggerated manner. She turned and smiled at her companion in a way that seemed to promise mischief. Regina suppressed a giggle.

'You!' Sister Ulla said to Ianthe. 'You've washed? Come with me.'

The Testing Room was further along the corridor from the dormitory. It was bare but for a table and two chairs in the centre of the floor. Tall windows overlooked an empty courtyard flanked by colonnades and facing a wall with an iron grate leading into the forest. Sister Ulla told Ianthe to sit, and then left the room.

Ianthe waited.

The courtyard outside grew steadily lighter. Ianthe watched the shadows draw back towards the easternmost colonnade. Birds hopped along the forest wall. Half the morning passed by, and still nobody came. She wondered if this was part of the test. If she stood up and walked over to the window, would she fail? Perhaps she was *supposed* to make a decision and leave? Were they watching her? She got up and listened at the door but heard nothing. She sat down again.

The morning dragged on. Noon came and went. It must have been early afternoon when Sister Ulla returned. The little old woman carried a glass bell jar, which she placed unceremoniously on the table as she sat down. In the jar was a frog.

Sister Ulla regarded Ianthe for a long time. Her crumpled face was unreadable, but her eyes were small and cold. Finally she said, 'Know where you are and who you are with. This organization gives nothing. If you want to be a part of it, you will accept that.'

Ianthe looked at the frog.

'Some members of the Guild like to think they can bend the rules,' the old woman went on. 'They expect me to make concessions for students. But I don't hold with that. The Guild is not a crown to be worn or a sword to be wielded. It is an ideology. Do you understand?'

Ianthe thought she should nod, so she did.

The old woman's eyes narrowed. Then she tapped the glass jar and said, 'I want you to kill this creature.'

Ianthe just looked at her.

'Psychic communication requires the lightest touch,' the old woman said. 'The ability to sense thoughts without disrupting the transmitting mind in any way. Psychic warfare, on the other hand, is all about causing *stress*. One forces one's own thoughts into the recipient's brain with the *intention* of causing disruption. A competent practitioner can alter the mood of another psychic . . . evoke depression . . . or rage. But a skilled warrior . . .' Her wrinkled lips made a semblance of a smile. 'A skilled warrior can cause actual damage.'

Ianthe glanced at the frog again. 'What about *control*? What about getting someone to do what you want?'

The old woman made a sound of disapproval. 'You can't etch glass with a sledgehammer, can you?' She gestured towards the frog. 'Psychic warfare techniques are more effective than the communicative disciplines precisely because there is *no need* to read the intricacies of the target mind. One's victim need not even be sensitive. Even a mindless ugly little creature like this is vulnerable.'

'But I don't want to hurt it.'

Sister Ulla stood up. 'I think it extremely unlikely that you will. Now, I have a class to teach. I'll be back before supper to check on your failure.' She headed for the door.

Ianthe called after her, 'I'm just supposed to *will* it to death?'

'Do what you like,' Sister Ulla replied.

'But how? I don't—'

The old woman slammed the door.

Ianthe stared at the frog. The frog blinked. She allowed her mind to connect with the creature's perceptions and peered up at herself through its marbled eyes. *Poor little thing.* She sighed, then got up and walked over to the window. A brown pigeon had perched on the forest wall at the other side of the courtyard. It pecked at some moss near its feet, then fluttered off into the trees. Ianthe opened the window and breathed deeply of the cool green air. She could hear other pigeons cooing above her and the restful chuckle of a stream coming from the woods beyond the wall.

She glanced back at the frog. Then she stormed over, threw herself back down in her seat and stared at the miserable little creature, willing it to die.

Time dragged on. No matter how much hellfire and agony Ianthe wished upon the frog, it simply crouched there, staring dumbly out of the jar. Its throat bobbed, and it blinked, and, once, it turned slightly. By mid afternoon a headache had crept into Ianthe's skull. She let out a long breath and rose from her seat, stretching her arms and neck.

Aria was standing in the courtyard outside, looking in.

Ianthe hurried over and opened the window. 'What are you doing here?'

The big red-haired girl glanced back at the courtyard wall, where she had propped the gate open with a wicker basket. 'We're supposed to collect mushrooms in the woods,' she said, 'but most of the girls just go back to the dorm. No one ever checks up.' She looked past Ianthe into the room behind. 'Is that a frog?'

Ianthe followed her gaze. 'I'm supposed to kill it.'

Aria frowned. 'Why a frog?' she said. 'Normally it's a mouse. Not that anyone ever kills it the first time. Sister Ulla likes to say it's easy, but it isn't. Animal minds are much harder to destroy than Unmer ones.'

'Have you ever killed an Unmer?'

Aria shook her head. 'The dungeons are full of stock, but you're only supposed to torture them,' she said. 'There's barely enough to go around. If we killed them all, we'd need to bring in more from the ghettos and that would mean less income from the empire.' She looked suddenly serious, and lowered her voice. 'Constance killed one by accident, and Sister Ulla was so furious she nearly expelled her.'

Ianthe thought back to the illicit excursion her mind had taken through the palace the night before. The palace had extended as far underground as it had reached skywards. Had *all* those people she'd sensed down there been Unmer?

'Do you want to walk in the woods with me?'

Ianthe snapped out of her reverie. 'What?'

'Sister Ulla wont be back for ages.'

'What about the test?'

'She's not expecting you to pass anyway.' She held out her hand. 'Come on, it's a lovely day. I'll show you the glade.'

Ianthe accepted Aria's hand and climbed out through the open window.

Aria picked up her mushroom basket and closed the courtyard gate behind them. Gold-green light filtered down through the forest canopy, dappling the mossy ground and picking out bursts of white and pink wild-flowers. Yellow butterflies fluttered to and fro. The air smelled of warm summer pollen. Numerous trails wound through the ancient oaks, and Aria led Ianthe along one of these down a steep slope towards a spur of granite. As they drew nearer, Ianthe heard the sound of a rushing stream. Steps cut into the living rock took them down one side of the spur to a shady pool surrounded by walls of smooth grey stone. The sunshine fell on a flat expanse of granite beside the water's edge, so smooth and round it might have been carved by the gods as a seat for bathers. In the shadows at the rear of the glade, a small waterfall chuckled into the dark waters.

Ianthe crouched at the edge of the pool. It was so clear she could see light rippling across pebbles two fathoms down. She hesitated, then dipped her hand into the cool water.

Aria flopped down onto the rocks behind her. 'Some of the girls come here to swim,' she said. 'Do you swim?'

Ianthe shook her head.

'Me neither.' Aria rummaged in her basket, pulled out a handful of red berries and began to eat them.

'Weren't you supposed to be collecting mushrooms?'

'These taste better,' Aria said. 'Do you want some?'

Ianthe realized she was ravenous. The only food she'd eaten since she'd arrived at the palace had been the chicken leg Aria had given to her the night before. She scurried over, and soon the two girls were sitting side by side, their chins running with red berry juice as they devoured Aria's hoard.

'Look, Regina,' said a voice from behind. 'A pig and a peasant.'

Ianthe turned to see two girls standing on the rock steps above them. The small blonde, Constance, stood with her chin raised and her blue eyes lit with arrogance, while her clumpy, brown-haired companion shifted coyly on the rock steps a few paces behind. Both girls carried baskets similar to Aria's.

Constance strolled down the remaining steps, stopped before Ianthe and peered at her as one might peer at an insect. 'I suppose Unmer eyeglasses are fashionable in Evensraum,' she said to Regina. 'These peasants have always had quaint ideas.'

Regina giggled.

Constance reached for Ianthe. 'Let me see them,' she said.

Ianthe turned away.

Constance gave a snort of disapproval, then grabbed for Ianthe's spectacles. Ianthe pulled away and tried to shove the other girl back. Constance grabbed a handful of Ianthe's hair. Ianthe lashed out wildly with the back of her fist.

Constance recoiled, and stood there for a moment – an expression of shock forming on her pretty face. She touched a thin scar across the bridge of her nose, and her fingers came away bloody. 'You broke my nose,' she said. 'You broke my nose!'

Ianthe fumbled to adjust her lenses. She didn't see the other girl charge at her until it was too late. With an angry shriek, Constance pushed Ianthe into the pool.

Freezing water engulfed Ianthe. The shock of it took her breath away. She thrashed about, struggling to right herself, then broke the surface, heaving for air. And all at once she felt herself begin to slip under again. She opened her mouth to call for help, but swallowed water and gagged.

Constance smiled at her from the bank.

Ianthe slipped under the surface of the pool again. Her nose filled with water. She kicked and flailed her arms madly, trying desperately to reach air. Her heavy Haurstaf robes seemed to drag her down. For an instant her face broke free and she sucked in a breath before the waters closed around her once more. She felt something solid smack against her head and grabbed it. Suddenly she felt herself being pulled along.

Aria was using a branch to drag Ianthe through the water. Ianthe held on fiercely. She reached the edge of the pool and clung on to the rock, breathless and shaking.

Constance laughed.

Ianthe tried to pull herself out of the water.

Constance crouched over her. 'You can't get out here,' she said. 'This is our area. Go around the other side of the pool.'

'Leave me alone,' Ianthe said. She struggled to climb up, but the blonde girl held her firmly down.

'You need to learn your place,' Constance snarled, forcing Ianthe back down into the cold water. The scar across her broken nose looked livid and angry. 'Peasants don't belong in the Guild. You're not fit to clean the drains.' She wheeled around and flashed her teeth at Aria. 'Give me that stick.'

Aria hesitated.

Constance struggled with Ianthe as she tried to stop her from climbing out. But Ianthe, in her desperation, managed to force her way up past the smaller girl. Constance broke away, snatched the branch from Aria, then swung it round hard.

It struck Ianthe a stinging blow across the cheek. Dripping wet, she turned and fled towards the rocky steps, where Constance's companion, Regina, waited.

'Stop her,' Constance yelled.

Regina moved to block Ianthe's way, and Ianthe tried to push past.

'Grab her.'

Regina seized the hood of Ianthe's robe.

Ianthe lost her footing on the wet rock. Suddenly the glade whirled around her. She fell backwards and struck her head on something hard. A moment of darkness and confusion passed, and then she heard someone breathing heavily close to her ear, grunting, gasping.

'Leave her alone.'

'In the water.'

Fists grabbed Ianthe's robes. Someone pinned her arms down. Regina loomed over her, her hair dishevelled, her face flushed. Constance wore a savage grin on her face. They began dragging her back towards the pool. Terror gripped Ianthe's heart, and she kicked and punched and screamed, 'No!'

Something strange happened. Ianthe sensed Constance's perceptions, as she always had, and yet in that instant of fear and struggle she caught a rare glimpse of the mind behind them. It was as if the world had *flipped* abruptly. Instead of simply peering out through the other girl's eyes, she found herself engulfed by the whirlwind of Constance's emotions. *Hatred, desire, envy.* Ianthe's own consciousness lashed out instinctively . . .

Her cry seemed to hang there in the silence of the glade. And then Ianthe became aware of the thumping of her own heart, the frantic sound of her own breathing. Shakily, she sat up.

Constance was lying a few feet away, unmoving, a trickle of blood coming from the corner of her left eye. Regina lay curled up on the ground beside her, with her face clamped behind her hands. She was wailing softly like a young child. Aria sat on the ground behind them, gazing at the two stricken girls with wide, fearful eyes.

'What did you do?' she said.

Ianthe got to her feet and ran.

'*You* do not summon *me*, Mr Maskelyne.'

Maskelyne looked up to see Briana Marks standing at the open doorway of his suite. 'Did I summon you?' he said, feigning confusion. 'Honestly, I can't now remember why.'

She shook her head, but failed to entirely hide her smile. 'Are you comfortable here?'

The suite occupied two floors of one of the palace towers and boasted fine views across the mountains and valley from its garden terrace. Elegant dragon-bone furniture rested on moss-deep carpets. Crystal chandeliers hung from silk-draped ceilings. Maskelyne had counted seven couches, twelve armchairs and no fewer than twenty-two mirrors bouncing light from window to wall. His bed was big enough to accommodate ten people. 'Comfortable enough,' he said, 'although the bed feels cold at night.'

'Your wife will remain in Port Awl until your case is decided,' Briana said. 'And that won't happen until we determine Ianthe's worth to the Guild.'

Maskelyne grunted. 'You intend to hold me here until you decide whether or not Ianthe has talent? What difference does it really make? She's unharmed. Is this justice, or are you simply waiting to see if you can lawfully acquire leverage?'

'There are worse places to be.' Briana strolled over towards the glass doors leading to the terrace. 'That's one of my favourite views,' she said. 'You can see the Culche Pass from here, Mian Morre and the Folded Wings. Don't you think the four mountains opposite look like a dragon's spine?'

'I find the view somewhat spoiled by the acres of burned forest, razor-wire and concrete bunkers surrounding the palace,' Maskelyne replied. 'Do you know that a cockerel crows every morning in one of the camps? The sound is always followed by a single shot, and then silence. I can't help but wonder if it's one, trained, bird, or if there's a supply of them.'

Briana closed her eyes for a moment. 'A supply,' she said.

'Did you just ask your associates?'

'All three thousand of them,' Briana replied. 'The great benefit of telepathy is that one is able to obtain information whenever one wishes. A psychic is never surprised.' She reached the glass doors, opened them and stepped out onto the terrace. There she stopped dead. 'Where did you get all this stuff?'

Maskelyne joined her. A small collection of Unmer trove lay spread across the flagstones, most of it located amongst potted plants and flower troughs, although he had set out many of the more useful pieces for disassembly on the stone breakfast table. 'After so many months at sea,' he said, 'I find it refreshing to work outdoors.'

'*Work?* Where did this trove *come* from?'

'The palace storerooms.' He made a dismissive gesture. 'The Unmer won't miss objects you've already confiscated. Most of it is simply junk, but there are a few pieces that may prove vital to my research.'

Briana simply stared at him.

'The Unmer are able to manipulate Space and Time,' Maskelyne explained. 'To transfer energies across vast gulfs. I have been trying to determine how they accomplish this.'

'You were supposed to remain locked in this suite,' Briana said.

Maskelyne waved his hand irritably. 'Yes, yes. My point is this: What we perceive as *sorcery* is merely a method of juggling entropy. The Unmer transmit energy and matter from one place to another, most likely from one *universe* to another, through some sort of aspacial conduit. The Unmer's strength lies in their ability to plunder what I have chosen to call *cosmic remnants.*'

'How did you get past the guards?'

Maskelyne sighed. 'You're not listening. Our present universe is merely the latest configuration of energy and matter formed within a never-ending cycle of cosmic inflation. Like the ripples formed beneath a dripping tap – as the outer circles fade they are replaced by new ones. If my—'

'Did you *bribe* someone to bring all this equipment here?'

'If my theory is correct, then . . .' He paused and frowned at her. 'Of course I bribed someone. When dealing with the Haurstaf, it is practically immoral *not* to bribe someone.' He smiled thinly. 'If my theory is correct, it means that certain aspects of Unmer sorcery are not only detrimental to our universe, but completely impossible without assistance from beyond our universe.'

She just looked at him.

'Imagine a bathtub full of water,' he said.

She continued to stare at him.

'Now imagine there are two plugs in the bath, one at either end,' he went on. 'When we pull out both plugs, the water begins to drain through both openings at once. If the holes represent vast clusters of matter and the water represents the space between those clusters, then the flow of water represents the force of gravity.' He glanced around the terrace, looking for something he could draw a diagram with, but there was nothing to hand. 'In this analogy, the bathwater would flow out, leaving no *space* between the holes, no cosmos. But what is space? Is it tangible, like matter? Or does it merely represent a sea in which the *potential* for material interactions exists? What if, as the bath drained, the volume of water it contained did not diminish? What if the area of space between the holes actually *stretches*? If

SEA OF GHOSTS

the holes remain unchanged, the distance between them must increase.' He nodded. 'So the universe expands.'

'I really wish I hadn't come here,' Briana said.

Maskelyne walked over to the terrace balustrade and sat down. 'Have you ever wondered *how* the Unmer came to possess the ability to remove matter, to turn flesh and stone into vacuum? This talent requires no device, no sorcerous ring or pendant.' He shook his head. 'It is *inherent*, and therefore like nothing else we have ever seen.'

'It's just a gift,' Briana said. 'Like telepathy.'

Maskelyne threw his hands up. 'It is nothing like telepathy,' he said. 'Telepathy does not add or subtract anything from the universe. Look.' He walked over to the table and picked up a partially disassembled gem lantern from among the clutter of machine parts and tools. 'These burn for, say, a thousand years,' he said. 'Do you have any idea how much energy that requires? It's enough to blow a battleship to pieces, and it has to come from *somewhere*.' Next he untied a burlap sack from the leg of the table and opened it. Three small concrete spheres floated up out of the bag and rose gently towards the sky. Maskelyne scooped them back into the bag before they drifted too high. 'Air stones,' he said, 'or chariot ballast, or whatever name you want to give them. The repulsive force comes from *somewhere*.' Next he snatched up a stoppered ichusae. 'You recognize this, of course?' He set the bottle down again when he saw fear light Briana's eyes. 'Ichusae introduce poisonous matter to our world, matter brought from *somewhere* else. You see? Most of what the Unmer create *sucks* matter or energy from somewhere and dumps it into our world.'

'Void flies—' Briana began.

'Void flies are not *created*,' Maskelyne cried. 'Void flies are creatures which possess the same *inherent* ability the Unmer do. And that's the key. Where did they suddenly appear from? What

359

becomes of the matter they remove from our universe? Where does it go? There's a balance in all of this. A trade.'

Briana frowned.

Maskelyne's gaze travelled across the objects on the table. 'The universe expands in all directions,' he muttered. 'Elemental particles of matter cool and cease to fluctuate. But space cannot exist between identical particles. As variance decreases, more and more particles must find themselves occupying the same point in the universe, regardless of how far apart they are. Vast swathes of the cosmos begin to gather in one place, a single, tiny place that exists almost everywhere at the same time. Unimaginable pressure builds, and builds, and builds, until eventually . . .' He looked at her expectantly.

She shrugged.

Maskelyne felt deflated. 'I can see you're not taking this seriously,' he said.

'You weren't brought here to study the cosmos at our expense, Mr Maskelyne.'

'At your expense?' He shook his head in disbelief. 'Miss Marks, if my theory is correct, then it is very likely that there are still scraps of former universes adrift out there.' He jabbed a finger at the sky. 'Frozen, dying and *utterly* alien to anything we could imagine. If the Unmer have communicated with the inhabitants of one of these cosmic remnants and, indeed, have actively been *shifting matter* back and forth between here and there, then we need to consider any consequences that the subsequent enslavement of their race might have had.'

She sighed. 'Go on.'

'Our world is drowning,' he said. 'Whatever deal the Unmer made with the far side of the cosmos has evidently turned sour.' He sighed. 'I'm no merchant, but I know that when one party fails to adhere to a trade agreement, the other party gets angry.'

CHAPTER 16

PERTICA

Violent juddering woke Granger. He sat up abruptly, momentarily disorientated, then remembered where he was. Green light filtered through the windows of the deadship cabin, bathing the shelves of trove and Unmer experiments in a queer underwater luminance. Granger got up, wincing as his dry flesh cracked, and took a moment to work the numbness out of his arms and legs. It was freezing in here. His breath misted in the air before him. He wrapped a blanket around himself and shuffled over to the window.

Green ice floated upon a green sea. Outside the window stretched a frozen expanse of the Mare Verdant, the brine littered with broken slabs of ice and great nebulous snow-dusted masses with facets as deep and dark as bottle glass. From the bow of the ironclad came a dull pounding sound as the ship smashed its way through more of the ice field. Granger took out a fur-lined jacket from the captain's dressing room and forced his heavy joints into it as he stomped up the steps that led above deck.

It must have rained during the night. Fronds of clear ice crystals had formed on the metal tower in the centre of the deck and on the torn remnants of the spinnaker attached to it. The wind had blown them into crazy shapes. A sugaring of white snow crunched under Granger's boots. He scooped some up and ate it as he paced the deck. Vast ice-fields lay ahead of the deadship, a glittering expanse of emerald and white. In her wake stretched a channel of dark green water where she had punched through the surface ice. Granger walked to the bow of the ship and scanned the horizon. Basalt cliffs rose out of the sea a league to the north, their storm-cracked aspects mortared with snow. Upon the edge of this landmass perched a single building, a drab and windowless cube supporting a vast steel tower on its roof.

A sense of dread seemed to roll down from that structure and creep into Granger's bones. That building was the source of the deadship's power and could only be its ultimate destination. The force that had steered the icebreaker towards his own wooden lifeboat, and then brought him inexorably north, must emanate from there. In order to gain control of this ship, he must disable that interference. He gazed up at the building for a long time, watching for signs of life, but saw only white flurries of snow blowing across the black and green.

Constant snapping and pounding noises came from the prow as the deadship smashed a channel through the ice. The air remained as cold and sharp as a knife edge. Granger rubbed his hands and stamped his boots upon the deck, trying to coax some feeling into his body. He spotted an old wharf, partially hidden behind the headland of a sheltered natural harbour. The ice was thinner here and bereft of snow, its surface etched where the frozen brine had cracked and reformed. The ironclad slowed as it drew near, until the whining from the ship's tower suddenly stopped.

The ship coasted the final few yards and then bumped against the wharf. Silence fell over the deck, broken only by the hiss of the wind through frozen metal.

Trying to ignore the uneasy feeling in his guts, Granger hitched a canvas bag over his shoulder and, after weeks at sea, finally stepped onto dry land.

A stairway zigzagged from the wharf up into a deep cut in the cliff. Twisted iron railings bordered the steps in places, but many had sheared away and now lay at the bottom of the gully among tumbles of ice-fused rock. Granger edged his way upwards with one shoulder against the wall of the defile, testing each step before trusting his weight to it. Icicles overhung the trail in places, forming glassy passages. The wind keened like a grief-stricken child.

At the summit he paused to catch his breath. The air hurt his lungs. No other living thing was breathing this, and perhaps never had. Down below, the ironclad waited in that smashed green bay, as dark and empty as a coffin. To the north stretched a howling landscape of emerald and white, the snowfields sculpted by constant gales into scalloped ridges and dream-like shapes with razor-blade edges. From here Granger could see the transmitting station tower rising above a snowy bluff to the east. Perhaps a hundred and fifty feet high, it was far larger than the one aboard the deadship, supporting a torus three times the size of its smaller twin. A faint whining sound came from its summit.

Granger's boots sank into deep powder as he struggled up the bluff. At the summit he was rewarded with a clear view of the Unmer station. A square grey block with a huge round metal door, it occupied more than an acre of ground. Snow drifts engulfed its windward side, partially burying the whole structure. As Granger studied the landscape, he perceived other objects partly buried in the surrounding snow. *Dragon armour and bones*. Conquillas's Revolution, it seemed, had reached even this distant place.

And yet *this* station continued to transmit power. The attackers had failed to shut it down.

The hinges had frozen solid, and it took considerable effort to pull that massive door open. Granger chipped away at the ice with his knife until, finally, it gave way. With a metal groan, the door swung open a few feet before lodging itself in snow. A dark tunnel lay behind, wide enough to drive a horse and carriage down. Granger took out his gem lantern and held it high. There were signs of violence. Black stains spattered the curved floor. The concrete had been scorched by dragonfire and heavily scarred by impacts from blades. A single thigh bone lay in a frozen puddle, and yet, strangely, he couldn't see any other human remains.

Close fighting in here, several opponents.

Twenty paces further along, the passageway swelled into a spherical chamber lined by coils of copper wire. The humming sound was more intense here, the air noticeably warmer. Melt water had leaked in through the apex and collected in a shallow green pool in the hollow below. Granger stepped carefully around it. Several objects lay under the water – metal brackets or machine parts, all furred with verdigris. Two further openings led deeper into the station. He listened at each for a while, then lifted his gem lantern again and took the first passage.

This conduit took him to another wire-walled sphere where the passage branched again. Again, Granger chose the opening from which the humming noise seemed louder. He passed through four more of these junctions before he began to perceive a tremor running through the floor. It was accompanied by an uncomfortable tingling sensation in his fingertips. His gem lantern seemed brighter, too. In places he found round metal plaques set into the curving walls, each inset with a small clear lens. He passed four or five, before something about them began to bother him. When he found yet another, he stopped to inspect it more closely. As he lowered his eye to the lens at its centre, he glimpsed another eye withdrawing abruptly from the other side.

Granger shuddered and moved on.

Eventually, the concrete maze opened out into an enormous cylindrical space like the inside of a tower. Scores of other conduits led away from its base. The humming sound he had been following reached a fierce resonance here; he could feel it reverberating in his teeth and bones. Great mounds of trove covered the floor, some twenty or thirty feet high in places. Pistols and cannons and suits of armour lay among piles of wrecked war machines: arbalists and turtles and drop-forged rams. His gem lantern shone so brightly it illuminated the whole vast space from wall to wall. There were ballistic weapons and energy weapons, and countless burned and twisted metal pieces of indeterminable purpose – a bonfire of scrap and used weapons, of flanged tripods and serrated fins, with bursts of wire, glass shields, goggles, gauntlets and cannon barrels protruding like giant steel fingers. Upon a nearby mound lay an ancient sky chariot, heavily dented and fire-blackened, but seemingly intact. Granger's gaze travelled up the walls, and higher still, to the ceiling far above, where similar mounds of wreckage had floated up and gathered there in sorcerous defiance of gravity.

He frowned. Had he been descending underground all this time? From the outside the building hadn't seemed tall enough to contain a space this large.

Amidst all this trove, one area in the centre of the chamber had been left clear. Here a single stone pedestal supported a crystal as large as a man's head. It was glowing brightly, radiating shafts of ever-moving light, like a lighthouse lantern. The humming noise seemed to emanate from its facets. Granger let his kitbag slide down from his shoulder to the floor, then tucked his seeing knife into his belt.

He wandered over to the nearest heap of trove and reached in to pull out a sword. But the instant his hand closed on the grip, something remarkable happened.

One moment he was alone, the next he was surrounded. Out of thin air they appeared – six men dressed in bulky Unmer furs, brutally thin, with howling red eyes and brine-scorched skin.

And every one of them was pulling a sword from the surrounding scrap.

Sorcery.

Granger swung his stolen blade up at the nearest figure, but his opponent parried instantly. The two blades clashed. Granger sensed movement all around him. He leaped back, and his opponent did likewise. And then Granger recognized him.

His opponent was the very image of himself, identical in every way, from the fur jacket he had taken from the deadship down to the sword he carried. Granger turned his head to examine the other five, and as he did so these five turned *their* heads in unison. Every one of them was *him,* and every one continued to mimic his every move. He lifted his sword, and the others lifted *their* swords. He lowered the sword again, watching as the simulacrums copied him. On their faces he saw six mirror images of his own startled expression. He dropped the sword . . .

. . . and the men vanished.

He picked up the sword again, and they reappeared.

A cheerful voice called out, 'You found my Replicating Sword.'

Granger, and his six replicas, turned to see an old man standing in the corner of the chamber. He was short, stooped and grey of face, and he wore an old suit of mail several sizes too large for him. A simple tin crown sat low upon his brow, balanced above his prodigious nose and ears. Tufts of yellow hair clung to his head the way dead weeds remain clinging to a mountainside. If a man's attitude to life leaves its mark in his face then this crooked figure had found much to smile about over the years. And he was smiling now, a huge smile that reached all the way from his lips to his honey-coloured eyes.

'It's designed to allow a warrior to fight multiple enemies at once,' he said. 'But controlling them is tricky. You have to think of multiple manoeuvres at the same time or the simulacrums just mimic you. I could never completely master it myself.' He chuckled. 'And I've got the scars to prove it.'

The man looked vaguely Unmer, but he spoke Anean like a Losotan. His crown rested low on his brow, and Granger thought he knew why. If this man had fought during the Uprising, it would be covering another scar.

'Some of the other inventions are even harder to wield,' the old man said. 'You're lucky you didn't pick up any of the Sniggering Blades. A sword like that will trick you into cracking open your own bones and sucking out the marrow if you give it half a chance. Even Brutalists are frightened of them.' He nodded amicably. 'And then there are the Phasing Shields and Void Blades, of course. To call them *terrifying* doesn't even begin to do them justice.'

'Who are you?' Granger said. He was startled to hear his own voice coming out of six mouths at once, but not startled enough to drop the weapon.

'The name's Herian,' the old man replied. 'I'm the operator here.'

'I didn't think there were any free Unmer left,' Granger said, 'except Conquillas.'

Herian's smile withered. 'Conquillas will be judged by powers greater than us,' he said, strolling forward. 'He gave up the right to call himself Unmer a long time ago.'

Granger noted that the old man's crown only partially covered a red welt above his left eyebrow. *Not exactly free, then.* Herian had been leucotomized by the Haurstaf. But if he'd been captured and deliberately crippled at Awl, then how did he find his way out here?

The old man picked his way across piles of trove. 'A lot of these flowspaces were used for storage during the war. Dragons don't much like to venture inside them. Not against a gradient of this magnitude.' He stubbed his foot on something and let out a curse, then picked up the offending object and flung it away. It was a skeletal box of some sort. 'It's all clutter to me now,' he said. 'I swear there's more of it every time I come in here.' He approached the crystal and examined it carefully, allowing curtains of shimmering light to bathe his face. For a moment he seemed to forget himself, but then he said, 'Have you looked at this closely, yet?'

'How do I get out of here?' Granger said.

Herian didn't answer.

'How do I gain control of the ironclad?'

The old man continued to gaze into the crystal.

'The icebreaker,' Granger insisted. 'Tell me how to steer it.'

'You don't steer it,' Herian said. 'Only the captain can do that.'

'The captain is dead.'

Herian smiled again. 'That didn't stop him from delivering his package and then bringing you here, did it?' His gaze returned to the jewel, which was now shining even more brightly than moments before. The colour and texture of its light had altered, too. A scattering of pink and orange rays swept across the old man's mail suit, his weathered face and his tin crown. 'Don't you find it mesmerizing?' he said. 'The light, I mean . . .' Radiance flooded over the mounds of trove behind him. As the rays touched the Unmer devices, many of them activated. Deep within the heap it seemed that embers began to glow. Energy weapons hummed and crackled. To Granger's astonishment, additional copies of himself began to appear. He moved towards Herian, and his simulacrums moved too.

'Draws you in, doesn't it?' Herian said.

Granger stopped.

'Time's horizon,' the old man went on. 'Entropaths use it to control the gradient, the rate of aspacial flow. You can't see it, but it's all around us now. If this device let it all through at once, our universe would collapse like that.' He glanced up at Granger and snapped his fingers. 'Bang. Crushed in a blink.'

The radiance from the crystal now filled the entire chamber. Through its facets Granger spied an image of a black plain under a burning sky. Curtains of red and pink light tore across the horizon. Lightning flickered. He took another step forward and then stopped himself. Had he meant to approach? His instincts screamed at him not to get any closer. The sky within that jewel continued to pulse and writhe. All around him, his simulacrums began to walk forward. And Granger found himself following them.

He halted beside Herian, without having made the decision to approach. And now he saw that the plain within the jewel was not land at all, but a great black sea, empty but for a single cone of rock rising above the tarry waters. Upon this solitary island stood a cylindrical metal tower as tall and broad as the interior of this chamber. 'What is that place?' he said.

'It's this place,' Herian said, 'and yet it's not. It's a fortress, a refuge, a doorway, the last bastion of thought in a dying universe.'

'The source of brine?'

Herian chuckled. 'Do you even know what *brine* is?'

Granger hesitated.

Herian grinned even more fiercely. 'What happens when the seas rise?'

'We drown.'

'That's the sort of limited answer I'd expect from a human,' Herian said. '*The seas rise, the land shrinks, and woe to all mankind.*' He laughed. 'Brine *never* stops flowing. Not in a hundred years, nor in a million; not when our air thins and boils away and this bloated planet pulls the moon and the sun down from the sky. It will fill the vacuum between the stars long after *my* race has

departed this world and yours has perished. It isn't a weapon, it's
a catalyst – the broth from which a new cosmos will be manufac-
tured.'

'Who sent it here?'

Herian shrugged. 'We made a deal.'

'With whom?'

At that moment the whole chamber gave a sudden shudder. Light burst from the trove all around, as though those dull
embers within the mountains of scrap had suddenly been fanned
into flames. Herian cocked his head to one side and grinned.
'You're about to see for yourself,' he said. 'They've sensed you
and activated the conduits.' He gestured towards the nearest
wall, where a dim green glow now pulsed within the passageway
openings. 'They don't like trespassers.'

Granger grabbed the old man's mail shirt. 'Who are they?'

Herian beamed. 'Your race would call them gods,' he said.
'Mine think of them as masters of entropy. They have stalled the
end of their own universe.' His eyes sparkled with awe. 'Can you
comprehend the sheer magnitude of that achievement? To actually *resist* the formation of a singularity . . . even for a moment?'

Granger shook him. 'You invited them *here*?'

'Not me,' Herian said. 'I'm just an operator.'

At the old man's words, someone seized Granger from
behind. A strong arm gripped his neck, dragging him backwards.
Granger reacted at once, driving his elbow into the unseen
opponent's ribs.

Something struck him hard in the gut, punching the air
from him. The blow had come from nowhere. Granger hadn't
even seen whatever had hit him, but he felt his opponent's grip
slacken. He wrestled free, spun round . . .

. . . and found himself facing one of the simulacrums.

This copy was no longer mimicking him. It was bent over,

clutching its ribs. And, to Granger's astonishment, so were all the others. At least a dozen copies stood around him, every one of them doubled over in pain.

Had Granger struck *himself*, along with all the others? He raised the sword, but none of the simulacrums copied his gesture. Many of them had already recovered. They were edging closer from all directions at once. For a moment, Granger stood there, uncertain. Then he dropped the sword.

The simulacrums vanished.

Herian laughed. 'If you don't make decisions for your own swordsmen,' he said, 'then there are always others who'll do it for you.' He indicated the scrap pile. 'Please, help yourself to something else. Plenty more weapons to choose from.'

Granger stooped to grab a different sword but hesitated. He glanced at Herian.

Herian shrugged. 'It wouldn't be *my* choice.'

Granger walked up to him and punched him in the face.

The old man fell back into a pile of metal. His crown fell off, revealing the leucotomy scar on his forehead. He spat blood, then gave Granger a red grin. 'A hundred years ago I'd have made you suffer for that,' he said. 'Old age has mellowed me.' He reached over into a heap of trove and grabbed a heavy flintlock pistol with a barrel big enough to ram a fist inside. He swung it round to bear on Granger.

Granger forced his boot down on Herian's arm, pinning the weapon. He crouched over the old man and slugged him again, breaking his jaw. Herian howled. He managed to squeeze the trigger and the pistol gave a soft hiss, like an exhalation. A *haze* passed through the air, scattering the trove beyond the weapon's barrel in all directions. The flying scrap turned to dust even as Granger watched. He slammed Herian's wrist down, again and again, until the old man dropped the pistol. Then he kicked the damn thing away. He punched Herian's face a second time, and then a third.

Herian sputtered and coughed, but then he grinned once more. 'Beating me doesn't even scratch the cosmos, you know?' he said. 'The wings of a fly make as much damage. Look around you, man.'

The crystal was blazing now, filling the whole room with the radiance of that alien sky trapped inside. And something equally strange was happening within the mouths of the conduits. Green light flickered within each of those portals, accompanied by a furious crackling sound and a deeper, more regular mechanical *shunting*. Was this whole tower a *machine*? A piece of trove itself? Many of the surrounding weapons began to glow and shiver, as weird fires danced across their metal surfaces. Granger could feel the energy crawling across his skin.

A bolt of lightning shot from one of the conduit doorways and struck the crystal, followed a heartbeat later by dozens more in rapid succession. The air fizzed with power. Herian shrieked with laughter, his bruised and swollen face contorted into a rictus of joy. His tongue lolled in his mouth; his eyes stared madly at the lightning. Granger released him and searched around frantically for something, anything with which to protect himself. He hauled out a heavy glass shield and raised it before him. Looking through it was like looking through an old, warped window, and yet the landscape he saw through that shield bore no resemblance to the chamber around him. Instead, he perceived a winter forest, the trees like charcoal dashes on a white page.

Herian growled, 'Beware of wolves.'

Granger spied movement in that world beyond the shield – grey shapes loping through the snow. Something flashed by to his immediate left, and he spun the shield around to follow the movement. Through the woozy glass he saw a wolf pounce at him, its red eyes agleam, its fangs bared. The beast slammed against the shield, knocking Granger backwards. And suddenly he felt its weight on top of him, pinning him down as it slavered and snapped at the other side of the glass.

Herian laughed. 'How does it feel to hold something that's in two places at once?'

Granger heaved the shield aside and the weight abruptly disappeared. The wolves and their bleak forest remained inside the glass.

Electrical fluids were now streaming between the crystal and the mouths of the conduits, forming a blazing net that filled the centre of the chamber. The air smelled of storms. As Granger watched, the energy began to coalesce in front of the crystal, forming a discernible shape. It seemed to him that he could see the outline of a female figure in that chaos – white and luminous with lightning for hair.

'She's reversing entropy,' Herian said. 'Recreating *herself* in this place.' He scrambled to his feet and laughed again. 'You needn't bother arming yourself – flesh, steel, bullets, it's all just matter to her.'

The woman amidst the lightning was becoming more solid with each passing moment as energy hardened and took the shape of flesh and bone and armour. Her mirrored plate had been crafted to resemble the facets of a crystal and shone with the brilliance of a thousand gem lanterns. She wore a glass shield strapped to her back, and carried a whip that sparkled with energy. Her long hair blazed and snapped, the electric fluids arcing in every direction. As the energy dissipated around her, Granger saw that her face was old and grey and haggard. For an instant he thought that she was weeping, but then he realized the truth. Those weren't tears he saw, but brine leaking from the corners of her eyes and trickling out of her open mouth. She looked and smelled like one of the Drowned.

'Those tears will burn,' Herian said. 'But I see you've had some experience of that already.' He was sitting on a nearby mound of trove with his chin resting on his fist. 'You look like a man who's already had a taste of the world to come.'

Granger tore his eyes from the woman. Frantically, he eyed the trove around him. *Swords, shields, pistols, armour.* He didn't know what any of it *did.* He reached for another sword, but then stopped when Herian began to snigger. This was Unmer weaponry. Most of it would be beyond him. He spied the kitbag he'd brought from the deadship. He'd packed it with tools he'd found aboard. But they were Unmer too. He snatched it up anyway and threw it at the entropath in wild desperation.

She cracked her whip. The kitbag fell in two pieces, spilling its contents onto the floor.

Shit.

He glanced back at the conduits leading into the chamber. Green fires now burned deep inside them with such savagery that each opening looked like the mouth to a strange chemical furnace. Streamers of lightning flowed from every one of them, feeding the crystal which fed the manifestation before him. He wheeled round and fixed his gaze upon the Unmer chariot lying at a shallow angle upon a heap of trove. Blue and pink electrical auras fluttered across its egg-shaped hull.

Granger bolted across the room and, chased by the sound of Herian's laughter, ducked inside the open hatch of the flying machine. The floor sloped sharply down towards the stern. Dozens of switches, dials, rollers and levers occupied a console that swept across the bow of the vessel, each marked by Unmer glyphs and numbers of indeterminable meaning. Several panels beneath the console had been removed, leaving the internal mechanics exposed. Lights of all colours flickered within that mess of wires. Above the console, three glass panels hinged like winged dresser mirrors offered views of the chamber beyond. Through these Granger watched the entropath approach. Brine continued to pour from her mouth and eyes; it trickled from her fingers and through the spaces in her armour.

Granger studied the console. None of the controls made any immediate sense. He placed the heel of his hand against a roller and eased it forward. The chariot bucked suddenly and then shuddered, but did not move from its position. The machinery within the console gave out a painful screech. He began trying each control in turn, flipping switches in sequence, pulling levers and spinning rollers in all directions. The chariot jerked suddenly to port, slamming Granger against the bulkhead. He heard laughter behind him.

Herian was holding onto the hatch. 'I don't know what you hope to accomplish,' he said, smiling. 'There's enough energy pouring through the conduits to burn this ship to nothing. My lady will simply absorb the residue.'

Granger located the roller that had sent the craft to port and turned it in the opposite direction. The chariot lurched suddenly to starboard, causing Herian to tumble head over heels in through the open hatch. He landed on the floor, striking his head, as the flying machine burst free of the scrap pile and careened across the chamber. Granger rolled the control wheel back to its central position. *That's lateral control.* Carefully, he turned a second wheel, set several inches above the first. The chariot responded by rising quickly through the air. *Vertical control.* Now, where was thrust? Two large hand-grips caught his attention. He eased them both away from himself, and the craft surged forward, trembling slightly.

Herian groaned. 'You're wasting a perfectly good chariot,' he said.

Granger ignored him. Through the glass panels he watched the entropath diminish below him as the craft rose higher and higher. She had strapped her glass shield to one arm and carried her whip in her free hand. Brine continued to pour from her, forming an expanding pool around her boots. She lifted her gaze to the chariot and then lashed out with the whip.

The flying machine should have been well beyond the range of that weapon. But as Granger watched in horror, the lash extended upwards like a bolt of black lightning.

He spun the lateral control wheel to port, but he wasn't fast enough. The whip struck the craft, opening a thin crack in the port side of the hull. Light shone through.

Herian began to chuckle again. 'She's toying with you,' he said. 'That lash could cut the world in half.'

Granger spun the vertical control wheel, and the craft shot upwards at breakneck speed. Through the view screens he watched the floor drop far away. The entropath was drawing back her whip to strike again. Granger waited a heartbeat before halting his ascent. As the woman struck out a second time, he sent the chariot plummeting downwards like a stone.

The force of acceleration almost lifted him from his feet, but he clung to the console. He heard the whip crack somewhere overhead. A yard from the floor, he brought the flying machine to a sudden halt, then sent it barrelling sideways towards the centre of the chamber, towards the entropath herself. If he'd judged his heading correctly . . .

The lower edge of the chariot hatch crashed into the pedestal, shattering it and toppling the crystal balanced upon its summit. As the craft's momentum carried it onwards, the great jewel flew in through the open hatch, bounced off Herian's prone body and came to rest against the port side of the hull.

Herian's expression turned fearful. 'What are you doing?'

Granger slammed the thrust levers forward. The jewel rolled to the back of the control room and clunked against the rear bulkhead. If the damned thing was acting as a bridge between the entropath's universe and this one, then he had to hope she wouldn't risk its destruction. He spun the lateral control again, slewing the chariot in the direction of the nearest conduit.

'You'll burn us alive! Herian cried.

And the crystal too.

The lash snapped again, and this time a thin slice disappeared from the starboard side of the hull. The blow had cleaved through the edge of the console itself. The chariot stuttered and yawed suddenly to port. Granger wrestled with the controls to bring it back on course. Ahead through the view screens the conduit mouth loomed like a green inferno. Sparks burst from the console under Granger's fingers. Engines screamed. The whole ship began to judder madly.

'Stop,' Herian cried, trying to rise from the floor.

But by then they had reached the portal.

A storm of energy poured into the chariot through the open hatchway, arcing between the bulkheads. Green flames tore across the console. The view screens blazed like suns. Granger cried out as electrical fluids shot through his body. His muscles began to spasm uncontrollably, and for a heartbeat he was aware of nothing but light and agony and the smell of his own burning flesh.

Abruptly, the light vanished.

It was as if someone had thrown a switch. The surrounding inferno simply ceased to be, leaving the view screens dark and the craft flying on through gloom. Granger eased back the throttle levers, slowing their forward momentum. Apart from the hum of their engines, the conduit was silent.

Herian groaned from the floor. 'You've no idea what you just risked.'

Granger halted the flying machine. He stepped past the old man and retrieved the jewel from the rear of the cabin. It had ceased to glow, and he could no longer perceive the alien landscape within its facets. It looked like an ordinary crystal. He wedged it behind one of the view screens and gunned the engines again.

'Let me take it back,' Herian said.

Granger just grunted. He flew the chariot onwards at a much slower pace, threading his way through the conduits and junction spheres until her reached the transmitting station's main entrance. All appeared as dark and desolate as it had at first. He brought the craft's bow gently up against the outer door and then eased the throttles forward. With a shudder and an almighty groan, the door scraped open, and the small vessel moved out into sunlight.

Snowflakes swirled across the view screens and blew in through the open hatch and the gaps in the hull. Granger's hands danced across the controls as he brought the flying machine up and over the building in a slowly rising spiral. He passed the white, lace-frill skeleton of the transmitting tower and the great torus upon its summit, where he let the chariot come to a halt. The northern ice fields shimmered like emeralds and diamonds, a jewelled coast abutting the bottle-green waters of the Mare Verdant. Awl lay somewhere to the south-west. He might reach it in a few days, but then what?

The Haurstaf had an entire army at their disposal, while Granger had one half-wrecked little chariot. He didn't know if the craft would even make it that far.

He stood there for a moment, thinking.

'Let me go,' Herian said. He sat on the floor, shivering, with his shoulders slumped in an attitude of defeat. Snow was already gathering on his hair and mail shirt. 'I'm no danger to you. Keep the chariot, let me take the jewel back.'

Granger picked up the jewel and carried it over to the hatch. An icy gale blew around his shoulders. A few yards below him, the toroid gleamed dully under the monochrome sky. Not a single snowflake had adhered to that metal surface.

'What are you doing?' Herian said.

Granger pitched the jewel out of the hatch. It landed in the depression in the centre of the toroid with an almighty *clang*, rolled one way, and then the other, before finally settling.

Herian crawled over, then let out a groan.

'You'll get it back,' Granger said. 'But I want something in return.'

The old man stared after the jewel.

'That sword I picked up,' Granger said. 'The simulacrums . . .'

'What about them?'

'Show me how to use it properly.'

'That's all?' Herian said. 'You want to wield a Replicating Sword?'

Granger grunted. 'That's just the beginning.'

The room looked like a lecture theatre to Ianthe, with wooden seats rising in curved tiers before her. It was empty apart from a panel of four Haurstaf witches. Subtle changes in their expressions told her they were having a discussion, even if she couldn't hear them. Briana Marks glanced at Sister Ulla, who gave an almost imperceptible shake of her head. The remaining two spinsters simply glared down at Ianthe as if they knew the secrets of her soul. They were older than anyone Ianthe had seen before, balanced there like pinnacles of weathered rock.

'Really,' Briana said suddenly. 'This is beyond tiring. Why not let the girl hear what you have to say? I'm not going to go over this twice for her benefit. If the point of psychic warfare is to inflict pain, suffering and death, then she's done exceptionally well.'

Sister Ulla snorted. 'We can't have lawlessness and anarchy within our own ranks.'

Briana looked at the old woman with an expression of incredulity. 'Anarchy? Don't be so dramatic, Ulla. The loss of one brat is not going to make any difference to the world. She was hardly an asset.'

'The parents!' Sister Ulla protested.

'*Why on earth* would you want to inform them?'

'They'll find out eventually—'

Briana batted a hand at the other woman. 'We have finances set aside to deal with these sorts of problems. Don't bore us all with your peacock morality. Her parents ought to be glad she was given an opportunity here in the first place.'

Sister Ulla fluffed out her chest, as if she was going to protest, but then she sank back into her chair.

Briana looked at Ianthe. 'Mara said you turned that girl's brain to paste.'

Ianthe felt her face turn red. She shuffled from one foot to the other. She wanted to say that she hadn't meant it, that it wasn't her fault and if they would let her go home she'd never bother the Haurstaf again. But that wasn't going to happen now. She lowered her head.

Briana laughed suddenly. 'You think so, Ulla?' she said. 'I'd like to see *you* do it.'

'Don't tempt me,' Sister Ulla growled.

Nobody spoke for several minutes, and it seemed to Ianthe that the witches had fallen back into psychic communication. But then Briana turned to her and said, 'Sister Ulla is of the opinion that you had help. Did you have help, Ianthe?'

Ianthe said nothing.

'If you don't mind,' Briana went on, 'we'd like to examine those eyeglasses of yours.'

'They're just eyeglasses.'

'Then you won't mind—'

'No!' Ianthe cried. 'They don't belong to you.' Tears welled in her eyes, blurring her vision through the lenses. These old women had no right to ask her to give up her sight, no right at all. All of them except Briana were glaring furiously at her now.

Sister Ulla looked as if she was ready to explode with indignation. 'You'll hand them over now,' she said, 'or I'll come down there and take them from you myself.'

Ianthe spoke through her teeth. 'Try it.'

Briana raised her hands. 'That's enough,' she said. She glanced from one sister to another, before returning her attention to Ianthe. Her expression softened. 'There's a place for you here, Ianthe, but only if you work with us. I won't tolerate threats. I expect you to be as civil and honest with us as we've been with you.' She gave her a half-smile. 'We can't put you back into the classroom now.'

'But I didn't mean to harm—' Ianthe's voice broke and she began to cry.

Briana left her seat and walked down the central aisle of the theatre. She wrapped her arms around Ianthe and held her. Ianthe couldn't stop herself. Her whole body began to convulse with sobs. Tears flowed freely until she could no longer see through her lenses. She clung fiercely to Briana. 'I'm sorry,' she said. 'I'm sorry.'

The Haurstaf leader smoothed Ianthe's hair. 'Shush,' she said. 'You've done nothing to be sorry about. All you need is a little guidance.' She held Ianthe for a long time. Finally she squeezed Ianthe's shoulders and gently pushed her away. 'If you can do that to a human,' she said, smiling, 'think what you could do to the Unmer.'

Ianthe sniffed and shook her head.

'This is what we do, Ianthe,' Briana said. 'It's what your classmates have been training towards, what poor Caroline sacrificed her life for.'

'Constance,' Ianthe said.

Briana nodded. 'And when you see what the Unmer are capable of, you'll understand why the Guild is so vital. Women like us keep the world from falling apart.' She turned to the other three witches. 'I think she's ready to see the dungeons now.'

Sister Ulla shook her head, but her two companions looked at each other for a few moments. 'There's no going back if you decide to take that route,' one of them said. 'She'll be bound to us for good or ill.'

Briana made a face. 'Don't be so melodramatic, Bethany,' she said. 'We can always kill her later.' She moved her lips close to Ianthe's ear. 'I'm joking. But your acceptance into the Guild will have other consequences. Maskelyne will be executed for his crimes.'

Ianthe looked up at her for a long moment. 'What about his wife? His son?'

Briana looked surprised. 'You want them dead, too?'

'No, I mean—'

'We must protect our family from the Maskelynes of this world,' the witch said. 'Family is important, don't you think?'

Ianthe's eyes filled with tears again. She nodded.

Briana extended her hand. 'Then come with me.'

What happened next happened quickly. Ianthe found herself whisked away from that room. Briana Marks led her on through the palace, through glassy black corridors and halls and rooms where women Ianthe did not know looked on in grim silence. They descended one stairwell and then a second and a third and a fourth, until Ianthe lost count and it seemed to her that they must be deep with the earth itself. Finally they came to a nondescript door in a small stone antechamber. Briana turned a key in the lock.

They stepped out onto a balcony set high on one wall of an enormous, brightly lit chamber – one of four platforms connected by a cruciform steel catwalk. Thousands of gem lanterns depended from the vaulted ceiling overhead, filling the entire space with harsh white light. Below the catwalk lay a maze of roofless concrete cells, each about six feet to a side. Hundreds of small openings, barely large enough for a man to squeeze through, connected each cell to one or more of its neighbours in a seemingly haphazard fashion. Ianthe strolled to the edge of the balcony and looked down. A network of pipes suspended beneath the catwalk fed an array of shower heads, one located above each cell. Their purpose was presumably to wash the occupants below.

Hundreds of Unmer filled that grey labyrinth, either alone in a cell or gathered together in small groups. All were naked and painfully thin. They slouched against the bare walls or sat on the floors or lay sleeping. The murmur of conversation gradually ceased as they became aware of their observers in the gallery above.

'It used to be a mental faculty test,' Briana said, her voice echoing far across the chamber, 'but we ended up using the place to store the breeding stock. They're all leucotomized, of course, so security isn't much of an issue here. Food can be thrown down, filth washed away, and we use acid to direct test subjects to the gate for removal.'

Ianthe's throat grew dry. They were all looking up at her.

'The leucotomy procedure allows them privacy,' Briana said. 'We don't need psychics to monitor them constantly.'

'They look so miserable.'

'Misery is the price of freedom,' Brian replied. 'We can't have them walking through walls or vanishing matter at will. They're happy enough. Come now, I'll take you to the zoo.' She set off across the catwalk at a brisk pace.

Ianthe hesitated. 'The zoo?'

'That's where we keep the able-minded ones,' the witch called back.

Ianthe waited a moment longer, then ran after her. The catwalk rattled under her boots. She kept her gaze level, afraid to look down at the pitiful creatures below. She caught up with Briana just as she reached the opposite balcony. Briana unlocked another door and ushered her into a corridor lit by gem lanterns recessed behind copper mesh. A door at the end of this passage led to yet another stairwell, which descended even further beneath the earth.

By the time they reached the bottom, Ianthe was quite out of breath. They had reached a circular chamber with walls clad in blood-coloured seawood inlaid with curlicues of copper. Recessed lanterns threw cross-hatch patterns across the living rock floor. At least a dozen exits surrounded them, each blocked by a door made from different coloured glass. The air was much cooler here and carried the scent of perfume.

Ianthe could sense large numbers of people behind each of the doors. Her inner vision fluttered with the lights of their perceptions: a hundred of them, maybe more. And yet she held back in spite of all her nervous excitement – forcing her mind to remain in her own body. She was about to witness the Haurstaf's greatest secret with her own eyes.

Briana opened the door.

Ianthe' first impression of the chamber beyond was that it was upside down. Light poured into the room through huge slabs of glass set into the floor. These panes were all of various shapes and sizes: squares and oblongs and long strips. In the centre of the room stood a tall, thin wooden structure, like a small watchtower or an improbably large high-chair. A ladder on the near side gave access to a cushioned seat at its summit. Upon this sat a young witch in plain white robes. She had been peering down into the glass floor below her but now glanced up as Briana and Ianthe entered.

'Any mischief?' Briana asked.

The witch on the high-chair did not reply.

'Verbally,' Briana said

The other woman cast a curious glance at Ianthe. 'Not in here,' she said. 'But we had an incident in suite seven.'

'Who was in the chair?'

The younger woman shrugged. 'Some new girl. She over-reacted.'

'Did the prisoner survive?'

'Sort of.'

As Briana and Ianthe approached, Ianthe looked down through the glass pane under her feet. Below lay a bedroom, as richly furnished as any other in the palace, with silken sheets and plump pillows on the bed, Evensraum rugs on the floor. Paintings and tapestries adorned the walls, giving the room a rather stately feel. One of the two doors led to a bathroom, with a smaller glass pane for a ceiling. Ianthe walked over it and found herself gazing down at a huge copper bathtub with a matching sink. The other bedroom door opened into an enormous lounge, also roofed with glass. Through this pane, Ianthe could see a young man reclining on a red settee, reading a book. He glanced up at her without expression, before returning his attention to the pages. To the right of the lounge lay a small library containing a writing desk flanked by bookshelves. The witch's high-chair allowed her to look down into any of the rooms below.

Briana stood directly over the man in the lounge. She tapped her heel against the floor and said, 'How is the prince today?'

The young man yawned, but didn't look up.

'He's been ignoring me for months now,' said the witch in the high-chair. 'Not so much as a glance.'

'But you must be used to *that*,' Briana said. 'A face like yours . . .'

The witch did not reply.

Ianthe walked across the glass floor. She couldn't take her eyes off the young man. He couldn't have been much older than her, and yet he appeared so much more relaxed and confident in his surroundings. *A touch of arrogance, even?* He was clearly aware of the women in the chamber above him, but chose to dismiss them, casually turning the pages of his book with long white fingers. He had a pale, slightly effeminate face framed by an unruly mop of hay-coloured hair, and he wore a flamboyant smoking jacket of red velvet trimmed with gold.

'He hasn't been leucotomized,' Ianthe said.

Briana looked up. 'We couldn't do *that* to the king's son. It wouldn't be civil.' She glanced down again. 'Not as long as he behaves himself.'

An Unmer prince? It seemed odd to think of the Unmer having a kingdom of their own.

'The first emperors tried for years to devise a physical prison to contain the Unmer,' Briana said. 'No psychics, no monitoring, just walls. They submerged their prisons under the sea. They used chains and cables to suspend them over pits.' She paced the glass floor, watching the young man below. 'Nothing worked.'

'Wouldn't they just fall *through* the ground at the bottom of the pit?' Ianthe asked.

'Oh, they can keep that up for a while,' Briana replied. 'Fifty feet into solid rock, a hundred feet, maybe more. But there's a limit to the amount of matter they can destroy before they get tired. Sooner or later, the fall catches up with them.' She stopped pacing. 'No, that wasn't the problem. The problem wasn't what they destroyed, but what they *made* when you weren't watching them.'

'Trove,' Ianthe said.

'They'll sit for days over a chunk of stone or scrap of metal, running their fingers over it, chanting and muttering to themselves. It's almost as if they're praying. And when they've finished, the piece of stone or metal isn't a piece of stone or metal any more.'

'So you watch them *all* the time?'

'For their own protection,' Briana said. 'Otherwise we'd have to kill them.' She tapped her heel against the glass floor again. 'Isn't that right, Marquetta?'

The young man continued to ignore her.

Briana's lips narrowed, and all of a sudden Ianthe sensed *something* in the air around her – a reverberation like a musical note too low to hear. The young man in the room below cried out suddenly. He dropped his book, clamped both hands against his temples and rolled over in agony.

'Their minds are like wine glasses,' Briana said. 'Easy to crack, easy to shatter.'

'Stop it!' Ianthe cried.

Briana exhaled, and the sensation in the air abruptly disappeared. Down below, the young man slumped forward and held his face in his hands. He was breathing heavily, his shoulders trembling slightly.

Briana turned to Ianthe and smiled. 'Now let's go find you one to practise on,' she said.

CHAPTER 17

OVER AWL

Dear Lucille,

~~*Let's not be under any doubt that some trumped-up, officious envelope-steamer who has been awarded her pointless role within the Haurstaf due to a lack of any real psychical ability will have read this letter before it reached you.*~~ *If said person realizes the truth of that statement, and if she is insecure enough to feel threatened by it, she will undoubtedly wield what little power she possesses by immediately utilizing her censoring pen. However, upon realizing her pettiness was predicted, she should then feel embarrassed enough to wish to destroy the entire letter.*

But she won't.

She won't do this because I coated the envelope in a fast-acting anemone poison capable of being absorbed through the skin. Our envelope-steamer will be dead in minutes. I have arranged for the letter itself to be removed from her corpse by a highly paid accomplice, who will pass it on to you, my dear, in a plain blue, non-toxic envelope. If the envelope containing this missive was not blue, then something has gone fearfully wrong, and I apologize.

I miss you and Jontney terribly. Awl Palace is an empty shell without you here. There is an academy – in which our vicious little trove-hunter has been enrolled – and a modicum of artefacts for me to study. The sisters float around in their robes as aimlessly

as whiffs of cloud, soaking up gossip from the ends of the world.
They have no interest the greater mysteries of life, but, like the
majority of their sex, are content to twitter vacuously among
themselves. It's a blessing I cannot hear telepathic conversation,
for every spoken conversation I have overheard eventually leans
towards the subject of hair.

Briana Marks is different. She is cruelly unsubtle, but clever,
and finds deep enjoyment in the power games between her own
organization and the empire. A woman like her expects to find
treachery in every shadow. Sadly, because of her distrust I have
failed to impress upon her the importance of my work.

Nevertheless, I believe I have achieved a major breakthrough
in my understanding of the Unmer's source of power. If I cannot
convince Sister Marks of the importance of this, I must leave at
once for Losoto to gain an audience with Emperor Hu. Be ready,
Lucille. I will soon come for you both.

Maskelyne was pacing his room when someone slid a piece of
folded paper under the door. He raced over and snatched it up.
He had been expecting a reply from Lucille, but this note startled
him. It was a coded message from his contact.

32/3/44/51/163/33/29/29/32/19/32/3/67/8/56/9/163/3/7/80/17/1
8/3/89/18/76/33/88/1/50/127/43/2/16/127/22/21/70/246/70/13/
3/18/33/9/29/79/11/263/99/3/32/101/106/61/119/32/12/44/3/57

Maskelyne cursed. His contact had repeated several of the
numbers, which meant that any fool might decipher the message
without the pass. How many times did he have to tell the man?
Even the staff who delivered the messages might easily unravel
such an obvious formula. He went over to the bookshelf and
pulled out a volume of *Clarke's Almanac*, then sat down, turned
to page 412 and began counting through the script to find the

letters corresponding to each number. A short while later, he had his answer.

> *Ianthe officially Haurstaf. They're going to execute you.*
> *Awaiting signal.*

Maskelyne crumpled up the paper and popped it in his mouth. While he chewed, he decided it was probably a good idea to leave sooner rather than later.

He went out onto the terrace, where his scattered trove gleamed in the bronze evening light among potted plants and stone garden furniture. Reefs of golden cloud filled the western sky behind the mountains. Maskelyne leaned on the balustrade and looked out across the valley. Smoke rose from a dozen military encampments located in cleared areas of forest below the palace. Several artillery emplacements occupied strategic ridges and hilltops, their steel barrels trained on the heavens. A foot patrol was marching south-east along the banks of the Irya towards Port Awl. He filled his lungs with cool mountain air, so sharp with the antiseptic scent of pine, and he waited for the sun to set.

Mountainous shadows crept across the valley floor. A few lights winked on in the military bases, and fires flickered between the trees. The sky grew darker. Maskelyne watched the first stars appear overhead. Cloud cover would have been better, but there wasn't anything he could do about that. He licked his finger and held it up to test the direction of the breeze. The evenings frequently brought cool air down from the mountains towards Port Awl and the sea, and he was relieved to find such conditions tonight. He picked up the gem lantern from the table he used as a workbench, opened the shutter so that its light spilled out and went back inside.

From under his bed, he took out a brown paper parcel and tore it open to reveal a Guild soldier's uniform and a specially adapted leather harness. Maskelyne stripped, then donned the uniform. The heavy cotton was lined with wool and fitted him snugly. Warm enough, he supposed. Then he secured the harness over the jacket, tightening its padded straps around his waist and under his arms. Its many pockets had originally been used to hold ammunition, but Maskelyne's contact had had these enlarged and reinforced with wire. A further addition had been the ring of brass hooks around the base, each of which supported a small burlap sack full of sand.

Finally dressed, he checked all of the straps a second time. The harness was heavy and cumbersome, and the weight of the sandbags put an uncomfortable strain on his shoulders. He wandered into the bathroom and set the gem lantern on top of the cistern. He lowered the commode seat and stood on top of it. From here he could reach the eight chariot ballast spheres resting upon the ceiling. One by one, Maskelyne took them down and fed them into the pockets on his harness, securing each firmly with a brass buckle. The harness began to strain upwards against his chest, wanting to rise, but his weight kept him grounded. When the last sphere was in place, he stepped off the commode.

He drifted slowly down the floor.

No good. He had to shed some weight.

He raised the commode seat again and unbuttoned his fly. A few moments later, his head touched the ceiling. He buttoned himself up again, then grabbed the gem lantern. Its extra weight was just enough to bring him back to earth. By traversing the bathroom in a series of slow leaps, and by pushing himself along the walls, he made his way back through the doorway and into the bedroom. At the door to the terrace, he stopped and reached inside the gem lantern, making a small adjustment to the feedback mechanism he had fitted inside. The light began to grow brighter immediately. Quickly, he set down the lantern and pushed himself through the terrace doorway. His boots scraped the flagstones for an instant, but then he was rising swiftly into the star-encrusted sky. Up past the palace pinnacles he soared, watching the terrace drop away below him. The breeze carried him southeast, out over the forest towards the army encampments and the coast. The palace dwindled behind him, its windows all glimmering like the facets of a jewel.

But the light from his bedroom already outshone all others, and was growing brighter still.

Maskelyne drifted out across the valley, enjoying the cold, pine-scented air. Acres of dense woodland swept by under his feet. To the east he could see the mercurial ribbon of the Irya gleaming faintly among patchwork fields, with the dark mass of the mountains towering behind. His flight path would take him directly over a Guild army camp, but that couldn't be helped. He had to hope that any spotters would have their telescopes fixed on the palace by now.

The light from his gem lantern was blazing like a small white sun. Even from this distance he found it difficult to look at directly. The feedback mechanism couldn't last much longer. Maskelyne knew it had to fail, and fail soon.

Any moment now . . .

The light flickered. And then a fireball bloomed in the heart of the palace. A heartbeat later, the sound of the concussion reached Maskelyne: a sharp crack, followed by a prolonged rumble. The blast wave punched through the air around him, pushing him onwards with a noticeable jolt. A cry came from one of the military camps down below, followed moments later by the rising-falling cycle of an attack siren. Maskelyne drifted onwards, out into the night, a single tiny mote among billions of stars.

The higher he rose, the colder and thinner the air became. It soon felt like ice in his lungs. The harness was starting to chaff and pinch under his shoulders. He blew into his hands and rubbed them constantly to try to keep the blood moving through his veins. His lips and face already felt completely numb. After a while, he unbuckled one of his harness pockets and released a chariot stone, which duly shot up and away to be lost forever in the heavens above. Maskelyne wondered how many there were, floating up there in the vacuum between worlds. He began to descend again, more rapidly than he would have liked, so he opened one of the sandbags and scooped out handfuls of ballast until his descent slowed.

On he drifted, over fields and hedgerows and hayricks, floating through the darkness like some strange wandering sorcerer. He passed over a farmhouse with bright windows spilling firelight across an empty yard. No one was around to notice him. He crossed the River Irya and followed a country lane for a short while, before the breeze carried him back out over the water and the farmland beyond. At one point he sailed above a clump of woodland, his boots skimming the tops of the trees, while he frantically bailed out more sand.

Eventually, he came within half a mile of the Crossing Inn, where the palace road crossed the river. The breeze was blowing him west, further away from the road and his arranged meeting place, so Maskelyne decided to land. He released another chariot sphere, controlling his quickening descent by dropping more sand.

He landed easily in a grassy field several yards behind the road, whereupon he rubbed his hands and set off for the inn.

His contact was waiting for him in a corner of the bar. Firelight played across the roughcast walls. A few long, dusty tables lined the walls, but the communal benches were all empty at this late hour. Even the innkeeper had retired for the night, leaving his single guest to pour his own mead. He looked up when Maskelyne entered, grinned and then shoved a clay goblet across the table towards him.

'Cold outside?' he asked.

'Good to see you, Howlish,' Maskelyne said, rubbing his hands fiercely. 'Be a good fellow and put some more wood on that fire.'

The captain leaned over and pitched a few logs onto the fire. Flames snapped and crackled.

Maskelyne joined him at the corner table. 'You've seen my wife?'

'Recovering well, by all accounts.'

'And Jontney?'

'Fine, fine. They're expecting us before dawn.'

Maskelyne took a sip of mead and leaned back in his chair. 'I was thinking we might postpone our escape.'

Captain Howlish looked at him.

'For a few days, at least,' Maskelyne added.

The other man took a long draught of mead, then set down his goblet. 'It's your money, Maskelyne, but I think you're making a mistake. News travels fast here. There are a lot of psychics on this island.'

'Those psychics have taken something that belongs to me,' Maskelyne said. 'A man in my position simply can't allow thefts like that to go unpunished. It's a matter of my own survival.'

'They're not going to give you the girl back.'

'No,' Maskelyne admitted. 'I don't expect they will.' He took out a scrap of folded paper from his uniform jacket pocket and handed it to the captain. 'I wonder if you could collect some more items for me.'

Howlish unfolded the paper and read through it. 'The rifles are easy,' he said. 'Cutting tools, brine gas, ichusae if you have the money. No problem.' But then he shook his head. 'Forget void flies. I didn't even know there were any left in the world until you brought out that damned blunderbuss.' He grunted. 'And what's with all these lanterns? Are you planning a war or a party?'

'A little bit of both.'

'It would easier to explain this without a pistol pointed at my head,' Herian said.

Granger kept the pistol aimed at the old man. It was the same weapon Herian had tried to use on him earlier and, as far as he could tell, the only thing in this godforsaken trap he could be sure didn't have a nasty surprise in store for an unwary handler.

They were standing beside the shattered pedestal in the transmitting station's main chamber. It was reassuringly gloomy in here without the crystal's radiance, however most of the trove around him now appeared to be defunct. Herian had assured him it wasn't.

The old man threw up his hands. Then he wandered over to the nearest pile of trove and sat down. 'There's a story about a human who once made deal with the Unmer,' he said. 'He was a slave, of no real value to anyone, but he proposed something that piqued the interest of the greatest entropic sorcerer of the age. You see, the slave thought he had devised a method by which he might live forever.'

Granger listened.

'He imagined that if he could trap his reflection between two mirrors,' Herian went on, 'then it would remain there indefinitely. And so some part of him would always be preserved.' He shifted uncomfortably, frowned and moved some shiny piece of trove out from under him. 'However, although he could place two mirrors so that they faced each other,' he said, 'the slave could never duck out from between them quickly enough to leave his reflection behind.' He looked up at Granger. 'But the sorcerer decided that if he could slow down light enough, the reflection might remain. He didn't care about the slave, of course, only the problem he presented.'

Granger sat down nearby. He balanced the pistol on his knee.

'So the sorcerer tried everything to slow down light. He filled the space between the mirrors with all sorts of gases, liquids and prisms. Nothing worked. And then he had an idea. He didn't have to slow down light. All he had to do was increase the distance between the mirrors. If the light from the slave's face took long enough to reach the mirror and rebound, the slave need not even be there when the reflected light returned. The hard part would be to create two perfect mirrors, and place them far enough apart.

'After many years of labour he finally created the mirrors. But he knew that the distance he required between them would be phenomenal. There wasn't enough space in all of Anea to place the mirrors far enough apart. So he put the slave and the mirrors in a chariot. And then he flew up into the void beyond the earth.

'The sorcerer had constructed a suit to supply him with all the air and food and water he'd ever need, and to keep him warm during his journey across the freezing wastes. The slave didn't have a suit, of course, and died quickly, but that didn't matter. He didn't actually have to be *alive* to cast his reflection. The sorcerer set one mirror adrift in the void, and then he took the slave's body and the other mirror away with him deep into the unknown.' Herian shrugged. 'And nobody ever saw him or heard from him again.'

Granger grunted. 'Is there a point to all this?'

'The point is,' Herian said, 'don't get involved with things you don't understand. The artefacts you call trove were designed to study different facets of the cosmos around us. You are no different from the slave. You cannot wield any these weapons safely unless you understand the forces at work.'

'So teach me.'

Herian shook his head. 'It took me years to learn. It would take *you* a lifetime.'

Granger got up and walked over. He placed the barrel of his pistol against the old man's head. 'This gun turns things to ash,' he said.

Herian snorted. 'Ash? It increases *entropy*.'

Granger's finger tightened on the trigger. 'I don't care what you call it,' he said. 'It'll hurt just the same.'

'You have no idea what you're getting into.'

Granger shot him in the foot.

Herian howled as half his toes vaporized in a puff of grey-coloured ash. He clamped his hands across the stump, but there was no blood at all. His crown fell off, and he began to shudder and wail.

'I think I just increased some entropy there,' Granger said.

'You bastard.'

Granger grabbed the old man's neck and lifted his face so he could look into those terrified eyes. 'Tell me how these weapons work,' he said. 'All of them.'

Herian just stared at him with utter contempt.

Granger raised the pistol again.

'All right,' Herian said. He let out a growl of pain and frustration. 'There are two main schools of Unmer sorcery: Entropic and Brutalist. Brutalist sorcery concerns the movement of energy. Gem lanterns, wave cannons, air stones, perception devices, they're all made using those principles. Entropic sorcery focuses on matter, its destruction and creation. It's how trove is made.'

'How do I use the Replicating Sword?'

'I'll come to that!' Herian cried. 'Just give me a moment. Give me a moment!'

Granger had no means to judge the passage of time inside that gloomy tower. He sat and listened for hours as the old man talked about the principles behind many of the artefacts around them. Most of it he didn't understand, but he learned enough to be both frightened and respectful of these things the Unmer had made. Some objects, it seemed, had no discernible purpose other than to test a theory about the cosmos, while others had been deliberately crafted to torture and kill. The deadliest weapons were not always the ones that looked dangerous. Seemingly innocuous objects worked horrors Granger could scarcely comprehend. There were pins that turned flesh to gemstones and screaming rings that, once worn, could never be removed. In one corner Herian unearthed a crib once used to smother human children. Devices for exchanging perceptions abounded, and Granger wondered if he might use one of them to communicate with Ianthe. But he was afraid to try anything in the old man's presence that might affect his own mind in ways he couldn't predict.

It must have been late into the night when Herian finally slumped to the ground and begged Granger to let him rest. Granger left him alone and took the chariot back out into the frozen wilderness to find a place where he himself might sleep safely.

The sun was rising over the Mare Verdant, and the waters lay under a veil of green vapour. Not a breath of wind disturbed the snow. Granger flew the chariot leagues into the north until he could no longer see the transmitting station tower. Still the ice stretched on forever. The curve of the world bowed before him under ink blue skies.

There he slept, wrapped in his fur jacket and clutching his pistol, while the chariot hovered twenty feet above the bitter ground.

At dusk, he turned the machine around and headed back to the transmitting station. He had no doubt that the old man would by now be armed and waiting for him, but Granger decided to take that risk. He had so much more still to learn.

Two soldiers strapped the Unmer man to a chair, then ripped off his blindfold, revealing the leucotomy scar on his forehead. He was a rag of a man, skeletal, limp-haired and savage-looking. He glanced feverishly around the room, before his gaze settled on Ianthe.

Briana paced behind Ianthe's chair. 'Just do what you did with Caroline, but tone it down a thousandfold.'

'Constance,' Ianthe said.

The man's eyes filled with fury. His cheeks moved rapidly behind his gag. His naked chest rose and fell. Sweat dripped from his forehead, causing him to blink. Behind him, the Guild soldiers retreated to the far wall. One of the pair brushed a speck from his blue uniform sleeve and then stood to attention. The other man yawned. They were young, these two, but their blank expressions verged on boredom. They'd seen torture before.

Mirrors covered the three walls of the room facing the prisoner. Ianthe could see nothing in them but the room's reflection, and yet she sensed dozens of figures waiting behind those huge panes. She cast out her mind . . .

. . . and found herself among a group of old women seated on tiered benches, their faces rapt as they studied the young Evensraum girl in a room behind a glass wall. The mirrors worked in one direction only. Ianthe flitted between the minds of her hidden observers, watching them through the eyes of their own peers. They were ancient, older than any Haurstaf Ianthe had seen. She sensed expectation, perhaps even excitement, in that secret room. She could see it in their eyes, in the twitching of skeletal fingers, the pursed lips.

'Start with . . .' Ianthe returned to her own body, '. . . a point behind his eyes,' Briana said. 'Sometimes it helps to picture a tiny tuning fork located there. Concentrate on the image until you begin to hear the fork vibrate. Haurstaf use such techniques to visualize and manipulate unconscious processes.'

Ianthe tried to picture a silver fork between the Unmer man's eyes. Immediately, he began to struggle against his restraints, thrashing his head left and right. Had he been sensitive to that simple act of visualization? She wasn't convinced. She imagined the fork vibrating, and she imagined the sound it made, but it didn't seem to affect him in any way. 'What do I do next?' she said.

'Visualize pain in your own head,' Briana said. 'You can imagine someone driving a nail into your skull. As soon as you start to feel it, push the sensation across into the tuning fork. If you've made a connection with the subject, he'll feel that pain, greatly amplified.'

Ianthe found it hard to comply with the witch's instructions. No matter how many imaginary tortures she inflicted on herself, she couldn't spark the merest glimmer of a headache. After a while, she gave up. Thankfully, the Unmer prisoner appeared not to have suffered any ill effects from her efforts. She looked up at Briana. 'I can't do it.'

'You did it with Car . . . Constance.'

'That was different.'

'How?'

'She angered me.'

Briana snorted. 'That's easy enough to fix.' She nodded at one of the two Guild soldiers. 'Remove his gag.'

The soldier untied a knot at the back of the prisoner's head.

The Unmer man spat out his gag. 'Mutants,' he said. He spoke Anean clearly, but with a heavy accent. 'This is what happens when entropy is retarded.' He shook his head in exasperation.

'Unsterilized, unchecked, a rotten branch poisoning the whole tree. Your own deformity prevents you from recognizing the truth!' For a long moment he regarded Ianthe with narrow, cynical eyes. And then his expression softened. 'Little girl,' he said. 'Look at yourself. Look at them. Do you want to be like these old women?' He was almost pleading with her. 'For the sake of the cosmos they should all have been drowned at birth.'

'The tragedy is,' Briana said, 'that he genuinely believes what he's saying.'

The prisoner shook his head again.

'He was part of what the Unmer called their Branch Evaluation and Reintegration Programme,' Briana said, 'one of three thousand workers, tasked with altering aberrant "low entropy states". Ask him how he accomplished this.'

'There was nothing immoral about it,' the Unmer man said.

'Then tell her.'

The man shrugged. 'We drowned people.'

Ianthe stared at him.

'Thousands of people,' Briana said. 'They were experimenting with brine long before they dumped all those bottles in the seas.'

The man gave a bitter smile. 'Brine is simply a medium for re-working dangerously retarded entropic states. Would you rather we extinguished you altogether?' He looked down wistfully at his bound hands and feet. 'And this is how you reward our restraint? With imprisonment, torture and degradation? That's the difference between us. You lock up everything that threatens you. We set it free.'

Ianthe felt Briana's hands on her shoulders. The witch leaned close and whispered, 'Picture a fork behind his eyes.'

But Ianthe couldn't. The prisoner's frank admissions had provoked the anger that Briana had doubtlessly intended, and yet those feelings weren't directed at him. They were directed at herself. She had allowed herself to pity the young Unmer prince in the palace dungeons, to be fooled by his beauty, to spend so many waking moments thinking about him. And now she felt betrayed and humiliated by a man she'd never even met. She closed her eyes and let the world's perceptions flood into the darkness around her.

And she could see the dungeons down there through the eyes of the Unmer, the concrete maze under its cruciform catwalk, its starved and naked inmates. She allowed herself to drift down through the unperceived void below it, down to the glass-floored suites where the witches sat on high-chairs. *Twelve suites.* Ianthe had been foolish not to show herself the extent of it before. She wandered from one Haurstaf mind to another, until she found the chamber Briana had shown her. The prince was sitting at a desk in his library, writing a letter. With a hammering heart, Ianthe slipped into the mind behind his eyes.

Dearest Carella,

This ugly language frustrates me. It lacks the finesse to fully express my feelings. And yet you must not forget that the Haurstaf, by binding us within their petty laws, admit their own weakness. As much as they grub through each other's minds, they can never peer into ours. They can only see what we choose to let them see.

How can what we show them not shame them?

Your last letter filled me with such despair I felt that I must surely destroy this place or die in the attempt. My rage would carry me through the heart of the world. Only your strength holds me back. Every day I kneel before the gods and beg them to transfer your suffering to me. Every night my dreams bring me to your bedside so that I can hold and kiss you, and mop the sweat from your fevered brow. We lie in each other's arms and talk

*about that summer in Forenta: the old dragon cave that father
showed us, Mistress Delaine waddling around without her shoe,
our lunches in the rose gardens, the field behind the orchard.*

*Have hope, my love, and do not be afraid. My arms are
always around you.*

'Ianthe?'

The voice came from a world away. Ianthe opened her eyes
and found herself back in the mirrored room. Briana was looking at her strangely. Her thoughts, however, remained with the
Unmer prince and his letter. Those had not been the words of a
heartless fiend, but of a thoughtful and caring young man. Ianthe
couldn't help but wonder who the real monsters were.

'Ianthe? What's wrong? You're a million miles away.'

Ianthe glared at the witch. 'I can't do it,' she said.

'It takes time—' Briana began.

Ianthe rose from her chair. 'I don't want to do it!'

'Ianthe?'

She strode towards the door. 'Leave me alone.'

Briana hurried after her. 'Listen . . .'

Ianthe rattled the door handle, but it was locked. 'Let me out
of here.'

'. . . I only want to—'

'Open the door!'

Briana put a hand on her shoulder. 'Ianthe, please.'

That single touch was a spark to a flame. Ianthe spun round,
her anger bunched like a fist inside her. She threw the witch's
hand aside and cried out, 'Leave me!' And in that moment something happened that she did not plan and could not control. She
compressed all of her rage into a single, desperate thought, like a
mental scream, and released it.

The wall-sized mirrors exploded. In the galleries behind,

Ianthe glimpsed the witches reeling and clutching their heads. Many had bleeding, lacerated hands. Sobs, wails and groans came from their midst. Briana Marks took three steps back, her face white with shock. She wiped away blood from her nose and gaped at it dumbly. The Unmer man lay slumped forward in his chair, unmoving. Only the two Guild soldiers seemed unaffected. For a moment they looked on in stunned disbelief, and then one of them unstrapped a baton from his belt and came for Ianthe.

She cried out, raised her hands to defend herself.

He swung the baton, and everything went dark.

'This is an Unmer infiltration,' Commander Rast said, 'The girl is a spy and an assassin, the explosion . . . clearly designed to distract our troops while she carried out her mission.'

'Designed to distract troops by drawing their attention to the palace?' Briana said.

The commander's face reddened, and his lip-whiskers twitched. Murmurs swept around the table, vocally among the other Guild commanders and mentally among the Haurstaf contingent. Seven combat psychics were in attendance, led by Sister Ulla, although in light of recent events, the term *combat psychic* now seemed little more than an embarrassing misnomer. Ianthe had wrecked the minds of six of their best with one thought.

One thought. Briana was still reeling from the girl's attack. The sheer scale of the power she'd sensed coming from Ianthe had shocked her to the core. It had been like catching a glimpse of a howling abyss, some raw, savage, primordial vortex of energy. Even now ripples still spread through the entire Harmonic Reservoir, that abstract plane the Haurstaf used to envision the telepathic network. Ianthe could not have generated such a force herself, Briana felt sure. The girl had to have accessed and channelled it – much as the Unmer channelled their sorcery – from somewhere else. They had been naive to try to bring her into the Haurstaf. This girl was on a different level altogether.

'What about the eyeglasses?' she asked.

Torturer Mara looked up. 'A simple perception transference device,' he said. 'They appear to contain the mind image of an Unmer sea captain – one of the old Brutalist sorcerers who fought Conquillas's dragons at Awl. One can look back through his eyes into past moments of his life, which is somewhat unnerving, but not particularly useful to anyone except a historian.' He tapped his pencil against the table. 'Nevertheless, two odd things about them *have* come to light. Ianthe had the focus wheel set to the present time, which meant she was essentially looking at the world around her through *his* perceptions rather than her own. The sorcerer's image in turn must have been able to see through her eyes.'

'Then she was spying,' Rast exclaimed.

Mara snorted. 'Spying for a ghost,' he said. 'And an impotent ghost, to boot. That Brutalist is merely an image, an optical illusion trapped forever within those lenses.' He raised a hand to stop the commander's objections. 'If you listen, Rast, I have better ammunition for your cause. What's more perplexing is that Ianthe managed to wear the lenses at all. Because the mental link happens both ways, she sees through his eyes and he sees through hers. But the Brutalist's mind is essentially trapped in the past. He *cannot* perceive events in our present time without creating a paradox that the lenses don't allow. Any attempt to do so produces an unbearable strain on the wearer's mind. The human volunteers we used to test them could not bear to wear the blasted things for more than an instant.'

'And what effect on Haurstaf?' Briana asked.

Mara rolled his pencil between his fingers. 'We did try them on one girl, but I should probably speak to you about that in private. The results were . . . dramatic and rather messy. Suffice to say, a sensitive mind reacts much more severely to the lenses, which begs the question as to why Ianthe should be immune to their effects.'

Rast gave a bellow of frustration. 'The lenses were obviously created *for* her. The facts here are clear. She attacked a room full of Guild psychics and left the single Unmer prisoner unharmed.'

Briana thought about this. 'He survived because she didn't target him directly,' she said. 'But he didn't escape unharmed. His mind lost all of its higher functions.' She leaned over the table. 'Ianthe's anger was directed at the room, at those who were pushing her to do something she didn't agree with. I was there. What I saw was an emotional outburst from a sixteen-year-old girl, not a carefully engineered plan.' She left the rest of her reasons for doubting the commander unspoken. It had seemed to her that Ianthe had *held back*.

And yet she couldn't deny that the girl had much in common with the Unmer: her resistance to any ill effects caused by the lenses, her channelling of power from somewhere outside her own body, her uncanny ability at finding lost trove. Had Maskelyne spotted the connection, too? Briana had been foolish to underestimate him once, and now she had a sixty-foot-wide hole in the side of the palace to remind her of that fact.

'And what news of Maskelyne?' she said.

The Guild commanders shook their heads. Rast himself looked suitably ruffled. 'He couldn't have passed through the lines,' he exclaimed. 'Either he's still in the palace, or he martyred himself in that explosion.'

'He didn't seem like the martyr type,' Briana muttered.

'If he's alive,' Rast added, 'then he'll stay close to the girl. The two of them are in this together.'

Briana experienced a moment of doubt. Could the commander

be right, after all? Maskelyne's timely disappearance suggested that *someone* had informed him of his impending execution. She shook her head. She simply couldn't imagine Ianthe in that role. Given Maskelyne's background, the traitor was more likely to be someone in the military. After all, back in Ethugra, he had recruited mercenaries and privateers as a matter of course.

'What do you want me to do with the girl?' Torturer Mara said.

'Execute her,' Rast said. 'No fuss, no ceremony, just put her down before she wakes up.'

'Not yet,' Briana said. 'She's channelling power from somewhere. I'd like to know *where* she gets it from and *how* she does it, before any of our other girls learn how to do the same thing. Her powers are growing stronger all the time. We don't yet know what else she's capable of.'

Sister Ulla sat up. 'I agree,' she said. 'We have a chance here to study something completely new.'

'A thorough dissection would tell us a lot,' Mara said.

'You'll get your moment, Torturer,' Briana said. 'But in the meantime, I want her broken, stripped down. Peel back the layers until you've bared her soul. I want to know what's in there.'

Ianthe dreamed she was in a ballroom with tall shuttered windows and golden chandeliers hanging from the ceiling. A blonde Unmer girl sat on a three-legged stool, gently plucking a harp. She was pale and terribly thin, and her physical weakness translated into the music she played. Every fragile note seemed to quiver on the edge of oblivion.

Ianthe had never heard anything so sad and so beautiful before. She stood there for a long time, listening. And then the music suddenly stopped, and the girl was looking at her defiantly. 'Who are you?' she said.

'Just a friend.'

'What are you doing here?'

'I came to deliver a letter.'

The blonde girl shook her head. 'You're with them,' she said. 'Don't you know that I could destroy you? As easily as this . . .' She moved her hand through the harp strings, and they snapped one by one with a series of sharp, discordant sounds. 'I'll take away your fingers and pieces of your skin.' She stood up, knocking the harp away so that it crashed to the floor.

Ianthe was suddenly afraid. She turned to flee but halted when the door swung open behind her. A procession of revellers poured into the room, young men and women in fancy party clothes and exotic bird of paradise masks – a squall of peacock feathers and silvered beaks, gemstones and perfume. They were drunk and laughing. The men led the women, who shrieked and giggled and stumbled in their arms. They flowed around Ianthe, filling the room with their breathless gaiety.

A man in a white mask rapped a staff against the floor and said, 'Music! We must have music!'

The harp began to play, but this time the music was brisk and lively. It did not seem unusual to Ianthe that the broken instrument could produce these sounds. She could no longer see the blonde girl, for the revellers had formed a circle around Ianthe. As the music soared they started to dance. They moved in pairs, each man holding his partner's hand high. Their bird masks dipped and flashed under the chandeliers – a whirlwind of feathers and jewels. Their heels struck the floorboards with staccato barks. They clapped and laughed and bowed. None of them appeared to notice Ianthe at all.

Ianthe wanted to leave, but to do so would mean breaking through the circle. The music became louder and more delirious, and the dancers kept pace, spinning wildly in a great vortex of colourful silks. Ianthe moved towards the door, but the dancers forced her back. She tried to find another way through, and yet another, but there was no space among the flailing arms and stamping heels. And no space in the music. Notes clashed with their neighbours as the whole merged into an appalling cacophony. Like the shrieking of wild birds. Ianthe could hardly tell one dancer from another. They seemed to merge into one great fluid entity, circling her faster and faster, revolving out of control. And someone screamed.

But the dance went on. The cry became part of the music, just another hideous note swept away by the shrieks and laughter that followed. A girl was pleading: *Please don't, please don't.* Ianthe spied blood on the floor. The dancers' shoes slid through it; bloody heels clacked down, and up, and the men clapped their hands and carried their swooning partners' along. Some of the ladies were unconscious. Some were struggling to break loose. All were bleeding from countless wounds. And as they danced on their masks and frocks began to fall away like feathers. Scraps of silk and lace fluttered around them or lay strewn across the wet floor.

The laughter died. There was no longer any sound from the ladies, only the stamp of feet and the chaotic music as the bird-masked men whirled their naked, mutilated partners around and around the ballroom.

'You don't have a partner.'

Ianthe turned to find the man in the white mask standing next to her. He extended a slender, almost effeminate, hand. 'Please, will you honour me with a dance?'

'Ianthe?'

She was looking down at herself lying in hospital bed. A yellow gem lantern made a pool of harsh illumination in the otherwise dark ward. The sheets and pillows smelled of soap. Someone wearing Haurstaf robes was tugging at the straps securing her hands to the bed frame. And whoever it was was acting as a host for Ianthe's own befuddled mind.

Ianthe suddenly put a name to the voice she'd heard. 'Aria?'

'Shush. They'd kill me if they knew I was here.' Aria freed Ianthe's other hand, and stood back. 'We have to leave.'

Ianthe watched herself sit up. One of her eyes looked black and swollen. 'What happened?'

'Don't you know?'

Ianthe recalled the room of mirrors, and her heart cramped. 'I hurt Briana,' she said.

'She's all right,' Aria said. 'But everyone knows. It's not safe for you here.'

'My lenses? Where are they?'

Aria rummaged in her robe pocket and brought out the Unmer spectacles. 'Torturer Mara's office,' she said. Ianthe thought she heard a smile in the other girl's voice. 'I spotted them when I got the key. I knew you'd want them back.' She handed them over to Ianthe, who put them on at once.

Then she left Aria's body and flitted back into her own. And suddenly she could see Aria standing over her, her eyes twinkling, and a broad smile on her earthy face. Ianthe breathed a sigh of relief. She pulled back the covers and got out of bed. Her robe flapped around her ankles. The cold tiled floor under her bare feet sent a shiver up her spine, but she couldn't see her shoes anywhere.

'I didn't try them on,' Aria said.

'What?'

'The eyeglasses. Do they make it easier? Everyone thinks that's how you did it.'

Ianthe shook her head. 'They just help me see. I'm blind without them.'

410

Aria's expression became grim. 'Then you're in even more trouble than I thought.'

They left the ward and hurried along the adjoining corridor. Windows looked into white rooms full of metal tables. Most were empty, but in one Ianthe glimpsed the partially dissected corpse of an Unmer man. Something about him seemed familiar. Did he have a scar on his forehead? She paused, but Aria just grabbed her and dragged her onwards. 'We have to hurry,' she said. 'A driver is waiting to take you to Port Awl. He's a friend. He'll get you through the checkpoints. From there you can take one of the merchant transports to Losoto. John knows someone who can sneak you aboard.'

'Why are you doing this?' Ianthe said.

'Because you're the only one who would have done it for me,' Aria replied. 'I don't have any other friends here.' She stopped suddenly, pulled a small roll of gilders from her pocket and thrust it into Ianthe's hand. 'You'll need this. I'm sorry it's not much. It's all I have.'

Tears welled in Ianthe's eyes. 'Thank you.'

Aria smiled. 'Come on, we're nearly there.'

They took a left down another corridor, then reached a sturdy metal door.

'Wait,' Ianthe said. She sensed people waiting on the opposite side of the door – two men, their perceptions as bright as lanterns in that perpetual gloom beyond her lenses. *A military uniform.* She reached out to stop the other girl. 'Aria, there's someone there.'

'It's just the driver' Aria said. 'He's meeting us here.' She took Ianthe's hand, opened the door, and led her through.

It wasn't the driver at all. The door opened into a small round cell with a concrete floor and walls. A drain occupied a depression in the centre of the floor. The space was bare but for a metal chair and a coil of hosepipe connected to a tap. Torturer Mara waited

411

beside a large soldier in Guild uniform. The man was loosening his shirt collar. In one hand he clutched a wooden baton. Ianthe heard a click behind her.

Aria had closed the door.

'What is this?' Ianthe said.

The other girl just lowered her head.

Torturer Mara cleared his throat. 'It's the start of a very long process,' he said. 'Please take a seat.'

CHAPTER 18

AN EXPECTED DEATH

Dear Margaret,

I can't imagine that this letter will ever find its way to you, which is, in itself, enough to give me the courage to write it. I've been lying to you all this time. I never did escape from my Ethugran cell. I don't know why I lied – it was a moment of weakness and euphoria when everything seemed possible. Over the years it seems as if I have forgotten who I was. Desperation can do that to a man. It looks as if I'll die in here, and I didn't want to leave you with false hope. If the truth is crueller, then I'm sorry. You don't need to send any more money. Mr Swinekicker has taken charge of another jail, and his replacement has more resources at his disposal.

Love,
Alfred

The covered wagon bumped along the forest trail, rocking the four soldiers in the rear to and fro. One of the two men up front slouched over the reins; the other leaned back and warmed his face in the sunlight filtering through the trees. This was old woodland, a tangled landscape of roots and weary oaks draped with veils of eidermoss. Butterflies fluttered across the green verges on either side of the dirt road. Swarms of midges hung in the air like puffs of smoke. Maskelyne closed his eyes and breathed in deeply. He smelled wood smoke long before they reached the checkpoint.

The Guild soldier standing beside the barrier raised his hand. The wagon creaked to a halt. 'Lazy day,' Maskelyne said.

'Don't let the sergeant hear you say that,' the checkpoint guard replied. 'He's determined to scrub a promotion out of all this.'

'And where's he now?'

The guard grunted. 'Sleeping. Where you headed?'

'Eagle One.'

'What's in the back?'

'Disgruntled men,' Maskelyne replied. 'Commander Rast volunteered us to help with the search.'

'Lucky you.' The guard wandered to the rear of the wagon, lifted the flap, and peered in. 'I need to check this trunk,' he said.

Maskelyne called back, 'You think our man is trying to sneak back in?'

'I just work here,' the guard said.

Maskelyne heard the man unbuckle the trunk in the wagon bed and throw back the lid. Then he heard the guard whistle softly. 'Looks like you fellows have a long night ahead,' he said.

'You're welcome to join us,' Maskelyne said.

The guard strolled back to the front of the wagon. 'I don't like heights,' he said. 'You know the strangest thing about gem lanterns. Moths never circle them. Why do you think that is?'

Maskelyne frowned. 'You know, I can't say I've ever thought about it before. Maybe they've just got better things to do?'

The guard laughed. He lifted the barrier and waved them through. 'Good hunting.'

The driver snapped the reins, and the horses clopped forward. Once they were out of sight of the checkpoint, he turned to Maskelyne and said, 'Why *don't* they circle gem lanterns?'

'Truthfully, Mr Mellor,' Maskelyne replied, 'I don't know. But I suspect it's one of those mysteries where the answer either means nothing at all, or else holds one of the fundamental truths of the universe.'

'Like the keys of the Drowned?'

'Exactly, Mr Mellor. Everything warrants investigation.'

They passed through two more checkpoints. Closer to the palace, the army encampments became larger and ringed with palisades and razor-wire. Acres of forest had been burned to scrub to make way for the barracks, bunkers and gun emplacements. Guild soldiers drilled on quadrangles of dirt. Steel warmed in patchy sunlight. Pickets watched the road and the skies from wooden towers.

In places, the trail joined others circling the palace. Towards the end of the afternoon, the wagon reached one such junction, where Maskelyne ordered them to leave the Port Awl road and head north. The road became rougher, gouged by heavy use and then filled with rock. Occasionally through breaks in the forest he spied the palace towers and pinnacles rearing up like some great black crown. A quarter of a league beyond the junction the road came to an end.

Here a flat outcrop of rock overlooked the valley to the north. A wooden palisade ringed the whole area, encircling a group of low earthen buildings and a huge cannon set against the very edge of the precipice. As the wagon drew up before the encampment barrier, a soldier came out of a nearby hut and hailed them.

'If you want the captain,' he said, 'he won't be back till seven.'

Maskelyne climbed down from the wagon and stretched his arms. 'Commander Rast sent us to assist with the search. We'll be tramping the road tonight from here to Eagle Three.'

The soldier came over. He was a middle-aged man with a thin moustache and a nervous demeanour. 'Nobody told me anything about that,' he said, eyeing Maskelyne's uniform with distaste. 'Kind of old to be a lieutenant, aren't you?'

'Reserves,' Maskelyne said. 'I shouldn't even be here.'

'What do you do in town?'

'Mostly, I keep to myself.'

The soldier looked between Maskelyne and Mellor. 'I know a lot of Guild reserve men. You two don't look familiar.'

Maskelyne yawned. 'Your captain will vouch for us,' he said. 'Let us through so we can unload this gear.'

'What gear?'

He jabbed a thumb towards the back of the wagon. 'Lanterns.'

The moustached soldier wandered round to the back of the wagon and checked the cargo in the trunk, before returning to the barrier. 'Nobody and nothing gets in here without advance notice,' he said. 'You'll need to wait until I can verify this with the palace.'

Maskelyne sighed. 'Where's your telepath?'

'She's with the captain,' the man replied.

Maskelyne raised his eyebrows. 'And where would we find them?'

The soldier said nothing.

'Maybe we should go and ask Commander Rast if *he* knows where they are?'

The man folded his arms. 'You don't think the commander knows what goes on?'

'What's your name, soldier?'

He didn't reply.

Maskelyne turned to Mellor. 'Turn us around. The commander can get this man's name from the Haurstaf. Let them ask why Eagle One's captain leaves one cannon unattended to attend to another.' He climbed back into the wagon.

The soldier shook his head. He hesitated a moment, then strode over to the barrier and raised it. 'I want your attachment verified as soon as the telepath gets back. You can put your gear in the store.' He pointed at one of the earthen buildings, then turned around and marched back towards his hut.

'You heard him, Mr Mellor,' Maskelyne said.

The wagon moved forward into the encampment and into the shadow of the gun.

'The Haurstaf abandoned you,' Torturer Mara said. 'Which, I am sorry to say, means you are now under the protection of the Guild military.' He inclined his head at the large soldier, who lifted his baton and struck Ianthe across the face.

Ianthe fell off her chair and hit the floor. She couldn't stop sobbing. The soldier picked her up again and shoved her back into the chair. Perspiration covered his broad forehead and dripped down his heavy jaw. He had taken off his jacket and shirt, and his muscles shone like marble under the harsh cell lights.

'Your friend abandoned you,' Mara went on. 'Aria chose to deliver you here in exchange for an assured future with the Haurstaf.' He glanced at the soldier again, who struck Ianthe across the face a second time.

Her jaw cracked against the floor. She clutched her spectacles to her face and wailed miserably, her whole body convulsing with sobs. The concrete floor swam behind a haze of blood and tears. Through the ringing in her ears, she heard them turn on the tap. They hosed her down, blasting her body with freezing water until her limbs were numb.

'Briana Marks abandoned you,' Mara said. 'She ordered me to carry out this procedure. The faster we get to the end, the faster we can proceed with your dissection. For me, that's where the real interest lies. I expect to find some Unmer in your brain.'

The soldier picked Ianthe up from the floor with one hand. Then he stove his forehead into her nose. She heard the cartilage snap. Her spectacles flew off, and she was plunged into darkness. He let her drop.

She jumped into his mind only to see her own miserable body scrambling across the wet floor. Her robe hung from her like a torn rag; her elbows and knees were bruised and bloody. She picked the spectacles up again and fumbled to put them back on.

The torturer peered down at her, his face expressionless. 'Your own father abandoned you,' he said. 'Did you know he arranged to sell you to the Haurstaf? I've seen the letter myself. Of course the Guild does not negotiate with people like that.'

The soldier kicked Ianthe in the stomach.

She felt his boot break her rib. The pain made her vomit. Her lenses shifted to one side, and she felt herself slipping into darkness. She reached up and dragged them back over her streaming eyes. She coughed and sputtered and drew in a shuddering breath. The air tasted of bile.

'Your mother abandoned you,' Mara went on. 'Didn't she fail to protect you when the Hookmen came?' He made a sweeping gesture with his hand. 'She simply allowed herself to slip under the brine.'

Ianthe screamed. She tried to crawl away, but the soldier dragged her upright once more. He punched her in the face, then let her drop. Pain filled every fibre of her body. She couldn't move, but simply lay on the floor and stared at the drain, shivering uncontrollably.

'Even Maskelyne abandoned you,' the Torturer said. 'Like everyone else, he saw you as a means to an end, a tool to increase his personal fortune. Up until now that's really all you've ever been, Ianthe – something to be used by others.'

He crouched down beside her and spoke softly. 'But I'm not

like them, Ianthe. Can't you see that I'm the only one who wants to understand you?' He brushed back her hair. 'I want to help you achieve something with your life. I'm finally giving you a purpose.'

She closed her eyes.

Mara sighed. 'Again,' he said.

While his men unloaded the trunk of gem lanterns from the wagon, Maskelyne went to explore the three carthen buildings within the cliff-side compound. The first held stores of food, water and ammunition. The second turned out to be a small barracks in which he found the gunnery sergeant asleep on his bunk, while two other soldiers played dice on top of a crate. Maskelyne nodded amicably. He tapped the metal door lightly and then ducked back outside and wandered over to the last building. Here he found a tidy chamber containing a single bed, table and chair, and a wardrobe full of pressed linen – evidently the captain's quarters.

He returned to his men. 'All good,' he said. 'Howlish deserves a medal.'

Mellor looked up from the contents of the trunk and inclined his head in the direction of the hut beside the barrier. 'What about him?'

Maskelyne puffed out his cheeks. 'It will have to be done quietly.'

One of the four others slipped a knife from his belt, but Maskelyne shook his head. 'I'll deal with it.' He walked over to the hut and opened the door.

The soldier with the thin moustache was seated at his desk, writing out a report. He put his pencil down when Maskelyne came in.

'Your gunnery sergeant wants a word,' he said.

The soldier hissed. He got up and followed Maskelyne out. They walked over to the earthen bunker, whereupon the soldier ducked inside. Maskelyne pulled an ichusae from his jacket pocket, unplugged the stopper and tossed it into the building after the man. Then he closed the door and locked it with the padlock he kept in his other pocket.

'Watch the door,' he said to Mellor, 'in case they try to shoot out the lock.'

His first officer nodded.

The men in the bunker screamed for the first six or seven minutes and then fell silent. Soon afterwards, an endless stream of brine flowed out through the gaps between the door and the frame. Countless gallons of the toxic water surged over the rocky ground and washed along the bottom of the palisade wall, before leaking through and cascading over the edge of the precipice in a honey-coloured waterfall.

'So much for Awl,' Mellor said.

'All good things, Mr Mellor,' Maskelyne replied.

As two of his men opened the trunk and began lifting out gem lanterns Maskelyne, Mellor and the others dismantled the wagon bed with crowbars. They ripped up planks from the floor, revealing the hidden compartment where they had stored the gas tanks and cutting torches. And then they carried the lot over to the cannon.

Ianthe lacked the courage to return to her body and so she drifted in a sea of ghosts. She floated through a darkness patterned by the things that other people saw. She was a passenger, riding in carriages that didn't belong to her, a thief who stole moments from other people's lives, and that knowledge filled her with shame. Deep down she knew that Mara was right. The world she inhabited had never embraced her. She'd never really been a part of it. She would return to him in time and beg him to end her life quickly. By sifting through the wreckage of her life, they might even find some purpose.

420

But not yet. Her fear held her back, even as it deepened her shame. And so she wandered on through the darkness, a ghost afraid of her own death. She saw the Haurstaf scattered throughout their grand palace, the thousands in the woodland camps outside and the nebulous haze of the millions in the world beyond. She drifted down through the unseen spaces between occupied rooms, past the bright arena of the Unmer rat maze and down to the glass-roofed suites in the foundations.

She found him kneeling on the floor beside his bed, sobbing into his hands. Scraps of a letter littered the floor around him. The shock of seeing him like this almost broke her. All of his armour had gone. He was naked before her, naked before the gaze of the Haurstaf witch in the high-chair above. He had covered his face, as if that could somehow hide his despair.

A sudden fury gripped Ianthe. What gave the Haurstaf the *right* to preside over the lives of others? Over *his* life? Over *hers*? They weren't mankind's liberators but its new enslavers. Ianthe reached out into the mind of the witch, gathering together all of the woman's perceptions and thoughts into a single all-enveloping embrace.

And then she snuffed them out.

'If you knew how much money I've spent on that pirate Howlish,' Maskelyne said, 'then you wouldn't have sold yourselves so cheaply.'

The gunnery captain shrugged. He put his arm around the young Haurstaf telepath. 'I think we got a bargain, Mr Maskelyne.'

Maskelyne eyed them both. She couldn't have been older than sixteen, and him eighteen. If he was smart enough to attain his rank at that age, then he was smart enough to know he could have taken Maskelyne for much more. Which meant his reasons for helping them had to be personal. Or was *she* the one with the reasons? The two of them looked on as Mellor and his men cut through the last of the cannon's securing bolts.

'You know Ianthe?' Maskelyne said to the girl.

The telepath hung her head.

'You don't need to know why we're doing this, Mr Maskelyne,' the captain said. 'The money is enough to give us a fresh start.'

Maskelyne grunted.

Mellor switched off his gas torch. 'That's us, sir.'

'Good. Now hitch up the horses.'

The men brought the two horses round and used the wagon hitch to secure them to one side of the cannon. Mellor grabbed the reins and pulled, urging the heavy beasts forward. Nothing happened at first, but then a low scraping sound came from the base of the gun. Slowly, the whole cannon revolved on its vertical axis. When it was more or less facing in the opposite direction, Maskelyne walked around the weapon, checking the new trajectory with a compass.

'That will do nicely, Mr Mellor,' he said. From his jacket pocket he took out a map, heavily marked with pencilled circles, lines and crosses. He studied it while the men unhitched the horses and steered them away. Then he made an adjustment to the cannon's elevation by turning a brass wheel in the side of the gun carriage. The barrel dropped gradually lower.

'How do you intend to get her out?' the telepath said.

'Brute force,' Maskelyne admitted. 'It's the only way to deal with the Haurstaf, present company excluded.'

'But what if you hurt her?'

'That's a risk I'm prepared to take.'

The captain held his girlfriend closer. 'He knows exactly where they're keeping her, Regina.'

She didn't seem convinced.

Mellor handed one of the gem lanterns to Maskelyne, who

opened it up and made a small adjustment to the mechanism inside. Then he pulled out his pocket watch and noted the time. Mellor loaded the lantern into the cannon.

'You know the demands?' Maskelyne said to the girl.

She nodded.

'Word for word?'

'Word for word.'

Maskelyne covered his ears. 'Fire.'

Mellor pulled the lanyard, and the cannon barrel retracted with a sudden, violent *boom*. A flare of light shot skywards, arced over the trees covering the hillside above them and disappeared from sight. Maskelyne turned to Mellor's men and nodded. They set off at once in the direction of the road.

'I was expecting more of a bang,' the gunnery captain said.

At that moment, the skies above them erupted with fire. The ensuing blast wave ripped the tops from hundreds of trees, blowing tons of debris far over their heads as a thunderous concussion shook the valley. Maskelyne, Mellor and the young couple dived for the ground. The whole mountain continued to shake for several heartbeats, and then finally settled. Scraps of burning forest drifted down past them.

'Send the demands, please,' Maskelyne said to the girl.

She got to her feet shakily, then took a deep breath. After a moment, she said, 'It's done.'

'Any response?'

'Give them a minute.'

They waited.

The telepath suddenly blew through her teeth. 'They say . . .' She paused and shook her head. 'They say no, they say . . .'

'Word for word.'

'There's a lot of it. A lot of argument, hold on . . .' She raised her hand. 'They want you to stop . . .'

'Word for word.'

'You will halt your attack immediately. The Haurstaf do not negotiate with terrorists. They're . . . They're bombarding me with questions, about you, about our location.'

'That's to be expected.'

'They don't know where the shell came from.'

Maskelyne turned to Mellor, who began to reload the cannon immediately. 'Tell them the next shell destroys the mountain above the palace,' he said to the girl.

'But what about Ianthe?'

'Do as I say.'

She paused a moment. 'Wait. They're willing to talk. They've offered to meet you.' She shook her head again. 'There's a lot of confusion. Something strange is going on in there. I'm losing contact everywhere.'

Maskelyne snarled, 'They're shutting me out.'

'No . . .'

He picked up another gem lantern, set the feedback mechanism and tossed it over to Mellor. 'Five degrees lower. They've had their warning.'

'What are you doing?' the telepath cried.

The captain grabbed his arm. 'This isn't what we arranged.'

'It's in the tube now,' Maskelyne said. 'Tick, tock.'

Mellor pulled the lanyard, and the second shell blasted into the air, tracing a fiery arc across the blue sky. This time gunfire crackled on the hillside to the south.

'They're on to our position, sir,' Mellor said.

A second concussion tore across the roof of the world, its flash illuminating the snow-clad mountain peaks. The sound of impact was much heavier than before. The ground shuddered under their feet.

'That was rock,' Maskelyne said.

A great grey cloud of ash rose over the forest ridge. Moments later, a hail of small stones pinged against the outcrop all around them. Maskelyne stood where he was, listening intently. 'They're still firing,' he said. 'Why are they still firing?'

He could hear it more clearly now that the echo of the gem lantern explosion had diminished – the constant *rat-a-rat* of small-arms fire, accompanied now and then by the distant booming of cannons.

He turned and looked out across the valley. And there he spotted a tiny craft glinting in the sunshine high above the valley floor. It dodged and weaved between puffs of smoke. The Guild military were trying to bring it down. It was an Unmer chariot, and it was heading this way.

Ianthe drifted through the dark spaces of the palace, no longer as a lost and frightened ghost, but as a harbinger of death. While her body lay broken in the torturer's cell, her mind remained free to travel wherever she wished. And she used it now to wreak destruction. She moved from room to room, possessing Haurstaf minds and shattering them. Their perceptions vanished in her wake, leaving only swathes of darkness.

From the kitchens to the banquet hall she flitted, through floors and walls, snuffing out lives like candle flames. She watched girls fleeing, screaming as their companions fell around them. Hundreds of them fought to get out of the palace. But they were as slow as they were vulnerable and she tore through them like a gale. Their minds were windows they couldn't close. They could not keep her out and they could not hide.

The palace grew darker as its corridors filled with the dead. Soon the only lights came from the dungeons where the Unmer dwelt, and the scattered human servants who still wandered among their masters' corpses. Ianthe became weary. She allowed the survivors to leave unimpeded. And then her attention returned to the torturer's cell.

The torturer's accomplice was sharpening a knife.

Blasts shook the flying machine as Granger tried to steer it past another Guild compound. The view screens flickered and then settled down again, still focused on a single artillery position at the northern end of a long ridge. Maskelyne had rotated the cannon 180 degrees, so that it now aimed towards the Haurstaf stronghold. Its last shot had brought down half the mountainside. If he lowered the barrel again, his next shot would obliterate the palace itself.

He hunched over the steering console, his feverish eyes darting to and fro as he used one brine-scarred hand to spin the controls erratically in order to keep the craft on an unpredictable course. In his other hand he clutched the grip of the Replicating Sword he'd taken from the transmitting station. He wore a suit of mechanical nerve armour that clicked and whirred softly whenever he moved. His belt held an assortment of small blades, pistols and other small artefacts. And he wore a blood-red crystal shield strapped across his back.

A series of concussions battered the chariot's hull, knocking it momentarily off course. Smoke blotted the view screens and wafted in through the open hatchway. The engines howled and began to judder violently. Sparks erupted from the console. Granger shut down systems and readjusted the controls with lightning speed, the metal nerves in his mechanical suit compensating for the limits of his own tortured body. The shield on his back started to glow with alternating colours as it absorbed the smoke, using the sudden rise in entropy to energize its sorcerous portals.

As the fumes cleared, Granger spied the artillery position once again, now less than two hundred yards below him. Maskelyne's man was frantically spinning the gun carriage wheel, trying to bring the cannon's barrel round to bear on the rapidly approaching craft. But where was Maskelyne himself? Granger grinned. *There.* He spotted the metaphysicist fleeing for his life across the compound. Granger was going too fast to stop now, so he threw the craft sideways to intercept him.

The rock outcrop filled the view screens.

The chariot struck the ground like a meteor, exploding into a cloud of pulverized rock and metal.

Granger watched the impact from a spot several hundred yards above the compound. The seven simulacrums who stood in the forest around him watched it, too, but none of their positions offered him a better view of the events that had just occurred. It had all happened too quickly. He couldn't see Maskelyne. But had he actually hit the man? He felt a sudden vibration in the grip of his sword, and his eighth simulacrum appeared. This copy of himself cricked his neck and flexed his shoulders. *Good.*

That made nine of him again.

He turned away and headed for the palace at a run.

Ianthe's pain returned the moment she slipped back into her own body. She was lying on the floor. Her chest convulsed and she retched up blood. Every nerve felt shredded. Tears streaked her face. One of her eyes had swollen shut behind its lens, and through the other she saw Mara and his accomplice leaning over her.

'I thought I'd lost you for a moment there,' the torturer said. 'My assistant was a little too eager.' He scraped the chair through the blood on the floor and sat down. 'Step one was less successful than I'd hoped,' he said. 'But I think we'll see more results with step two.'

Ianthe tried to speak, but no words came out. Instead, she threw herself into the torturer's mind.

427

The sight of her own ruined body lying on the floor sent a pang of despair through her heart. They had been beating her in her absence. Her legs and buttocks were dark with purple bruises. Her robe lay in bloody tatters around her. One of her arms was clearly broken, and lay at an odd angle against her chest. From the torturer's perspective, she watched herself start to weep.

'That's much better,' he said.

Ianthe reached out, as she had reached out into the Haurstaf minds, trying to embrace the whole of the torturer's thoughts and emotions. But there was nothing there for her to sense. His human mind would not allow her inside.

'We're going to try something different now,' Mara said. 'I want to try to associate certain words I say to the particular sensation my assistant makes you feel when I say them. It's like a game. The idea is to break down any previous associations you have already made with the words, so we can start anew.' He sniffed and rubbed his hand under his nose, then glanced up at the soldier. 'The first word will be *mother*.'

The soldier crouched down beside Ianthe and placed his knife gently into the hollow behind her knee. He gave the torturer a quick nod.

'Mother,' Mara said.

The cell door burst open with such force it flew off its hinges and slammed into the opposite wall. A man stood in the doorway, clad from head to foot in metal. Brine burns covered his naked scalp and face. His eyes were as red and wild as those of a ber-serker dragon. In one gauntleted fist he held a green alloy sword. He was as grotesque a figure as Ianthe had ever seen.

Mara and his assistant retreated as the man strode into the cell, his boots clanking on the concrete floor. He glanced at them and then looked down at Ianthe. The tiny metal plates and filaments in his armour seemed to whirr and chatter as he bent down and picked her up.

And then he carried her out of the door.

She was drifting in and out of consciousness by now, and she must have muddled her dreams with reality, for she saw two impossible things before the armoured man carried her away from that place.

In her first dream she imagined she saw multiples of her rescuer in the corridor outside the cell. Seven or eight of them, identical in every way. Each wore the same armour and carried the same green sword. They looked on as he walked between their ranks. And then they turned away and filed into the torturer's cell. The last of them closed the door behind him.

She must have woken and blacked out again.

In her second dream he was carrying her through the main palace entrance hall. The sound of his boots rang out like a bell in that huge space. Dozens of bodies lay strewn across the black marble floor. Smoke drifted in through the open door, and she could smell fires burning outside. But before her rescuer reached the door, he halted at a sound behind him and turned around.

The young Unmer prince stood in the shadows, watching them. Ianthe's vision was blurred and she couldn't see his face clearly, but she thought that he was smiling. 'Is she the last of them?' he said.

'She was never one of them,' Ianthe's rescuer replied. 'But, no. Others survived.'

The prince nodded slowly. His gaze lingered on Ianthe for a long time, and then he turned away and walked back into the shadows.

EPILOGUE

Maskelyne spat out dust and rolled over on to his back. Above him, smoke boiled behind the shattered remains of a wooden roof. He raised his head and winced as pain shot through his neck. He was lying on the floor of what was left of the guards' hut. Through the open doorway he could see fires burning around a lump of twisted metal half-buried in the ground.

The chariot?

Maskelyne got up. His limbs felt beaten and raw. He staggered over to the door and looked out.

Dust and smoke filled the air. The horses stood a short distance down the trail. The wagon they'd been hitched to had smashed through the compound barrier and broken an axle. Now it lay collapsed at the end of a long dirt furrow. He spotted Mellor and two of his men, sitting under the palisade wall behind the crashed Unmer vessel. They looked stunned. The body of a third man lay on the ground before them among fallen debris and burning scraps of wood. The gunnery sergeant and his girlfriend were nowhere to be seen.

Maskelyne eased himself down the steps outside the guard post and limped across the ground towards the stricken chariot. His ankle buckled whenever he put any weight on it. He reached the craft and peered inside the open hatchway.

Empty. Nothing remained but a mangled mass of metal and wire. He was about to turn away, when he spotted something glinting among the wreckage. Carefully, he climbed inside and retrieved the object.

It was a crystal, as large as a man's head. Maskelyne turned it over in his hands, marvelling at the multitude of perfect facets. In each one he could see a reflection of his own bruised and dusty face. He tucked it under his arm and then ducked back outside.

'Mellor,' he said. 'We're leaving.'